MURDER

in BELLEVILLE

Also by Cara Black

Murder in the Marais

MURDER
in BELLEVILLE

Cara Black

Published by
Soho Press
853 Broadway
New York, NY 10003

Library of Congress Cataloging-in-Publication Data

Black, Cara, 1951–
    Murder in Belleville / Cara Black.
        p. cm.
    ISBN 1-56947-279-3 (alk. paper)
    1. Private investigators—France—Paris—Fiction. 2. Belleville
(Paris, France)—Fiction. 3. Paris (France)—Fiction. I. Title.

PS3552.L297 M79 2000
813'.54—dc21

                                                    00-041012

Printed in the United States

10   9   8   7   6   5   4   3   2

Dedicated to all the ghosts, past and present

Thanks to so many who helped: Karen Fawcett; Joanna Bartholomew and Gala Besson in Menilmontant; Bertrand Baché *merci*, soul-*soeurs* Dot Edwards and Marion Nowak; Latifa Eloualladi; Claude and Amina; Julie Curtet, *agent de recherche privée*; Jean-Jacques and Pascal; Jean Dutailly; the Saturday group; Andre Valat, Police Attaché French Embassy Ivory Coast; Thomas Erhady, Police Attaché French Embassy Washington DC; sgt. Mike Peck, Bomb Squad; Carla; Terri Haddix, MD, Forensic Pathologist; the Noe Valley librarians; Denise Smart, MD; Isabelle *et* Andi; *encore* Denise Schwarzbach Alice; Michael Harris of DRG Digital Resources Group for his patience; Jean Vargues and the Electricité de France group; Jane; the B's; the woman on the Oujda train; Grace Loh for her generosity; James N. Frey *toujours* and without whom; Linda Allen for her encouragement; a deep thanks to Melanie Fleishman who makes it all clear; my son Shuchan who lets me; and always to Jun.

As welcome as a hair in one's soup
—a French saying

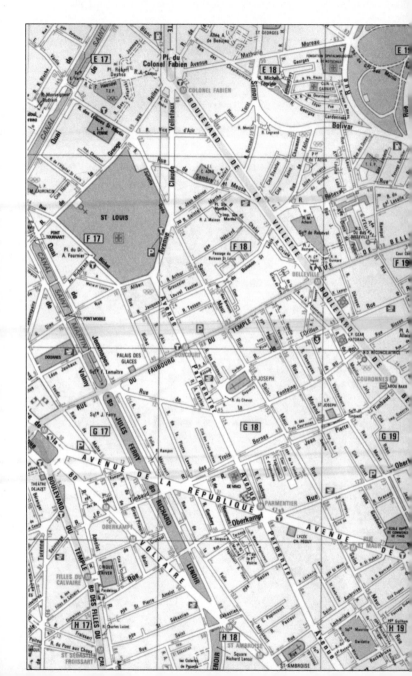

PARIS

APRIL 1994

AIMÉE LEDUC'S CELL PHONE rang, startling her, as she drove under the leafy poplars tenting the road to Paris. For a moment she'd felt as if she were flying—flying into spring, away from the winter, when her broken body needed to heal.

Aimée groped around in her backpack until she found her phone wedged next to her ultrablack mascara. Freeing it from her extra sweater, snarled on a software encryption manual, she finally flicked it open.

"Aimée!" shouted a woman's voice. "It's Anaïs."

"*Ça va?*" Aimée said, surprised to hear the voice of her friend Martine's sister. In the background Aimée heard loud voices. "Anaïs, let me call—"

"You have to help me," Anaïs interrupted.

Several years had passed since Aimée had seen her. "What's the matter, Anaïs?"

"I'm in trouble."

Aimée pushed her black sunglasses down on her nose and ruffled her short, spiky hair. How typical of Anaïs—everything revolved around her. A dull pewter sky blanketed the suburb of Aubervilliers. Within minutes the sky opened, and rain blanketed the road.

"Right now I've got to drop some work off, Anaïs," she said with growing impatience.

"Martine talked to you, didn't she?" Anaïs asked.

Impatience turned to guilt. Despite her promise to do so, she'd never called Anaïs after Martine spoke with her. Anaïs suspected her husband, a government minister, of having an affair. Computer security, Aimée had protested, was her field—not spousal surveillance.

The phone reception wavered and flared.

"Right now it's difficult," she said. "I'm working, Anaïs."

She didn't want to interrupt her work. Thanks to a client referral, she was dropping off a network systems security proposal at the Electricité de France. Aimée prayed that this would get Leduc Detective back on its feet after a lean winter.

"Please, we have to meet," Anaïs said, urgency in her voice. "Rue des Cascades . . . near parc de Belleville." Anaïs's voice came and went like a piece of laundry whipping in the wind. "I need you."

"Of course, as soon as I finish. I'm on the outskirts of Paris," Aimée said. "Twenty kilometers away."

"I'm scared, Aimée." Anaïs was sobbing now.

Aimée felt torn. She heard a muffled noise as if Anaïs had covered the receiver with her hand.

Birds scattered from hedgerows. Along the gully budding daffodils bowed, skirting a mossy barge canal. Aimée pressed the Citroën's pedal harder, her cheek reddening in the whipping wind.

"But Anaïs, I might take some time."

"Café Tlemcen, an old zinc bar, I'm in the back." Anaïs's voice broke. ". . . get caught. . . ." Aimée heard the unmistakable shrieking of brakes, of shouting.

"Anaïs, wait!" she said.

Her phone went dead.

MORE THAN an hour later, Aimée found the café with dingy lace curtains. She eased out of her partner's Citroën, which was fitted to accomodate his four-foot stature, and smoothed her black leather pants.

Strains of Arab hip-hop remix drifted in from the street. The narrow café overlooked rue des Cascades; no entrance to a back room was in evidence at first glance. Pinball machines from the sixties, their silvered patina rubbed off in places, stood blinking in the corner.

Aimée wondered if she'd made a mistake. This didn't seem the kind of place Anaïs would frequent. But she remembered the panic in Anaïs's voice.

Apart from a man with his back to her, the café's round wooden tables were empty. He appeared to be speaking with someone who stood behind the counter. Old boxing posters curled away from the brown nicotine-stained wall. She inhaled the odor of espresso and Turkish tobacco.

"Pardon, Monsieur," she said, combing her fingers through her hair. "I'm supposed to meet someone in your dining room."

As he swiveled around to look at her, she realized that there was no one else behind the counter. He put down a microphone, clicked a button on a small tape recorder, and cocked a thick eyebrow at her.

"Who would that be?" he said, amusement in his heavy-lidded eyes. His thinning gray hair, combed across his skull, didn't quite cover the bald top of his head.

A long blue shirtsleeve pinned to his shoulder by a military medal concealed what she imagined were the remains of his arm. Behind the counter sepia photos of military men in desert jeeps were stuck in the tarnished, beveled mirror.

"Anaïs de . . ." She stumbled trying to remember Anaïs's married name. She'd been to their wedding several years ago. "Anaïs de Froissart—that's it. She said she'd be in the back room."

"The only back room here is the toilet," he said. "Buy a drink, and you can meet who you like there."

A *frisson* of apprehension shook her. What was going on?

"Perhaps there's another Café Tlemcen?"

"*Bien sûr*, but it's three thousand kilometers from here, near Oran," he said. "Outside Sidi-bel-Abbès, where I lost my arm." He nodded to his tape machine. "I'm recording the truth about the Algerian war, anticolonial struggles from 1954–61, and how our battalion survived OAS friendly-fire bombardment."

Why had Anaïs suggested this place? Had she made a mistake?

Aimée stepped closer to the counter. "I might have misunderstood my friend. Did a woman use your telephone recently?"

"Who are you, Mademoiselle, if I may ask?"

"Aimée Leduc." She pulled a damp business card from her bag and laid it on the sticky zinc counter. "My friend sounded agitated on the phone."

He studied her, his hand wiping a falling strand of hair back over the bald dome of his head. "I've been busy with deliveries."

"This isn't like my friend Anaïs," she said. "She was very upset. I heard car brakes, loud voices." She searched his face, trying to ascertain if he was telling the truth.

He hobbled out from behind the large chrome espresso machine to where she stood.

"A blond, wearing designer clothes and gold chains, came in," he said. "She looked like she'd made a wrong turn coming out of the Crillon."

That must have been Anaïs. Aimée maintained her composure—this man was proving to be a helpful observer.

Torn between searching for Anaïs and hoping she'd return, Aimée decided to wait. She drummed her chipped red nails on the counter. She remembered Martine complaining about her sister: It was always hurry up and wait.

"Did you see her leave, Monsieur?"

He shook his head.

She was dying for a cigarette. Too bad she'd quit five days, six hours, and twenty minutes ago.

"She told me to meet her here. She'll be back."

"Doubt it," he said, studying her as if coming to a decision.

"Why?"

"She gave me a hundred francs," he said. "Said for you to meet her at 20 *bis* rue Jean Moinon."

Aimée stiffened. "Why didn't you say so?"

"Had to be sure you're the impatient one with big eyes," he said. "She said to make sure it was you."

He nodded his head toward the street. "She knew she was being followed."

Aimée felt the first hint of fear.

The man gave a half bow. "Retired Lieutenant Gaston Valat SCE, formerly with the intelligence branch of the Franco-Algerian police," he said. He stood to attention as much as a one-armed man with a limp could. He noticed her gaze. "A *votre service*. Not half bad, eh?"

Not all that surprised by his change of attitude, she figured an old vet like him would welcome action on his doorstep.

"When did Anaïs leave, Gaston?"

"Close to an hour ago," he said.

She shouldered her bag.

"And like I told her," Gaston said, studying her, "*adieu*."

AIMÉE HURRIED into the sheets of rain. Her edgy feeling had been growing all week. Paris was bracing itself for terrorist attacks, the radio warned, due to enforcement of the anti-immigration policy. The *flics* were nervous and, as Aimée knew, when nervous they tended to overreact. Shopping on the quai, she'd noticed the darting *flics'* eyes. She'd seen the dark blue suited CRS riot police in her Métro station with machine guns questioning random riders. Even *boulangerie* patrons in line ahead of her had jumped, startled by the sudden banging of trash cans. It seemed like everyone vibrated with fear.

By the time she reached the boulevard the downpour had ceased. Twilight covered Belleville. Parents tugged children from shop to shop under umbrellas or placated them with baguettes at the crowded bus shelters.

The aroma of cumin from the corner Lebanese restaurant perfumed the rain-freshened air. Aimée had forgotten the bustle and energy in Belleville. African dialects reached her ears. She walked by abandoned, graffiti-covered turn-of-the-century shop-fronts. Taxi *klaxons* honked, and old men bargained in Arabic at fruit stands. Senegalese women clad in bright-patterned cloth-ing and headresses shared the Métro stairs with black-on-black Parisian sophisticates.

A neighborhood of *caractère*, she thought, but its working-class origins had suffered the onslaught of the trendy. Chunks of the grime-blackened eighteenth-century buildings in Edith Piaf's for-mer neighborhood had either been torn down or renovated.

The saucerlike April moon had risen by the time she'd reached the narrow street. In contrast to the busy boulevard, rue Jean Moinon lay quiet. Aimée paused. The smell of wet dog mingled with rosewater from a nearby passage. She wondered why Anaïs would come here.

The streetlamp's yellow cone of light revealed broken pave-ment. Parked cars filled one side of the narrow street. Number 20 *bis*, or 20 and a half—as Aimée remembered her mother explaining the term—consisted of two floors with many bricked-up windows. That was one of the few things she recalled her American mother joking about. Number 7 *bis*, their old apart-ment, had been referred to by her mother as "half here and half not, like me." Not long after that, when Aimée was eight, her mother had tacked a note on the apartment door telling her to stay with the neighbor until her father came home. Her mother had never returned.

Aimée stood back and looked up at the nineteenth-century building. Dark and silent. Only one floor had open windows, their shutters weathered and broken. No concierge or *gardien*. Just a massive wooden door defaced by silver graffiti.

Gaston could have given her the wrong address.

"Anaïs?"

Had Anaïs ever come—or had she already left?

Aimée didn't know the code for entry so she rang the service bell. She waited, watching the streetlight's reflection dance in the oily puddles between cobbles. Opposite, several buildings advertised apartments to rent.

No answer. She shifted in her boots, looked around. The street was deserted. Apprehensive, she felt like leaving.

Aimée walked up the uneven pavement to the end of the street, regretting her impulsiveness in following Anaïs's trail. This wild goose chase had led nowhere. She wanted to kick herself—why had she agreed to help? She needed to hustle for the EDF contract!

Spousal surveillance really wasn't her field. Next time she'd think twice before she ran into the rain. She turned to retrace her steps. On her way back to the car she'd try one more time.

In the distance she saw two women emerge from the door of 20 *bis*. Aimée recognized one as Anaïs, her blond hair illuminated by the streetlight. The other, a dark-haired woman, wore a shiny black raincoat that swung as she moved. The woman opened the driver's door of the car parked in front, reached in, then shoved something across the car's roof to Anaïs, who waited on the curb.

As Aimée walked closer, she saw that the car was a powder blue Mercedes. Anaïs stuck the object in her shoulder bag, put on her sunglasses, then rushed off without saying good-bye. Odd, Aimée thought, since it was dark and rainy.

"Anaïs!" Aimée called out, hurrying to catch up with her.

Anaïs turned, noticed Aimée, and waved in recognition.

Strains of Arabic music suddenly blared from nearby, loud and piercing. "Shut that crap off!" someone shouted from a window.

The dark-haired woman slammed her car door and started her engine, and with a blinding flash the Mercedes exploded. With a deafening roar, the car burst into a white-yellow ball of flame. Aimée faltered, and everything seemed to move in slow motion, but it could only have been microseconds. Terror flooded her. Tires and doors blew off like missiles, into the stone buildings.

She saw Anaïs rise in the air, as if she were flying, then disappear. The ground reverberated.

The pressure wave knocked Aimée off balance in mid-dive, as she aimed for the nearest car. The backdraft sucked the air as if trying to vacuum her body into a smaller space. Tighter than she could stand. Steel fragments and bloody viscera rained over the street.

Aimée landed on wet cobblestones praying that nothing else would explode. Her heart hammered. She tried to cover her head with her hands. Memories of the Place Vendôme terrorist explosion that killed her father came back: his burned body ejecting from the surveillance van, her hand holding the molten door handle, and the fireball that engulfed the van as it smashed into the Place Vendôme column.

And then she realized the danger—gas tank vapors from the parked cars could ignite from the flames. She pulled herself up. Made her legs move. Made them go past the Mercedes's metal skeleton, burning furiously and bulging like an accordion. The intense heat singed her eyebrows. She had to find Anaïs, get out of here.

Her ears rang, and she choked on the billowing smoke. She tripped on the cobblestones, greasy with oil and antifreeze. Her hands were bloody and shaking. Like five years ago when her father had been blown up in front of her eyes—the same horrible nightmare.

BERNARD BERGE, FORTY-FIVE YEARS old and prematurely gray, stared out from his ministry office window onto Place Beauvau, dreading the imminent phone call. He pushed his round-rimmed glasses up on his forehead and rubbed his weary eyes. He felt in his pockets again for the blue pills. Only two left.

Across the square the flickering blue lights of the Elysée presidential palace blurred in the spring night. Bernard hadn't slept in days. Sixty-two hours, to be exact, and he didn't think he would ever sleep again. The sleeping pills had stopped working.

A loud knock sounded on his office door. He'd left instructions not to be disturbed. Who could this be?

"*Oui,*" he said. "Is this urgent?"

In answer the heavy wooden door opened slowly. His mother, a small white-haired sparrow of a woman with deep-set black eyes, strode in. Without removing her wrinkled raincoat, she planted herself in front of his desk in the chilly office.

"Maman!" he said. "What are you doing here?"

From the reception area beyond his open door, several heads looked up. He hurried to the door and shut it.

"Bernard, as God is my witness," she said, "I can't believe you will allow this."

"Sit down, Maman."

His mother remained standing and pulled open her bag with difficulty, then set a much-thumbed *carte de séjour* down on his desk. "Your stepfather earned this residence permit. And Bernard, you studied the Bible. You know God's higher law." Her voice quavered, but her gaze held steady. "Put your hand on it; swear to me you will not deport any victims."

"Be reasonable, Maman." Bernard Berge sat down heavily in his chair. How could she confront him like this?

"Did nothing you saw of the repressions make sense?" Her hands shook. "Forget this business, but not your conscience."

"Right now that's impossible, Maman."

"How can you say that?" She sat down. "You were born in Algiers." She shook her head. "You spoke Arabic as fluently as French until we got to Marseilles."

"This immigration issue is different," he said. "These *sans-papiers* stayed after their visas expired. They're illegal. Not like us *pieds-noirs*; we were born in Algeria."

"Did our little André die in vain?"

Bernard flinched as though she'd slapped him. His younger brother, André, had been torn from his crib by rebel *fellaghas* and hurled down the village well. Lots of babies had, in retaliation for the French massacres of whole villages in the countryside. But it had been years before he'd learned this. He never ceased to wonder how his mother could live with such pain.

"Maybe I've been silent too long," she said, as if she could hear his thoughts. "I instilled values, raised you as a socialist." She shook her head. Her eyes darkened. "What happened?"

"I'm just a *fonctionnaire* responsible for unpopular policy, Maman. Antoine has lived your dream," Bernard said. He stood up, bracing himself for their ongoing argument. His half-brother Antoine ran the pediatric ward of a major hospital and a free clinic in Marseilles.

"But these *sans-papiers* Africains, these Arabes . . . they are just people, *non?*" Her voice softened, pleading. "As *pieds-noirs* we came to France, but we were not welcomed as real French. We were outsiders, and still are in some places."

"It's the law, Maman. If I don't do this, someone else will."

"The Nazis said that, too," she said, shaking her head.

Bernard paced to the tall ministry windows and looked down on rue des Saussaies. Once the Gestapo had detained whomever they wished in the police headquarters a block away. Lantern lights reflected long quivering rectangles in the Elysée's fountain-fed pools.

Why couldn't she understand?

"Mothers and children," she sighed. "How can you deport them?"

Bernard's head was splitting. He rubbed his eyes again. Why wouldn't she leave him alone?

"We have laws in France assuring *liberté, égalité, fraternité*," he said. "My job is to protect that, follow the ministry policy. You know that, Maman. I don't design these directives."

"You look like you haven't slept," she said. She rose slowly, her eyes boring into his. She turned and walked to the door. "If I had your job, Bernard, I wouldn't be able to sleep either."

"Maman, please be reasonable," he said. "I've served in the Palais de Justice, presided as a *juge d'administratif*. I must follow the law."

"Bernard, you have a choice," she said, turning to face him again. "But if you make the wrong one, never defile my house again."

He stood at the window and listened to her shuffle away. Buried fragments from his childhood rose up in his mind—the muezzins' call to prayer at sunrise, the long, dusty lines for bread, the blue mosaic fountain trickling in their arched courtyard, the cries in the darkness as the *souk* in their *quartier* burst aflame during the riots.

His phone rang. Bernard debated whether or not to answer, then picked it up.

"*Le Ministre* Guittard regrets to say that immigration orders can be ignored no longer," came the smooth voice of Lucien Nedelec, the undersecretary. "Your department, *Directeur* Berge, has been ordered to uphold the deportation policy. Please proceed."

There was a long pause.

"I understand," Bernard said.

The peach-colored sunset had already dipped over the Seine outside Bernard's window when his intercom buzzed an hour later.

"Shall I send in the *caporal, Directeur?*" his secretary said. "He has no appointment."

The Elysée Palace must have come up with a plan and wanted his input.

"Tell them I'll join them in a moment."

Would he be served up to the country and the media on a platter, a convenient scapegoat for the controversial policy? He'd already been denounced by his mother. Could it get any worse?

He buttoned his collar, reknotted his tie, and slipped his suit jacket on.

The RAID paramilitary team stood in the vaulted hallway.

"*Directeur* Berge, accompany us, please," said a steel-eyed man dressed in riot gear.

Bernard stood, holding his head high, then nodded. "Lead the way, Monsieur."

Bernard followed them past halls carpeted with eighteenth-century rugs and mirrored walls opening onto a sweeping staircase and a soaring, thirty-foot ceiling. More like a museum than a working ministry, he'd always thought. In Place Beauvau, he was bundled into a waiting black Renault. Once inside, the steel-eyed man pointed to the hazy northeast of Paris. "We're escorting you there."

"Aren't we going to the Elysée Palace?"

"They're waiting for you at the church," he said.

"Who's waiting?" Bernard asked, puzzled.

"The hunger strikers in Notre-Dame de la Croix."

"Aren't there trained negotiators there?" Bernard said, his voice cracking. He knew a crowd of *sans-papiers* had taken over a church in Belleville. Some were staging a hunger strike to protest deportation.

"Seems you've been requested."

"Requested?" Bernard asked.

"You're special," he said, nodding to the driver who pulled into traffic.

He had been right, Bernard thought woefully. Things could get worse.

"ANAÏS, WHERE ARE YOU?" Aimée shouted. At least now she could hear herself. The intense heat drove her to move, to shake off the memories of her father.

She crawled along the cobbles, then pulled herself up. Someone was crying; she heard yelling in the distance. Her body felt as if someone had beaten her all over with a bat. Long and hard.

"Over here, Aimée," Anaïs moaned, sprawled on the sidewalk. She was pinned down by a large *appartement à louer* sign, ripped from an adjacent building. The rental sign had probably saved her life, Aimée thought.

Aimée felt for a pulse. It was weak, but steady. Aimée shook Anaïs's shoulders. She groaned. Strands of gold chain, muddied and twisted, drooped from her neck. Her pigeon-eye pink Dior jacket was dotted with bloody red clumps and her blond hair was matted. Black vinyl fragments littered the street.

"Can you hear me, Anaïs?" she asked, her voice soothing, as she pulled the sign away. She knelt down and took off Anaïs's sunglasses. Luckily for her, they'd shielded her eyes from the blast.

Anaïs blinked several times, her eyes regaining focus.

"Where's S-S-Sylvie?"

"Was Sylvie getting into the Mercedes?"

Anaïs nodded.

"She's gone, Anaïs," Aimée said, taking Anaïs's chin in her hands and making her meet her gaze.

Anaïs blinked again and focused on her, growing lucid.

"Your hands are shaking, Aimée," she said.

"Explosions do that to me," Aimée said, aware of the burning car just meters away. "Let's get out of here."

Anaïs saw that there was blood on her skirt. She looked up, past Aimée, her eyes widening in alarm.

"They're coming back," Anaïs said.

Aimée scanned the street. People peered from their windows. Several men were running down the street.

"Who?"

But Anaïs had scrambled on all fours, pulling Aimée after her into the number 20 *bis* door, which had blown ajar.

"Close the door before they see us!" Anaïs panted.

Out of breath, Aimée crawled in, then pushed the massive door shut. Ahead, the red button of a timer light switch gleamed, and she pressed it. The damp floor and dented wall mailboxes were lit by a naked bulb overhead. Of the several mailboxes only one held a name: "E. Grandet."

To the right of the staircase, a narrow drafty passage led to the rear courtyard. Newspapers, thrown in a dusty heap, sat under the spiral stairwell.

"Who are those men?" Aimée asked.

"The ones who followed me," Anaïs said.

Loud shouting came from the street. What if the men broke down the door? Torn between confronting them or looking for an escape, Aimée froze.

Now the voices came from outside the massive door. Loud whacks made the door shudder, as if they were attacking the door's kickplate. Her fear propelled her to action.

"Let's go," Aimée said, pulling out her penlight.

"My legs . . . don't work well," Anaïs panted.

Aimée helped her stand up.

"Put your weight on me," Aimée said. Together they hobbled down the drafty passage leading toward the back.

Her thin beam flickered off the dripping stone wall; moss furred in green patches. The walls reeked of mildew and urine.

April in Paris wasn't like the song, Aimée thought, and couldn't remember when it had been.

Something glinted in the cracks, where stone joined the gutter. She bent down, shined her penlight. In the yawning crevice, an indecently large pearl shimmered.

She pried it out and rubbed the slime off with her sleeve.

"Anaïs, did you drop this?"

"Not my style," she said, breathing hard.

Aimée slipped the pearl into her back pocket. As she edged past the rotted wooden door, she was glad she'd worn leather boots. Too bad they had two-inch heels.

"Who are they, Anaïs?"

"Just keep going, Aimée," Anaïs said, panting.

She headed for an old metal *fonderie* workshop in the courtyard. The fluttering of disturbed pigeons greeted them.

The building smelled of garbage. Her small penlight beam revealed several blue plastic sacks of trash. Unusual, she thought. The building appeared deserted. Not only that, but the garbage in Paris was collected every day.

Slants of moonlight illuminated part of the rain-slicked cobbles and wet walls inside. Empty green Ricard bottles lay strewn in what appeared to be the main part of the old workshop.

She helped Anaïs sit down.

"Let me check for a back exit," Aimée said. "Take a rest."

On Aimée's left, twisted pipes and a network of frayed electric lines trailed up the building interior to the remaining bit of black roof.

Through the hole above loomed the dark dome of the sky, and a yellow glow outlined the rooftops of Belleville. Aimée stumbled on the slippery concrete, caught her heel and lurched outside. She grabbed hold of something rusty that flaked in her hands. Straightening up, she took another step. She skidded and lost her balance but held on to her penlight, shining the beam ahead.

A stone wall five or six feet high stood in front of her. Jagged glass, like a string of grinning teeth, lined the top.

No exit.

Aimée tried not to panic.

Returning to Anaïs, she noticed the buttery leather Dior bag strap tangled around Anaïs's shoulder. The last time Aimée had seen Anaïs she'd also been in Dior, radiant and walking down the steps of St-Séverin on the arm of her new husband, Philippe, as the cathedral bells chimed over the square on the *rive gauche*. Aimée remembered dancing with Martine and her father at the candlelit reception at the Crillon, and Anaïs giggling while Philippe drank champagne from her silk shoe.

She shook Anaïs's shoulder. "Please, Anaïs, tell me what's going on," Aimée said. "Were these men trying to kill you?"

Anaïs gagged, turned, and threw up all over the empty Ricard bottles in the *fonderie*. The delayed reaction worried Aimée— had the realization just hit Anaïs, or did she have internal injuries?

Anaïs wiped her jaw with her sleeve and nodded. Then she burst into tears, sobbing.

"I wish to God I knew," she said.

Aimée pulled out her phone to get help, but her battery was dead. They were stuck.

"*Nom de Dieu!*" Anaïs said. "That *pute* Sylvie, she's the cause—" Anaïs choked.

"How—who is she?"

"The sow my husband slept with," Anaïs said, catching air. She straightened up, then took deep breaths through her nose. "On a regular basis. Sylvie Coudray. It was over. But I think she blackmailed him." Anaïs began sobbing again. "Philippe, he's such a weakling."

Aimée wiped Anaïs's mouth clean and smoothed her hair back. She knelt closer, trying to ignore the stench.

"What did Sylvie give you?"

"Who knows?" she pleaded, her eyes wide in terror. She reached inside the handbag. Her hand came back with something metal, the size of a makeup brush, and passed it to Aimée.

Aimée recognized the five-fingered brass hand covered with Arabic writing, a good luck 'hand of Fat'ma' strung with hanging blue beads and a third eye. A talisman to ward off evil spirits.

Sirens sounded in the distance; the hee-haw got closer. Aimée figured they came from the boulevard. More pounding came from somewhere outside the building. Louder and stronger. Startled, Aimée almost dropped the Fat'ma symbol.

"Open up!" shouted a loud voice.

Aimée stuck the charm back in Anaïs's purse.

"We've got to get out of here," Anaïs said.

Aimée steadied her hand on Anaïs.

"What kind of hell is this?" Anaïs said, covering her ears with her blood-spattered hands, and rocking back and forth. "You've got to help—so sordid," she gulped, grabbing Aimée's arm.

Aimée brushed Anaïs's skirt off and helped her to stand.

"Philippe's a minister. I can't let them find me here!" Anaïs's knees buckled.

"Can you walk?" Aimée asked.

Anaïs nodded.

From the passage, she heard scraping metal noises and footsteps.

Aimée looked around the courtyard. They were hemmed in by the U-shaped building and stone wall.

Behind Aimée and Anaïs, the passage's wooden door banged. The footsteps pounded closer. Aimée figured the only way for them to escape was over the stone wall topped by jagged glass.

Aimée helped Anaïs to the wall, then cupped her hands. "Climb. Be careful of the glass."

Aimée winced as Anaïs stepped a high heel on her hands. She heaved her up and heard Anaïs groan. Aimée braced herself and pushed Anaïs's slender frame over the wall. For a small woman, Anaïs felt heavy.

"Go on," Aimée hissed. "Let yourself drop to the other side."

She heard wood splintering and figured Anaïs had landed.

"Run toward the boulevard. Whatever happens, just get to the Métro," Aimée said. Getting back to the car would be impossible.

Aimée climbed and gripped the jutting stone. She shimmied herself up trying to find footholds, afraid to cut herself to shreds on the glass if she got stuck. Her fingertips had just reached the ledge with broken glass when she heard voices. She had to move and forget the pain.

Stretching her leg as far as she could and scraping her heel across the stone, she hit something flat and pulled herself up.

She took a deep breath, then pushed off the wall into the yard of the next building. She landed on her feet. No Anaïs. Aimée took off, running, into a disused garage lot, but slowed down to avoid banging into something and alerting the neighbors. A heap of rusted bicycles and once-chrome car bumpers were piled close to each other.

"Over here," Anaïs whispered.

Aimée narrowed her eyes and saw Anaïs crouched on her knees in the mud behind a faded Pirelli tire sign.

"Let's go," Aimée said.

Anaïs crawled on her hands and knees, low moans escaping from her. When Aimée reached to help her, she realized that Anaïs's legs were cut to ribbons from the glass.

"I tried to walk, but my legs won't hold me," she said, her face a chalky white in the moonlight.

Aimée looked again and saw blood oozing from Anaïs's thigh, soaking her skirt. If she didn't stop it, Anaïs would pass out. She couldn't get Anaïs this far and leave her. Aimée quickly looked around—why didn't Anaïs wear a silk *foulard* around her neck, like every other Parisienne? She grabbed the closest thing—a deflated tire tube—and looped it around Anaïs's leg as a tourniquet. She tightened it, and the bleeding stopped.

Anaïs managed a weak smile. "Forgive me, Aimée, for pulling you into this."

"You're being really brave," Aimée said, hoisting her up and linking her arm around Anaïs. She brushed the hair from Anaïs's eyes. "I know it hurts. Try to walk; we'll get to the Métro. It's not far."

"But look at me! What will people think?" Anaïs asked, gesturing toward her leg and blood-spattered suit.

She was right, Aimée thought. But what choice did they have?

Aimée half dragged and half carried Anaïs several meters through the abandoned lot, puddled and muddy, past the semi-roofed garage. She couldn't keep this up all the way to the Métro, and she doubted the chances of catching a taxi here. Not to mention staying out of the sight of curious neighbors. Running away from an explosion wouldn't look good to the *flics*.

Anaïs grew heavier, more like dead weight. Aimée noticed that Anaïs's eyes were closing, and her body went limp.

Aimée set Anaïs down under a corrugated overhang jammed with old bikes and mopeds. They were stuck in a muddy garage lot.

She couldn't leave Anaïs here. She tried to think, but her shoulders ached, her legs were scratched with glass cuts, and she wondered what in hell she was doing with a minister's wife who was being chased by men who'd probably planted the car bomb under his mistress's car.

What could she do now?

Barbed wire crested the chain-link fence. But only a Bricard lock held the gate. She kept Anaïs's bag around her, then reached for her makeup bag inside her backpack. She found the Swedish stainless-steel tweezers. Within two minutes she'd jimmied the lock open, muffling the clinking sounds with her sweater sleeve. That done, she wiped the sweat off her brow with her other sleeve and surveyed the bikes strewn around Anaïs.

No way would she be able to pedal, steer, and grip Anaïs. She was exhausted. She noticed a beat-up but serviceable Motoguzzi moped by an oil can. It was like her own moped, but a lot older. And with more horsepower. One thing she knew about mopeds—they could run on fumes for several kilometers, and if the spark plug was still good they might make an escape.

After unscrewing the spark plug, she blew on it to get rid of the carbon, scraped corrosion off the pronged head with her tweezers, and screwed it back on. She shook the body from side to side to slosh any gas around, pulled out the choke, and prayed. She started pedaling. Silence. She kept pedaling and was finally rewarded by a cough. Good, she thought. Temperamental as these Italian bikes might be, with patience and coaxing they would deliver. With much more encouragement, the cough had developed into a full-throated hum, and she hoisted Anaïs up and urged her tourniqueted leg over the moped's passenger ledge. Anaïs's eyes fluttered, then widened. She pushed Aimée's shoulder and tried to get off.

"No!" Anaïs yelled. "I can't do this."

"Got a better idea?" Aimée asked.

In the distance the sound of a siren came closer.

"I hate motorcycles," she wailed.

"*Bien*, this is a moped," Aimée said, gunning the engine and popping into first. "Hold on!"

Anaïs grabbed Aimée's waist.

"No matter what," Aimée said, "don't let go!"

Aimée reached rue Ste-Marthe as the SAMU emergency van turned into rue Jean Moinon. Odd. Why hadn't the fire truck arrived first?

A black-and-white *flic* car cruised from rue de Sambre-et-Meuse, blocking the shortcut to the Goncourt Métro.

"Let's ask them for help, Anaïs."

"*Non*, nothing must connect to Philippe," Anaïs said.

Aimée's heart sank as Anaïs's fingers squeezed her in a steel-like grip.

She kept an even speed, afraid that going faster would invite curiosity. The *flics* veered in the other direction. Aimée turned into Place Sainte-Marthe, a small rain-soaked square, its single café closed for the evening.

She noticed a dark Renault Twingo turn after her at the far end of the square. By the time the verdigris art nouveau Métro sign came into view, the car had edged close behind them.

As if reading her thoughts, it pulled ahead. She drove near the closest Métro entrance, and the car cut in front of her. Its doors popped open, and two burly men jumped out.

She veered away from them at the last minute but a bearlike man obstructed the wet sidewalk. The padlocked newspaper kiosk and the Métro stairs were in front of them.

Aimée scanned the intersection, registering a few cars paused at the red light and Métro entrances on the other corners. Ahead a Crédit Lyonnais bank stood opposite Crédit Agricole, with a gutted café still advertising horseracing and a FNAC Télécom store facing that.

"Anaïs, grab me tighter."

"No, Aimée!" Anaïs yelled.

"You want to spend the night with these *mecs?*" Aimée asked. "Or in the *Commissariat de Police?*"

"*On y va*," Anaïs whimpered in answer, digging her fingernails into Aimée's stomach.

Aimée cornered the kiosk, zigzagged across the narrow street, and headed down the Métro steps, honking and screaming "Out of the way!" It took a minute before the thugs realized that the moped had plunged down the stairs and ran after them.

Exiting passengers yelled and moved to the railing as she and

Anaïs bumped and wobbled their way down. Aimée squeezed the brakes.

Thank God Anaïs was a small woman! Even so Aimée's wrists hurt from braking so hard with the handlebars. At the landing by the ticket window, plastic sheets and barricades for construction blocked their way. A uniformed man in the window shouted at them, shook his head, and pounded on the glass. The burning rubber smell from the moped's brakes and black exhaust filled the air.

The turnstiles were being repaired at night—just their luck, since the Métro carried fewer passengers than usual. But, Aimée also realized, she and Anaïs would be thug bait unless they could reach a platform, ditch the moped, and get on a train quickly.

Blue-overalled workers, under glaring lights, drilled and hammered. Several of them stopped their work, snickering and catcalling. They grew quiet when they saw the smeared blood on Anaïs and her look of terror.

"*Tiens*, this section's closed," one of the workers said. "Use the other entrance."

"Her *salop* of a boyfriend beat her up," Aimée improvised.

"No mopeds, *mesdemoiselles*."

"He's trailing us—vowing to kill her," she said. "We need help."

A large bearded man set down his drill and stood up.

"Can't you let us through?" she asked. "Please!"

The man stepped forward, pulled the plastic sheets aside with a theatrical gesture, and bowed, "*Entrez, mesdemoiselles*, courtesy of the RATP. Please be our guests."

"Gallantry lives. *Merci*," Aimée said.

She revved the motor and shot past the construction. Hot air dusty with concrete grit met her. The moped shimmied as she drove through a puddle, the back wheel almost dovetailing. They sped along the tiled tunnel past Canal 2 posters to a fork.

She paused. Two choices lay ahead—direction Châtelet or Mairie des Lilas. Which train would come first?

The late-night Métro ran infrequently. No matter which train they took, Aimée thought, the men would split up and each take a platform. Even if she and Anaïs managed to get on a train, they'd be followed easily. If only Anaïs could walk or navigate!

Either way they wouldn't get far.

To the right sat a man cross-legged on a sleeping bag. His shaved scalp shined in the overhead light. He watched them with an amused expression, pointing to his begging bowl.

The tiles gleamed in the warm Métro. Blue-and-white signs proclaimed *accés aux quais* and *sortie* to avenue Parmentier. Her only solution would be to go up the exit steps on the left. Would the moped have enough juice to mount the stairs? Aimée doubted it.

"Go for it," Anaïs said, surprising Aimée.

But how could she get Anaïs up the stairs on the moped? Her arms hurt, and with both their weights would the wheels go up?

Shouts came from the ticket area.

"Help us out, and I'll make it worth your while," she said to the homeless man.

"How much worth my while?" he asked in a bargaining tone. But he'd stood up and dusted off his worn trousers.

"This moped's yours," Aimée said, running her sleeve over her perspiring forehead and thinking fast. "If you help me get her to the top of the stairs. Deal?"

"Why not?" He grinned, quickly gathering his bedroll.

"Come with us to the stairs," she said. "Quickly."

He ran toward the exit. Behind them she heard heavy footsteps.

Aimée revved the motor and shot forward. The tunnel curved and she followed his trail. "If we just get halfway up, Anaïs, jump off, we can drag you the rest. Now lean into me and pray,"

Aimée yelled. She'd worry about the Twingo if they ever made it to the top.

At the first flight of stairs, she jerked up on the handlebars as much as possible and felt the bike respond. The tires churned, climbing several steps, the engine strained. But the moped climbed. Higher and higher. Aimée saw the dark tent of sky through the exit.

The bike had almost reached the last set of steps when she felt the tires buck.

Aimée had the sickening feeling of the bike rearing like a horse. She decelerated.

The homeless man reached over and steadied Anaïs. "Get off; it's too heavy!" he shouted. "We'll guide her up."

Anaïs loosened her grip on Aimée.

"Hold the handlebars, Anaïs," Aimée said, getting off and putting her arms around Anaïs's shoulders.

Time slowed as she and the homeless man guided Anaïs on the moped up the Métro steps.

The engine whined, snarled. Out of the corner of her eye, she saw the man steady Anaïs so she didn't topple into him.

But the moped tipped over. Like a felled animal, it whined uselessly on its side.

"*Allons-y!*" she yelled.

Only a few more steps to the top.

She grabbed Anaïs under the arms and together with the homeless man helped her hobble up the last stairs.

"*Merci,*" Aimée said. "Tell them we took the Métro toward Châtelet."

"And they just missed you," the man said, righting the moped. He took off down the sidewalk. Aimée hoped he'd keep their pursuers busy for a while.

"*Attends,* Anaïs," Aimée said lying on her stomach, peering around the cement divider near the Crédit Lyonnais.

She saw the Twingo, parked illegally on the opposite curb,

and a dark-suited man watching in all directions. If she and
Anaïs could join passersby and cross to the taxi stop on rue du
Faubourg du Temple, they'd escape. Traffic idled at the inter-
section. Tree-bordered Canal Saint Martin lay in the distance.

Aimée's hopes fell as Anaïs moaned again. No way could she
get her up and across to the taxi stop. A couple emerged from
an apartment building, laughing and kissing each other, as they
walked to the Métro.

Aimée crawled around the divider, then helped navigate Anaïs behind some bushes. Cardboard was piled next to the kiosk,
hiding them from view.

"Keep low. I'll get a taxi," she said taking off her sweater and
covering Anaïs. Aimée shivered in her damp silk shirt and spread
a piece of cardboard across a major puddle. She crawled across
to the curb, then crouched behind a plane tree. When another
couple walked by she stood up, kept her head turned and crossed
the street abreast of them.

By the time the taxi driver, to whom she'd promised a good
tip, pulled up on the sidewalk to pick up Anaïs, the driver of
the Twingo had noticed them. He jumped in the car and started
his engine.

"Lose that car," Aimée said to the taxi driver.

Anaïs reached in her purse and pulled out a wad of franc
notes. "Here, use this." She shoved them in Aimée's hand.

"Here's a hundred francs," Aimée said. "There's more if we
make it out of the *bas quartier* without our friend."

"*Quinze* Villa Georgina," Anaïs managed, then collapsed on
the seat. Aimée loosened the tourniquet, glad to see the bleeding
had stopped, and elevated Anaïs's leg.

As they sped up the Belleville streets toward Parc des Buttes
Chaumont, Aimée slouched down. The streetlights flickered
through the taxi windows. Cafés and bistros held lively crowds
despite the cold, wet April night. Aimée paused, remembering
the mailbox with "E. Grandet" on it.

"Why did you meet Sylvie?" Aimée asked.

"I'd like to forget about it," Anaïs said, holding back her sobs.

"Anaïs, of course it's painful, but if you don't talk to me," Aimée said, "how can I help?"

Poor Anaïs. Maybe she felt guilty. Didn't wives harbor thoughts of killing their husband's mistress no matter how civilized the arrangement?

"Sylvie arranged to meet me," Anaïs said, rubbing her eyes. "Said she didn't trust telephones."

"What happened?"

"The entry door was open," she said. Anaïs licked her knuckles, rubbed red raw in the dirt. "I went upstairs. The landing was spattered with pigeon droppings."

"The building looked ready to demolish," Aimée said. "Did Sylvie live there?" Why would a woman who drove a Mercedes live in a dump like that?

"Sylvie told me to meet her there. That's all I know," Anaïs said, her eyes downcast. "We argued right away."

"You argued?" Aimée said.

The lights of Belleville blinked as they wound up the hilly streets. Aimée poked her head up, but saw no Twingo behind them.

"My fault. I got angry," Anaïs said, shaking her head. "All those years of lying . . . I couldn't calm down. Sylvie kept going to the window. She made me nervous. I got mad and ran out the door."

Aimée wondered what Sylvie had been trying to tell Anaïs. Sylvie could have gone to the window to see if she'd been followed or was afraid Anaïs had.

"Was Philippe aware you were meeting her?" she asked.

"Why should he be? Philippe told me he finished with her months ago," Anaïs said. "Things between us were getting better."

Aimée stared at Anaïs. Had she gone to make sure he'd kept his word?

"Why did you want my help?"

"Call me a coward," Anaïs said, biting her lip. "I'm ashamed I thought she wanted money. But she asked me to forgive her."

"You mean forgive her for the past?"

"Told me how sorry she felt over things escalating," Anaïs said, breathing quickly.

"Escalating?"

"That's the term the *pute* used. Can you believe it?" Anaïs shook her head. She leaned back and took more deep breaths.

By the time they'd reached the angle where the streets met at Jourdain, the driver had definitely lost the Twingo. But he circled the winding streets around Saint Jean Baptiste Church several times to be safe.

The taxi followed the terraced streets intersected by lantern-lined wide stone stairs. Nineteenth-century rooflines faded below them. At rue de la Duée, they turned into narrow, cobblestoned Villa Georgina. This little-known area, she realized, was one of the most exclusive and expensive pockets of Belleville.

"I'm hiring you," Anaïs said, "to tell me what this means."

She reached in her bag, pulling out the Fat'ma and another wad of francs. "Consider this a retainer."

"The Fat'ma?" Aimée said, as Anaïs put the bronze, blue-beaded talisman in her hand.

Anaïs stuffed the francs in Aimée's pocket.

"Maybe this means nothing, but I want to know who killed her," Anaïs said. "Find out." Her eyes shuttered.

"Anaïs, talk to Philippe. You're in deep water," Aimée said, exasperated by her reaction. "If they blew up Sylvie's car and saw her pass something to you . . ."

"That's why you need to keep it," Anaïs said, her eyes black and serious.

Too bad this hadn't helped Sylvie, Aimée thought.

"My little Simone will think I've forgotten her," Anaïs said, worry in her voice. "I always put her to bed."

Lights blazed brightly from the upstairs windows as the taxi pulled up.

"*Quelle catastrophe*—Philippe's hosting a reception for the Algerian Trade Delegation!"

"Worry about that later," Aimée said. "Look, Anaïs, we've broken a chunk of the penal code tonight, I want to stop while I'm still free on the street."

"You're in this with me," Anaïs said, her voice cracking. "I'm sorry I dragged you in, but you can't stop."

True. But Aimée wanted to run into the dark wet night and not look back.

"Right now," Aimée said, "we've got to get you inside."

She turned to the taxi driver and slipped him another of Anaïs's hundred-franc notes. "Please wait for me."

She helped Anaïs to a cobalt blue side door, set back along a narrow passage. After several knocks a buxom woman opened the door, silhouetted against the light. Aimée couldn't see her face but heard her gasp.

"*Madame . . . ça va?*"

"Vivienne, don't let Simone see me," Anaïs said, as though accustomed to giving orders. "Or anyone. Get me something to put over this."

Vivienne stood rooted to the spot. "*Monsieur le Ministre . . .*"

"*Vite, Vivienne!*" Anaïs barked. "Let us in."

Mobilized into action, Vivienne opened the door and shepherded them inside. She thrust an apron at Anaïs.

"Help me get my jacket off," Anaïs said.

Vivienne gingerly removed the blood-stained jacket and dropped it on the kitchen floor.

Anaïs staggered and clutched the counter, where trays of hors d'oeuvres were lined up. Vivienne's lips parted in fear, and she clutched her starched maid's uniform.

"But you must go to *l'hôpital*, Madame," she said.

"Vinegar," Anaïs whispered, exhausted by her efforts.

"What, Madame?"

"Soak the bloody jacket in vinegar," Anaïs muttered.

Aimée knew Anaïs was fading fast.

"Vivienne, tell *le Ministre* she's had a sudden attack of food poisoning," Aimée said. Aimée surveyed the plates. "Those," she pointed. "Tainted mussels. Apologize profusely to the guests."

"Of course," Vivienne said, backing into kitchen drawers.

"I'll get her upstairs," Aimée said, worried. "Bring some bandages. Towels if you have to; she's bleeding again."

Aimée grabbed the nearest kitchen towel and tied it tightly around Anaïs's leg.

Vivienne picked up a tray of *crudités* and bustled out of the kitchen.

They made it upstairs and down a dimly lit hall, the wood floor creaking at every hobbling step.

"Maman!" said a small voice from behind a partially open bedroom door. "Where's my *bisou*?"

The child's tone, so confident yet tinged with longing, rose at the end. Aimée melted at the little voice.

"*Un moment, mon coeur*," Anaïs said, pausing to regain her breath. "Special treat—you can come to my room in a minute."

Had she ever asked her mother for a goodnight kiss? Had her mother even listened? All Aimée remembered was the flat American accent saying, "Take care of yourself, Amy. No one else will."

In the high-ceilinged bedroom, with pale yellow walls and periwinkle blue curtains, Aimée helped Anaïs out of her clothes.

She wiped the blood from Anaïs's legs, helped her into a nightgown, then got her into bed. Aimée set several pillows beneath her leg. Again, after she applied direct pressure, the leg stopped bleeding. Thank God.

Aimée tied her own damp sweater around her waist.

A great weariness showed in Anaïs's sunken face. But when a carrot-haired child, in flannel pajamas dotted with stars, peered around the door, her face brightened.

"Maman, what's the matter?" asked the child, her brows knit together in worry. She padded in bare feet to her mother's side.

"Simone, I'm a little tired."

"I couldn't wait to see you, Maman," said the child.

"Me neither," Anaïs said, opening her arms and hugging her daughter. "*Merci*, Aimée. I'm fine now."

Aimée slipped out of the room, passing Vivienne who cast a large shadow, carrying antiseptic and towels.

"Please call Anaïs's doctor," she said. "The bleeding's stopped for now, but she should be checked for internal injuries."

Vivienne nodded.

"Keep checking on her, please," Aimée said. "I'll call later."

Down at the kitchen doorway Aimée paused and peered at the reception in progress. A mosque fashioned out of sugarcubes, with details painted in turquoise and embellished with a gold dome, stood near chilled Algerian wine and fruit juice. Knots of men, some in *djellabas*, others in suits, clustered under the de Froissarts' eighteenth-century chandeliers. Conversation buzzed in Arabic and French.

She hadn't seen Philippe de Froissart since the wedding, but she recognized him huddled among uniformed military men. He'd aged; his beaklike nose was more prominent, his mottled pink cheeks lined, and his black moustache graying. His thick black hair, white around the temples, curled over his collar. A member of the aristocracy, he'd once been a card-carrying Communist. Now he'd become a watered-down socialist, she thought, like everyone else.

She didn't want to crash the reception, smeared with mud and blood—his mistress's blood. But she had to get his attention and tell him what happened. She waved at him, standing partly behind the door.

Finally Philippe saw her. He reluctantly excused himself, causing several of the men in his group to turn and stare in her direction.

"Why, Aimée, it's been a long time, the food poisoning—is Anaïs all right?" Philippe said, surprised.

"Vivienne's calling the doctor," she said as she pulled out a stool by the counter and closed the kitchen door with her foot.

He noticed her outfit, and his eyes narrowed. "Of course food poisoning is serious, but how are you involved?"

"Sit down, Philippe." She leaned on the glasslike granite counter, her mouth dry. She chewed her lip.

"The minister's here—what's the matter?" he asked, watching her intently.

"Philippe, there was a car bomb," she said.

"Car bomb—Anaïs?" he interrupted, his eyes flashing. He started for the door.

"Hear me out. Sylvie Coudray's dead."

Philippe paused. "Sylvie . . . No, it can't be," he blinked several times.

Aimée read shock on his face. And sadness.

"I'm sorry," Aimée said. "Sylvie turned on the ignition and then—"

He sat down heavily, shaking his head. "*Non*, not possible," he said, as if his words would negate what happened.

"Philippe, her car blew up right in front of us."

He sat, stunned and silent.

"Do you understand?" Aimée said, her voice rising. "We were thrown by the blast; Anaïs might have internal injuries."

He looked as if he'd hit a cement wall. Full force.

"What does it have to do with you, Philippe?"

"Me?" Philippe rubbed his forehead.

The clink of melting ice cubes accompanied the hum of voices from the other room. Platters of wilted salad sat by the sink.

"Sylvie tried to tell Anaïs something."

Philippe stood up, anger flashing in his eyes.

"So?"

She wondered why Philippe was reacting this way.

"Anaïs could have been in that car," she said.

"Never," he said. "They didn't get along."

What an understatement.

"I helped Anaïs escape—"

"Escape? What do you mean?"

"Some men followed her," Aimée said. "They came after us when your mistress was murdered."

"But Sylvie's not my mistress," he cut her off. Philippe paced past the stainless-steel refrigerator. Preschool paintings with 'Simone' scrawled in pink marker covered most of the door.

"You shouldn't be here," he said.

"But Philippe," she said, "Sylvie tried to tell Anaïs—"

Aimée was interrupted by two men, their arms around each other, who burst through the kitchen doors.

"Why all the secrecy, Philippe? Eh, hiding in the kitchen," said a smiling man with curly hair and flushed cheeks, pushing up the sleeves of his *djellaba*. He had laughing eyes and cinnamon skin. He saw Aimée and his brows lifted.

"Call me a party crasher," Aimée said, wishing they would leave. "Excuse my appearance, I'm in rehearsals," she said to explain her outfit. She wanted to keep it vague. "A German miniseries—a Brecht adaptation."

"Aren't you going to introduce us?" asked the man. Of the two, he appeared the more personable.

"My wife's friend, Aimée Leduc," Philippe said reluctantly. "Meet Kaseem Nwar and *le Ministre* Olivier Guittard."

Both men smiled and nodded to Aimee. Guittard gave her a

once-over. Already she didn't like him. It had nothing to do with his Cartier watch or perfectly brushed hair. She imagined him having a matching blond wife and 2.5 blond children.

Kaseem turned to Philippe. "Of course, you're announcing the joint venture with continued funding of the humanitarian mission tonight?" He spoke with a slight Algerian accent and seemed intent on cornering Philippe.

She saw Philippe stiffen.

"*Tiens*, you're impatient, Kaseem!" Philippe said, his tone even. He put his arm around Kaseem and shot a look back at Aimée that read, *Keep your mouth closed.*

Aimée didn't like this, but she gave Philippe the benefit of the doubt. No reason to blurt out what had happened to these men.

"You know that's a quality I admire, but the Assembly thinks along different lines," Philippe said. "Last night we recommended that the delegation count on next year."

"Kaseem's plan depends on the dry season, Philippe," Guittard said. "We don't want to disappoint him or his backers."

"Social gatherings require wine, Olivier, don't you agree?" Philippe said, reaching to uncork a bottle of Crozes-Hermitage on the counter. "Or juice for Kaseem?"

Aimée couldn't see Philippe's face while he redirected the conversation. Or tried to.

"What about your wine, Philippe," Olivier said. "Has Château de Froissart yielded a good vintage yet?"

"Soon," Philippe said. "Winemaking takes time, everyone struggles the first few years."

"So you keep your women in the kitchen like we do, Philippe?" Kaseem grinned. He turned to Aimée. "Don't be offended, I'm joking. Some women feel more comfortable."

Aimée gave a thin smile. She didn't think she looked like the domestic type.

Philippe rubbed his white, fleshy thumbs together. A bland, masklike expression came over his face.

"Excuse us." He motioned his guests in the direction of the dining area.

Philippe returned, his eyes dark.

"I'll take care of Anaïs," he said, guiding her toward the back door.

"Philippe, why are men after her?"

His face was flushed. "How do I know what you're talking about? Let me speak with Anaïs."

And he shut the door on her.

In the taxi on her way back, Aimée wondered what Philippe was hiding. And she realized she hadn't seen one single woman at the reception.

ON ILE St. Louis, Aimée asked the taxi driver to stop around the corner from her flat. Dropping change on the floor, she couldn't stop her hands from trembling. She needed a drink. The dim lights of the bistro *Les Fous de L'Isle* shone on rue des Deux Ponts. She tucked a hundred francs under his lapel.

"Call me next time," the driver said, giving her his card, which read "Franck Polar."

"Don't log the fare, Franck," she said. "That's if you want me to call you again. *Merci.*"

She got out and inhaled the crisp air, her bruises and cuts smarting. Dankness emanated from the leaning stone buildings and she pulled her sweater tighter. Ahead, leafy quaiside trees rustled, and the Seine lapped below Pont Marie. She narrowly missed stepping on dog droppings, which reminded her of Miles Davis, her bichon frise—time for his dinner.

She heard strains of music wafting over the narrow, wet street. Outside the bistro a blackboard announced in blue chalk, QUIN-TET JAZZ! She opened the glass doors plastered with accepted bank cards and edged past the tall potted plants. The warm, hazy smoke hit her. She'd chew nails for a cigarette right now.

The quintet had paused while the female drummer did a solo. The piano player sat upright, eyes closed, with a cigarette stuck in the corner of her mouth, while the saxophonist, trumpet player, and contrabass player stood together, swaying to the notes. Every table was full of patrons eating. A standing crowd overflowed the bar. The beeping cell phones, blue cigarette haze, and familiar gap-toothed grin of Monique at the bar made Aimée feel at home.

She squeezed in at the counter between a *Bourse* stockbroker type with a nice profile and an aging longhaired man. He proudly told anyone who'd listen that his daughter Rosa played the saxophone, even though she was in the *Conservatoire de Musique*.

"*Ça va*, Monique?"

"*Bien*, Aimée. You working?" Monique eyed her, setting a glass of house red in front of her.

Aimée nodded.

"*Et aprés?*" Monique asked.

"Steak tartare to go," she said.

Monique nodded solemnly.

"*Une tartare pour Meels Daveez,*" Monique said turning to the chef, her brother, also gap-toothed. Maybe it was genetic.

"For me a cheese *tartine*," Aimée said.

"Your usual, eh?"

Aimée nodded, sipping the heavy *vin rouge* and drumming her fingers in time to the beat.

The stockbroker lit a cigarette, talked earnestly into his cell phone, and smiled. He exhaled a snake trail of smoke near her ear. She wanted to grab his filter-tipped Caporal and suck the tobacco into her lungs, but instead she reached into her pocket for Nicorette gum.

He raised his wineglass in salute, his dark blue eyes holding hers. She raised her glass, then ignored him. Not her bad-boy type.

The solo ended; then the quintet resumed, with the piano player singing a smooth, unsentimental variation on Thelonious Monk's version of "April in Paris." Her voice was low, almost a whisper.

Aimée didn't want to hear any more. She picked up her food, wedged the franc notes under her glass, and slipped into the crowd.

Miles Davis greeted her at the apartment door, his wet black nose sniffing her package of steak tartare. She kicked the hall radiator in her twenty-foot-ceilinged entryway twice until it sputtered to life, pulled her damp wool sweater off, and stepped out of her leather pants. She sniffed. Something smelled musty.

"Time for dinner, Miles Davis," she said. She scooped him into her arms and carried him to the dark kitchen at the back of the apartment. The Seine flowed gelatinous and black below her tall windows. Lantern lights dotted the quai, their pinprick reflections caught in the heavy water. Almost as though they were drowning, she thought.

Bone weary, she peered outside to look at the quai, her nose touching the cold glass. The only person she saw was a figure walking a German shepherd. She couldn't explain why, but she felt she wasn't alone. Foreboding washed over her.

Miles Davis licked her cheek.

"A *table*, furball," she said, and hit the light switch. The chandelier flickered, then emitted a feeble glow.

She took his chipped Limoges bowl, spooned in the steak tartare, and set it down for him. After changing his water, she plopped her *tartine* down on the counter, too tired to feel hungry.

Her thoughts turned to her last boyfriend. She pictured Yves, his large brown eyes and slim hips. When he'd accepted the Cairo correspondent post, she'd stuck pins in a Tutankhamen doll until it resembled a pincushion. Right now the only male in her life was on the floor at her feet with a wet nose and wagging tail.

Aimée heard the cat door thump shut. The hairs on her neck stood up. Miles Davis growled but didn't abandon his steak tartare. Who could that be?

On her way to check the front door in the hallway, she smelled an odor. Had something died between her walls? Visions of decaying, rabid creatures in death throes wafted before her. She grabbed a broom and one of her boots as weapons, gingerly stepping down the hallway. The odor grew stronger.

The ripe, sweetish tang alarmed her. A bulky envelope had been wedged through the cat door she'd installed for Miles Davis. She hadn't noticed the envelope when she entered.

She pulled on the first thing hanging from her coat rack, a blue faux-fur coat, then opened the door. Cold and musty drafts tunneled down the hallway. Her bare-legged reflection, in the worn mirrors opposite, stared back at her. Was she this rooster-haired, skinny creature armed with a broom and high-heeled boot?

Miles Davis's low growl amped to a high-pitched bark. With the broom she prodded the envelope, feeling around. "Back off" was smeared in brown letters—a deep dark brown. She looked closer. Dried blood.

She stepped back.

Her poking had dislodged the contents of the unsealed envelope. Something gray slid onto the black-and-white diamond tiles. Mottled and furry. The odor, strong and rank, filled her hallway.

At first she thought a stuffed animal had emerged, but it was the biggest gray rat she'd ever seen. At least it would have been if the head had been attached to a body.

She turned cold inside. The head was as big as a kitten. She hated rodents, fat or skinny.

She scanned shadowy corners but saw only the dusty niched statues that spiraled the wall of her staircase.

No one.

She had to get rid of it. The putrid stench filled the landing. She pulled a pink TATI plastic shopping bag from her coat rack and shoved the dripping head into it with a broom. Using the broom handle, she carried the bag at arm's length down her marble stairs.

She watched for an attacker but figured they'd gone—the "message" had been their goal. Miles Davis barked, keeping up the rear under the dim hall sconces. By the time she dropped the bag in the trash, a slow anger burned over her fear. Her thoughts skipped back over the events since Anaïs's call. Did this have a link to Sylvie or Anaïs?

Her evenings hadn't been this eventful in a while, she thought. A dead woman and a dead rat all in one night.

BACK IN her apartment the musty smell lingered. Outside her bedroom, at the far end of her hallway, stood a small yellowed statue. Beside it lay a pile of what looked like tea-stained bandages. She froze. Voodoo . . . evil spirits.

The rustle behind her caused her to turn and swing.

Yves jumped aside, wearing her father's old bathrobe and a smile. She almost beheaded the marble Napoleonic bust in the hall beside him. He leaned against the door frame, his tan body and damp hair silhouetted in the bathroom light.

"So that's how you greet someone, after a long flight, who's brought you priceless Egyptian artifacts?"

She took a deep breath.

"Just unannounced ones," she said, setting the broom against the wainscoting. "Did I give you a key?"

"Your partner René had an extra one," he said. "Maybe you should check your messages," he said, coming closer. His dark sideburns snaked to his chin.

"I've been a little busy," she said, realizing she was still barefoot and in a faux-fur coat.

"Something's spoiled," his nose crinkled.

"Rat tartare," she said. "Someone's trying to scare me."

"Scare you?" he asked. "Aimée, what's the matter?"

She almost told him right then about the explosion and the rat. But she hesitated. He was dangerous to her psyche. A soul shaker and troublemaker.

Yves searched her eyes, sniffed her breath. "Busy enough to have a drink around the corner?"

She shrugged.

"Why haven't you come to Cairo?"

"*Ecoute*, Yves," she said, pulling her coat tighter. "Parts of Paris are Third World enough for me."

But that wasn't totally true. It had to do with commitment. Her inability to commit made it difficult to visit another continent.

"*Et, voilà.*" He pursed his mouth. "I'm just another notch on your lipstick case."

"If I remember correctly, you moved, Yves. Not me," she said. "Then you pop into my life and disturb my concentration."

"Maybe I need to disturb it more."

"I haven't heard from you for ages," she said, rubbing her legs in the frigid hallway. "Suddenly you appear. I don't owe you an explanation."

Yves turned away. There was a lot more she could say, but she didn't feel like addressing his back.

"Like you, I've been busy," he said, turning around and edging closer. The fresh scent of her newly laundered towels clung to him. "Civil wars and guerrilla encampments in remote outbacks don't leave me a lot of time for chitchat."

"Chitchat?"

She'd dealt with a dead rat and found a live one in her apartment.

"I've got no excuse," he said. "Forgive me?"

"That's all you can say?"

"I'm sorry," he said.

"How sorry?"

She couldn't believe she'd said that.

"Let me show you," he said, with a small smile. "After all, I have a lot to make up for."

She ran her fingers through her hair. They came back sticky. "I need a bath. Want to scrub the motor oil off my back?"

"Good place to start." He took her in his arms, noticing the bloodstains and scrapes on her legs. "I suppose you're going to tell me about it."

"Later," she said with a half smile. "We better catch up first."

AIMÉE WOKE UP WITH a start to pounding on the door and Miles Davis barking.

Alone.

A sheet of papyrus was pinned to the pillow with "Charged your phone—try to keep out of trouble, Yves" written on it.

She'd fallen into bed with him again. Sometimes she amazed herself.

The pounding got louder. She pulled on a suede button-down shirt from the chair, grabbed a pair of black velvet jeans from her armoire, stuck the cell phone in her pocket, and stumbled barefoot to the door.

"Mademoiselle Leduc?" said a smooth-faced plainclothes *flic*. His clear eyes and matter-of-fact expression contrasted with those of his partner, older and heavier, who paced the chill landing with a sour expression. His exhalations showed in breathy puffs. Both wore suits: cheap ones.

Her heart pounded. Maybe this was a bad dream. She wanted to shut the door in his face, go back to bed.

"You are Mademoiselle Leduc?"

"I think so, but after coffee I'll know for sure," she said, scratching her head. "And you gentlemen might be . . . ?"

"Sergeant Martaud of the Twentieth Arrondissement," he said. "But of course we're happy to accommodate you at the *Commissariat de Police*."

Her words caught in her dry throat. A sinking feeling came over her. The talisman poked out of her backpack on the claw-foot marble table in plain view. She reached out and slipped it under her blue faux-fur coat which was lying on the chair.

The sergeant opened his suit jacket with a flourish. In one fluid movement he removed his badge from a vest pocket, displayed his photo ID, then slipped it back in. She figured he practiced this in front of a mirror before work.

"Identities are so important," Sergeant Martaud said.

"Sergeant Martaud, I'm particular about my coffee." she managed a smile. "Almost obsessive, my colleague tells me, so you'd need a warrant to get me to Belleville without my customary cup."

His sour-faced partner returned the smile and waved a piece of paper. "Matter of fact, Mademoiselle, I happened to bring one with me."

BERNARD STOOD IN FRONT of Notre-Dame de la Croix Church. Chanting protesters in bright-patterned Mali cloth tried to block his way. The men, North African Tuaregs called "blue men," for their traditional indigo blue veils and turbans, marched with women in black chadors and stout nuns in habits.

Arms crossed, Bernard waited as the negotiator checked off concessions for the sanctuary seekers. Last night a group holding a candlelit vigil had refused him entrance. He'd been relieved when the minister told him to postpone meeting the leader. But when the car picked him up this morning, he'd felt the same dread. Only worse.

On the way he'd heard the radio alerting the city to repercussions from the ministry's decision finally to enforce last year's anti-immigration laws. Had France's recent triple-digit unemployment tipped the scales?

Tension rippled, too, across the Mediterranean, from Algeria, where an undeclared civil war still simmered after the military's cancellation of the 1992 elections. The military's hold over the strong fundamentalist factions was tenuous at best.

Bernard wondered again why he, and not his boss, stood in the drizzle to negotiate. Bernard's sleep, his first in days, fitful and broken, hadn't been restful at all. His left eye had begun to twitch, a sign of extreme fatigue.

"We know Mustafa Hamid, the Alliance Fédération Libération leader, bowed to internal pressure in taking over the church," said the sharp-nosed negotiator, studying Bernard. "He organized the *sans-papiers*, but he's a pacifist leader from way back."

Notre-Dame de la Croix stood before them, an anomaly of vaulted stone and lead-paned windows in the heavily Muslim immigrant *quartier*. Around them the air was redolent with spices and Arab music.

"Future residence priority—there's your give point," the negotiator continued. "If you get that far."

Now Bernard understood: Dangle the carrot of future residency before the immigrants. This disgusted him. Once the zealots agreed to leave the country, he knew they'd never be allowed back in. These people might be stubborn, but not stupid.

"Where's *le Ministre* Guittard?" Bernard asked.

"Staying informed," the negotiator said. In the glare of the police-car lights his crew cut glistened with tiny rain droplets. "*Monsieur le Ministre* awaits the negotiations breakthrough."

It made sense. Guittard would watch the outcome, then either step in to claim credit or remain on the sidelines if a bloody confrontation occurred. Having been a midlevel *fonctionnaire* for years, Bernard understood how the ministry worked.

"*Le Ministre* Guittard hopes for your successful negotiations," the man said, as if an afterthought. "The Naturalization Committee needs leadership."

Here were the wily workings of a modern-day minister, Bernard thought. Delegate the dirty jobs and offer higher rank if the job proved well done. If the dirty job backfired, so did the *fonctionnaire*. Last year one of his ministry counterparts had been banished to the Ivory Coast in a similar fracas.

Bernard's mother's words played in his head as he entered the church. "These . . . Africains, these Arabes . . . they are just people, *non*? . . . Like us, Bernard."

Tuesday Midday

AIMÉE BANGED ON THE cell bars, demanding to speak with the commissaire. The blue-uniformed *flic* lowered the radio volume on his desk, smoothed the red hair under his *képi*, then took his time walking to her cell.

"Cool your heels," the *flic* said. "Everyone's busy right now."

"Monsieur, please let me talk with the commissaire."

"He's dealing with the immigrants taking sanctuary in the church," the *flic* said. "Too busy to take much interest in you right now."

"A bizarre mistake has been made," she interrupted.

"You're a troublemaker," the *flic* said, pushing the brim of his *képi* back. His eyes were bloodshot. "We like things calm in here. Peaceful. And if you don't shut up, there's a a cell where types like you can meditate and reflect. It's our *première* accommodation with no telephone privileges." He grinned. "Come to think of it, no privileges at all."

"My father was a *flic*," she said. "Those 'meditation' cells disappeared after the big reform."

"Care to find out?" he said.

She'd like to report this tyrant. *Flics* like him gave the force a bad name; ones who enjoyed having suspects in pretrial detention and making them sweat before being charged. Procedurewise, she knew that she could be held up to seventy-two hours, like suspected druggies or terrorists, with only the prosecuter's signature. He seemed the type who'd take advantage of the penal code.

Worried, she drummed her fingers on the bars. Why hadn't Morbier come?

"My godfather's a commissaire in the Fourth," she said. "He's en route."

The *flic* stared at her, his eyes like hard green stones. "If you're asking for special treatment, I told you, the 'meditation' cell can be arranged."

She shut her mouth.

The *flic* grinned, "If you change your mind, let me know. We like to accommodate all our clients." He strutted back to his radio. Only two cells in this criminal-holding commissariat, but he acted as if he presided over a private prison.

Aimée tried to piece it all together: the explosion, Anaïs's story, the moped escape, and the rat. She sat down on the wooden cot hanging from the brick wall by metal chains. A coarse institutional brown blanket was folded in a neat square in the middle. Not even a *pissoir*, Aimée thought. Sticky, smudged steel bars three centimeters apart were bolted into the stained concrete floor that angled into a drain. Her feet were wet, and her stomach growled. Her teenage cellmate wasn't much of a conversationalist; she crouched in the corner, in black overalls and with needle tracks visible on her bony ankles, drooling and nodding off.

How had she ended up in a vomit-laced cell with a junkie who couldn't be more than sixteen?

"Couldn't you at least have waited until I finished my poker game?" Morbier grumbled, grinding out his Gauloise with his foot. "I'm on medical leave."

He nodded his salt-and-pepper-haired head to the *flic*, who got out his keys. The *flic* examined Morbier's ID, then unlocked Aimée's shared cell.

"What's the uproar about?" Morbier demanded.

The *flic* handed Morbier a clipboard, and he scanned it.

"*Et alors?*" Morbier asked. "Suspected robbery, télésurveillance photos, obstruction of RATP personnel, neighbors' grievance. You can't hold her with this."

"The commissaire issued holding instructions," the *flic* said, standing his ground.

Morbier passed the clipboard to Aimée. She read it quickly.

"Circumstantial evidence! My business card and smudged fingerprints won't cut it with the *police judiciare*," Aimée said, handing back the clipboard. "And you know it."

The *flic* squared his shoulders, his gaze rigid.

"My commissaire's instructions were specific," he said.

"The report indicates two women and a man," Aimée said. "Where are they? Not only that, Sergeant Martaud failed to note I'm a licensed detective."

"Your commissaire might have misunderstood the report," Morbier said, riffling through an empty pack of Gauloises. He shrugged. "Happens all the time with field reports—clarity issues."

The *flic's* gaze wavered. Morbier was giving him a way out.

"Let me talk with him," Morbier grinned. "We handled a case last year, very confusing. I'm sure he'll remember my cooperation in the Marais."

There it was—the old network—scratch my back and I'll scratch yours. Now the *flic* had to give in or saddle his commissaire with a bad name.

"Confusing, that's the word I was searching for," he said. "A confusing report."

"Put her on my tab," Morbier said. "And lose the paperwork. Next time your commissaire's on my manor, I'll reciprocate. *Comprends?*"

"*Oui, Monsieur le Commissaire!*" The *flic* nodded and kept his eyes averted from Aimée's.

Aimée picked up her personal effects: her Hermès bag, a flea-market find, leather coat, and damp ankle boots.

The other small holding cell around the next corridor was full of working girls from a roundup.

"Your *souteneur?*" one of the girls said, adjusting her black garter belt and bustier for all to see. "Let me introduce you to mine. He's younger, much better looking. Yours seems kind of long in the tooth, eh?"

"*Merci,*" Aimée grinned. "Maybe next time."

She stopped to lace her boots and Morbier went ahead.

Morbier's flesh-colored body brace was visible under the rain-coat draped over his shoulders.

"How's the *bébé?*" he said to a honey-skinned prostitute in the opposite cell combing out her blond wig.

"*Merci bien, Commissaire,*" she smiled. "He's making his first communion soon! I'll send you an invitation."

"*Nom de Dieu*—how time flies," Morbier said wistfully as he walked stiffly to the foyer.

"Haven't seen you since Mouna," the discharge *flic* said to Morbier.

Aimée didn't hear his reply.

"Who's Mouna?" she asked, standing near the discharge desk.

Morbier didn't answer.

Aimée stared at him, "What's the matter?"

"Mouna helped me out," he said, wincing and looked away. "You can handle yourself from here. I'm late for physical therapy."

By the look she'd caught, she realized he'd known her quite well. "You're still friends with Mouna?" she asked.

"Mouna's gone." His face reddened.

Surprised, Aimée paused. She'd never seen Morbier react this way before.

"What happened, Morbier?"

"She happened into crossfire during the 1992 riots."

"I'm sorry," she said, watching his expression.

"Mouna wasn't the only one," he said. "Events got messy."

For Morbier to even mention it, things must have been bad.

She and Morbier stood filling the scuffed wood-paneled entrance of the *Commissariat de Quartier* on narrow rue Rampo-neau.

Aimée hesitated, unsure how to respond to this new facet of Morbier.

"You've never talked about her," Aimée said, her voice tentative.

"That's not the only thing I keep to myself," he said, irritation in his voice. "Don't let me catch you behind bars again. What would—" he stopped the words catching in his throat.

"Papa say?" she finished for him. "He'd say getting me from behind bars is my godfather's duty."

"Leduc, stay out of Belleville. The Twentieth Arrondissement isn't your turf," he said. "And since when have you taken to riding a moped through the Métro, using it to rob people at the ATM, and ditching it around the corner?"

She kicked a loose cobble on the curb. It wasn't her fault the homeless guy used the bike to steal.

"Morbier, the Métro was unavoidable but I never robbed—"

"Stop. I don't want to hear this," Morbier said, covering his ears. "Heavy hitters play dirty here. They have their own rules."

"This concerns a minister's wife."

"Tiens!" Morbier said, rolling his eyes. "With you, everything has to do with politics. Let the big boys handle it, Leduc," he said. "Stick to your computer. Go home."

"It's not that easy," she said.

"Consider this what I owe you," he said. "Since I didn't make it when you played footsies on that Marais rooftop." He referred to her case last November, when an old Jewish woman was murdered in the Marais. Morbier glanced at his watch, an old Heublin from the Police Nationale graduation. Her father had kept his in the drawer. "We're even."

"Morbier, let me explain—"

"Leduc, you're a big girl," he interrupted, "I want a full pension when I retire. *Comprends?*"

Arguing with him would get her nowhere.

"Merci, Morbier," she said, pecking him on both cheeks.

She joined the crowd on boulevard de Belleville. At the Métro entrance, the cold spring rain pelted her black velvet pants and beaded her eyelashes. She debated, standing in the drizzle, while commuters veered around her, a wet island in a sea of umbrellas.

The smart course of action would be to leave Belleville, escort Anaïs to a lawyer, and follow up on the Electricité de France job proposal. And she was smart. She had a business to run and a brilliant partner who more than helped shoulder responsibilities.

Yet every time she closed her eyes she saw the burning ball of white-yellow heat, felt the clumps of flesh raining down on her, heard blood sizzling on a car door. Her hands trembled, though not as badly as last night. And she couldn't get Simone's voice or Anaïs's white-faced horror out of her head.

AIMÉE STEPPED into a phone cubicle on avenue du Père Lachaise to save her cell phone battery. On her left a florist's sign above baskets of violets promised tasteful funeral arrangements.

"Résidence de Froissart," a woman's voice answered.

"Madame, please," Aimée said. "Is this Vivienne?"

"Who's calling?"

"Aimée Leduc," she said. "I helped Madame last night."

A pause. Pots clanged in the background. The voice sounded different, unlike Vivienne.

"How's Madame feeling?"

"Madame's unavailable," she said.

She could understand Anaïs not feeling well, but she wouldn't give up that easily.

"Unavailable?"

"I can take a message."

"Did the doctor visit?"

"You'd have to speak with *le Ministre* about that," she said.

Most likely Anaïs had slept and recuperated. But the guarded tone bothered her. She heard a loud buzzing.

"May I speak with *Monsieur le Ministre?*"

"Not here," the woman said. "*Pardonnez-moi*—someone's at the door."

Before Aimée could ask her to have Anaïs call her, the woman hung up. She stared out into gray rue Père Lachaise where rain pattered over shop awnings. She noticed a cat peering from a window. The cat looked dry and well fed. She tried calling again but the line was busy.

Frustrated, Aimée punched in Martine's number at *Le Figaro*.

"*Mais* Martine's at a board meeting," said Roxanne, Martine's assistant.

"Please, it's important," Aimée said, "I must talk with her."

"Martine left you a message," Roxanne said.

"What's that?"

"I wrote it down," Roxanne said, her tone apologetic. "I'm sorry to be cryptic, but Martine made me repeat this: 'Start where Anaïs told you; there's a lot more in the *pot-au-feu* besides vegetables.' She said you'd understand."

Understand?

Aimée thanked Roxanne and hung up.

She didn't like this. Any of this. She felt torn after vowing to stick to corporate work and build her computer security firm.

The plastic surgeon who'd pieced her together after the Marais case told her to be careful—next time might not find her so lucky. Her stitches had healed nicely. He'd done a good job, she had to admit; no one could tell. He'd offered to enhance her lips gratis. "Like the German models," he'd said. But she was born with thin lips, and figured she'd exit with them.

Someone once told her the Buddhists believe if you helped someone you were responsible for them. But she wasn't a Buddhist. She just hated the fact that someone could blow a woman up and get away with it, and put a little girl's mother in peril. And for what or why she didn't know.

At the shop next to the florist, she bought an umbrella and then entered a nearby café. She used the rest room, washing her face and hands, to try to get rid of the jail cell odor—a mix of sweat, fear, and mildew. Refreshed after a steaming bowl of *café au lait*, Aimée boarded the bus for the apartment on rue Jean Moinon.

The cold wind slicing across lower Belleville didn't feel welcoming. Nor did the gray mesh of sky.

Through the bus window Aimée saw the store with a hand of Fat'ma talisman in the window. She stood, gripped by the image of the small metal hand with turquoise stones and Arabic sayings to ward off evil words.

Just like Sylvie's—the one Anaïs gave her.

Hopeful, Aimée got off the bus and went into the store. Maybe she would find an answer about Sylvie's Fat'ma.

The crammed store was lit by flickering fluorescent light strips.

Her heart sank.

Hundreds of Fat'mas lined the back wall. They hung like icons, mocking her.

The owner sat on the floor. He ate his lunch off a couscous platter shared with several other men, who appeared disturbed at her entrance.

Aimée pulled the hand of Fat'ma from her bag.

The owner stood up, wiped his hands on a wet towel, and slid behind the counter.

"Sorry to interrupt you, Monsieur," Aimée said. "Do you recognize this Fat'ma?"

He shrugged.

"Looks like the ones I carry," he said.

"Perhaps this one is distinctive. Could you look?"

He turned it over in his palm, then gestured toward the wall. "The same."

"Perhaps you remember a woman who bought this—long dark hair?"

"People buy these all the time," he said. "Every other shop on the boulevard carries them as well."

Her hopes of finding out more about Sylvie had been dashed. Aimée thanked him and went out into the rain.

She crossed Place Sainte Marthe, the small, sloped square with dingy eighteenth-century buildings. Wind rustled through the budding trees. A knot of men clustered near the shuttered café, smoking and joking in Arabic.

Blue-and-goldenrod posters plastered over abandoned storefronts proclaimed: FREE THE *SANS-PAPIERS*—JOIN HAMID'S HUNGER STRIKE PROTESTING FASCIST IMMIGRATION POLICIES. Behind Place Sainte Marthe seventies-era housing projects loomed, jagged and towering.

She walked over the same route she'd driven with Anaïs. The April wind, raw and biting, pierced her jacket. Her ears felt numb. As she entered rue Jean Moinon, she curled her hands inside her pockets, wishing she'd worn gloves.

Pieces of blackened metal bumper and a charred leather armrest remained from the explosion. Almost everything else had been cleaned up from where Sylvie Coudray had gone up in a shooting ball of white fire and flames. The only other evidence was the oily, blackened residue filming the cobblestones. But after a wet spring that too would be washed away.

A dark curly-haired custodian swept the Hôpital St. Louis side entrance near the apartment. His plastic broom, like those used by street cleaners, had known better days. Wet leaves clumped together, refusing to budge over the cobble cracks. He wore a woolen turtleneck and headphones, the wires trailing to his blue work coat pocket. He seemed oblivious as she approached. Something familiar—what was it?—stuck in the back of her mind; then it disappeared.

"*Pardon*, Monsieur," she said, raising her voice, stepping into his line of vision.

He looked up, his prominent jaw working in time to what she imagined was the music beat. She saw the name, "Hassan Elymani," embroidered in red on his upper pocket.

"Monsieur Elymani, may I have a moment of your time?"

He pulled out his headphones, set the broom against the crook of his arm, and lifted a bracelet of worry beads from his pocket. Brown and worn, they slid through his fingers.

"You a *flic?*" he asked.

"My name's Leduc; I'm an investigator."

"*Tiens*, they don't do business there anymore," he interrupted. "Scattered. I told the police," he shrugged. "Like the clouds on a windy day."

"I'm not sure what you mean, Monsieur Elymani."

"Over there," he said, pointing beyond the day-care center to the narrow passage jutting into rue du Buisson St. Louis, with buildings slated for demolition.

"*Voilà.* The slime hung out near rue Civiale," he said, as if that explained everything.

"Catch me up, Monsieur," she said, scanning the street. The view from Sylvie Coudray's window, she imagined, looked over those rooftops dotted with pepper-pot chimneys. She wanted to know what he saw.

"Who exactly are you referring to?"

"*Les droguées,*" he said, his cork-colored fingers coaxing the worry beads through his hands.

Junkies? Parts of the area, she knew, held pockets of them. Morbier, a commissaire, had told her *flics* often let junkies carve out a corner for themselves. "For efficiency," he'd said. "We keep tabs on them, and they don't venture further for clientele. Designer drugs come and go, but there're always addicts with habits who work, pay bills, and stay afloat." His tolerant attitude surprised her. "Fact of life," he continued. "When they wash up on my turf, I put them back out to sea."

Elymani ran his eye over her clothing. "You undercover?"

"You might say that," she said, realizing her appearance could give rise to that conjecture. "I'm interested in Sylvie Coudray," Aimée said pointing to the first-floor windows.

"I'm not a betting man," he said, his eyes narrowing. "But does this have to do with the explosion?"

The rain had ceased, and weak sunlight filtered through the seventeenth-century hospital arches.

"Sylvie Coudray's murder—" she began.

His eyes had narrowed to slits. "Who do you mean? They said Eugénie was killed."

"Eugénie?" Aimée paused. Had Elymani gotten her confused with someone else? "Monsieur, can you describe her?"

Ahead, opposite them, a car pulled up.

"My hours change a lot," Elymani said. "I'm not sure who you mean."

A stocky man in a tight double-breasted suit alighted from the car and waved at Elymani.

Elymani slipped the worry beads back in his pocket and began sweeping. "Excuse me, but the *patron*'s here, and I haven't hosed down the lockers."

"Monsieur Elymani, does she live at number 20?" Aimée asked. "That's all I want to know."

"Look, I'm working," he said bending down, scooping a clump of leaves into a plastic bag. "I need this job."

"Monsieur Elymani, who's Eugénie?" Aimée said. "Please, I'm confused."

Elymani shook his head. "Lots of people come and go," he said, motioning her toward the gate. "I get mixed up."

Fine, she thought. Clam up when it suits you. She'd follow up later. She'd often found that witnesses who grew uncommunicative turned helpful later.

"May I talk with you after work?" she said, handing him her card.

"Don't count on it," he said.

"Please, only five minutes of your time."

"Look, I work two jobs," he muttered, glancing at the man who'd motioned to him a second time. "I'm lucky to do that."

Aimée decided to cut her losses. She turned and walked over to the entrance of 20 *bis* and studied the nameplate. Out of the corner of her eye, she saw Elymani in conversation with the man. He tossed her card into his garbage bag.

She ran her fingers over the name E. Grandet. Her mind teemed with questions. Why would Sylvie Coudray insist on meeting Anaïs here? Had Elymani mistaken Sylvie for Eugénie? Too bad the building had no concierge whom she could question. Concierges were a vanishing breed in Paris these days, especially in Belleville.

She had ventured one door down when a young woman with a stroller burst from the doorway. Empty string shopping bags twined around the handles.

"Excuse me," Aimée said. "I'm investigating the death of a woman next door. Did you know her?"

The baby's coo escalated to a higher pitch, and the woman's mouth formed a *moue* of distaste. "I work the night shift," she said glancing at her watch. "My husband too. We don't know anyone. Or see anyone."

The sky darkened, and a light patter of rain danced on their umbrellas.

"I'm sorry, I must bring the baby to the *crèche*, give my mother-in-law some peace. Talk with her; she's home all the time. *Belle-mère*, some *flic* wants to talk with you."

She punched in the four-digit code, the door clicked, and she motioned Aimée inside.

"First floor on the right." And the woman was gone.

The foyer, similar to next door's, held piles of bundled circulars and newspapers in the corner. Aimée stuck her umbrella in a can with the others and tramped upstairs. A stout woman, her grizzled gray hair in a hairnet, beat a small carpet on the landing. The dull, rhythmic *thwack-thwack!* raised billows of dust. From the apartment interior, Aimée heard the *Dallas* theme song blaring from the television.

"*Bonjour*, Madame," Aimée smiled, pulling out her ID. She felt the chill from her damp boots rise up her legs.

"You don't look like a *flic*," the old woman said, scanning Aimée up and down.

"You're perceptive, Madame, I can tell," Aimée said, edging up the stairs toward the door, trying to ascertain the view from inside her apartment. "I'm a private detective, Madame . . . ?"

"Madame Visse," she said, drawing out the *s*, her tone rising. "God's got chosen helpers. Those he uses in emergencies."

Aimée nodded. The old woman seemed a slice short of a baguette.

"May I come in?" she asked.

"Edouard—that's my son—says people will think I'm *folle*, they'll put me away," she said, showing Aimée the way inside. "But that's their problem, eh. I know what I know."

Aimée looked around, noticing the boxlike front hall with rain boots, a crowded coatrack, and a crushed box of Pampers.

She moved into the kitchen. On the left a row of spice jars ringed the galley-style kitchen. Pots bubbled on the cooktop, curling steam fogged the only window. Rosemary and garlic aromas filled the air. Aimée's stomach growled in appreciation—all she'd eaten today was a croissant. A patched lace panel hung over the open window, fluttering in the wind. To the left, inside a dark room lined with bookshelves, toys littered the floor. Cardboard boxes were piled everywhere.

"My son and daughter-in-law's name are near the top of the housing list," she said, her thin mouth curling as she frowned.

"When they get the call, they're packed." The woman returned to her cooking and stirred the pot.

"Madame Visse, did you know the woman killed in the car bombing?" she asked, hovering in the doorway to the kitchen. She wanted to see if Madame Visse's window looked into her neighbor's courtyard. The window was to the left of the cooktop. It overlooked number 20's back courtyard.

"Edouard's eyes will open up," the old woman said, lifting the lid on a pot. She smiled knowingly. "Yolande can't cook to save her life."

Why did Madame Visse ignore her question? The woman's left hand shook with a slight, constant tremor Aimée hadn't noticed before.

"That smells wonderful," Aimée said, sidling toward Madame in the narrow kitchen. "Were you home when the car exploded last night?" She asked in what she hoped was a casual tone.

"Monday-evening rosary, dear," Madame Visse sighed.

"Did you see anything happen in the courtyard last night?"

"All I saw was that idiot man across the courtyard exercising his cockatiel *comme d'habitude*, like he does every night." She lifted a lid and stirred a simmering cassoulet. She controlled her tremor well.

"Did you notice anything unusual on the street?" Aimée asked. "Any strangers?"

"You look hungry," Madame said, filling a bowl and thrusting it at her. "Sit down. Tell me if it needs more *herbes de Provence*. I have recipes I can share with you."

"*Non merci*, Madame," Aimée declined, perching on a stool at the narrow table. Exasperation was creeping up on her. It had been a long day. She was in no mood for this woman.

She was sure the steaming cassoulet would melt in her mouth. A crusty baguette poked out of a bread basket.

"Try this," the old woman said, proffering a bit of stew.

Aimée shook her head. "I'll just take a bit of baguette."

"Ah, you're just like Eugénie. Too polite," she said.

Aimée sat up, alert. First Hassan Elymani and now this old woman had mentioned Eugénie.

"We look alike too, eh?" Aimée said, in what she hoped was a tone inviting conversation.

Madame Visse crinkled her eyes, surveying Aimée from the stove. "That wouldn't have been my first comment." She set the lid down with a clang on the pot. "Your face and big eyes are similar, but Eugénie's hair was . . ." she stopped and reached for a spice jar.

Aimée remembered Sylvie's hair as long and dark, when she stood by the Mercedes.

Madame unscrewed the lid, sniffed, and slowly put the cap back on. "Stale."

"You were describing Eugénie's hair?" Aimée let the question dangle.

"Red, *bien sûr*," she said. "And short like yours."

Aimée gripped the tabletop. Red. Had Sylvie worn a wig? Or was this another person?

"Now I'm confused," Aimée said, "Did Eugénie live in number 20?"

"Everyone had moved," Madame said. "Eugénie was the only one left."

If Sylvie lived a double life, it could have been a rendezvous spot with Philippe. However, she doubted that this part of Belleville was to his taste.

"Why would someone get murdered here?"

"Good question," Madame said, slamming the baguette on the table, attacking it with a steak knife, and carving uneven slices. "Never seen her before. No one had."

"Who?"

"The dead woman, God rest her soul."

"Madame, you said you never saw the murdered woman!"

"Why should I?" she said. "But people who live here don't drive Mercedes!"

The woman had a good point, Aimée thought.

Madame opened the silverware drawer, pulling out a long-handled serving spoon. Amid the cutlery Aimée saw a distinctive silver box with "Mikimoto"—the famous pearl store on Place Vendôme—embossed across the top. She doubted Madame Visse would own expensive pearls.

Then she remembered the odd-shaped pearl she'd found in the mucky passage. When Anaïs had denied it belonged to her, Aimée had slipped it in her pocket and forgotten about it.

"I love pearls," Aimée said, inclining her head toward the drawer. "I see you do too."

Madame glanced at the box.

"Just the boxes," she said, wiping her hands on her apron. She picked up the distinctive rectangular box, surveyed it. "Eugénie was throwing some away. I kept this one."

Owning Mikimoto pearls and living in Belleville didn't add up, Aimée thought, unless one was a wealthy mistress.

Mikimoto was in Place Vendôme near the bronze-spiraled column melted from cannons Napoleon captured at Austerlitz. Again the carnage of her father's explosion revisited her. She pushed those thoughts away. Reliving the past would get her nowhere.

"Pearls aren't cheap, Madame," she said. "Eugénie has expensive taste, wouldn't you say?"

"She kept to herself," Madame Visse said.

Madame motioned her to the door. "My boy will be home soon. He doesn't like me to have guests. It's up to God, my dear," she said. "Good day."

At least she'd found out Madame Visse knew Eugénie, corroborating Elymani's comment. And she liked pearls. But was

ıgénie\Sylvie? Eugénie lived in a building ready for the wreck-
ng ball and had expensive tastes. That's if Elymani and Madame
Visse were telling the truth.

Back on rue Jean Moinon, Aimée buzzed the remaining apartment buildings. No answer. Most had bricked-up windows. She
figured soon they would all be gone and the area would look like
the day-care center nearby: concrete, squat and ugly.

Several more attempts at ringing doorbells on the back street
brought no luck.

Aimée tried reaching Anaïs again to check on her health, but
the person who answered stonewalled her, saying Anaïs couldn't
be disturbed. Why hadn't Vivienne answered the phone? she
wondered.

Since she'd discovered Madame Visse's box she felt it all connected. She decided to call Mikimoto.

Monsieur Roberge, the Mikimoto appraiser, declined to answer her questions or give an appraisal over the phone. "Liabil-
ity," he'd sighed. "Bring the piece in." Aimée had wanted no
part of Place Vendôme or the memories it carried for her.

But she'd made an appointment for later in the day, picked
up her partner René's car and driven the winding Belleville
streets. She parked by Leduc Detective on rue du Louvre.

State-of-the-art computer monitors and scanners lined their
art deco office walls. Sepia-tinted Egyptian excavation photo-
graphs and digitally enhanced African maps hung beside a poster
of Faudel, a French-born star of Algerian descent, René's favorite. Beside that was a Miles Davis poster, her favorite, from his
performance at the Olympia.

"What happened to you last night?" René asked as she burst
through the door.

A handsome dwarf with large green eyes, black hair, and a
goatee, René enjoyed comparisons to Toulouse-Lautrec. The
hem of his Burberry trenchcoat, tailored for his height, had

dripped a puddle on the parquet floor under the coatrack by the door.

"Sorry, René," she said. "I had guests."

"I've refined our Electricité de France systems vulnerability scan," he said. He sat on his customized orthopedic chair, clicking on his keyboard, eyes fastened on the flashing screen in front of him.

"Any word on the EDF probationary contract?" she asked, picking out her black leather coat from the rack.

"The EDF manager liked you—liked you a lot," he said. "He had some questions."

Too bad she hadn't spent time discussing their services with him since she'd hurried to meet Anaïs.

"But it's the big guys at headquarters who need persuading," René said. "I'm meeting EDF's lawyer later."

"Did you check the data report?" she asked. "See any virus?"

"So far the EDF system looks clean. But there's a nasty little virus going round," he said. "Think I've isolated its birth mother. She's uglier than her spawn!"

"You're the terminator at the terminal." She grinned. "The virus's days are numbered."

René watched her. "Anything else you want to tell me?"

"I had visitors last night," she said. "One thanks to you. Yves."

"Did everything work out?" René said, a smile in his voice.

"Let's say Yves took my mind off the first one. A rat. Sorry I didn't make it—long story."

He hit Save. "Want to talk about it?"

She told him. Most of the story, anyway. She kept her hands in her pockets so he wouldn't see them tremble.

René shook his head.

"No wonder you look like you've been hit by a truck," he said. René swiveled his chair toward her. "You, of all people, get nervous with things that ignite. Can I help?"

"*Merci*, I'll let you know," she said. "Time to change."

She wedged her feet out of the damp chunky-heeled boots, setting them by the door. In the storage room she changed into her Chanel suit. It was black, tailored, and short, the one classic she owned. Her father's face had lit up whenever she wore it. "That fits the Parisian in you," he'd always said.

"Who died?" René asked, his eyes quizzical when she emerged.

Startled, Aimée almost dropped her Hermès bag.

"You only wear that to funerals," René said.

She doubted one would be held for Sylvie Coudray: There wouldn't be anything to bury.

"I've got an appointment with a pearl expert," she said. "See you later."

STANDING ON RUE DU Louvre, Aimée took several deep breaths. She told herself she could do it, and began the ten-block journey.

It was time.

It had been five years since she'd walked up rue St-Honoré toward Place Vendôme. She concentrated on keeping her high-heeled feet one in front of the other, planning what she'd say. But, as if it were yesterday, she saw her father's half grin, heard his low voice say "*Attends*, Aimée, let me check. Wouldn't want anything exciting to happen."

But it had.

The bomb exploded into a fiery ball of metal, blowing him and the surveillance van through the fence and into the column base. The blast slapped her backward with the van door handle in her hand, still burning. Debris rained over the column. Glass shards, burned bits of rubber and flesh—just like the explosion that killed Sylvie.

Aimée turned her head away; she still couldn't look. She hurried to Mikimoto, where she stepped into the high-ceilinged foyer lined with mirrored doors. She was glad to be off the street, away from the painful memories and with a purpose. How Sylvie and Eugénie connected was what she hoped to find out at Mikimoto.

"Mademoiselle, do you have an appointment?" the blond coiffed receptionist asked, looking Aimée up and down.

Aimée smoothed her skirt and smiled at her. "Monsieur Roberge at two o'clock," she said.

"Let me confirm," the receptionist said with an intake of

breath that brooked no argument and was meant to reveal how busy she was at the same time. Her glossy coral-manicured nails clicked over the keyboard, consulting her computer screen.

Aimée wondered why she couldn't just check an appointment book—even in this part of Paris she doubted that too many sheikhs or billionaires beat down the door to purchase rare pearls at the same time.

Her idea of jewelry shopping was bargaining at the antique stalls in the Porte de Vanves flea market. She rifled through her Hermès bag and touched the pearl she'd stuffed in the small plastic bag. It felt bumpy and cold.

"You may go up," the receptionist said.

Aimée mounted the stairs to Roberge's upper floor office.

"*Bonjour*, Mademoiselle."

Pierre Roberge stood and greeted her. A tall man, his bony shoulders were hunched, giving him a stooped look. Aimée figured him to be in his sixties, and with a good toupee. He smiled and motioned for her to sit down. The plush Aubusson carpet absorbed her footsteps. Roberge's tall gilt-edged office windows overlooked the Ritz Hotel and the verdigris statue atop the Vendôme column.

"Thank you for seeing me, Monsieur Roberge, on such short notice."

Below, a fleet of chauffeured Mercedes waited by the entrance of a bank so discreet that no name was posted out front. Aimée shifted in the little gold chair to avoid the view.

"To be honest, Mademoiselle Leduc, I was intrigued by your call," Roberge said fitting the jeweler's loupe over his eye. He adjusted the thin halogen lamp and donned a pair of white gloves.

She set the odd-shaped pearl, fat and tumescent-looking, on the black velvet tray.

Roberge sat forward and peered closely.

"Mikimoto is renowned for cultured pearls, Mademoiselle," he said. "Unlike these."

"Monsieur Roberge, I was told you are a pearl expert. I appreciate your kindness," she said. "I hope I haven't wasted your time."

Politeness would prevent him from agreeing with her even if she had.

He turned the pearl, luminescent under the light, in his gloved hand.

She studied the framed Provençal landscapes ringing the room. Impressionist by the look of them, less known but original. She figured everything in the room was authentic except her story.

"Les maudites," he murmured. The damned.

What did he mean by that?

"Comment?" Aimée asked.

"Forgive me," he said.

Roberge's voice had grown tight, she noticed, his tone more clipped.

"That's the term we use," Roberge said. "May I ask where you obtained this pearl?"

Irritated, Aimée wondered why he'd started posing questions. Instead she smiled and crossed her legs.

"All in good time, Monsieur Roberge," she said. "I'd like your impressions. Tell me what you think first."

"To be honest, Mademoiselle," he said, fingering the pearl once more before setting it down on the black velvet, "the value diminished once this piece was removed from the setting."

She kept her surprise in check and nodded. "And the setting—?"

"But you're a thief," he interrupted, "you should know."

"Hold on, Monsieur!" she said, alarmed. "I didn't steal this."

"Security will deal with you," he said, reaching for the phone.

Alarmed, Aimée stood up, putting her hand on his glove. "Why do you think this is stolen?"

He didn't answer.

She saw his eyes flicker with fear, but she kept her hand on his.

"You know whom the pearl belongs to, don't you, Monsieur Roberge?"

"I'm an old man," he said. He blinked so much that his jeweler's loupe fell on the velvet. "Don't threaten me."

"Tell me who it belongs to, Monsieur Roberge," she said, perching on his desk. "And I'll take my hand off yours and tell you who I really am."

He looked unsure.

She let go, fished in her bag, and pulled out her ID. "I'm a private investigator, Monsieur Roberge."

He stared at it, his jaw set and stubborn. Maybe he didn't like the unflattering photo on it.

"From what I've discovered so far, Monsieur, my next stop will be the morgue."

"What do you mean?"

She stood up and walked to the tall window. But after staring at the Place Vendôme, she didn't have the heart to tell him the truth. Thinking back to Madame Visse's conversation about Eugénie, she had to be sure of the dead woman's identity.

"I believe the woman who owned this could be there," she said, and turned to him. "Your information might help me avoid that process. Her toe tag will probably say Yvette, what the *flics* label unknown dead females. A number will be penciled next to that indicating the order in which her corpse was delivered."

"So she's dead?" he asked.

"A woman's been murdered," she said. "I've been hired to find her killer, but her identity is unclear. I just want to know if this pearl belonged to her."

"Mademoiselle Leduc, you could have told me this before.

However, we are under no obligation to provide confidential details to you."

"Exactly," she said. "However, I told you who I was. It's your turn."

Roberge stared out the window, his eyes reflected sadness. "*Tiens*. I don't normally perform appraisals or commissions for the money," he said. "When something exquisite crosses my path, I find joy in sculpting and weaving the piece to highlight the beauty. With Biwa pearls, its simple. Set off their uniqueness." He paused. "Not hard to do."

His Gallic evasiveness bothered her.

"Why won't you tell me her name?"

Silence. She kept her steady gaze on him.

"I only pay attention to the work." He shook his head. "I am a craftsman. When the piece speaks to me, I listen."

Aimée reasoned that few patrons would argue with Roberge's dictum after that speech, impassioned but spoken with an honesty she rarely heard.

"Are you trying to protect her, Monsieur?" Aimée asked. "She's beyond caring, I'm afraid."

Outside, shadows cast by the column lengthened across the Place.

"She came to me with loose pearls in a jumble," he said. "There were four, an unlucky number for Japanese. I suspected their origin. But when I examined them I knew."

"Knew what, Monsieur?"

And why did that unlucky number mean anything, she wanted to ask, but she held her tongue. Maybe he was trying to tell her in his own convoluted way.

"*Les maudites* are the last natural pearls gathered from Lake Biwa," he said. He set the jeweler's loupe down on his desk. "No more exist. At least none we know of. Now they're cultured in mass freshwater farms nearby. But it's not the same. Connoisseurs know this."

"Why the term *maudites?*"

Roberge's forehead wrinkled. "Luck evades the possessors, you might say. Fortunes shift and change."

Like the Hope diamond, she thought. Many believed a curse followed the owners. Aimée paused; another angle occured to her. Had Sylvie been killed for the pearl?

"Won't you help me?" she asked.

He shrugged.

Aimée leaned forward and stared at Roberge.

"Japanese numerology has its own rules." He gave a thin smile. "Mademoiselle, the pysche is not an exact science like your science of criminology."

She stood up. "So you're saying rich people are superstitious?"

"More so than most," he said. "And Sylvie Coudray belonged to that category."

At last! Without missing a beat, Aimée sat down. "Tell me about Sylvie."

"I never asked about her bank account," he said. "Or her profession."

"According to my client, it was the oldest one in the world," Aimée said. "But I'd guess that could be said for a portion of your clientele."

"My services don't require accounting," he said. "But Sylvie loved good things. Especially pearls. And against her flawless skin . . ." He let the sentence dangle.

Had Roberge secretly desired Sylvie? Or had they been *intime?*

"She had a good heart," he said.

A whore with a heart of gold—such a cliché!

"She came to me several years ago with a single strand of black pearls," Roberge said. "Of the kind I'd seen only once before. After my credentials were established, she let me restring them. An honor."

"Did she mention a woman, Eugénie? Or perhaps bring her?"

"Always alone," he said. "Sylvie had a rare appreciation of beauty. Something shared by so few people. I will miss her."

Aimée could see in his eyes that he would.

"Where did she obtain such pieces, Monsieur? Surely you wondered, *non?*"

"At first. But that's not my business. As I told you," he said. "Beauty attracts beauty. A pearl's essence is of life—a once living coral, ossified into a grain of sand, enveloped and loved by the oyster and reborn as a pearl. An irritant transformed. Like Sylvie."

"Like Sylvie?" she asked.

Roberge waxed poetic concerning pearls, but she hadn't seen the connection to a highly paid mistress. A murdered mistress, she reminded herself.

Roberge didn't answer. His gaze riveted on the pearl still lying on the black velvet, he seemed lost in thought.

"Monsieur Roberge, I'm not sure I follow you," she said, trying to coax him to speak.

"Pearls are to the ocean's geology as gems are to the igneous strata in the earth."

"How does that relate to Sylvie, Monsieur?"

"We only talked of pearls. And such discussions we had," he said, his tone wistful.

"How does Sylvie remind you of pearls?"

"A rare woman is like that," he said and shrugged. "What more can I say?"

His desk buzzer sounded. "Your next appointment's arrived, Monsieur Roberge," the clipped voice of the receptionist announced.

Aimée left. She doubted Sylvie had been murdered for her pearls, but experience had taught her not to discount anything. Most of all, she wondered why it had happened in Belleville.

As she passed through Place Vendôme on the way back, she

felt different. As if she was pursuing justice as her father would have, but in her own way. Step by painful step. And for the first time in a long time, she remembered her father's laugh with dry eyes.

She'd be floundering in the dark, until she saw the police report of the explosion. Time for answers. Her next stop was the morgue.

YOUSSEFA PULLED THE BLACK chador over her head. The long draping wool felt hot and heavy. She found it ironic, having worn one rarely in Oran, she wore it almost every day in Paris. But it made the perfect cover. Too bad it couldn't disguise her limp.

Youssefa prayed Eugénie would show up this time. She had to. Everything depended on it. Over and over in her mind Youssefa replayed Eugénie's instructions: Meet Monday in the grotto at Parc des Buttes Chaumont. But Eugénie hadn't showed. Failing that, the back-up plan had been to meet at the Parc de Belleville summit same time on Tuesday.

If only Eugénie would use a cell phone, she thought. But Eugénie didn't trust them. She told Youssefa the encrypted channels weren't secure; France Télécom just liked everyone to think they were.

Youssefa shivered in the doorway, scanning rue Crespin du Gast. France was so cold. Did the sun ever shine? She waited for the old woman walking her well-clipped terrier to pass. Then Youssefa followed the narrow street, clutching her packet tightly.

She kept her head down, passing the chanting protesters in front of the church.

"The AFL protests for your rights, *mon amie*," a dreadlocked young man said thrusting a flyer into her hand. "Take one. Come to our vigil."

Youssefa scurried by, afraid to touch it. Where she came from, such protesters would have been mowed down like wheat before the harvester.

Keep to yourself, Eugénie had instructed. Trust no one.

At the Parc de Belleville summit, the Paris skyline, dimmed in fog, was lost on Youssefa. She paced rue Piat, which crowned the park. No Eugénie. Fear mounted inside her.

Three hours later her sense of dread turned to despair. Youssefa had been in Paris only five days. Her contact, Eugénie, was gone. The link severed—she'd be next.

INSIDE THE CHURCH BERNARD paused under mullioned windows catching and refracting the green light. The whites of people's eyes caught the gleam from dripping wax candles. Murmured conversations echoed off vaulting pillars supporting the nave.

Bernard's credentials were checked at the damp vestibule door by a woman wearing a yellow Mali cloth headress. A thumbed copy of Frantz Fanon's book, *The Wretched of the Earth,* was crooked under her arm. Beyond her Bernard saw mattresses lined along the Gothic stone walls.

"Mustafa Hamid represents us," she said. Her other arm swept over the wooden pews where children played and men lay on mattresses. "We speak as one. As French people, not as *beurs*," she said, using the word applied to second-generation North Africans, French born. *Beur*, the masculine form of butter, was used in *verlan*, the language developed in the suburban housing projects.

Doomed already, Bernard thought. The ministry had a plane waiting for these immigrants of Algerian and African descent, without papers.

Under the nave the uneven mosaic tiles were covered with muddy footprints. The glass-framed paintings of saints reflected sputtering votive candles and blue gas burners with huge pots simmering on them. The scent of melted wax and the sweat of many bodies hung over the pews.

Appalled, Bernard realized the church had by necessity become a day-care center and campground for the hunger strikers. If the French press described this scene, the whole cause would backfire on these people. Even as a lapsed Catholic, he knew church sanctity struck a chord with Christians—fallen-away Catholics most of all. And the real issue of the hunger strikers would tumble aside.

He felt an insistent tug on his trouser and looked down. A bug-eyed toddler, no taller than his knees and with a runny nose, was pulling himself up. His diaper hung loose, his small chest labored under a skimpy shirt. It was food stained and not warm enough for this dank church, Bernard thought, feeling the chill radiating from the stone. The toddler let go and took a few lurching steps, then crumpled, landing upright with a surprised smile on his face.

"Akim's first steps, Monsieur," said a chador-clad woman. At least he thought those words came from behind the black mask. He turned around to see a dark-eyed young woman, with a scarf tied around her face, addressing him.

"I speak for his mother, who may not address you without her husband," she said bending down and helping Akim.

Akim grinned and pointed at Bernard.

A salvo of Arabic erupted behind the chador. The young woman nodded. "His mother asks, Monsieur, if you could please help her. Akim was born in Paris but not she or his father. They are political refugees from an oppressive regime."

More torrents poured forth, and the young woman bent forward to listen.

"If they are forced to go back, they face prison and Akim an orphanage. He has"—she stumbled in French—"how do you say it?—*un coeur fragil*, a weak heart."

Bernard wished he could back out the way he came in, pretend he never heard this story and find safety behind his Regency office desk overlooking the Elysée Palace. But he couldn't. He stood rooted to the spot.

Akim crawled over to Bernard's leg and started the laborious process of standing again.

"Monsieur, Amnesty International isn't allowed to visit prisons in their country," she said, looking up, her dark pupils reflecting the flickering votive candlelight. "His mother begs you to help them. Akim is their only child to survive infancy."

Bernard couldn't avoid Akim, who clung to his trouser legs. Maybe he could help, he thought, find Akim a decent children's home with a medical facility. And then he saw the line forming behind the mother, stretching from the nave along the full length of the church.

"What's this?" he asked.

"They all want to tell you their story," the young woman said. "Akim's family is . . . *comment?*" she searched for the words. "How do you say, the tip of the iceberg?"

Bernard wanted to tell her it didn't matter anyway. Everyone had to leave. He wished he were made of the stone that lay below his feet.

"Mademoiselle, I'm representing the Ministry of the Interior. I don't make the decrees, but I'm here to speak with Mustafa Hamid," he said, trying to affect a sincere tone. "We have much to discuss."

He heard little Akim's whimper as he was shown the way to Hamid. Suddenly Bernard was transported to his own childhood, trudging knee-deep through the charred timbers of the *souk*, stung by the blowing sand, and smelling seared flesh. His feet so heavy and tired, the waiting boat at the port so far away, the sky stainless steel, and the wind whistling through the barbed wire.

"*Bonjour, Directeur* Berge," said Walid, a bearded man, interrupting his thoughts. "Come this way. Mustafa Hamid wishes to present demands to the ministry. Reasonable and just."

"I'm here to open negotiations," Bernard said.

"Meet our terms," he said. "I'm sure time, stress, and police power will be saved."

"NO STIFFS SINCE LAST Saturday," the morgue attendant told Aimée, stifling a yawn.

"Are you sure?" Aimée asked. "Would you mind checking again?"

He looked her up and down, lingering on her long legs, then ran his pudgy finger down the entry ledger. "Try the lab. Sometimes they're slow with the Yvettes if we've had an HP."

"Meaning?" She felt as if he were waiting for her to ask.

"High-profile death."

Once she'd arrived at the police lab, she found the carved doors padlocked and a small sign indicating that the facility had relocated due to retrofitting. That meant more walking.

She'd gained more than a kilo recently, and her Chanel suit knew the difference. The waistband cut into her and she wished she had worn jeans and hightops. She also wished she had a cigarette. En route she'd checked her machine, but no voicemail from Yves.

After an hour she ended up back in Belleville, the lab's temporary space on the edge of Bastille, where the *quartiers* joined. She recognized the building as her cousin Sebastien's former *lycée* from ten or more years before. Turreted and medieval, the surrounding wall crumbled in bald spots, revealing naked stone. She'd often met him here after class when they took fencing lessons together.

There was something appealing, she thought, about the quiet air of neglect. Inside the courtyard hung peeling school posters of tutorials. Behind cobwebbed plate glass were the weekly luncheon menus. Aimée had always preferred to eat at home, as her friends did, so she could be with her grandfather. But since her grandmother died, he'd taken to eating out. Every day. He'd also acquired a younger girlfriend, whom she suspected fed him.

At the vacant meshed window of the concierge's loge, she saw a hand-lettered sign instructing her to ring. She put her finger on the buzzer. A loud echoing trill reverberated off the stone. Pots of budding red geraniums leaned against the rusted bicycle rack.

No one.

Silence except for the high beep of a truck backing up in the distance. Suddenly the gush of water, from the *bouches d'égouts*, startled her. The *égoutiers*, sewer men, had diverted the flow with their sewer rags.

Then a face in shadow appeared behind the window. She couldn't decipher the gender.

"*Oui?*"

"Have the criminology personnel transferred here?" Aimée asked.

"Depends," the person said, "on which branch."

"*Tiens*, I'm looking for Serge Léaud, the Luminol expert."

"Aha," the person said, warming up. "Name sounds familiar. Let me search."

The loge light flicked on. Inside stood a blue-uniformed *flic*, "Police Nationale" stitched on her lapel. A lollipop stick poked from the side of her mouth.

"You know half the lab moved to Bercy," the *flic* said. "Ask me why, and I'll tell you I don't know. No one else does either."

The usual bureaucracy screw-up between the branches, Aimée figured. She heard papers rustle as he turned pages.

"Why move the other half here?" Aimée asked.

"These days," said the *flic*, who'd grown quite chatty, "much of the work's on contract. Several labs operate here, so it's easier to move the stiffs from floor to floor rather than across the Seine."

"Good point," Aimée said, wishing the *flic* would get to the point.

A gray-spotted cat slinked behind the geraniums.

"According to the new *renseignement*, Léaud operates offices in both buildings."

Aimée groaned. She'd counted on Serge to show her the report on Sylvie's explosion. Informally, with no fuss, no paperwork. He owed her big-time from the Marais, where, with her help, he'd leaped up several notches in his criminology career.

"So Léaud's working today?" she asked.

"You're in luck, he's here, and he's there," the *flic* chuckled, opening her mouth. Her tongue was blue. "Wouldn't you know it, he's also scheduled at the same time for an inquest in quai des Orfèvres—the Brigade Criminelle screws up again!"

"I'll find him later," she said, exasperated. "Seems you're backed up, and the Yvette I'm looking for—"

"You have clearance, I presume." The *flic's* voice changed, becoming businesslike. She pulled the lollipop from her mouth.

Aimée had to think fast.

"Commissaire Morbier cleared me," Aimée said. "Check the report on the Yvette, a car-bomb victim on 20 *bis* rue Jean Moinon in Belleville."

"That would be nice," he said, taking a pencil and scratching her neck with the eraser. "But I don't have it."

Of course, she wouldn't. Procedure would have it at the autopsy table or in the Medical Examiner's Office.

"Who does?"

"Intake's slow," the *flic* said. "The HP took up their time."

"Look, I'm working on other investigations too."

"Show me your clearance, and I'll check."

"Like I said, the clearance goes with the report," Aimée said maintaining her cool with difficulty.

"Says here Commissaire Morbier's on disability."

"Par for the course, wouldn't you say?" Aimée grinned. "Like Serge Léaud's whereabouts." Trying to play fair with this *flic* hadn't worked. She reached into her Hermès tote and fished for the alias she reserved for special occasions.

"Marie-Pierre Lamarck," she said, flashing the ID she'd altered from her father's old one. "Internal Affairs."

Marie-Pierre, according to Aimée's computer investigations had returned from maternity leave to very part-time.

The *flic* studied the ID, looked up the name, then looked at her. "Eh, you could have told me," she said, punching in numbers on the phone.

And spoil the fun? Aimée almost added.

"No one answers in Léaud's office."

After coming so far and going through this charade, she wasn't going to give up now.

"Fine," Aimée said. "I'll leave some things for him in his office. What floor?"

"Third floor," she said. "Take the stairs, the elevator's broken."

Serge's office door, by the birdcage elevator, had CRIMINO-LOGUE taped below the DÉPARTEMENT DE PHILOSOPHIE stenciled on the glass. Aimée pulled her black leather coat tighter while she waited in the frigid, damp hallway. She wondered why most institutions of learning retained the cold so well.

"Serge could be anywhere," the harried young woman said, looking up from her microscope inside the room lit by wide skylights. She consulted a schedule from her lab coat. "They've got him running from lab to lab." She threw her hands up. "All this consolidating service!"

"I'm sorry, but it's important that I talk with him," Aimée said, nodding in sympathy.

"We're run off our feet, and Serge has to be in two places at once. Work grinds to a halt when that happens."

"I'm looking for the report on the car-bomb victim," Aimée said.

"Oh, yes, parts of an unclaimed Yvette came in," the busy woman said. "Just bits and pieces, you understand."

Aimée hoped the woman didn't notice her wince.

"Try the basement. The formaldehyde smell isn't hard to miss," she said, peering back through the microscope. "If you see Serge, tell him he's got a four o'clock appointment with the *médecin légiste* about the HP autopsy results."

By the time Aimée took the creaking stairs to the basement, she'd realized she might as well try to find the *médecin légiste* herself.

Down in the chill basement, she heard the gallows-humor *argot* uttered by the group of medical students in the hall. She followed them and found an autopsy being performed. Inside the gray-tiled room, a bitter pine disinfectant competed with the reek of formaldehyde. The dampness mingled with the smell she remembered from when she'd identified her father's charred remains.

The balding *médecin légiste* looked up, his gloved hands weighing a tan-yellow organ, huge and glistening. Below, on the enamel trough lay the pasty corpse, its chest cavity open, skin and muscles filleted back.

"Enlarged fatty liver, notice the greasy, doughy appearance," he said, his voice clear and echoing off the tiled room, to the surrounding white-coated students. "He lived the good life."

Snickers greeted his remark. "In more ways than one," one of the students said.

The *médecin légiste* noticed Aimée and nodded.

"*Bonjour*. Marie-Pierre Lamarck," she said, flashing the ID.

"The paperwork isn't ready," he said. "This procedure will take another hour."

He assumed she was here for this corpse.

"*Pas de problème*, but I'm picking up the report for the Yvette brought in last night."

"We're backed up here," he said. "That report will be submitted shortly."

"But the—" Aimée said.

"Scalpel," he interrupted. A medical student handed him the diamond scalpel.

The neck vessels, she noticed, were clearly well preserved for better embalming. Care had been taken to conceal the scalp incision in his sparse hair.

Very careful job, she thought. More appropriate in a private funeral parlor for concerned relatives than in a morgue. Or maybe she was being too hard on the public morgue.

Aimée noted the expression on the corpse's face. A lopsided grin. She wondered why.

"Some of us dream of going like this," the *médecin légiste* said, noticing her gaze. "This chamber deputy had a heart attack in the arms of his mistress. During the heat of passion, we'd say. Scandal or not, he doesn't care anymore."

Major coitus interruptus, Aimée thought.

"Frightened the lady out of her bustier," a student added, grinning. "It took a paramedic to untangle them."

Aimée wasn't keen to hear the details.

"Do you do such a good job for the Yvettes?" she asked.

The minute she'd spoken she willed the words back into her mouth. Embarrassed, she looked down. René often pointed out how her reactions got in the way.

Apparently they hadn't registered, for the *médecin légiste* ignored her remark. The scraping and clang of stainless steel instruments echoed off the tiled walls. Aimée shifted uncomfortably in her damp heels. The formaldehyde reek, the crowding medical students, and the open dissection of the corpse's innards made her claustrophobic. She wished he would hurry up.

"About that report?" she asked.

"I'm not finished," said the *médecin légiste*, waving aside her question.

"He's got an open-casket state funeral," he said in a matter-of-fact tone. "And the family wants him, let us say, dignified." He explored a smooth red-brown organ with the scalpel, then sniffed. "I need a resident student to weigh this spleen."

A large-boned woman, her ponytail crushed in a hairnet, volunteered.

"Léaud's checking the unusual results," he said. "*Et voilà*, then the report will be yours."

"Unusual results, doctor—can you explain?" Aimée asked.

The organ scale's chain creaked with the spleen's weight as the student weighed it. Aimée pulled her coat tighter in the frosty room.

"We found traces of Duplo *plastique*," he said. "Embedded in part of a leg."

"Duplo *plastique*?"

"Duplo's an English cousin of the cheaper Czech Semtex," he said. "You'll have to wait for the report."

Puzzled, she stepped out into the hallway.

Out by the dark stairwell, she ran into a figure who rounded the corner at the same time.

"*Merde!*" he murmured, flicking away a cigarette.

"You're a hard criminologist to find," she said, staring into the bearded face of Serge Léaud.

"And I like to keep it that way, Aimée," he said with a half smile. "I'm doing two jobs and filling in for someone on leave."

"Which you thrive on," she grinned. She looked down. "Smoking in the lab?"

"Ever since I published the Luminol paper about that fifty-year-old blood, I've had no peace," he said. His full face, pinkish and scrubbed shiny, was framed by the beard flowing from his curly hair. "I've started smoking again. *Tiens*, my wife won't let me near the twins when she smells smoke on me."

"Sometimes the gods punish us by giving us what we want, as Oscar Wilde pointed out," Aimée said. "In your case, making police bulletins around the world."

"Why do I have the feeling you're after me?"

"But I am," she said, tugging his sleeve and pulling him toward a slitlike basement window. "Just as a bad *centime* you throw away keeps coming back. Tell me about Duplo *plastique*."

Serge's pager beeped.

"I'm late," he said, glancing down and reading the message. "What's your interest in it?"

"The victim got blown up in front of me," she said. "I've been hired to find who did it."

"I didn't hear that," Serge said, shaking his head. "You know I can't say anything."

"Don't speak," she said. "Just let me see the report when you're finished."

"I'm due at quai des Orfèvres," he said, rolling his eyes. "There's another inquest in an hour, and I promised my mother-in-law I'd pick her dog up from the groomers'."

"I think we can work something out," Aimée said, taking his arm. "What's your mother-in-law's address?"

BERNARD STUDIED MUSTAFA HAMID. He marked Hamid's large black eyes, sallow complexion, and the dried lace of spittle on his beard. Took in his hollow-cheeked profile and bone-thin arms.

The cold and damp called for Bernard's lined winter coat, not the skimpy suit jacket he wore. He wondered at Hamid's simple white cotton knee-length shirt and his smocked leggings. He wore a *chechia*, a white crocheted cap, and a prayer shawl covered his shoulders.

The old familiarity gnawed at Bernard, intrusive and intimate. Memories of what he'd tried to forget came back to him. The wild-eyed holy man proclaiming doom in the deserted streets of Algiers. How a sniper's bullet silenced him at Bernard's mother's feet in the long lines snaking to the port of Algiers.

Bernard watched Hamid's hands trace worry beads as he sat on a thin mattress. With a deft movement Hamid touched Bernard's hand then his own heart.

"*Salaam aleikum, Directeur* Berge," Hamid said, addressing him formally, his voice deep. "Forgive me for not rising to greet you."

"*Aleikum es-salaam,*" Bernard replied. That much of the Arabic greeting Bernard remembered. "Monsieur Hamid, I appreciate your time and hope we can arrive at fruitful negotiations."

"Please excuse my appearance," Hamid said. He gestured toward a tray laden with a teapot and mint sprigs in thin gold-rimmed glasses. "You are my guest. May I offer you tea?"

Bernard nodded. "Monsieur Hamid, won't you join me?"

"Unfortunately my fast allows only weak tea."

Not wishing to tower over Hamid, Bernard sat down on a nearby tattered cushion.

"Monsieur Hamid," he said, "my ministry wants to provide for your people. We wish to work with you. After the dust settles, so to speak, we'll make sure provisions allow for their return."

Bernard had spoken quickly, dropping the bad news. He clung to the idea that Hamid would hear the sincerity in his voice. Somehow miraculously believe him and shuffle the *sans-papiers* down the aisle and into the planes.

Hamid shook his head. His eyes mirrored the sadness Bernard felt. "I apologize in advance for whatever happens," Hamid said, bowing his head, flecked with gray under the *chechia*. "Violence is never called for."

"I'm sure you're not threatening retaliatory force, Monsieur Hamid," Bernard said, recovering quickly. "That would surprise me, coming from a leader and a man known for peaceful negotiations."

"I speak not so," Hamid said. "The teachings of Allah embrace the family of man, evidenced by those you see around us. Not distinguishing us as Hindu, Muslim, or Christian."

Hamid raised his arm, then dropped it. The effort of exertions appeared to tire him.

A man with a heavy beard, dressed in the same style, appeared. "Monsieur Hamid's health bears watching," he said. "I'm sorry, he's very weak. Please discuss with him later."

"*Bien sûr*," Bernard agreed. "A very delicate situation."

The last thing Bernard wanted was for Hamid to become a martyr. Visions of the Ivory Coast Bureau, manned by disgraced bureaucrats at half their pension, danced in his mind.

He retreated to the vestibule, seeking a silent spot.

What had Hamid insinuated by mentioning violence? The hidden fundamentalist cells dotting Paris and their retributions loomed in his mind . . . Métro bombings, explosions in department stores . . . innocent people commuting to work, families buying school clothes, killed due to fanatics. His heart hardened. He'd thought Hamid was different, from a peaceful sect.

"Get me access to *le Ministre*," Bernard said, eyeing the buses lining rue de la Mare. Their rumbling engines and exhaust fumes filled Place de Ménilmontant.

"As you wish," the lantern-jawed CRS captain said.

By the time *le Ministre* came on the line, Bernard had rehearsed his plan mentally several times. He'd avert a crisis the only way he could think of and get Hamid out of the church. Hopefully the *sans-papiers* would follow.

"Hamid's weakened condition demands attention," Bernard said to *le Ministre*. "Setting him up as a martyr, canonized by the immigrants, is the last thing we want."

"And what do you propose to do about that?" *le Ministre* asked.

A rustling came from the minister's end as he put his hand over the phone. Bernard heard applause and murmuring voices in the background.

"A tactic to diffuse his power," Bernard said.

He explained his plan.

Three minutes later the minister agreed, with one caveat. "He's out, Berge. Or you are."

AIMÉE HAD DEPOSITED MOMO, a well-coiffed shih tzu, at Serge's mother-in-law's, declining tea despite the insistent invitation. More than a month had passed, she realized guiltily, since she'd taken Miles Davis for a trim.

In her office, she rang Philippe again, but he was out. His secretary promised to reach him and have him get back to her. She worried. Anaïs hadn't returned her calls either.

Aimée stood reading Serge's unfolding fax over René's shoulder.

"The Yvette's identity hasn't yet been established," Aimée said as she read the report. "But Anaïs identified her as Sylvie Coudray. Yet the neighbor and the custodian referred to her as Eugénie. According to this the *National Fichier* in Nantes hasn't ID'd her, either."

She shook her head, unable to figure it out. The *Fichier*, known for quick response time, held all kinds of information: drivers' license number, *carte bancaire*, and *carte nationale d'identité* among others.

"What's next?" René asked.

"Why don't you try to access Sylvie Coudray's *Sécurité sociale* and Eugénie Grandet's—if she exists—while you're at it."

"You mean the name 'Eugénie,' the alias she used?"

"So far that's the only thing I have to go on," she said. "But we need proof."

"I used to have a friend in Nantes," René said. "Let me see if she's still there." He made a face. "Saves me much more time if you've got the woman's *carte bancaire*." His eyes gleamed. "I could hack the chip on her card and get into her account."

"Wish I did," she said.

"*Tiens*, Aimée, I prefer that to the 128-bit encryption system at Banque de France."

"I'm impressed, René," she said, letting out a low whistle.

"Banque de France is a royal pain to maneuver!" he said. "I haven't cracked all their encryptions yet." He spread his arms from the edge of her desk indicating as far as the wall. "Only about that long. But take away the best years of my life and I will."

"Save your brain for the important stuff, René," she said. "Like our rent!"

"*Bien sûr*, but I'll stop at your apartment for some software. If I get hold of my friend, I might be able to navigate the *Fichier* in Nantes," René said. "Besides, I've got a bag of bones for Miles Davis."

"You're just trying to get on Miles Davis's good side," she said.

"Check out the Duplo," René said. He scanned the fax. "Interesting explosive to use."

She'd wondered about that, too.

"Why use Duplo?" Aimée asked.

"Instead of the more easily available Eastern-bloc explosive, Semtex? Good question." René replied. "Word is the fundamentalists like Semtex."

Aimée's eyes widened at René's knowledge.

"Have the *flics* blamed it on the fundamentalists yet?" she said. "That's standard procedure." Every time there was a bombing, the media referred to it as an Arabe incident in the same breath. The inherent racism made her sick.

She walked to their oval window overlooking rue du Louvre, giving herself time to think. The truth could lie somewhere in between. If the fundamentalists wanted to kill Anaïs, a minister's wife, they'd botched the job. But why? The victim hadn't been identified, Anaïs's name hadn't been mentioned, and no group had claimed credit.

"Let's say the fundamentalists want no connection to this," she said, "or they have no connection."

"Life is full of possibilities," René said. "But I'd say the latter. Mafioso-types and the criminal element use commercial stuff like Duplo."

"Look here," Aimée said, pointing at the last paragraph in the report. "Traces of a circuit board found indicate it was Swiss-made—an electronic switch manufactured in Bern. They meant business."

"The timing feels off, Aimée," René said, cocking his head sideways. "I thought you left Gaston's café around seven-fifteen, which gave you time to walk there, try the door, go up the street, and then return to number 20 *bis*." He paused and pointed to the report. "According to this the explosion occurred at eight o'clock. First on the scene were the *pompiers*, then a SAMU at eight-twenty followed by the bomb squad, which arrived at eight thirty-five. The bomb squad did its documentation and recovery; then the chemical analyses began two hours later."

"*Attends*, René," Aimée said. She grabbed a black marker, taped a sheet of newsprint to the wall, jotted down 7:15, then drew a thick arrow.

"Go on," she said.

"Didn't you say that when the *flics* came you hopped like a bunny over the wall?" René asked.

The grunting, heaving lunge of a sea lion seemed a more apt description. But she kept that to herself.

"Well, I heard sirens and they said, 'Open up!' " She stopped writing, her marker held in midair. As she and Anaïs pulled into rue Sainte-Marthe, she remembered seeing a SAMU van and thinking how quickly someone had called the ambulance. It would have been 8:10 at the latest.

"According to this report," René said, "a tenant, Jules Denet, one street over, said that after the explosion he heard suspicious noises in the courtyard.

Rene punched the paper with his stubby fingers.

She thought back to the SAMU, then nodded. "Then there were two SAMU vans," she said. "The other one came at eight-twenty."

"It's pretty coincidental that another SAMU van would respond but not be listed on the report or log in with the other SAMU crew. So if it wasn't emergency or the *flics*—who was it?" René asked.

Aimée tacked the fax next to the timeline. Stared at it. Not only were the times off, but something didn't add up. She stood back and opened the oval office window, letting in dull light and diesel fumes from rue du Louvre. She paced to the door, flicked on the office light, then paced back to her desk.

"Follow this logic, René," she said. "Say whoever planted the bomb hung nearby to activate it or make sure the thing went off. I remember hearing some Arabe music just before the bomb exploded. Maybe they planned on blowing up Anaïs too—are you with me here?"

"Go on," he said.

"What if they used a SAMU van as a fake, maybe parked nearby to set off the bomb," she said. "Or they wanted what Sylvie gave Anaïs and figured on grabbing Anaïs."

"But you disturbed the scenario?" René interrupted excitedly.

"Exactly," she said. She closed the window and faced René. "I think what the neighbor Denet heard was Anaïs and me. I wonder if he saw something more than that?"

René nodded.

"I better go find out."

Wednesday

AT DAWN, UNDER ORDERS from the Paris prefect, uniformed police swept Notre-Dame de la Croix. They took Mustafa Hamid and the other nine hunger strikers to waiting SAMU vans, which carted them to nearby hospitals.

The prefect issued a statement saying that the raid had been ordered for humanitarian reasons after he'd heard alarming reports about the health of the hunger strikers from doctors attending them at the church. However, the acting director of Paris emergency medical services said the hunger strikers had been taking tea and water with sugar and vitamins.

"We were not consulted about evacuating them," said a doctor who preferred to remain nameless. "The low ketone level tested in their urine was not considered life threatening, but characteristic for the body's acid balance at such a stage."

By afternoon no one had left the church. Seven of the hunger strikers had signed themselves out of the hospital. They returned to the church to applause from the others who'd vowed to take up the hunger strike in their place. Mustafa Hamid was among them.

AIMÉE PAUSED AT THE entrance of 34 rue Sainte Marthe. KROK spelled out in rainbow colors spread across the door. A middle-aged man wearing an undershirt answered, a frosted white cockatiel perched on his shoulder. The man's stomach protruded over his stained pants, and he looked vaguely uncomfortable.

"*Eh*, sorry about the noise," he said quickly. "I'll keep her quiet. She's a bit agitated, that's all."

"Monsieur Jules Denet?" Aimée asked. She kept the disappointment from her voice. Denet looked the reclusive type. Too bad. His presence would make things difficult. She needed to break into Eugénie's apartment, which lay behind his back courtyard.

"*Oui*," he said, starting to close the door. "Like I said, I'll keep her quiet."

"Monsieur Denet, you misunderstand," she said showing her card. "I'm a private detective. If you'd be so helpful as to answer a few questions about the incident you reported, I'll be on my way."

"I thought you were from the tenants' association," he said. "There's nothing more to say." He stroked the cockatiel, which pranced back and forth on his shoulder. Dark circles hollowed under Denet's eyes. He seemed as nervous as his bird.

"Please, spare me just a few minutes of your time," she said.

"My bird's upset with all this commotion. I need to calm her down." He grabbed the door handle to shut the door.

She had to think of something that would make him talk.

"What's your bird's name, Monsieur Denet?" she said. "I love cockatiels. People say I have a way with them."

Denet paused, interested, his hand resting on the handle.

"Blanca," he said. "*Espagnol* for white. My wife came from Madrid."

"Blanca's a lovely bird, Monsieur Denet," she said. "Very healthy. Obviously you must take wonderful care of her. Won't you let me come in? The hall is too drafty for her."

Denet shrugged, then motioned for her to come inside. He stifled a yawn.

"I'm sorry but I've got to nap. I go to work at ten o'clock."

"Why's that, Monsieur?"

"So Belleville residents get their *croissants, baguettes, et pain levain* bright and early at the *boulangerie*, Mademoiselle."

No wonder he looked tired. He baked all night.

"*Eh bien*, Monsieur, one simple question." She edged toward his entryway. "You keep baker's hours and sleep during the early evening. How would you see disruption in the courtyard that I believe your dining area looks over?"

"Eh, who did you say you work with?" he asked.

She showed him her ID with the less-than-flattering photo.

"Did you hear the explosion, Monsieur Denet?"

"Those people!" he said. He pointed to what Aimée figured was the Visses' back window. "The screaming brat woke me up, and the lady with her prayers all night. She makes sure I hear her praying for my soul. My sinful soul."

Aimée controlled a smile, stuck her arm out, and restrained her squeamishness as the bird's sharp talons clamped her wrist. As Blanca hopped over to Aimée's sleeve an admiring look showed on Denet's face.

"Blanca never goes to anyone else," he said, his voice wistful. "Only my wife and I."

"Nightingales nest in the pear tree outside my bedroom window," she said, slowly stroking Blanca's feathers. "They let me hand-feed them. Why don't you show me the view, Monsieur?"

Denet led her inside. His apartment, a capsulelike affair remodeled in the seventies, overlooked rue Jean Moinon's rear courtyards. Several large windows composed most of the wall of his dining area.

"Too much light for me," he said, gesturing to the skylights and tall windows. "I can't sleep in the daytime. My health's being ruined—working by hot ovens all night. Only Blanca enjoys such a warm place."

Many Parisians would kill for such a light-filled modern apartment, she thought. Warm and toasty with a working heater, plentiful electrical outlets. Even closets.

Her own Ile St. Louis apartment had a temperamental electrical system, archaic plumbing, and warped seventeenth-century parquet floors overlooking the Seine.

"Tell me what happened, Monsieur," she said, as Blanca strutted up and down her arm. The pincerlike talons pierced through Aimée's blue wool sleeve, the bird's white feathered crest rippling as Aimée stroked it. Blanca's pigeon-pink eye reminded her of Anaïs's suit after the explosion. The suit clumped with blood. Sylvie/Eugénie's blood.

"Blanca likes you," said Denet, sitting down heavily in a tubular chrome chair at a glass-topped table.

Good, Aimée thought, hoping the bird didn't need to relieve herself soon.

"I'm moving to a hotel if I can't get some sleep," Denet said.

"You told the police of a noise or some disturbance?"

"Sorry, Mademoiselle, even if I saw something, I stay away from gossip."

Jules Denet, sallow-faced and paunchy, seemed out of sync with his furniture. And his apartment. A true denizen of *populaire* Belleville, the socialist working class, he belonged more in the last century.

Aimée wished she could offer him space in her dark cavernous and drafty apartment. He might feel more at home. Maybe he'd be more cooperative.

"You'd like my flat, Monsieur Denet," she said. "Dark and quiet, no heat to speak of," she smiled. "But Blanca might object."

Denet's eyes softened. For a moment she thought he would open up. He had to be lonely. Then his eyes hardened.

"Bad business," he said. His mouth set in a firm line.

"Routine questions, Monsieur, are my job," she said. "I'm hired to find the truth. Not manufacture a theory like the *flics* often do to keep their statistics high."

Denet nodded; he understood. Working-class folks were known for their mistrust of *flics*.

"I'm sorry I can't help you."

C'est dommage, she thought. A crying shame.

And a dead end.

Besides requestioning the devout Madame Visse and Elymani—the custodian with two jobs who wanted no part of her investigation—she didn't know where to go from here. She tried one last question.

"Too bad, Monsieur," she said. "I suppose you can't tell me about Eugénie?"

"Aaah, the red-haired one . . ." Denet trailed off.

Her heart skipped. Blanca still on her arm, she sat down, containing her excitement. "Eugénie lived across at 20 *bis*, didn't she?"

"Eugénie told me too much *télé* was bad for my eyes," he said.

Not what Aimée expected to hear, but she agreed.

"How did Eugénie know that, Monsieur?"

"Last summer—you know how it stays light so late in the evenings—I tried everything to block out the light. But I couldn't sleep. And that baby had colic, crying all the time . . ."

Aimée leaned forward, resting her arm on the table, Blanca

content to be continuously stroked. She listened, nodding encouragement from time to time.

"So I watched the *télé*, something my late wife and I never did. We always had so much to talk about . . ." He trailed off and looked down at his large hands. "She passed away a year ago yesterday."

"*Désolée*, Monsieur Denet," she said.

Jules Denet, a lonely widower plagued with insomnia . . . Aimée wanted him to finish painting this picture.

"Until Eugénie—an angel, that one," he said, spreading his fingers over the coffee table.

Aimée's response caught in her throat. She took a deep breath. "Eugénie sounds very thoughtful, Monsieur Denet."

Denet's eyes held a faraway look.

"I told her about the *boulangerie*," he said. "Looking back, if she was bored, she never let on. Told me it was better than waiting for her boyfriend."

"Her boyfriend?"

"I never saw him," he said. "Seems he was married. You know the type!"

Aimée nodded, unsure that her meaning of the "type" matched Jules Denet's.

It was hard for Aimée to picture Philippe de Froissart, an aristocrat gone socialist, having a rendevous with Sylvie/Eugénie in this dilapidated building. Why not a hotel? Then again maybe he'd liked slumming in *bas* Belleville.

"But you saw her girlfriends, of course," Aimée said. "Did she have a friend with long dark hair?"

"Not that I remember," he said. "I'd see Eugénie every few weeks. Maybe a month would pass."

"What about her friends?" she asked. "Did you see them?"

Denet's face fell. "I wouldn't call them friends."

Aimée sat up. "How's that, Monsieur Denet?"

"Arabes," he said, his mouth tight.

"Young or older?" Aimée asked.

"Eugénie had a good heart," he said and sighed.

Aimée remembered that Roberge the jeweler had said the same thing.

"She helped anyone," Denet said. "I told her, 'Don't let those types hang around. They'll take advantage. Steal.' "

"What did she say to that, Monsieur?"

"She'd smile. Say everyone deserved a chance in life. Everyone." Denet shrugged. "Who can argue with that?"

Aimée saw that it bothered Denet.

"Eugénie liked pearls, didn't she, Monsieur?" she asked.

He seemed taken aback. "She wore overalls—like my baker's ones—we used to joke about that. Very down-to-earth." His smile turned bittersweet. "She seemed sad sometimes. There was a big hurt in her."

Was she sad that Philippe, a minister with a family, wanted only an affair in *bas* Belleville while he lived in the heights?

Aimée noticed Denet's tapered fingers, trimmed nails, his graceful little movements illustrating his words. Here was an artist who used his hands. Every day.

She tried to question him further, but he protested, finally revealing he'd seen nothing, only heard noises, and he hadn't been sure of *that* since he'd been watching a Jet Li action flick. She wondered how that soothed his nerves to sleep.

"Here's my card," she said. "If you remember anything else, please give me a call."

But he'd seemed more concerned about his noise trouble with the Visse family. And that bothered her. She figured he'd heard her and Anaïs in the old garage yard and wanted to get back at the Visses. But at least now she knew when to break into Eugénie's place.

BERNARD HAD FAILED TO deliver the immigrants to the airport. Now he'd be dismissed, relegated to some third-rate office at the ends of the earth.

Bernard walked away from the church. His feet carried him; his mind was blank. He wished he were numb. He found himself on familiar streets, the haunts of his later childhood. In *bas* Belleville, where his family had counted themselves lucky to find a cheap apartment after their exodus from Algeria. With no servants or belongings, only the clothes on their backs.

It had been a frigid, biting April, like this one. One of the coldest in years. Bernard had been surprised at the cold and gray of Paris. He'd never imagined the sheeting rain, density of human habitation, or so many vehicles. Not like Algiers, with the bleaching sun, the clamor of the medina, and the donkey droppings on the stone streets. He'd worn his coat in their small apartment, never feeling warm.

The nearby Belleville haunts of his childhood had changed. Now the narrow streets were full of discount Chinese shops, cell phone stores with signs in Arabic, even a M. Bricolage do-it-yourself home fix-it chain. Bright green AstroTurf lined the entrance. Once, he remembered, that had been a glass factory.

His first vivid memory of Paris was seeing the workers in overalls at the glass factory pouring sand into yellow cauldrons—huge, steaming pots made of black cast iron. On his way home from school, he wondered at the crisp and brittle glass sheets lined up for delivery. "Sand into glass?" he asked, and his mother had nodded yes. "But you told me you can't turn a sow's ear into a silk purse," he said. "Of course, that's different," she sighed.

"How?" he persisted, and she, weary or late for work, would say "Later, Bernard, later." No one had ever successfully explained it to him. At the polytechnic the dry professor had discussed the chemical process. Secretly Bernard had dismissed the theory, preferring to believe in magic, as he always had. Remembering the stories of the *djinn* from his Berber nursemaid, and the *Aïcha qandicha*, who, as everyone knew, had goat's feet and one eye in the middle of her forehead.

No magic lay in his old apartment building. A restaurant stood on the ground floor where formerly a dark wood brasserie had occupied the corner. The bright, gold-trimmed Thai restaurant advertised EARLY-BIRD DINNER SPECIAL 48 FRS. Memories drew him to the door.

His stepfather, Roman, a displaced Pole who'd joined the Legion in Algeria, had been a butcher by trade. Roman had supplied the meat and played cards with the owner of the old *brasserie*, Aram, a Christian from Oran. Roman, he remembered, had resented—as he resented so much else—Aram's buying the place cheap after the war. But his mother had countered: "The former owners are ashes, Roman, that's why." Roman's eyes had hardened. He'd been quiet after that. His mother too.

Bernard went inside the restaurant.

"Monsieur, a party of one?" the smiling black-haired woman asked. Her gold-flecked *patung* caught the light, a fuchsia band encircled her waist. The scent of lemongrass came from the kitchen. He remembered the wood-paneled walls, the dark interior, and the lack of windows.

Bernard nodded.

She showed him to a table set with chopsticks and blue-and-white porcelain bowls and plates. Gold-leaf dragons, like gargoyles, protruded from the ceiling. In the half-full restaurant, low conversations hummed and glasses clinked.

"Thai iced tea?"

He nodded again, happy to follow her lead.

She shoved a plate into his hands. "Help yourself, Monsieur."

The buffet table, with steaming soup and heated platters of rice noodles, spring rolls, lemongrass chicken, and other tantalizing dishes made him realize how hungry he was. He remembered that where the buffet stood had been the old birchwood bar. Oiled and polished by Aram every week.

Bernard was amazed. He hadn't thought of these things in years. Memories of people and the building opposite, victims of the wreckers' ball, flooded back to him as he ate. He felt almost giddy. Once it had been different, he remembered. Once it *had*.

He helped himself several times to the buffet. A calmness settled over him, like the way he felt from the little blue pills.

He went to the restroom, passing the kitchen, and looked in. The paint, the grease-spattered tile, even the pipes looked new. Only the arched ceiling downstairs in the lavatory was the same. Bland gray paint covered the old stones where Roman once hung his bloody aprons, the nights he stopped by after work to play cards.

"*Ça va*, Monsieur?" a shiny-faced Asian man asked, menus stuck under his arm. "Do you feel unwell?"

Bernard realized that he stood on the stairs, perspiring and shaking.

"I'm fine, sorry," Bernard said. He wiped his brow, then gripped the man's arm. "How long have you owned this restaurant?"

Apprehension shone in the man's eyes. He pulled away.

"Did you buy this from Aram?"

The man erupted in a volley of Thai, then disappeared up the stairs. Bernard slapped his forehead. How dumb! Of course the man was *sans-papiers*. And here he was accosting an illegal to find out about the past.

Upstairs the smiling woman who'd served him had turned into a businesslike hostess. Her command of French disappeared and she pointed at the bill, then her watch, indicating closing time.

His search for the past scared these people. He tried to explain one more time, but their impassive faces made him give up.

On rue d'Orillon, he paused and looked up at his old window. The peeling shutters were open, and a single line of wash hung outside. An African dialect reached his ears. A child cried, the mother's placating rejoinder quickly soothed it. Another wave of immigrants, Bernard thought. Some things never changed.

The pager on his hip vibrated. Nedelec's number at the ministry read ominously on the display. Bernard stopped at the corner phone.

"*Directeur* Berge, we're giving you a second chance," Nedelec said. "Mustafa Hamid wants to negotiate. We expect you at the ministry within the hour."

Before he could protest, Nedelec had hung up.

Bernard felt cornered again.

He stumbled and lost his dinner in the vacant lot, among the rubble and wire where his neighbor's building had once stood.

MORBIER HAD AGREED TO meet Aimée at a small brasserie on rue Pyrénées after his therapy. He was late. She'd been ordering steadily at the bar.

"My poker game's waiting, Leduc," Morbier said, after the smoked trout and *escalope de veau*. He set his napkin on the table. "Or did you have something to say."

She'd been debating whether to ask Morbier or not. Maybe it was the Pernod talking, but she had to know. "Why did Papa take the surveillance job? Looking back, it didn't seem like the ordinary contract."

Morbier exhaled, blue smoke spiraled in the close air of the brasserie. "Give it a rest, Leduc."

"How can I?" She leaned forward, her arms resting on the crumb-littered white tablecloth. "I wake up at night thinking there was something he didn't tell me. Something I missed . . . how tense he was, how he went first into the van . . ."

"You're thinking you should have gone first?"

Sometimes she wondered if she should have.

"If you had, Leduc," Morbier continued, "your papa, rest his soul, would have been right where you're sitting, *his* heart bleeding. Instead of yours. He'd have been hurt more."

"How can you say that?" She brushed the crumbs aside, forming them into small piles.

"Eh, young people!" he said simply. "Who gets over the loss of a child?"

Morbier had turned into a pocket psychologist. Maybe he'd attended too many sensitivity sessions at the commissariat.

"You know more than you're telling me, Morbier."

"And if I do, what would it change?"

She paused, then swept the piles of crumbs into her cupped palm below the tablecloth edge.

"I could sleep at night, Morbier."

He looked away.

"Going to Place Vendôme brought everything up for me again," she said. "Sorry." With a quick motion, she flicked the crumbs onto her plate, then got the waiter's attention.

"*L'addition,*" she said.

She pulled a Gitane from Morbier's packet, scratched the kitchen matchbox he always carried, and lit it up. Raw and dense, the smoke hit her as she inhaled.

Morbier eyed her. "Didn't you quit, Leduc?"

"I'm always quitting," she said, savoring the jolt.

After paying the check and struggling into her damp raincoat, she and Morbier stood outside on the glistening cobblestones. The yellow foglamps of cars blurred like halos in the mist. She realized Morbier was watching her.

"You've got survivor's guilt, Leduc," he said. "I've seen it too many times. So have you."

"So *that's* what it's called?" she asked, digging in her bag for her Métro pass. She held it up. Expired. "Morbier, I wasn't searching for a label. But thanks. Now I can catalog the volume and put it on the shelf, eh?"

"You've had too much Pernod."

"Not enough, Morbier," she said.

He shook his head. "Once your papa was my partner. It doesn't go away. But I move on. How do you think I felt?"

Stunned, she looked at him. He'd never alluded to his feelings. Not at the funeral, or the posthumous medal ceremony, or over the years. Never.

"*Désolée*, Morbier," she said.

A taxi, its blue light signaling it was free, cruised up the cobblestones. Morbier stuck two fingers in his mouth and whistled. *Loud.* The taxi halted in front of a large black puddle.

"Go ahead," he said. "I feel like walking."

She was tired. "Don't mind if I do."

She got in. "Seventeen quai d'Anjou, *s'il vous plaît.*"

Before she shut the door, Morbier leaned over.

"Come to terms with it, Leduc, or you'll be devoured."

THE TAXI sped along the darkened quai, punctuated by globular street lamps, their beams swallowed in a thick mist. Morbier was right. The time had come to move on. March forward.

The taxi stopped under the leafy branches in front of her apartment. Below flowed the Seine, reflecting pinpricks of light as mist forked under Pont Marie's stone supports. She paid and tipped the driver twenty francs. Insurance for good taxi karma.

The trouble was that she didn't feel like moving on. She felt like clinging to the memories, fading and more transparent every year, especially the image of her father's crooked smile. Most of all she wanted to know who had killed him. Then maybe she could come to terms with it in her own way.

Her apartment lay empty. No sign of Yves. She hadn't heard from him again. She'd tried forgetting, hard to do since her sheets and towels held a lingering scent of him.

After walking Miles Davis along the quai, she took him upstairs. But she couldn't face her dark apartment and walked over to her office. Work always put her back on track.

The phone was ringing as she opened her glass-paned office door.

"*Allô?*"

"You call yourself my friend, promise to help my sister?" Martine asked angrily as she answered. "But you get her hauled to the commissariat?"

Aimée froze. "The commissariat?"

"Philippe said it's your fault!" Martine said, her husky voice rising.

"He's lying, Martine," she said, startled. She wondered what tale Philippe had spun. But in a way it was true—if she had made Anaïs go to the *flics*—but then those men following them had diverted her. "I've been trying to reach Philippe and Anaïs for two days. They don't return my calls!"

"The only favor I've ever asked you, Aimée," Martine said, disappointment in her voice. "Couldn't you have helped me once?"

"*Mais*, Martine, I helped Anaïs escape," she said, exasperated.

"Escape?"

Aimée set down her bag and hit the light switch in her dark office.

"Sounds like Philippe neglected to mention the car bomb that exploded in front of Anaïs and me," Aimée said, sitting down at her desk, logging on to her computer. "The victim was his 'former' mistress."

Martine sucked in her breath.

"Or so Anaïs said, but there's more to it than that," she said, checking her answering machine. "Things are smellier than the rat's head delivered to my door on Monday. Are you sitting down?"

"I guess I better," Martine said, her voice sounding worried but calmer.

Aimée told her what happened since Anaïs had called her: Sylvie's possible red-haired alias as Eugénie, the Lake Biwa pearl, the Duplo *plastique*, and Sylvie's lack of positive ID.

"Look, Philippe's never been my favorite," Martine said. "He loves Anaïs, granted, in his own way. But I know he wouldn't put her or anyone else in danger. He's the original aristocrat turned bleeding heart liberal. Since Simone was born—well—Anaïs says, he's taken stock of his life, made changes."

Aimée remembered Anaïs in the taxi speeding through Belleville. Her bloody leg and her calm acceptance of Philippe's former infidelity.

"What charges did the *flics* pull her in on?" Aimée asked.

"I don't know, but you've got to help her," Martine said. "Please! We Sitbon sisters pick such winners, eh?" Her voice had grown wistful.

Was Martine thinking about Gilles, her former boss and lover at *Le Figaro* whose job she now held?

"My track record doesn't rate any better," Aimée said. "Yves returned unannounced, I let him spend the night, and then he disappears."

"He's in Marseilles, Aimée," Martine said. "Covering Mustafa Hamid's AFL branch in case of repercussions."

Mustafa Hamid—Aimée remembered seeing that name from the AFL posters plastered around Belleville.

She heard Martine take a deep breath. Instead of reassuring words, Martine warned her. "Yves's ex-wife's back in the picture," she said. "Seems she's making big noises about their apartment."

This surprised her. Yves had never mentioned it, but then again she'd never asked.

"How do you keep so informed?"

"Because he complained that going to Marseilles was going to get him into trouble with all the women in his life," Martine said. "Eh, if that's blunt, sorry. But I know you can take it. You don't rely on men."

Yves could have told her.

Next time he showed up she'd ask for her key back.

"Which commissariat's holding Anaïs?" Aimée said, hoping her tone sounded matter-of-fact.

"In the *quartier* Charonne, rue des Orteaux," Martine said.

"Good. I know someone there," she said. "At least I used to."

But she wondered why Anaïs was being held. Was this some kind of cover-up?

* * *

JOUVENAL, AN old colleague of Morbier and her father's, manned the night-desk phone at the commissariat in Charonne. Had done so for twenty years. Too bad he hadn't been on duty when Martaud had brought her in to the other station: She'd have called him instead of Morbier.

Jouvenal always kept anise pastilles from Flavigny Abbey, near his hometown of Dijon, in his desk. On the nights she'd done homework in her papa's office, he'd fill her palm with them.

She called him at the commissariat.

"Philippe de Froissart, *c'est lui*," Jouvenal said, his voice raspier than ever over the phone. He coughed and hacked, still a pack-a-day man, she could tell. She visualized his kind blue eyes.

She wanted a cigarette. In the background she heard voices raised in heated discussion and the scraping of metal chairs over the floor.

"I need to talk with his wife, get her released," she said.

"De Froissart's attempting to get her out," Jouvenal said. "Monsieur bigwig says his own recognizance should be enough even though she hasn't been charged yet. The night is young, eh? His status will work in his wife's favor."

"She's not involved, Jouvenal," she said. "I ought to know."

"How's that?"

"She almost got blown up as well," Aimée said.

"I know your old man trained you," he said slowly. Aimée could almost see Jouvenal's broad shoulders. When she was little, they'd seemed like blue mountains when he'd shrugged. "But even if that's true, what can I do?"

"Let me speak with Philippe."

"He's busy. Looks like he's going to smack the *judiciaire* in a minute if I don't curtail matters." Shouts erupted in the background.

"Jouvenal, I always liked you," she said. "Please, get Philippe on the phone."

"You only liked me for my candy," he said.

"That too," she said. "But after you explained long division to me, I finally got it."

"*Attends*, Aimée," he said. The phone scraped and she heard Jouvenal's calming voice.

She had to meet Philippe, ferret out what he was hiding.

Finally, Jouvenal got Philippe on the line.

"*Oui*," he said curtly.

"It's Aimée Leduc," she said. "I need to talk with you."

"You! Were you born an *imbécile* or did you grow that way?" he shouted. "What did you get my wife involved in?"

"Me?" she asked surprised. "Sylvie Coudray blew up in front of us! Anaïs involved me, not the other way around."

Muffled noises like a hand held over the phone interrupted her.

"Come to my office tomorrow." he said. "We'll talk."

"Today. Now," Aimée said. "You're in the Twentieth Arrondissement; so am I."

She lied but she didn't want to be put off any longer. A pause. She heard a woman crying in the background.

Was that Anaïs?

"What's going on?" Aimée asked him.

"78 Place de Guignier in thirty minutes."

He hung up.

AIMÉE KNOCKED on the gate of number 78, a two-story house set back from the square surrounded by ivy-covered walls. Through the mail slot she glimpsed yellow roses and greenery bordering a path to the glossy dark green door. Bright lights shone on her.

"Who's there?" asked a loud voice.

"*Le Ministre* de Froissart, please," she said, blinking in the harsh beams.

A long-faced woman opened the gate. She looked Aimée up

and down. "Tradespeople use the back door." She jerked her head toward the side brick entrance, dripping with ivy.

"I'll remember that," she said. "Meanwhile, his wife might be framed for murder."

The woman stiffened and let out a gasp. "He's at the ministry."

"He said to meet him here," Aimée said. She looked around but didn't see a mailbox. "Who lives here?"

"Come this way," the woman said and led her inside toward the side door.

More yellow roses climbed trellises in the manicured garden. A Renault pulled in at the small side drive. The chauffeur, blue cap cocked back on his head, stepped out scratching his temple. The backseat was empty.

"Where's de Froissart?" Aimée asked.

The chauffeur looked askance at the maid, who shrugged.

"Who wants to know?" he said.

"Aimée Leduc," she said.

"You can prove that, I suppose?" He pulled the cap down over his forehead and leaned against the car.

She handed him her card.

"Get in," he said, buttoning up his jacket and opening the Renault's back door.

"Wait a minute," she said, suspicious. "*Le Ministre* de Froissart agreed to meet me here."

"Plans change," he said, holding the door open for her. "Life offers chances for flexibility. One must take advantage."

She didn't like the turn of events or his attitude. But she got in, secure in the knowledge that her Beretta was strapped to her shoulder.

He sped out of the courtyard into sparse traffic. They passed the small darkened shops: a coiffeur, a Turc-Grec kabob restaurant, and a shuttered *agence immobilier* advertising apartments along tree-lined Place de Guignier.

Soon the chauffeur merged into teeming rue des Pyrénées. He

wove the Renault, downshifting among small trucks and late-night taxis.

"Where are we going?"

"The minister will inform me soon," he said, casting a glance in the rear-view mirror at her. His car phone trilled. "That should be him."

She studied the black-coated throng crossing the street. A rain shower sprinkled the windshield and stopped before the chauffeur could switch on his wipers.

De Froissart dictated the rules and remained in the shadows. She didn't like that.

The chauffeur murmured, then hung up the phone. He turned on rue des Couronnes. Aimée had forgotten the panoramic view afforded from the heights of Belleville on a damp April night. In the distance the lighted Eiffel Tower poked a few centimeters above the building horizon. Diminished and distant, just the way she felt at the whim of Philippe de Froissart's agenda.

"We'll meet the minister shortly," he said.

The Renault glided down the steep, narrow streets of Belleville.

A larger car with smoked windows pulled alongside, then took the lead. She noticed the government plates. The car turned onto quai Jenmapes, which fronted dark Canal Saint Martin.

This cat-and-mouse game made her uneasy. Why couldn't Philippe just meet her? The chauffeur braked, jolting her forward. Frightened, she threw her hands out to avoid smashing into the seat.

Suddenly a heavy-set man opened her door. He cast a glance over the area, then jerked his thumb toward the canal. His manner, neither polite nor comforting, gave her little choice but to comply.

He returned to the other car, leaned against the Renault's hood, and studied his fingernails. The car that brought her took off toward République.

A raw wind sliced through Aimée's raincoat as she walked down the embankment. She pulled it around her leather-clad legs. She was cold, damp, and fed up with Philippe's close-mouthed attitude—his mistress had been blown up, his wife and Aimée chased by big ugly thugs through the Métro, and that was just the top of the list. She needed him to illuminate what the hell was going on and where Anaïs was.

Algae smells, mingled with the odor of refuse, wafted from the canal. Raindrops pebbled the water's surface, then stopped. Quaiside lights reflected the metal of the locks on the narrow waterway.

Aimée wished she could change what happened, rewind life—take it apart frame by frame as if editing a film, and stop Sylvie from entering that Mercedes. She also wished she was stretched in front of a roaring fire with Yves. But she wouldn't hold her breath on that one. Yves couldn't be counted on to be there, and besides, her fireplace had been bricked in after the war. So she had to get on with investigating.

Shadows from the skeletal trees not yet dressed for spring waved above her. She crunched over the gravel toward a figure seated on a bench.

Philippe sat, his eyes bloodshot, staring at the water.

"Why all the secrecy, Philippe?"

"Aimée, take my word," he said. "Things are better this way."

"Where's Anaïs?"

"I've taken care of things," Philippe said.

"You seem very take-charge, Philippe" she said, sitting down next to him. "So take me with you—what the hell's going on?"

"She's safe," he said, standing up. He nodded to the chauffeur by the car. Immediately the engine started and the wheels moved, spraying gravel. "You don't need to worry."

Men who condescended bothered her. A lot. She stood up and moved near him.

"Anaïs hired me to find Sylvie's killer," she said. "I took the job."

Aimée saw Philippe's half smile in the dim lights.

"Only Anaïs would do that, but it's so typical of her," he said. "And I love her for it."

Maybe it was how the shadows angled his face or how he leaned forward expectantly, but for a fleeting instant she saw Philippe's vulnerability. She saw how it could appeal to women. Some women—not her.

"Sylvie was trying to protect you, wasn't she, Philippe?" Aimée continued, not waiting for an answer. "She used another identity, Eugénie, didn't she?"

His face darkened. "I'm late for ministry negotiations."

"Philippe, I'm not bothered by the fact that you don't acknowledge me rescuing Anaïs," she said. "I'm bothered by how you avoid telling me who got to Sylvie and why."

He walked away from her, his raincoat flapping in the wind. She followed him.

Acacia wisps from the budding trees fluttered past in the wind. Philippe paused by the canal edge, staring at the eddying surface scum, dotted by furry blossoms and leaves.

She got closer, stared into his face.

"Did Sylvie get involved with the *Maghrébins*? Were you embarrassed your name would come up?"

"Now I remember—you were a *flic's* kid, a pain in the ass," he said, shaking his head. "You haven't changed."

And you're still a rich kid, she thought, with socialist leanings and a ministry job. Didn't he have a vineyard?

"I know people," he said. He looked at his watch, an expensive sports type, then gave her a meaningful look. "Leave this to me."

"Do you think calling the *interministériel* hot line and pulling in favors will work?" Aimée asked, kicking a loose stone into the murky water. "You act as if this was some piece of legislation or trade bill." The stone skipped wavelets midcanal, then sank.

"You don't understand how things work do you, Aimée?" Philippe asked, turning away, his tone even more condescending.

"Have you ever seen a car explode, Philippe?" she asked, trying to stay calm. She didn't wait for an answer but turned to him. "Have you felt clumps of tissue rain down on you, slipped on the bloody pavement, seen an arm fried crisp when it . . ." she stopped.

He bent his head and had the grace to look ashamed.

She hated bringing all this up, seeing those awful images again in her mind. But she had to prod him, make him tell her why.

Silence, except for the slow gurgling of water.

"So I knew," Aimée said, letting her sentence dangle.

"Eh, knew what?" he said, looking up. In the brisk night air, he removed his hands from his pockets and rubbed his thumbs together. "Look, before you speculate, you should know that Sylvie and I parted months ago," he said. He waved his hands dismissively. "Anaïs knew everything was over."

"Sylvie's murder could make sense if she'd got you by the privates."

She figured blackmail would give Philippe a motive to murder his ex-mistress.

"Go back and do whatever it is you do." Philippe scanned the apartments across the canal, he chewed his lip. "Leave your ideas for fantasyland."

"What if Sylvie felt spurned, maybe hurt and angry?" Aimée continued as if he'd never spoken. She knew she was pushing his buttons; if she tried hard enough he'd reveal something. Sylvie had cared for him and he for her. She stepped closer to him. "So when she finally realizes the affair is over, she blackmails you with pillow talk."

"That's not very nice, Aimée," he said, snapping his fingers. His mood changed. Instead of revealing anything he looked angry.

Footsteps crunched on the gravel behind her. She turned to

see a man, his head shaved, wearing rimless glasses and the distinctive bulges of a bulletproof vest under his dark blue sweater. The man's eyes, glassy and emotionless, reminded her of a dead fish. His gaze focused on her. She returned his look, hoping he didn't notice her shiver.

"Meet Claude," Philippe said.

Claude's gaze never wavered.

Aimée shifted her boots on the gravel. Her throat tightened. She should have met Philippe on her own terms. Insisted on it.

"Claude pays great attention to detail," he said. "And he's turning his attention on you. I wouldn't want him to find something irregular and close down your business," he said. His eyes hardened. "Stay out of things you know nothing about."

Aimée heard the two-way radio squawking from the car. Philippe looked over, his attention taken by a police dispatcher announcing, "Fracas at the *sans-papiers* hunger strike at Notre-Dame de la Croix."

"*Merde!*" he muttered.

"Does Sylvie have something to do with that?" she asked.

She saw shock in Philippe's eyes. "I'm not the bad guy," he said.

"Prove it," she said.

But Philippe had turned, hurrying to the car, Claude behind him. The car sped off, popping gravel before the passenger door had even shut.

She didn't realize how much Claude's eyes bothered her until she climbed the humpbacked bridge over Canal Saint Martin, and calmed down enough to think.

If Philippe killed his mistress, pinned the murder on his wife, then tried to cover it up—that made no sense. He would bring disgrace on himself.

Whatever deal Philippe de Froissart had cut, and with whom, had to be dirty. She could smell it.

She thought back to Philippe's reaction at the car radio announcement of Mustafa Hamid and the AFL. Aimée paused on the metal bridge, above the swirling canal. She remembered seeing Hamid's hunger strike posters blanketing Belleville. Plastered over walls near Sylvie's/Eugénie's apartment. Coincidence or connection, she had to find out. Gaston, she figured, could be a mine of information.

She found the number for Café Tlemcen and called from her cell phone.

"*Bonsoir*, Gaston," she said. "Have you got some time for conversation about Mustafa Hamid and the *sans-papiers?*"

She heard Gaston suck in his breath. The hum of voices filled the background.

"Full house right now," Gaston said. "Where are you?"

"Canal Saint Martin," she said.

"Be careful," he said. "Not a nice place at night."

The whir of the espresso machine competed with the loud voices speaking guttural Arabic. She heard what sounded like a chair scraping back then hitting the floor.

"Tempers rising, a bit of turmoil here," he said. "I can't talk. Come tomorrow. Early."

Returning home, Aimée crossed Pont Marie, her frosty breath punctuating the night. Her apartment lay dark, no windows lit, no rooms warm or Yves waiting. Face it, she thought, she had been convenient, a pit stop for him coming from Cairo.

Her head down, intent on hurrying to walk Miles Davis before the rain started, she barreled into a figure.

"*Pardon!*" she said, looking up.

"In a hurry?" Yves said, standing on the quaiside wall opposite her apartment. He brushed her cheek with his fingers, traced her eyes. Below them, the Seine gurgled. "Where were you?" he asked, his coat bundled around him.

Her delight melted. Hadn't he been to Marseilles and neglected to tell her?

"You don't want to know," she said, her mind back on the Canal Saint Martin, Philippe's threat, and Claude's dead eyes.

His feet shuffled the wet leaves.

"Someone else, Aimée?"

She wanted to laugh. However, the benefits of keeping a straight face outweighed the truth. There were a lot of other things she wanted to talk about.

"Where have you been, Yves?"

"Editorial meetings," he said, his eyes not leaving hers. "Lots of dissension, jockeying for position. The usual."

Her face felt warm. She liked his fingers on her cheek. "Aren't you getting along with Martine at *Le Figaro?*"

He shrugged.

For a moment the streetlight on the quai haloed his head, throwing him into shadow. She couldn't read his face.

"We're two different sides of the coin, Aimée," he said. "but that makes it interesting."

"You're undercover again, aren't you?" Her uneasiness warred with a desire to burrow inside his coat.

He put his finger over her lips. "Let's say Martine and I agree to disagree."

"So she wouldn't like—" she said.

"Work's over," he said, tapping his watch. "I already took Miles Davis for his walk. Why don't we warm up together with this?" He pulled a bottle from a paper bag, then a champagne glass from his overcoat pocket. Slants of light angled across his face. "I only found one glass."

"We can share," she said, hooking her arm in his. "A *sommelier* taught me the secret of popping corks. May I demonstrate?"

"Your talents never cease to amaze me." He grinned.

They walked down the stone steps to the embankment. Yves spread his coat for them to sit on under the arched bridge. A lone family of ducks swam in silent formation before them, rippling Vs in the smooth water.

"Veuve Cliquot eighty-nine, nice year!" She used her thumbs and with two twists uncorked the champagne.

"To the ducks!" Yves said. He hooked his arm around her shoulder and they drank soldier style, sipping together. The champagne slid down her throat, giggly and velvet. Yves's body heat warmed her.

As they stared into the water, he told her about Cairo. His face changed recounting a motorcycle trip into the desert on an archaeological dig.

"You like it there, don't you?" Aimée asked, huddling closer.

"You would too, Aimée," he said. "The play of light on the dunes, the stillness . . ." his voice trailed off.

She poured more champagne into their glass.

"I'm not very good at relationships," she said.

"Makes two of us," he said. "Let's drink to that."

And they did.

She stood up, gripping the bottle. "Last one upstairs—"

"Opens the next bottle," Yves interrupted, "but first things first." He leaned against the arch and pulled her close. "I can't get you out of my mind."

They kissed for a long time under the bridge. Not even the toot of a barge or an old *clochard* straggling by disturbed them. They were laughing together as he gave her a piggyback ride all the way up to her apartment. And they spent an even longer time in a hot bath with the next bottle.

Wednesday Evening

BERNARD PACED OUTSIDE MINISTER Guittard's office, rubbing his eyes and trying to come up with an excuse to decline negotiating. The high, frescoed ceilings, painted murals with cavorting angels, and diamond parquetry flooring were lost on him—so intent was he on his thoughts that he didn't notice a man emerging from the office until he collided with him.

"*Je m'excuse,*" he said and looked into the face of Philippe de Froissart.

Philippe, his old classmate from École Nationale d'administration, looked older, dissipated, bags under his bloodshot eyes.

"*Ça va,* Philippe?" Bernard asked.

"Rolling with the punches," Philippe said, his smile forced. He gave Bernard a tepid handshake, then moved on.

Bernard remembered Philippe back in the 1968 Sorbonne riots, a fiery demonstrator on the front lines, passionate about his ideals. He'd also attracted the female students. After graduation Philippe had cast his lot with the Socialistes. Later, he'd emerged as *Secrétaire d'Etat à la Défense,* a governor in the Defense Ministry. He'd done well, ranking high in the food chain of power.

Where had their youth gone, Bernard wondered, and the feeling that they could make a difference?

"Minister Guittard expects you, Berge," Lucien Nedelec said, smoothing his thin moustache. He rose and gestured Bernard forward. "Your plan backfired," he added. "Miserably, in fact. But we know you can do better."

"Nedelec, why me?" Bernard said. "My job belongs with another ministry section."

"*Mais* you're perfect, Berge," Nedelec said, buttoning his double-breasted suit jacket and ushering him forward.

"I don't understand," Bernard said, halting at the door.

"You don't get it, do you?" Nedelec shook his head. "It's your background, Berge! The minister's enamored of how as a *pied-noir*, born in Algeria, you uphold the law."

Bernard saw the reflection in the glass-paned doors and briefly wondered about the old man with the haunted look beside him. With a start, he realized he was staring at himself.

PHILIPPE PEERED INTO SIMONE'S bedroom. Her soft breathing and dinosaur nightlight greeted him. Philippe's shoulders relaxed. His baby was asleep. Safe.

He shuffled downstairs, grabbed the bottle of duty-free Johnny Walker, bucket of ice, and headed to his home office. Inside the room, he pulled down the shades and poured a generous portion into a Baccarat tumbler.

Philippe unknotted his tie, then sank down on the silk carpet. He leaned his back against his desk and sighed. He stared at the saltwater aquarium wedged among his bookshelves. The only sound came from the tank's bubbling air filter and the ice cubes tinkling in his glass.

Ignoring the work on his desk and Sylvie's folder, which Anaïs had given him, Philippe pulled down his ENA scrapbook. He kept pouring the Johnny Walker, neglecting the ice cubes, and turned the pages.

On the page Bernard Berge—younger and with a lot more hair—stared back at him. The Woody Allen resemblance had been there even then. He'd always teased Bernard about it, saying they could be identical twins. Even when Bernard was in his twenties, his eyes had held that furtive look. No wonder he'd stayed a *fonctionnaire*, never risen high in the ministry.

Philippe saw a photo of himself posed on a rooftop terrace, the Seine behind him. His arms were around a long-haired girl. They both wore headbands, tie-dyed scarves, and not much else. He remembered that afternoon in 1968 but not the girl. Demonstrating at the Sorbonne, he'd thrown *pavés* at the *flics*. All hell had broken loose. His group took over the Arts Building, proclaiming free love, free wine, and freedom of the mind. They'd formulated a new bill of human rights. The only one he remembered was, "Let it hereby be proclaimed that all humanity listen to their heart and sing." They thought, in their arrogance and naïveté, they were changing the world. And he'd never felt better in his life.

Philippe's flat stomach and sense of freedom were gone. What had happened to him? Did he look like Bernard Berge—an old man before his time? Was he as dead as he sometimes felt? No, that couldn't be. He struggled with the vineyard, but he'd make it work. Joy flooded him when he saw the wonder sparkle in Simone's eyes, heard her laughter. He'd fallen in love again with his glowing wife when she'd nursed Simone.

He called to check on Anaïs. The nurse told him Madame slept. Philippe thanked her and sighed as he hung up the phone. He poured more Johnny Walker into his tumbler.

If only he had stayed in the commune in Normandy, joined his brother's pop group, or traveled to India and lived on an ashram.

The phone interrupted his thoughts.

"*Allô*," Philippe said.

"You are elusive, Philippe," Kaseem Nwar said. "Talk to me, please, I must give the investors hope."

Tired of Kaseem's continued persistence, Philippe wanted to hang up.

"What more can I say, Kaseem?" Philippe said, annoyed. "My committee passed on the funding reins. We have no more control."

The less Kaseem knew the better. The less anyone knew the better. Look at what happened to Sylvie.

"Can't you reconsider, Philippe?" Kaseem said. "My investments weigh heavily on the project."

"Kaseem, we're subject to the whims of the Elysée Palace," he said. "Like I've always told you, I do what I can. Now it looks impossible."

"Philippe, this isn't just for me," Kaseem said, his tone lower and more insistent. "Others rely on the project, the funding of the mission. They're depending on you for this!"

Philippe heard the quiet desperation in Kaseem's voice.

"I'll see what I can do," he lied.

Anything to get Kaseem off his back.

"*MERCI*, GASTON," AIMÉE SAID, accepting the espresso from him at the counter in Café Tlemcen. The café, with its worn linoleum and lace-covered windows, felt familiar, almost comfortable to her. Raï, a fusion of Western pop with Algerian regional music, pounded from an open window across the narrow street.

"Wasn't Raï outlawed?"

Gaston nodded. "The fundamentalists banned Raï as degenerate Western music. But I like it."

"Me too," Aimée said, tapping her foot as she sipped from the steaming cup. She reached for another lump of brown sugar. The odd look on Gaston's face alerted her.

"Where can I wash my hands?" she asked, making her voice louder than usual.

"Follow me," he said.

He nodded to the rear. Past the zinc bar were the toilet stalls and a passage to the back.

Old men dealt poker at the wooden tables. Several young men in tracksuits and rasta types with dreads played the pinball machines.

Aimée kept up with Gaston, who grabbed a mop en route. At a door opening to a back courtyard, Gaston motioned her to the right. Outside in the courtyard stood a wire-and-glass-roofed structure. Aimée figured it had once functioned as an iron forge or a blacksmith's, and retained its Belle Epoque charm. The double wood doors lay half open despite the chill drizzle.

"We can talk *chez moi*," he said, indicating for her to follow him inside.

They tramped through sawdust, around exposed iron beams, and a sawhorse straddled by a semifinished oak cabinet. Bits of stucco clung to her heeled boots. Above her, skylights rendered opaque with age filtered weak light across Gaston's spartan live-and-work space. She shivered and wondered how he stayed warm in this place.

An old curved alcove was set into what had been the brick oven used for heating and smelting iron or smithing horseshoes. Inside was an iron bedstead covered by a khaki-colored duvet, with a white Persian cat sleeping at the end.

Below the grimy window she saw a double-ringed cooktop connected to a blue *Butagaz* cylinder on the floor. The aroma of old grease underlay fragrant clay pots of fresh mint and oregano perched on the sill. The only heat source she saw was a small portable heater. In the middle of the room was a chipped Formica table, cluttered with notebooks and yellowed newspaper clippings in clear cellophane. The Persian cat blinked several times, sniffed, then resumed its nap.

"Someone said a car bomb exploded in *bas* Belleville on rue Jean Moinon . . ." Gaston began, his tone hesitant. "Did something happen to Anaïs?"

"Not Anaïs. Her husband's mistress," Aimée said. "I think the woman assumed another identity in Belleville."

"But why?" Gaston asked, smoothing strands of hair down over his bald patch.

She told him an edited version of what happened.

"Ever heard of Eugénie?"

Gaston shook his head. "But Aimée, after you called I searched my files. I recognized Hamid. There's something about him you should know," Gaston said. He pointed to a clipped newspaper photo, captioned "Souk-Ahras 1958," from *Le Soir d'Algérie*. In it a group of turbaned unsmiling men, clutching rifles, stood outside a bombed-out building.

"Mustafa Hamid's a *mahgour*," Gaston said pointing to a lean-faced teenager.

Curious, Aimée leaned forward. Hamid seemed to be the youngest among them. "This is a *mahgour*?"

"*Mahgour* means a 'defenseless one,'" Gaston said. He opened a small refrigerator and took out a jar. "In traditional Islamic society, the family is ruled by the Koran and *shari'a*, a code interpreted by legal scholars, regulating everything from male inheritance to what a woman can do in her own home."

Gaston managed quite well with his one hand, emptying scraps from the jar into the cat's bowl on the floor.

"Hamid's family was massacred during an early battle in the mountainous Kabylie region. He grew up on the streets—a *mahgour* without connection, family, or group that could provide security and protection in a society where individuals without such connections are defenseless."

"But he's part of this group," she said, looking at the photo.

"That's true," Gaston agreed. "And now Hamid speaks for the AFL, as a leader. His group embraces all 'African brethren,' as he says."

"He's accepted, then, isn't he?" Aimée asked. She figured Gaston had a reason for telling her all this.

"A *mahgour* who forges complex loyalties and connections survives, can even thrive. But he remains a *mahgour*." Gaston nodded. "*Anciens combattants*, like me, fought with many. They joined us because their people didn't trust them. Some became *Harkis*—paramilitaries who fought with the French."

"Seems rooted in tribalism," she said.

"Most Algerians descend from the Kabylie or Berber tribes," he said. "But if you understand this concept you understand the country."

She felt glad that Gaston was on her side.

"Who's this?" she said, pointing to the young man beside Hamid. Their arms laced around each other's shoulders.

Gaston scanned the names under the photo. "His brother."

"But you said Hamid was orphaned."

"Orphaned brothers, once close," Gaston scratched his head. "We had files on all the insurgents. A high percentage came from *mahgours*. Hamid's brother lived in Paris but returned to Algeria, I think."

"Djeloul Sidi—is that his name?" Aimée said, peering closer.

Gaston nodded.

"Did Hamid change his name?"

"Lots of *mahgours* do," he said. "People often do that if they're hiding."

"Or putting the past behind and starting a new life," she said. "Any idea what his brother's up to now?"

"I concentrate on anticolonial struggles from nineteen fifty-four to nineteen sixty-one," he said, "and friendly-fire situations."

"What do you hope to achieve with your memoirs, Gaston?" she asked.

"The truth," he said. "No one likes to talk about that time. But friendly fire happened to my troop. More than once."

"You're writing the history?"

"Internecine struggles between Algerian factions could fill volumes," Gaston said, pointing to the papers. "In here, too," he pointed to his gray temple. "Canal Saint Martin, where you called me from last night," he said, "was a notorious reckoning spot in 1960. With hideous regularity, bodies were found floating." Gaston shook his head. "The OAS hunted the Algerian underground, and the FLN militants policed their own."

"So you mean the French killed their own, and the Algerians did too?" Aimée thought of the quiet flowing canal and Philippe's threat.

Gaston nodded. "Ugly things happened."

Claude's fishlike eyes still bothered her. "Based on Philippe's reaction, I think somehow Eugénie/Sylvie had contact with Hamid," Aimée said. "But as a wealthy minister's mistress, I doubt she supported Hamid's cause. She had another identity; she had secrets."

"Everyone has secrets," Gaston said.

But not everyone has a double life, Aimée thought. She had to find out more.

"What do you hear about the *sans-papiers?*"

"Last night I broke up a fight," Gaston said, "between a fundamentalist and a pimp's brother." He rolled his eyes. "Both claimed that Hamid is a figurehead. One said the *mullah* Walid would take power. The other said his brother, the pimp Zdanine, had plans to divert the attention his way." Gaston shook his head. "Meanwhile Hamid's wasting away on a hunger strike, the focus of media attention. He's trying to keep his AFL united with all the *sans-papiers*, not just the ones from Algeria."

"So if an AFL faction splits from Hamid, they could rationalize that because he's a *mahgour?*"

"Depends," he said. "But I'd say that's a good guess. We used to say, 'Muck floats downstream, the good and bad, often together.'"

"What do you mean, Gaston?"

"Hamid's got a church full of people. Some are just there for the ride."

"Aren't the police going to evict them again?"

"There's another candlelight protest vigil tonight," Gaston said. "Hamid's granting interviews."

"Then I'll get one too," she said.

But before that she had to get into Sylvie/Eugénie's apartment on rue Jean Moinon.

YOUSSEFA HUDDLED IN THE back of the church, trying to make herself small. Hamid—she had to talk to Hamid. Eugénie had told her she could trust him. The problem was reaching him.

Ahead of her the hunger strikers who sprawled on the pews rested with their eyes closed. To her they looked like the dead.

Youssefa squeezed her eyes shut under the chador. But the images were burned into her memory. The surprised looks and the raw fear on the victims as the rifles pointed their way. How the bodies shuddered at the impact, then crumpled into the pits they'd been forced to dig. The flies, the heat magnified and radiating off the corrugated-iron Quonset huts.

She pinched her legs until she couldn't stand the pain, almost screamed out. The images faded. Youssefa forced herself to gain control.

So far she'd buried the terror when it seemed ready to engulf her. She kept her story to herself. No reason to endanger the women where she worked. They asked no questions, and she gave no answers. An unspoken agreement; life stayed safe that way.

She overheard that Hamid's strength had ebbed, only a few AFL members were allowed access to him. And they were all men. She didn't want to bring attention to herself and was afraid the mullahs would refuse her. Especially the one called Walid, with his officious air.

"Zdanine, do me a favor," said a voice near her. "Eat your pistachios somewhere else."

"*Je m'excuse,*" Zdanine said and stood, brushing the shells from his tracksuit. Charcoal-eyed and handsome, his gaze reminded her of an undertaker estimating the length of a person's coffin and shroud. One who lived by taking quick stock of future merchandise. Zdanine appeared sharper than the young *hittistes* in her village, unemployed for lack of jobs. Many made ends meet by the odd scam or lived off their girlfriends. But, like her cousins, Zdanine seemed to share a worldview limited to himself.

She watched Zdanine stroll over to Walid, hold a short conversation, then head toward the back of the church.

But Youssefa realized that if Zdanine had Walid's ear, then maybe he could help her.

TONIGHT WAS THE TIME to break into the apartment, Aimée thought. Time to check those blue plastic trash bags for clues in Sylvie's courtyard. Garbage was collected every day in Paris, but had the *éboueurs* hit Belleville yet? She called her cousin Sébastien. He was good at dirty jobs. But she'd have to sweeten the pot. Entice him. Invite him to dinner. And she was hungry.

"How about L'Estaminet or Café de Charbon?" Sébastien suggested. "Let's try a hot rue Oberkampf restaurant."

Aimée was wary of the studied chic of these restaurants, old shops gutted, then refurbished to look old again in a nineties way, crowded with those wanting to see and be seen.

"Favela Chic is better," she answered, comfortable with the childlike elegance of Brazilian saints and icons studding the walls, not to mention the steaming manioc, beans, and crusty fried *Bahiana* shrimp cakes.

In her room she opened her armoire, found the green street-cleaner jumpsuits she was looking for, and stuffed them in her bag. In the unused bedroom, once her father's, she looked in his art deco chest. She didn't like going in his room, much less through his drawers. Once they were opened, her father's scent assailed her. The familiar wool and cedarwood of her childhood. She found his lockpicking kit, the tools wrapped in dark blue velvet. He'd taught her how to wire an explosive, crack a safe, and tap her own gas meter/phone line. He'd said, "It's just so you know the score."

* * *

SEVERAL HOURS later she opened the creaking door of Favela Chic, smoky and lit by strings of tiny pink and melon-green lights. The early-evening beer drinkers sat at tables covered with floral oilcloth.

Sébastien was flirting with the young Brazilian waitress when Aimée sat down at his table by the window.

"Orangina, please," she said.

"Make that two." He smiled.

"*Muito obrigada.*" The ringlet-haired waitress nodded.

Sébastien turned his head to watch the waitress sway toward the kitchen. "She seems the rave party type," he said, stretching his long legs and leaning back dangerously in the small chair.

He'd discovered the art poster business after he'd gotten his nose out of the white powder. And the needle out of his arm.

Her little cousin was making good. Aimée felt happy for him. All six feet of him. He engulfed the chair and table like a big black bear. The black leather studded pants, biker jacket, and bushy black beard contributed to the illusion.

"I'm considering a lease on the shopfront at the rue Saint Maur corner."

"You must be doing well, Sébastien," she said.

"Not bad," he said. "Some nice museum orders came in."

"Congratulations. I'm proud of you." And she meant it.

After they ate, Aimée had paid the bill, and Sébastien arranged to meet Maria-João, the waitress, after closing. He lit a cigar.

"So what do you want me to do?" he asked.

"Help me collect some garbage," she said.

"The human kind?"

"More inane," she said. "And stinkier."

"Why am I not surprised at that remark?"

"We're going to break into someone's apartment," Aimée said. "You'll help me steal her trash."

"Not my first choice of evening plans," Sébastien said.

"Little cousin, you owe me at least one lifetime," she said. "I remember clearing your airways and getting you on your feet before the SAMU arrived," she said. "Not to mention ditching your stash in a roof rafter before the *flics* raided the place."

"And for that," he grinned, "I'm your slave."

"Good. Let's walk, digest our food before the job," she said. "Did you park your van in Place Sainte-Marthe?"

"*Bien sûr,*" he said. "And brought everything you requested."

Sébastien shouldered his bulging leather bag. They reached Eugénie's building on rue Jean Moinon. The narrow street lay deserted and dark. The streetlight bulbs had been smashed. Probably, she figured, so the junkies could do business without an audience.

"My old *lycée* is near here," Sébastien said.

"And it's changed," she said. "Now it houses the temporary part of the morgue."

"Hold on here, eh?" he said, recoiling. "I don't break into morgues."

"Don't worry," she said. "I already have."

He blinked, then shook his head. "Shouldn't we get to work?"

From her bag she handed him the extra-large green jumpsuit with *PROPRIÉTÉ DE PARIS* on the back, worn by the garbage collectors. She stepped into hers, zipped it up, and tied a scarf around her hair. He pulled a ski cap low over his eyes.

"We're going to use an American technique," she said.

Sébastien's eyes gleamed.

"Like Dumpster diving?" he said. "We're dressed for it."

"Nothing so glamorous," she said, her mouth crinkling in distaste. "Too bad. The garbage gets dumped every day. But since the building's slated for demo and there's no *gardien* we might find something."

Eugénie's apartment windows were shuttered and silent. A

striped tomcat slinking down the street was the only sign of life. Part of Aimée didn't want to do this. Hated to do it.

She inhaled, taking a deep breath. The frigid air hit her lungs. She stifled a cough with her gloved hand and slipped her digi-code enabler into the door's keypad to unscramble the entry code. She hit a button and the bronze handled, hand-carved building door clicked open.

Once inside the foyer, she set down the leather bag she'd asked Sébastien to bring. He stuck a miniflashlight in his mouth and shone the beam, keeping his hands free. From inside, she handed him several pieces of felt, some Intermarché plastic shopping bags, and rubber bands. She wrapped the felt around her feet, pulled the bags over each foot, rolled rubber bands around her ankle to keep the bags up and indicated he do the same.

"An American technique?"

"It's hi-tech all the way with me," she said then climbed up the stairs. On the second-floor landing, she set down her bag. A bluish shaft of moonlight from the cracked skylight shone over their heads to the warped wood.

"*Shhh,*" she said, putting her finger over her lips and unwrapping her lock-picking kit.

Thursday Night

BERNARD SCROUNGED IN HIS suit jacket pockets. Pills. Where were those pills? The little blue ones. The ones that calmed him down, marshaled his words into succinct phrases.

The bottle was empty. He panicked. He'd already had the hunger strikers removed to the hospital. But after several hours they'd checked themselves out and returned to the church.

Bernard paced back and forth in front of his desk. Rays from his weak desk light pooled on his worn office carpet. What could he do with these people? How would he get Hamid out of the church?

Finally he found a broken blue pill in his pocket lining, chalky and only half a dose. He swallowed it, lint and all. Maybe it would help clarify his thoughts.

The captain of the *Compagnies Républicaines de Sécurité* had disappeared; then the minister had paged him. But Bernard had no phone. No aide de camp. He just clung to a thin rope above the raging rapids of Interior Ministry politics.

Bernard knew Hamid was too weak to conduct negotiations. And the buses bound for the air terminal were pulling up outside the church in Belleville. He remembered their rumbling engines. Like roars of hungry beasts waiting to be fed.

Thursday Night

AFTER AIMÉE'S REPEATED GENTLE coaxing, the cylinder lock opened. Relieved, she took a deep breath, then pulled out her Beretta. Breaking into a dead person's apartment didn't guarantee it was vacant.

Eugénie's door creaked open. Aimée hoped the apartment would surrender the woman's secrets. Brisk currents emanated from the windows, hung with tattered lace. Aimée motioned to Sébastien.

Alert for another presence, they padded into the apartment. Aimée almost tripped over a pile of building notices. Luckily Sébastien caught her arm. A musty odor trailed by faint whiffs of decay hit her.

The place had been trashed. By the look of things, this was definitely professional.

Aimée saw the detritus of the woman's life in her ransacked apartment. It was as if Sylvie had been violated again, even in death. Aimée wanted to leave. But she had to put her feelings aside, get on with the job. Find something to point her toward the killer or killers whether it felt good or not.

She padded into the front room, its windows facing rue de Jean Moinon. A bottle of Evian water had fallen on the floor, its contents long evaporated.

The apartment reminded her of an old-fashioned waiting room in a doctor's office—impersonal, bereft of life. She wondered why a well-off mistress of a minister would use this place. If Sylvie stayed here as Eugénie, there had to be a reason. And if the ransackers had found something, she wouldn't have a clue.

Frustrated, Aimée scanned the rooms, but no answers came to

her. Looking down from the window into the courtyard, she felt a strange sensation. She pulled her jumpsuit collar tighter around her neck.

Aimée unrolled more sheets of felt. She nodded to Sebastien and they tacked them up over the windows. Better than the flimsy blackout curtains provided during the war, her grandfather had told her, and the felt material kept the heat inside. Always keep some handy, he'd winked. You never know when you'll need to make an unannounced visit.

Now she felt safer and took out her large flashlight. The period and layout of the apartment appeared identical to Madame Visse's. However, in contrast with Madame Visse's apartment cluttered with boxes, bright yellow walls, toys, and furniture, Eugénie's was austere. Stark and deserted.

Several cracks in the plaster flaked onto the floor. She figured the nicotine-stained brown walls hadn't seen a new coat of paint since the 1930s or before. In the hallway faint pink rose-patterned wallpaper peeled in places. Former gas fixtures converted to electricity showed frayed wires. To her this didn't seem like a love nest or rendezvous spot for a minister and his mistress.

Aimée nodded to Sébastien and pointed to the old workshop down in the courtyard. He'd agreed to search for the blue garbage bags if they were still there. He made an okay sign with his fingers, pulled out his tools, and padded downstairs.

Back out in the hallway, the air was stale and frigid. But her gloved hands, clammy and moist, and the perspiration sticking the jumpsuit to her neck, made her feel like she was in a steambath.

She shined her flashlight inside the narrow kitchen, with barely enough space for one person to stand and reach the drawers. A double gas ring cooker and scorched aluminum kettle were tossed on the floor. By the old enamel sink, an upside-down bottle of *Maison Verte* dish soap had run green in the sink, leaving a perfumed soapy gunk. Every drawer was pulled out. Strewn teabags littered the chipped Formica table. Grease-stained lino-leum tiles, curling up at the edges, lined the floor.

Apprehensive, Aimée stared at the bare hallway, noticing that chunks of the plaster were gouged out, creating gaping holes in the faded wallpaper. Whoever had trashed this place was looking for something—blowing up Sylvie hadn't been enough.

In the shadowy bedroom, a shredded black sleeping bag leaked feathers over the floor. An Ikea pine desk, the kind requiring self-assembly, had been pulled apart, one of the legs smashed and splintered against the wall. Below the window, she noticed a phone jack in the wall. She searched the room. No telephone.

She found it hard to imagine the woman hadn't had a tele-phone.

Inside the bedroom closet was an orange crate filled with a pair of denim overalls, white shirt, and black sweater, turned inside out and ripped at the seams. A long black nylon raincoat hung from the only hanger, slit to ribbons. Aimée looked for a label.

None.

Curious, she edged further. Inside the cubicle-size bathroom was a shredded two-roll pack of Moltanel pink toilet paper. Pink tissue bits and cotton balls carpeted the stained tub. A large pump bottle of Sephora makeup remover, the expensive kind, had been emptied. The aluminum pipe under the sink had been removed, clumps of black hair and wet matter lay on the old tile floor.

Aimée went to the window overlooking the courtyard. From below, Sébastien flashed a thumbs-up at her, then left to fetch the van.

She turned, ready to untack the felt from the windows and leave, when something red by the empty coatrack caught her eye.

She centered the flashlight beam and peered forward.

Long wisps of what appeared to be red hair peeked out from the hall closet door.

Why hadn't she asked Sébastien to wait? Her flashlight beam centered on the closet door. She willed her hands steady and slowly coaxed the door open wider.

A shag-style red wig lay on the warped linoleum.

Nothing else. Aimée peered closer. The wig looked as if it had been tossed in as a casual afterthought. It had to be the one Sylvie used as Eugénie.

A lot of things bothered her, but one thing in particular cried out. She walked back into the shadowed bedroom. It was the phone jack with no phone. But perfect for a modem. Had Eugénie used a laptop and gone on-line?

She searched among the clothes in the closet. In the back pocket of the overalls she found the phone cord. The laptop had to be somewhere close.

She shone her flashlight and began searching the closet. Testing each floorboard to see if it had been pried up recently, feeling each wallpaper seam for bubbles or uneven joining.

Nothing.

She sat back on her heels. Where would she have hidden a laptop?

What spot could she have shifted the laptop to if she'd been caught off guard, with only time to slip the phone cord in her pocket?

The battered desk had one drawer. She opened it. Empty. But the drawer stuck slightly as she pulled it out. Kneeling down, she pulled out her miniscrewdriver and poked the pine strut holding the drawer support. Cheap pine, staple-gunned in places. She felt around, found a knobby spot, pressed it. The pine strut flap popped open.

A hidden drawer in plain view. Aimée was impressed. And if Eugénie had a wireless modem, she would have been more impressed. In France few people did. She and René lusted for one but were waiting for the price to drop.

Aimée reached inside, exploring the crevices and ridges. She felt a smooth booklet and pulled it out. It was a manual for a new laptop. Either the men before had found it, or Sylvie had taken it with her and it had gone up in smoke.

Outwitted or too late; either way it was gone.

Dejected, Aimée knew the only place left to find answers was in the trash. Before she left, she unrolled the felt from the windows.

By the time she got to the corner, Sébastien had loaded two blue garbage sacks in back of his van. He gunned the engine as she opened the door. They took off down rue Jean Moinon, narrowly missing the striped cat.

"*Ça va?*" he asked, staring at her.

"I'll know after we check what you found," she said, the sodium streetlight glistening above her.

They sped into the raw Paris night along rainwashed, cobbled streets.

THE OLD tack room where they unloaded the garbage occupied a courtyard corner of Aimée's building on Ile St. Louis. Once used by horses stabled in this former Duc de Guise mansion, it now housed discarded window frames, a ganglion of PVC piping, and twenty-five kilogram *Placoplâtre Mortier adhésif sacs*. On one side stood an old porcelain stove, its broken tiles and legs tilted, canting lazily against the stone wall.

"Having fun yet?" Aimée said as they sifted through the bags of Sylvie's trash.

Sébastien, intent on his work, hadn't bothered to look up. They both wore gauze masks. But there was no way of getting around the smell.

"I'll need a *hammam* session," Sébastien said, "after this."

"Me, too," she said, visualizing the *hammam*: hot marble slabs, steam rising to the arched white marble ceiling, her grime scrubbed away by black soap and a loofah, the small cups of mint tea, her body rubbed to mousse-like consistency by the iron-armed masseuse.

"*Tiens*, Aimée," Sébastien said, holding up soggy sprigs of something dark green and slimy.

She nodded. "Let's keep the organic matter over there."

Aimée's flashlight shone amid the candles she'd lit, casting a medieval glow under the vaulted seventeenth-century ceiling. Over the industrial-strength clear plastic, they'd spread out the contents of the garbage bags on the stone floor. She and Sébastien were hunched over sorting the contents.

They'd gotten lucky, she realized, to find the uncollected trash. The *éboueurs* must have figured the building was uninhabited.

Thirty minutes later they'd sorted the bulk into three piles: paper, perishables, and other.

The other consisted of a pair of black Prada shoes. They were marred by a broken heel, but *à la mode*. The thin arched sole was barely scuffed. Hardly worn by the look of them, Aimée noted. And very nice. Sylvie had expensive taste.

The perishables: apple peels, almond shells, and the green slimy thing. She sniffed. Mint. Cotton balls smudged by tan foundation, sparkly blush and black mascara streaks.

She surveyed a half-used jar of Nutella, a white plastic Viva bottle of sour milk, and a smashed carton of strawberry Danette yogurt.

They bundled the piles back up and shot them in Aimée's trash bin.

"I know I owe you, Aimée," Sebastien said, "but next time let me repay you in other ways."

Together she and Sébastien sifted all the papers into several piles: Monoprix circulars advertising April sales, crumpled receipts and envelopes, and torn gray paper. Aimée picked up a goldenrod sheet, like those plastered on posts around Belleville. Printed on it: AMNESTY FOR THE *SANS-PAPIERS*—MAKE YOUR VOICE HEARD! JOIN THE THE HUNGER STRIKERS' VIGIL—PRESSURE THE MINISTRY—MUSTAFA HAMID'S FAST ENTERS THE 19TH DAY.

She sat up. Her heart quickened. She remembered Philippe's reaction to Hamid on the radio: his anger and how he'd taken off in the car. Had Sylvie picked up this flyer and tossed it—or had she kept it for a reason? Was there a connection?

Aimée turned it over. On the other side was smudged writing. The name "Youssef" and "01 43 76 89." She wondered if this could be a phone number of one of the Arabes, whom the baker Denet disapproved of, hanging around Eugénie's. Aimée put it aside.

Sébastien assembled the gray pieces on an ironing board while she smoothed them with a travel iron. After ironing the strips flat, she set them in rows, adhering them to a clear contact sheet. She did this several times until all the gray paper had a contact front.

"Now for the interesting part," she said to Sébastien.

They trudged upstairs to her apartment, the temperature only a few degrees warmer.

No welcoming lights, no heat.

And no Yves. Too bad. She'd tried to push Yves out of her mind. But thoughts of him kept popping back in.

Sébastien rubbed his gloved hands together and stamped his feet. They unzipped their jumpsuits and Aimée threw them in her laundry. Someday she'd get to the *lavomatique*.

Sébastien set the papers on the faded Gobelin carpet. Her grandfather had purchased it at the Porte de Vanves flea market. She'd been twelve and remembered helping him lug his fifty-franc find home on the Métro. "A classic, Aimée," he'd said. He'd filled the place with "classics"—a bit worn and frayed at the edges.

She flicked her scanner on and began scanning the contact sheets of paper scraps. Now she could bundle up at the computer and run some high-resolution software programs to match paper fibers. After that she'd run another program to fit spatial and numerical characteristics. With a little maneuvering she'd match the paper together in the right order and read the contents.

"Sébastien, why don't you warm up with some Calvados?" she said. "Or help yourself to *vin rouge*."

"And you?"

"Calvados, please, I need a toasty think-drink."

He poured them both large shots of the amber apple brandy. Tongues of light danced from the dim chandelier.

"*Salut.*" They toasted each other.

Computer applications clicked across her computer screen, a greenish light haloing her terminal.

"I've got a long night ahead of me," she said.

He grinned, glancing at his watch. "I hope I do too."

DAWN CREPT WITH TINY footsteps over the Seine. Aimée watched rose slashes paint the cloudless sky. Below her window the black iron boat moorings on quai d'Anjou glistened, beaded by last night's rain.

She remembered her father, in his old bathrobe, making coffee on mornings like these. He'd throw on a raincoat, nip around the corner to the *boulangerie*, and bring home warm, buttery croissants. They'd stand at the counter, the Seine glittering below them, and talk. Talk about a case, the price of dry cleaning, or a film she'd seen—all the small threads of life's fabric, a fabric she'd lost when her father died.

Tired but jubilant, she'd matched 80 percent of the gray paper. Enough to know these were Sylvie's bank statements from an account at Crédit Lyonnais. Finding a pattern to her withdrawals, her spending, and her habits would take time. Miles Davis stirred on her lap.

"*Alors*, furball," she said. "Time for your walk and for me to clear my head."

She hit Save, then Print. Her printer whirred into action. For backup she copied it to her hard drive and made a disk for René.

She slipped Miles Davis's tartan plaid sweater over his head. In the hallway she grabbed her faux-leopard fur and laced her red hightops. Forget the fashion police this early in the morning.

With her laptop in her bag, she and Miles Davis scampered over the grooves worn in the marble steps. By the time they reached the quai, the sky had lightened to a faint lick of blue.

* * *

YELLOW-AND-BLUE PROVENÇAL curtains softened the stark lines of the stainless-steel terminals in this Internet café.

"Fifty francs per hour," said the lavender-scented woman owner to Aimée, setting down her cigarette.

According to René, for hide-and-seek on the Web the best location was a *café ceebair*, cybercafé. She got to work with Miles Davis settled by her feet, sipping a bowl of water. After logging onto their computer, she accessed a university address in Teheran, from there she logged onto another address in Azerbaijan and worked her way, via Helsinki, to Barclays Bank in London.

As Edwina Pedley, a Barclays Bank alias she'd used before, Aimée accessed the Crédit Lyonnais accounts page in Paris. She typed in Sylvie's account number. The screen immediately came up "Password Required." Aimée sat back, feeling a glimmer of hope. Now, she knew, as she'd suspected from the bank receipts she'd pieced together, Sylvie banked on-line.

Guessing and trying passwords would be futile since banks generally tripped an alarm after four attempts, thereby freezing entry to the account. Aimée sipped her *grand café créme* and downloaded a password encryption program from the Web. By the time the program decrypted Sylvie's password, she'd finished her second croissant.

Beur was Sylvie's password.

She remembered in the street slang *verlan*, *beur* inversed became *erabe*, or what was pronounced as "*Arabe*."

Puzzled, Aimée hit Save.

Arabe.

Aimée accessed Sylvie's account. She saw that Sylvie's withdrawals and an active *carte bancaire* hadn't disturbed the five-figure balance in her account.

More puzzled, Aimée sat back in the café chair. A woman with a fondness for Prada shoes and Mikimoto pearls should have a healthier bank balance. More like in the six-figure category.

Around her early-morning café life buzzed: the whine of the espresso machine steaming milk, the delivery man heaving plastic crates of bottles onto the tiled café floor.

She signed out of the decryption program, printed out Sylvie's Crédit Lyonnais balance, then paid for her coffee. What had Montaigne said . . . then she remembered: "So it happens as it does with cages: the birds without try desperately to get in, and those within try desperately to get out."

The access word *beur* stuck in her mind. She also had to figure out why Sylvie Coudray had used that apartment building. The *Fichier* still hadn't ID'd Sylvie or discovered her primary residence, but she'd have to ask René to try again.

SHE STOPPED at her neighborhood *bibliothèque* and began checking the database for *beur*. Every entry that wasn't culinary came up cross-referenced with Algeria. She searched microfiche files for articles on Algeria. An avalanche of current articles existed.

Overwhelmed, she sat back and patted Miles Davis on her lap. Could the current events in some way have affected Sylvie?

She refined her search, narrowing articles to recent ones, and found an editorial from *Le Monde* dated the week before:

> Algeria plunged into violence in early 1992 as the regime—headed by the military—cancelled a general election in which the FIS, a fundamentalist group, took a commanding lead. The FIS was banned shortly after the polls were scrapped. Much of the fighting was fueled by 'les Barbes,' evangelical preachers, so named for their long beards and adherence to Islamic traditions. The FIS countryside support and the agitation of returned 'beurs' from France with patriotic leanings stimulated the continuing unstable political climate.

Aimée thought of *les Barbes* whom she'd seen in front of a mosque in Belleville. Engrossed, she read further:

> More than 50,000 people—rebels, civilians, and members of government forces—have been killed, according to Western estimates. The military, plagued with budgetary problems since few countries venture to buy oil and fill the coffers of an unstable country, has wrested control only to lose it periodically. Without the arms, unnamed government sources say, the military's ability to enforce order is in jeopardy. Massacres of villagers in the countryside remain commonplace.

She leaned back in the creaking library chair, chewed a paper clip, and thought. She knew the reputation of the network of North African immigrants, the *Maghrébins*, in Belleville.

Ruthless.

She remembered an incident where a *pute* and her pimp strayed out of their territory into a housing project off rue de Belleville. They hadn't lived to regret it.

She wondered what connection Sylvie, a minister's mistress acting as Eugénie in Belleville, could have. What had Anaïs said? Sylvie was "sorry the situation had escalated." A chilling thought occurred to her. Instead of an illicit affair, could Sylvie have been referring to something else? Did it have to do with the Arabes who'd hung around her place . . . the hand of Fat'ma . . . had she upset someone in the *Maghréb* system . . . had they come after her?

Aimée hunched forward, chewed the paper clip some more. She also wished she'd found the laptop.

These thoughts were a leap, but worth exploring.

Outside the wind whipped the budding branches as they thumped the rain-spattered glass.

A *Maghrébin* would know. Not that any one of them would tell her.

Another thought bothered her: Why hadn't Anaïs returned her calls?

She pulled out the paper and punched in the phone number 01 43 76 89, written above the smudged name Youssef.

"May I talk with Youssef?"

Someone shouted in Arabic and hung up.

Friday Midday

BACK IN HER APARTMENT, Aimée's cell phone trilled in her pocket. If it was Yves, she'd let him know how busy she'd been.

"*Allô, oui?*" she said, in what she hoped came off as hurried yet casual.

"Leduc," Morbier said. "How about lunch?"

"Lunch?" she asked, spilling Miles Davis's milk on her counter.

"Café Kouris," Morbier said. She could hear *klaxons* beeping in the distance.

"Where's that?"

"Near the market on boulevard de Belleville," he said. "By the *fromagerie* and beside the plastic shoes."

Why was he so friendly all of a sudden?

He hung up before she could ask him what time.

"RENÉ, ANY luck on the *Fichier* findings about Sylvie aka Eugénie?" she'd written on a Post-it, stuck it on the floppy disk with Sylvie's bank discoveries, and left it in René's mailbox. In his hallway mirror, she swiped Chanel red across her lips, brushed on mascara, and pinched her cheeks.

She took the Métro to meet Morbier. On the way she thought about Sylvie's bank account, the expensive Prada shoes, and the Lake Biwa pearl. None of them seemed to fit with a lifestyle in a condemned building, the *Maghrébins*, the hand of Fat'ma, or Hamid's group. But her instinct told her that they meshed. How and why were the questions.

Aimée blinked in the sunlight as she emerged from the Métro.

The sun wavered, then retreated behind a steel gray cloud shrouding Belleville.

Friday, market day, found a densely packed strip of stands on the long pedestrian islands, stretching from Menilmontant through Couronnes to Belleville Métro. Fruit and vegetable sellers and *poissoniers* carrying fish from Marseilles and Brittany mingled with merchants selling children's clothing, pocketknives, ornate Egyptian teapots, and hair ornaments.

The unmistakable squawking of chickens sounded in her ear. Aromas of fresh mint wafted. Hawkers cried *"Viens! viens!"* thrusting samples of glistening Spanish melons, a thimble of pistachios, or fifty-franc Piaget lookalikes at shoppers.

The humanity varied as much as the products, Aimée thought. Nearby was the home of the French Communist Party. She passed *bas* Belleville, once housing the *prolétariat français*—a working-class bastion—now home to crumbling *serrurerie* metal factories, partially bricked up. Their graffitied walls were surrounded by teenagers pushing strollers speaking a *patois* of Arabic and *verlan*.

A certain charm remained, and Aimée liked that. The charm of an old world, when life moved slower and residents had time for each other, spending most of their lives in the *quartier*. Narrow winding passages, cafés of former *époques* patinaed by grime, hidden courtyards, and overgrown gardens of small dilapidated villas tucked on the hillsides existed until the dreaded *permis de démolir* brought the wrecking ball. The steep staircases, joining one street to another, resembled those of Montmartre, their scrolled metal balustrades worn and chipped in places.

Ahead of her, Aimée marveled at how two piano movers carried a piano up five steep and narrow floors to an apartment hardly wider than two Citroëns nose to nose.

She wondered how Sylvie/Eugénie fit into the melange that swelled the boulevard: the Tunisian Jewish bakery where a line formed while old women who ran the nearby hammam conversed with one and all from their curbside café tables, the occasional roller blader weaving in and out of the crowd, the Asian men unloading garments from their sliding-door Renault vans, the Syrian butchers with their white coats stained bloody pink, the tall ebony Senegalese man in flowing white tunic, crocheted prayer hat, and blue jogging shoes with a sport bag filled with date branches, a well-coiffed French matron tugging a wheeled shopping cart, a short one-eyed *Arabe* man who hawked shopping bags hanging from his arms, and the watchful men in front of the Abou Bakr Mosque near the Métro.

By the time she reached that part of the boulevard, the vegetable stands were being dismantled and crates repacked. Honey drenched cigar-shaped pastries beckoned her from a Lebanese stall but she resisted. The stench of *ordure* rose from the cobbles.

Aimée heard the whine of Arabe music—the same tune from before. She shuddered: She'd heard it right before the explosion.

She scanned the corner. The trouble with car bombs was that they were impossible to see. She willed herself to relax; it wouldn't make sense for an Arabe to bomb an Arabe *quartier*. For a moment she felt ashamed; she was thinking like a *flic*.

MORBIER SAT at a café table under a white awning where rue des Maronites met the boulevard. Parked motorscooters lined the curb.

He sat smoking, fingers wrapped around a glass of *vin rouge*, his posture unnaturally erect due to the body brace. Normally his favorite pose was leaning back in a swivel chair at the commissariat, feet up on his cluttered desk and barking orders on the phone while chain-smoking. He still chain-smoked, and his socks were mismatched, but the suspenders were slack. He'd lost weight, she noticed. For once his wool pants stayed up on his belly without help. Sitting there he guarded his cigarette from the wind, cupping it in his palm like a street *mec*.

"What's so important, Morbier?" she said, sitting down.

"Besides keeping me company?" he asked.

She eyed the carafe of wine and extra glass.

He poured her a glass, raised his, and said, "*Salut.*"

Gesturing toward the boulevard, he said, "I hate to think that this is what retirees do—take a walk, go to market, prepare the midday meal, visit the girlfriend, stop in the square for an aperitif. Next day, they do it all over again. The golden years!" His mouth turned down in disgust.

For a career *flic* like Morbier, this kind of leisure was like a slow death. Wasn't he too old for *le démon de midi*—the midlife crisis?

"Forget about retiring," she said. He'd recited this litany whenever he'd been injured or on leave and didn't know what to do with himself.

"Morbier, soon as the brace comes off you'll be back in the saddle." She looked at her Tintin watch, which had stopped. "I'm curious about why you invited me to lunch."

"All in good time," he said, sipping his wine. "Since you're here, notice that *mec* over there?"

She followed his arm and saw a short middle-aged man with mouse brown hair and prominent nose in a blue work coat. He stood in front of a *tabac*.

"You mean the man in the crowd," she said. "The one I'd never notice or think twice about?"

He shrugged. "We call them Pierres, these market thieves. He's been shadowing his mark for a good while now, weaving, ducking, and helping load the poor sucker's van. Of course that was after he'd eyed the cashbox under the driver's seat."

"What are you going to do about it, Morbier?"

Morbier's eyes lit up.

"Leduc, you're going to go and whisper in the *mec*'s ear how my eyesight is perfect and it's trained on him."

She shrugged. "If it puts you in a good mood and makes you

feel useful, it will be my *plaisir*," she said and stood. She knew this was Morbier's form of manipulation—he'd make her "work" for any information he shared with her. It was just his way.

And she wanted to humor him. There was something unsettling about seeing him in the brace and alone with a carafe at the table.

A hoarse voice bellowed, "Get your burgundy onions!" and a crisp wind scattered leaves in a whirlwind dance. She had the sad thought that the only person Morbier cared about—Mouna—was gone now. And her father too . . .

She offered "Pierre" a cigarette. His eyes narrowed, but he accepted. She took him aside and gestured across the way toward Morbier, who winked and smiled. Aimée bent down and whispered in Pierre's ear, trying not to laugh at the look of alarm spreading on his face. His eyes widened, then he tipped his beret to Morbier and disappeared around the corner.

"Pierre's a quick learner," she said to Morbier on her return.

"They usually are," Morbier said, lighting a cigarette from a glowing butt in the Ricard ashtray.

She motioned to the waiter. *"Un café, s'il vous plaît."*

"Red wine's better for your heart," he said, pouring himself another glass. "I've already bailed you out, Leduc."

Her shoulders slumped. Was he just going to warn her off? Had she wasted her time?

"Look, Morbier—"

"Didn't I?"

"And I appreciate that." Without skipping a beat she kept talking. "You called me."

There was a long pause.

"You want to know about the plastique," he said. "So do I."

She kept her surprise in check with an effort. How did Morbier know?

"That's news to me, Morbier," she said. "I stay away from the stuff. It gives me nightmares."

Another pause.

"You, of all people," she said, "should know that."

"My vertebrae are out of whack, Leduc," Morbier said finally. "Every single one."

Disconcerted, she'd never heard him admit to a physical problem. Why was he ignoring what she said? He knew her fear of explosives. Had he gone soft, dragging her here on a ruse, needing some sympathy?

"I am sorry," she said and meant it. "How can I help?"

"Help me catch a big fish," he said.

Her eyes widened.

"*Tiens*, Leduc, you asked if you could help."

"What's going on?" she asked. Was he going to feed her a tidbit to whet her appetite, then warn her off again?

"Leduc, you're sniffing around," he said. "It's not my business if a minister's wife hired you—but if you want to nail the *plastique* source, lead me to it."

She dropped her spoon, splashing a bit of coffee on the table. She was aware of the waiter wiping the table with a damp cloth and a muttered *tsk*.

"Now I have your full attention, I see," Morbier said.

A warning vibrated in her.

"My God, Morbier, I'm not undercover," she said. "The fundamentalists are fanatics—why ask me?"

"Who said anything about fundamentalists?" He didn't wait for her reply. "Call me psychic," he said, lighting a cigarette. "But you've been out of kilter since your moped ride."

She couldn't meet Morbier's eyes. Her heart beat quicker. He didn't know everything—but he knew she was involved.

"Humor an old man, eh?" he said. "Think of it this way: You might feel better about the past if you deal with this."

"Forget it," she said, throwing ten francs on the table.

"Leduc, you want to find out who blew her up, right?" he asked, leaning forward. He didn't wait for her answer. "This is how. My way. I know the players and the score in Belleville. You don't. It's that simple."

She didn't want to do this.

Morbier exhaled a stream of smoke over her head. Aimée winced at the tangy, acrid scent and wanted to suck one of the butts in the yellow ashtray. But she'd quit. Again.

"Everything's set up," he said. "We fed Samia information."

"Samia?"

"Samia got involved with Zdanine, a *plastique* supplier, and he's trouble," Morbier said. "Zdanine is a tiny *poisson*. Martaud and I want the big shark."

"Quit the riddles, Morbier, please," she said.

"Zdanine deals in nasty things. Me, I don't care," he said. "Street vermin die, and new ones flood the sewer. My turf is the Marais. But I want the girl, Samia, protected."

"Tell me more."

"Samia's young. Zdanine's the father of her child," Morbier said. "She made a mistake. She never needs to know I'm involved."

Aimée stirred the clumps of brown sugar in her cup. "And why would they tell me about *plastique?*"

"Leduc, you're not a *flic*; they don't know you," he said. "That's why you're perfect."

"*Attends*, Morbier," Aimée said. "How am I going to bring up the topic of *plastique?*"

He wiped his mouth, then smoothed his napkin on the table.

"But they might sell you some, Leduc," he said.

Aimée paused in midsip; her eyes widened.

"Hold on, Morbier—"

Morbier eyed her closely. "But Samia's young. Like I said, the young make mistakes."

"You've picked the wrong person."

His eyes narrowed under his bushy eyebrows. "And Martaud's

testy—you know the type. Wants the commissariat stripes and a coronary before he's forty. I want Samia protected. If there's any evidence left, make it disappear. *Compris?*"

Aimée's antenna came to attention.

"What's so special about Samia?"

"Forget the questions, Leduc," he said. "If you want my help."

Now she was intrigued. Curiosity overcame her fear. At least some of it. And Morbier was right; she needed to track down the *plastique*. Aimée sipped her coffee, concerned about the turn the conversation had taken.

"What about Zdanine?"

"Call him a procurer if you want to get technical, Leduc," he said, blowing the air from his lower lip. "*Tiens*, this is Belleville, one works with the *système*. Zdanine's claiming sanctuary in the church with the hunger strikers."

Again the church and hunger strikers had come up. She hesitated.

"Call Samia. Tell her Khalil, Zdanine's cousin, sent you," Morbier said. "We know he's a procurer who's stuck in Algiers awaiting promised papers from his soon-to-be legal cousin."

"How do you know this?"

"Never mind," Morbier said, beckoning the waiter for *l'addition*. "But it's true, and Khalil's just as nasty. Martaud wants him bad."

Her cell phone rang.

"*Allô*," she said.

"Don't tell me you forgot," Yves said.

She flushed and turned away from Morbier. "What's that?"

"The appointment," Yves said. "At *Le Figaro*."

"Sorry, but we never reconfirmed," she said, keeping the disappointment out of her voice.

She didn't remember saying this, but she'd said a lot things the other night after the champagne. She'd even told him about the explosion and Anaïs. Is that all Yves wanted?

"But on my voice mail messages, which you don't seem to have listened to," Yves continued, "I indicated I had meetings in Marseilles."

"Meetings?" Was he undercover or working on something Martine didn't agree with—or both?

"I also mentioned how amazed I was by the way you changed the temperature, how you altered the color of things. And how I'd like more of that," He paused. "That's if I remember correctly."

She cleared her throat. "I'll have to check on that and get back to you," she said, quickly gulping the rest of her coffee, aware of Morbier's gaze.

"You do that," Yves said. "I'll be waiting."

They hung up.

"You're blushing," Morbier said, cocking his eyebrows.

"I do that when I drink fast," she said, rooting in her bag for a tip.

Morbier grinned and said nothing.

"Here's Samia's number. She lives above the *hammam* near the Couronnes Métro," he said. "Pack your swimsuit, there's a *piscine* adjoining the steam rooms."

Tempted for a moment, she paused. She hadn't swum her regular lap quotas for several days.

Morbier nodded. "Like I said, little fish lead to big fish."

"I don't have time for swimming, Morbier," she said. "Or to chase the Paris periphery for pond scum."

What was she doing at a café with Morbier wasting her time? She pushed back her chair, scraping the sidewalk, and tossed her phone into her Hermés bag.

"Don't go rushing off, Leduc," Morbier said, wagging his nicotine-stained finger at her. "Last time you did that you had more broken bones than usual, remember?"

She flinched, fingering her throat at the memory of the rooftop in the Marais. The concussion, the lacerations needle-like over her skin . . .

A glass was knocked to the floor at the next table, jerking her back to the present.

"Think of it this way, Leduc," Morbier said, lighting another cigarette from the smoldering butt in the ashtray. "If you trace the *plastique* to the source, you might nab the mistress's killer." He shrugged. "Get some shitheads off the street. The murderer could be, as de Gaulle said, '*Chier dans son propre lit*,' shitting in one's own bed. Criminals often do. A common mistake."

"I think de Gaulle was referring to the Algerian crisis in that instance, but you've got a point," she said, a smile fighting its way over her mouth. "But like Papa used to say, things don't always seem as they appear or he would have been out of business."

"Keep an eye on Samia, that's all," he said. "Samia grew up in the housing projects with gangs, Raï music and tattooed bleakness. But trouble, like Zdanine, tends to follow. Far as I'm concerned, Zdanine is scum, but he's connected."

"*D'accord*, I'll call and meet her," she said, "but I've got to change."

"Make sure," he said, wagging his finger, "you dress appropriately."

She walked toward the Métro. On the corner the outdoor tables at Chez Mireille Bistrot were full. The *halah boucherie Islamique* held a steady stream of shoppers. Petulant whines of tired toddlers in their strollers, and the rumble of the Métro below greeted her accompanied by fumes from the 95 bus, direction Austerlitz. She wondered how Sylvie could have hidden in this dense *quartier*, where a woman would be noticed. Especially a good-looking woman. She shouldered her bag for the Métro ride to René's.

Aimée paused at the stairs of the Couronnes Métro. She felt

someone's eyes sizing her up. The bearded men wearing *chechias* and flowing white *habayas* stared at her from the Abou Bakr Mosque entrance. Her shoulders tensed. *Les barbes*—the Islamic fundamentalists she'd read about. Their staring disturbed her, rattling in her brain all the way to René's.

RENÉ'S HAUSSMANN-ERA building fronted rue de la Reynie—a tree-lined strip Aimée regarded as a minioasis from the nearby Les Halles, with its cheesy clothing shops, discount CD stores, and young crowd. His apartment overlooked a quiet, geranium-lined walkway wedged between buildings.

René's parking space was the same size as his studio apartment. But it certainly had more room, she thought, considering René's obsession with the latest computer equipment.

Computers and monitors, raised a cushion's height from the carpeted floor, lined two walls. Books covered another wall. His window looked onto a hulking gray building, draped and scaffolded for renovation. From the stereo a voice rasped, "Serves you right to suffer" accompanied by a guitar riff filling the room.

"James Lee 'ooker," René grinned. *"Les blues."*

Aimée smiled. Last time Rene's infatuation had been Django Reinhardt.

Two futons were piled in the corner. A poster showing the 417 types of French cheeses hung on the wall of his cockpit-size kitchen. Bodybuilding weights sat on the low counter specially designed for René's height.

Miles Davis sniffed her with his wet nose from his pillow beside René.

"So far, looking for Sylvie I've hit the *Fichier* firewall," René said. "But this new software should help." He pointed to several zip disks, stacked between the monitor screens filled with encrypted algorithms.

"You're a genius," she said.

He nodded, his eyes bright as his fingers danced over the keyboard. "Tell me that after I crack the code."

He was in his *métier*. No one she knew came close to his expertise.

"What about the Swiss electronic switch on the explosive?" she asked.

"Curious, that one," René said, hitting Save. He stood up and stretched. He wore a grey tracksuit, the top fitting his long torso but the pants shortened. "Seems that circuit board hooked up to a relay—you know the kind in the movies where the *mecs* set the device to explode in ten minutes? Meanwhile they've driven five miles away and have an alibi."

She made a face, pursed her Chanel-red lips. That would complicate things.

"However, reading the report," René said, packing his practice bag for the dojo, "that doesn't seem to fit. Seems they activated it from nearby, like you suggested, from the 'fake' SAMU van."

She picked up Miles Davis. But her edgy feeling remained.

"Can you watch him some more?"

René's eyes narrowed. "What's up?"

She told him about Morbier's lead.

"Call me if you need backup," he said. "I've got another bag of shank bones in the fridge," he said as she made for the door. "You're welcome to hit the dojo with me."

"Next time."

"Be careful," René said, giving her a meaningful look.

AIMÉE HAILED a taxi at the roundabout that dropped her at her rue du Louvre office. By that time she'd arranged a rendezvous with Samia within the hour.

Inside her once elegant nineteenth-century office building, with the ancient dark green water spigot in the foyer, she was tempted to take the birdcage elevator. But the tightness in her leather trousers told her no. She hiked the three steep flights. On the landing opposite the smoky bevel-edged mirror, she unlocked her door.

She hurried past her desk, stacked with Paris *pages jaunes* and manuals on secure cryptosystems, to the back storage room. She never missed leaving criminal work, but the old regret hit her. To play it safe, she pulled on her bullet-proof vest, made especially thin, the spy-store clerk had told her, for those "special occasions."

She rifled past hangers containing a blue rubber-strapped fishmonger's apron, the traffic jacket with SUBURBAINE stencilled on back, her lab coat embroidered with "Leduc" from her premed year at Université René Descartes, and an acid green sequined feather-boa affair from a defunct sex club in Pigalle.

After some deliberation and flirting with the boa, she chose a black leather jumpsuit, a relic of a friend's drug-dealing days. The leather unitard, composed of zippered pockets and quilted patches, fit skintight. She struggled into the legs and zipped it over her black lace bra. A zebra-striped *foulard* draped around her neck completed her ensemble.

After applying makeup she stepped into slingback black heels. She threw her red high tops into her bag in case she had to deal with more slick cobbles. Quickly she painted her nails so they could dry in the taxi.

Forty minutes later she'd emerged from rue du Louvre, hailed a taxi, and arrived at Samia's.

The *hammam-piscine* turned out to be a bland, renovated eighteenth-century building with popcorn stucco facing the street. She handed the driver a hundred-franc bill and told him to keep the change, grinning at his comment on how well her business must be doing.

If only he knew.

She gave a small smile, bidding him *adieu* when he began offering to drop clients her way.

By the time she entered the courtyard of the *hammam-piscine*, she'd taken Morbier's suggestion to heart. Right now Samia was her entrée to the *plastique* and the *Maghrébins*, her only source other than Gaston in Café Tlemcen. Slim at best, but a start, she reminded herself. And more of a lead than she'd had a bit earlier when her only view had been seeing *les barbes* in front of the mosque.

A *tatouage* parlor stood next to a shop with dusty windows and a faded red sign with BOUCHERIE-VOLAILLE still visible. Besides the *hammam-piscine* in the *cour*, they were the only other occupants. There was something appealing about the quiet air of neglect, she thought. As if the buildings held together almost from force of habit.

Inside the unrenovated interior, the walls were covered with rainbow-colored graffiti of *Nique le flic*—screw the cops. Colored handprints were imprinted over doorways, in the Muslim style, to guard dwellings. A narrow winding staircase, the steps grooved and worn, mounted upward. She wondered what it would be like to live here. Or to grow up looking at this graffiti every day.

Samia Fouaz lived above the tiled *rez de chaussée*, on the first floor. A stroller, string shopping bag, and a shiny four-wheeled cart filled the landing. Once polished and exquisite, Aimée imagined.

After several bouts of knocking, the door opened to a curvaceous figure in a peach lace teddy unself-consciously scratching her rear. Samia's light-honey-colored face was puffy, her eyes bleary, and she yawned loudly.

"Sorry to disturb you, Samia—"

"*Pas de problème,*" Samia said, eying her up and down.

Samia took a breath, pursed her mouth, then seemed to come to a decision. "Let's make this quick."

Nonplussed, Aimée recovered quickly. "Sounds good," she said, aiming for casual.

Inside, trying to bury her nervousness, Aimée followed Samia's sashaying down the yellowed hallway, its walls littered with calendars from local Arabic butchers on boulevard Menilmontant. Samia's scent, a mixture of musk oil, sweat, and something by Nina Ricci, trailed in her wake.

Raï music pounded from a room in the rear. At the far end of the apartment Aimée saw violet gauze billowing from the ceiling, bordered by curtains embroidered with tiny mirrors.

Samia gestured to a chrome metal stool fronting a counter. A galley-style kitchen lay behind that, small, scrubbed, and spotless. On an upper shelf sat a glazed earthenware dish covered with a pointed lid, a *tajine*. Above that stood a *qettara*, a copper still for distilling rose- and orange-blossom water. Aromatics with rosewater, Aimée knew, drove away the *djinn*, protected against the evil eye, and attracted good spirits. Aimée hoped the good spirits were with her—she needed all the help she could get.

Against the gray linoleum, Aimée noticed Samia's bare feet hennaed with intricate swirling patterns.

Aimée wondered about Samia's connection to Morbier. Samia looked young and tired, like a housewife who'd tarted up for a husband with little result. She gestured again for Aimée to sit down.

"Tea?" She smiled, her face opening up like a flower.

"*Merci,*" Aimée said, accepting the *de rigeur* small glass of steaming mint tea, sweet and fragrant. Acustom, she knew, observed even among enemies at the Mideast peace talks.

The fading afternoon sun shone into an open window overlooking the courtyard. Several women, their Arabic conversation echoing off the stone walls, entered the *hammam* door below.

"You mentioned Khalil when you called," Samia said. She looked even younger in the kitchen's light.

"True. And Eugénie, part of Khalil's—"

"Tell him this for me," Samia interrupted, turning and pounding her fist into her palm. Her gold bracelets jangled. "Zdanine's doing all he can, eh? *Compris?*"

Surprised at Samia's change of manner, Aimée stopped short, her mind racing. She hoped Samia couldn't check with Khalil about her. Why had she accepted Morbier's story that he'd "fed Samia information?"

"I'm not sure what you mean." Aimée barely kept her voice steady.

"Last month was the last time," Samia said, determined. "No more. Lay off!"

For a vulnerable-looking thing she packed a punch, Aimée thought. Her friendly demeanor had vanished.

"*Tiens*, Samia," she said, trying what she hoped was a winning grin. "I'm just the messenger. Don't shoot me."

Samia expelled a *whoof!* of air in disgust. She talked tough for eighteen, Aimée thought, or however old she was.

"Khalil isn't patient," Aimée said, improvising as she went along. "Poor *mec*, he's stuck in Algiers."

She had to persuade Samia to talk, pass on her *plastique* connection.

"Not my concern," Samia said, a petulant edge to her voice. But her quick anger had deflated. "You tell Khalil to deal with me himself," she said. "I'll get word to Zdanine."

"Khalil said to tell you I speak for him."

Samia half smiled, showing the edges of little white teeth. One of them was gold-capped and caught the light. "I mean no disrespect to a fellow sister, *bien sûr*, but business is business," she said. "And time for me to get dressed." She was about to usher Aimée to the door.

I'm blowing this, Aimée thought. Time to forget subtlety when the opportunity is walking out the door. "Samia, let me speak for Khalil and you for Zdanine," she said. "I need to arrange more *plastique*. Eugénie was supposed to help."

Samia's eyes widened; her round shoulders tensed. "I don't like this."

"Who does?" Aimée made her tone businesslike and shrugged. "The last delivery man blew himself to Mecca before his ticket was punched."

"That's history. Zdanine was only a distributor," Samia said, shifting from one bare foot to the other as she scratched a calf with the opposite big toe. "He's washed his hands of it now," she said, her eyes level as she sipped tea. "Where it goes and to whom . . ." She let that hang in the musk-scented air of her kitchen.

"From what I hear," Aimée said, leaning closer, "this is the beginning."

Samia shook her head. "My clients are waiting. I've got to go."

Aimée wondered what kind of clients.

She lowered her voice to a whisper and brushed her arm against Samia's. "Wholesale," she said, nodding her head. "Khalil understands profit margins. Do you?"

Samia's gaze wavered.

"Wholesale," Aimée said, growing more confident at Samia's reaction. She drew out the word to underscore the importance. "No dropoffs. No francs and centimes. Just thousand-franc notes and bank accounts. Big ones. That's wholesale."

"Zdanine deals with this, not me," Samia said, but her dark brows wrinkled—unsure.

"Sounds like you're not equipped to handle orders," Aimée said, pulling back, glancing again at her watch. "Khalil misinformed me. Forget I came. I'll outsource this."

Aimée shouldered her bag and stood up. She'd put the offer out there, sweetened it, and waited expectantly.

Samia's full lips tightened.

"Outsource?" she said, pronouncing the word slowly.

"Khalil prefers to work with family, of course. However, it

looks like I've no choice," Aimée said and sighed. "Other roads lead to *plastique*. He assumed Zdanine's linked to the supplier."

Samia's eyes narrowed. "He doesn't tell me about business."

"Just remember we came to you first," Aimée said. "Later on, don't say Khalil didn't offer his family a fat slice of the tart." Aimée studied her nails, trying to remember graffiti slogans on the Belleville Métro. "Like he says, 'Brothers of the *bled* 'country-side' should unite!' "

Samia snorted. "*Bled*!? The closest we've been to the country-side was when the colonials massacred those who couldn't emigrate as servants. Khalil went back for his 'roots,' and now he can't wait to get out."

She had a point, Aimée thought.

"Am I too *blanc* for you, Samia, is that it?" Aimée asked.

Samia didn't answer.

Frustrated, she didn't know how to get information from Samia. So far she'd gotten zip. Aimée looked around, thinking furiously. She felt as if she'd gone north instead of south.

She ran her fingers over a small CD player on the counter, and noticed the big-screen TV in the next room. A red-bordered overdue France Télécom bill lay on the windowsill. Now she had an idea.

"You've got a nice life, Samia. Quite a class act." Aimée strolled toward an open pantry lined with pâté, Turkish halvah, and Iranian caviar. "Better life than most. I'm a working girl. Hundred-franc uprights were all I knew, and burned-out cars were my place of business until I met Khalil. He became my *patron*, taught me things, showed me how to bleed the johns and make more than my rent." She looked meaningfully at Samia. "I'll do anything the *mec* asks."

Samia looked away. Maybe the affluence was hard to maintain. Aimée saw a framed photo of an almond-eyed boy with a serious expression, the honey patina of his skin like Samia's. He wore the short pants of a Catholic-school uniform, a bookbag slung over his shoulder.

"He's gorgeous," Aimée said, and meant it. "Your son?"

Samia nodded, her eyes lighting up. "Marc after Marcus Aurelius," she said, a winsome expression crossing her face.

"Catholic school?"

"He's baptized," Samia said, a hint of pride in her voice.

"Must cost," Aimée said, rubbing her fingers together.

Samia stiffened and turned away. "Zdanine helps us; he furnished the flat."

"But he can't help you now, can he?" she said, not waiting for an answer. "He's stuck in the church."

She saw the struggle in Samia's eyes.

Aimée knew she'd reached her when she'd talked about her little boy. And she knew Samia had money trouble.

"Look, if you're not interested, at least help me connect with Eugénie," Aimée said.

Samia's blank look answered her.

"You've got to go, haven't you?" Samia said, her veiled politeness strained. "I'm late."

Aimée tore a paper sheet from her datebook and wrote her cell phone number down. "Think about what I've said. Call me in a few hours."

Disappointed that Samia hadn't taken the bait outright, Aimée went down the worn stairs, past the *hammam*, and onto the street. She hoped when Samia got desperate she'd call.

"How much?" Aimée asked the man with the armful of watches on rue de Belleville.

"Fifty francs," he said, brandishing his arm close to her nose. He jiggled a phosphorescent tangerine plastic band with a yellow happy face off his wrist.

"Not my style," she said.

Her cell phone rang.

"Didn't we have a meeting?" René asked.

She thrust fifty francs into the man's palm, grabbed the watch, laced up her hightops, and took off running.

By the time Aimée returned to the office she'd convinced herself she'd find Sylvie's killers through the *Maghrébin* network. However, at this rate it could take a year.

René looked up from his book, his large green eyes hooded. She didn't like it.

"Don't tell me," he said, looking her up and down. "You're supplementing our income?"

"Didn't we get the EDF contract?" she said, sitting down heavily.

"Like I said, the nervous little manager liked us," René said, leaning back in his orthopedic chair. "But the big EDF guy in the sky doesn't want to 'piecemeal' the security system, or so they say. He's got a point. The Seattle firm offered a bid on comprehensive services. Impressive."

Aimée stood up, fire in her eyes. "So can we."

"Already have," René winked. "I roughed a basic package together," he said, pulling out a thick folder. "A draft, of course. But I thought we might want to throw in something special. A little extra."

"Exactly. Some *pièce de résistance*," she said, tossing her leather jacket on the coatrack. She scratched her head, then opened their office window overlooking the Louvre. The knock of diesel engines and the occasional cry of a street vendor competed with the roar of Paris buses.

"Let's get to work, partner," she said, unsnapping the studs on her sleeves.

After an hour they'd redone their network vulnerability scan and thrown in maintenance too. A realistic offer. And at lower than what they figured the other firm would bid. She felt good, at last, to work on something concrete. Aimée took a deep breath and faxed their offer to the EDF.

Her cell phone rang.

She prayed that Samia was on the other end.

"*Allô?*"

"Philippe denies e-e-everything," Anaïs said, her voice thick and slurred.

Relieved finally to hear from Anaïs, she was startled at her tone.

"He won't s-s-speak of her."

"I've been worried, trying to reach you," she said, terrified by the way Anaïs sounded. She grabbed a piece of paper. "Let me come and get you. Where are you?"

"Somewhere," she said, her voice slipping away. "Martine and the housekeeper take Simone to preschool. But s-s-something's wrong. S-s-sent you a *chèque*. Philippe's afraid. I didn't tell you— S-Sylvie gave me the envelope—"

"I need to talk with you, Anaïs," she said. "Where is that envelope—?"

But Anaïs hung up before Aimée could finish. Worried, she called Philippe. No one answered at the de Froissarts.' She tried the ministry. Philippe's cordial secretary had no idea where Madame de Froissart could be reached but again promised Aimée she'd see that the minister got her message.

Fat chance. She'd begun to feel the only way to bag Philippe would be to grab a rifle and haunt the ministry.

She searched the mail on her desk and slit open a letter addressed to her. She waved Anaïs's check in the air.

"Our account's ten thousand francs richer," she said.

René blinked.

"Anaïs?"

She nodded. "Let's eat while I fill you in on the latest."

They ordered sushi from the new Japanese restaurant below their office, putting it under business expense.

Over a spider crab roll and *saba* marinated mackerel Aimée told René about Morbier's agenda and Samia, who baptized her son and wanted him to be French, while his father, a pimp and explosives conduit, claimed sanctuary in the church.

"What about the *Fichier* in Nantes?" she asked. "Sylvie must have another address."

"So far no luck, but I'll keep trying," René nodded. "My friend loaned me a new identity morphing software," René said, rubbing his stubby hands together. "For now why don't I try it out on Sylvie?"

"Be my guest," Aimée said, putting down her chopsticks. "What does it do?"

"A slight hitch remains," he said. "We need a photo."

"I think I can do something about that," Aimée said. She logged onto her computer, accessing the bank account with Sylvie's password, *beur*. She dug around for documentation used to establish the Crédit Lyonnais bank account. After ten minutes she got excited when she pulled up Eugénie's *carte nationale d'identité* photo.

"Look, René," she said, printing the image.

For the first time she got a good look at the woman, not just her dismembered limbs.

"Parfait!" René said. "Knockout!"

"She's good looking, striking—" She was about to add that no one, attractive or not, deserved to be torn apart by a bomb.

"Knockout's a new program. An image-masking software," he said, "which works for anything involved in digitally enhanced images."

"Meaning?"

"Watch this," he said, his eyes bright with anticipation.

Aimée slipped Sylvie's photo onto the scanner.

At his terminal René drew selection lines defining the inner and outer boundaries of Sylvie's face. Knockout outputted the processed foreground—the object with colors removed—and a grayscale alpha channel that preserved the transparency of the original.

"Short red hair?"

"Like mine," she said, remembering the wig. "Make it a bit more shaggy in the back."

He played around, then printed the image out. A seamless fit.

"You're a wizard, René!"

"Try jogging people's memory with that," he said. "You know, for the right price the *Maghrébin* network performs similar functions. A gold Eurocard, driver's license, even a *Sécurité sociale* number."

"*Merci*," she said, again surprised by René's depth of underworld knowledge. "I need to find out where this Duplo *plastique* comes from." She pecked René on both cheeks. "Time to get busy."

"Where are you going?" His green eyes widened.

"To jog Philippe's memory," she said. "Get his thoughts."

Before she'd unzipped her leather jumpsuit, her cell phone rang again.

"*Oui.*" She caught herself before she blurted, "Leduc Detective."

"I'm waiting for you," Samia said.

She'd expected Anaïs but recovered quickly, "Samia, you've reconsidered?"

"There's someone you need to meet." Samia's voice sounded strained, tight. "Hurry up."

"What about Eugénie?"

"He knows," she said. "I'm at the *hammam*. Can you meet me in fifteen?"

"I'm on the way," she said, reaching for her jacket and tucking the Beretta in her pocket.

This could be the break she was looking for.

Friday Late Afternoon

INSIDE THE *HAMMAM-PISCINE*, SAMIA slouched by the ticket booth overlooking the L-shaped pool. A thirties-style vaulted ceiling and salmon tiles housed the humid, chlorine-laced air. In the shallow end an old woman, her bathing cap's tight strap separating the fleshy folds of her neck, bobbed up and down.

Aimée's eyes darted around the nearly empty pool. She preferred the *piscine* at Reuilly; cleaner, newer, and a short bike ride from her flat. A middle-aged man, kneeling with a long handled net, was fishing for something on the dark green bottom.

"Do you have a car?" Samia asked. She'd changed into a narrow black trench coat.

Aimée nodded. René's Citroën sat parked nearby.

"Let's go," Samia said.

Wary, Aimée noticed her fluttery eyelashes, the orange-day-glo fingernails. Morbier was right. She was young. And Aimée was supposed to be protecting her.

"Tell me where."

"The circus," Samia said.

Aimée followed Samia's leather mules as they scuffed down the dank-smelling stone passage into the street.

In the Citroën, Samia's gaze wavered as Aimée adjusted René's customized seat and pedals.

"Which circus?" Aimée said, turning on the ignition and hearing the powerful hum of the engine.

"Cirque d'Hiver," she said. "If you don't hurry up, we'll miss him."

"Who?" Aimée asked, shifting the car down rue Oberkampf.

"The man you're dying to meet." Samia's full lips were set in a firm line. "He wants to see you, too. Just to make sure."

"Make sure of what?"

Samia shrugged. "To see that his wholesale line goes to good hands."

Aimée kept her surprise in check. Samia had found this connection fast.

Something about it made her uneasy, nervous. Didn't Samia know about the explosion?

"What about Eugénie?"

"My feelers are out," Samia said. "She owes me money."

Aimée wondered why the *Maghrébin* network hadn't spread the news about Sylvie/Eugénie's death. Odd—were they cagey because they'd sold the *plastique*?

Aimée found no parking spaces anywhere and *klaxons* blared in annoyance. She ended up parking under an ARRÊT GÊNANT towing sign, among several other cars on rue Oberkampf. They reached the Cirque d'Hiver, a circular nineteenth-century building resembling a tent, topped by a bronze statue of an Amazon on the roof and two bronze warriors on horses over the entrance. Circus posters proclaiming past glories—the Bolshoi Circus, Chinese glass balancers, Mongolian contortionists, Hungarian jugglers, and Canadian trapeze artists—were pasted outside.

The Cirque d'Hiver brought back memories to Aimée: traditional Christmas day visits with her grandfather, chewing the fluffy pink *barbes à papa* which turned fuchsia in her mouth. The monkeys sitting on the accordionist's shoulder as he played while strolling through the audience, the spotlight's glare on the rhinestone-studded trapeze artists. As a child she'd loved the ink-black darkness and heat from the spotlights trained on the big ring.

"Do what I say," Samia said, jolting Aimée from her reverie. Samia pulled her coat tight around her and stared at Aimée.

"So if we pass the test, the big man gives us a contract?" Aimée asked. "My client's picky. He wants Duplo *plastique*."

Samia looked at Aimée's wrist and grinned.

"*C'est chouette!*" she said tapping Aimée's new watch. "I need one," she said and strutted toward the red entrance doors.

Samia was a kid. Aimée didn't like this, but then she didn't like much of what had happened so far.

The Cirque d'Hiver nowadays rented the hall for everything from fashion shows to rock concerts in its one-ring circus. Aimée wondered why they kept the circus posters, mostly from the sixties and seventies, behind smudged glass in the carpeted lobby. Neglect or nostalgia for former glory?

Muffled laughter and applause came from behind greasy-looking doors. A private show of Stanislav the Stupendous—Budapest's third natural wonder, his name framed by tiny lights—was scheduled for the evening.

"Auditions for new acts," boomed a bored woman at the *barbe à papa* concession. She exhaled a funnel of smoke rings into the air and shook her head. "Sorry. *Pas possible*. Too many guests disturb the animals' concentration."

"We're a late addition to the guest list," Samia said, nudging Aimée.

Aimée slipped a hundred-franc note across the counter. "Of course," she said, "we won't disturb their concentration."

The cigarette hung from the side of the woman's mouth. Her blue shadowed eyes narrowed as she looked Aimée up and down. "We all need to live, eh?" she said, pocketing the note. "Enjoy the show," she said, jerking her thumb toward the doors.

They walked by gilt-edged walls with plaster chipped in a few places. The *cirque* seemed frayed at the edges.

But despite the deserted foyer, they weren't alone. She felt eyes following her.

Inside, she and Samia stopped, gripped by the scene under the elaborate chandeliers. Four children and four men in brown leather rode motorcycles into the ring. They parked their bikes and the men lay on top of them and juggled the children with their feet.

Scattered applause burst from the few onlookers in the worn red velvet seats. Samia tugged Aimée's arm and motioned for her to join the front row. They sat down, their faces highlighted by the ring lights. Aimée was struck by the soft contours and sharp edges shadowed in Samia's face. As if she were *mixte*, French and Algerian. Awe shone in her eyes.

Several large men in well-cut suits, one chewing a licorice stick, were seated to their right. Peering closer, Aimée realized that the stockier men on the aisle casually surveyed the crowd and exits.

The occasional tilt of their necks, and the thin wires trailing from their ears into their collars indicated that they wore radio receivers. Sophisticated security, she thought. What circus aficionados were they guarding?

"Wait five minutes," Samia whispered. "Then go to the bathroom."

"Why?"

"It's a test," Samia interrupted, standing up. She brushed imaginary lint from her coat, licked her finger, and wiped her brow with it. Then she was gone.

A large brown Siberian bear wearing a cone-like silver wizard's hat pedaled a tiny bicycle into the ring. The trainer's whip slapped the sawdust, creating dust puffs ahead of the bear in his line of vision. She wondered what the bear would do if he got out of line. Tear up the tiny bike, wreak havoc in the crowd, and other things she didn't like to contemplate. Like Sylvie's murderer had done.

Aimée heard loud, sustained clapping from the licorice-chewing man. Several guffaws sounded from the suits, who'd risen and enveloped him in a protective cocoon.

The suits sat back down, and some of the men evaporated toward the lobby. Aimée noticed that another man had joined the licorice chewer, addressing him as "General." He also sat stiffly. Light glinted off their lapels, and then she realized that they wore medals and were in some kind of stiff uniform. Russians, maybe?

Her idea was quickly dispelled when a man bearing a tray of small, steaming tea glasses appeared. She could smell the mint from her seat. A Moroccan delegation playing hooky from state affairs? Diplomats didn't wear uniforms, but the military did.

The General leaned forward, his posture stiff but his eyes alight. He chewed the licorice in time to the crashing cymbals beaten by a sad-faced clown, in a black-and-white Pierrot costume, standing in the center. Aimée realized that the bear's paws pedaled in time to the cymbals.

Aimée stood up and made her way to the lobby. On the restroom door hung a sign saying CLOSED FOR CLEANING. Aimée stuck her head in.

"Samia?"

No answer. Just the drip of water echoing off the tiles.

She wondered if this was a setup. Going in would be inviting trouble. Yet she worried about Samia.

She walked toward the red velvet drapes at the backstage entrance, giving herself time to think. This part of the *cirque* lay deserted except for a sixties-style vacuum cleaner, chromed and sturdy, propped against the wall next to assorted pails and detergents. In the dim light she could make out an exit door.

And then, on her left, Aimée heard the unmistakable sound of a safety being clicked off. Her pulse jumped as she dodged and reached for her Beretta. But from behind a large warm hand enclosed hers. She never managed a scream since another one clamped over her mouth.

She back-kicked her heel and tried to twist away. Her head

was slammed against the woodwork, hard. The pressure, like a band of white heat, tightened around her head.

Too bad her kicks landed in the air, not in the groin of whoever or whatever gripped her in a headlock. She jacknifed her body, turning until her spike heels impacted hamstring hard muscle. She heard the growl of pain, and ground her heels in harder.

Something glittered. For a brief moment she saw a huge hand, with a diamond ring shaped like a star. Then she twisted and kicked again. Anything to release that pressure on her head. She screamed, trying to get attention or help.

She tried to roll, but her legs didn't obey.

And then she poked and jabbed back, flailing at the air until she hit something soft like tissue. A man's cry reached her. She'd either gotten him in the eye or the nuts. Either way it had to hurt. But she was down on the floor, face to face with a hideous forties red floral carpet. Now her legs responded. She tried to push off the floor.

"*Bent al haram,*" a voice hissed in her ear.

With as much force as she had, she elbowed behind her and scrambled to her feet. She heard him crash into the metal pails and swear. Running and falling, she kept on going.

A loud roar sounded, like a high-speed TGV. Her chest reverberated as something punched her in the back. And she knew she'd been shot. The bullet-proof vest hadn't absorbed the whole of the bullet's impact. A burning sensation stung her hip. She stumbled but caught herself.

Wall plaster rained over her black leather. Don't think about the bullets, she told herself as terror gripped her—keep running. Don't stop. There were loud shouts, the sounds of someone running into the metal buckets. Applause reached her ears, the performance was over, patrons streamed into the lobby.

Screaming and barreling past the velvet curtains, Aimée ran into something large and furry. The Siberian bear growled, and then all she heard was white noise.

*   *   *

AIMÉE GREW aware of an odd taste in her mouth, grit on her face, and something wet on her chin. Drool. And slits of fractured darkness. Prickly stubs poked her ears and nose, sweet and crinkling. Hay.

By the time she realized she was under a burlap bag, she was ripping her way out with torn red fingernails. Her head throbbed. The ground shook. The earth was moving—not the way she liked it to.

At least the leather jumpsuit had protected her. The bear was gone.

Then she remembered.

She'd crawled into a feed trough for animals—the first thing she'd stumbled across after the stage entrance. She untangled her legs and reached for her bag, still strapped over her shoulder. Her side pulsed with pain. She took short breaths—big ones hurt—afraid to touch the spot where her bullet-proof vest had failed.

Despite her sore head and body, the ground shaking helped her get up quickly. Grabbing a ledge beside her, she plowed into the tail of a wrinkled gray elephant. She scooted out before the stamping feet got any closer. The elephant's trunk picked up the burlap, tossed, then stomped on it. Just in time, Aimée thought, trying to ignore her splitting headache.

A trainer led a pair of chestnut mares over the cobblestones. He clucked and said some soothing words. She followed the trio past the sign ENTRÉE DES ARTISTES and nipped into the first empty stall. It had a waist-high wooden partition and was vacant except for a pile of fragrant hay.

She knelt down and felt her head, gingerly. A bump had blossomed like a big onion. Carefully she smoothed her hair and unrolled a gray parachute silk raincoat from her bag. Her legs wobbled.

From the neighboring stall, she heard a horse slurping water and flicking its wire-haired tail against the buzzing flies. She slid out of her slingbacks, which had somehow stayed on her feet, and into her red Converse hightops and laced them quickly. For the last touch, she donned a pair of large-framed horn-rimmed glasses. Before her head split in two, she was going to go back inside and find who'd whacked her. But first she needed to deal with the bullet throbbing in her side.

At the Café des Artistes facing the cobbled back lane behind Cirque d'Hiver, she leaned against the bar. She ordered a pastis and *aspirine* from Inés, a pudgy woman, who sat doing a crossword in the corner.

"Slice of horsemeat works better on a shiner," Inés said, shoving two white pills across the soggy bar.

Aimée popped the pills and took a big swig of pastis, not feeling convinced.

Inés stared at Aimée. "Trapeze artists swear by it," she said. "Order steak tartare and I'll throw in the *frites*."

Soon she had a horse steak on her temple and the cell phone in her other ear.

No answer at Samia's. No Yves at her apartment.

She hobbled into the small bathroom, rolled down her jumpsuit, and assessed the damage. The Kevlar vest had absorbed most of the bullet, except for the painful shrapnel embedded a centimeter or so in her hip. The hollowed-out bullet had fractured on impact. Blood oozed stickily, making her feel faint in the close-quartered bathroom. She had to pull it out.

Her tweezers were history, lost at the yard getting the moped started. The only tool she could think of was the sugar tongs on the zinc counter. She had to do better than that.

Aimée stuck her head out.

"Would you have a first-aid kit?" she asked, her smile weak.

Inés took one look at Aimée and said, "Stay there." She came back with a first-aid kit and a small shot glass.

"Drink this," Inés said.

Aimée gulped and felt the malt whiskey burn down her throat, scalding and welcome.

"Would a doctor help—?"

Aimée reached for the kit. "I can handle this."

Inés nodded, her expression unchanged as she took in Aimée's bloody condition. "How about I catch you if you fall over?"

"Deal," Aimée said. "But only if you give me another shot of whatever that was."

Inés brought the bottle, another shot glass, and joined her. They stood in the small rest room, Aimée perched against the old marble sink and Inés leaning against the wall.

"During the battle for Paris, there was street-to-street fighting here," Inés said, watching Aimée pull out the cotton and anti-septic, then dab the blood away. "The circus animals had been slaughtered for food long before, but my mother refused to kill our ferret."

"Ferret?" Aimée asked, sticking the long-handled tweezers into alcohol. She liked hearing Inés talk; it helped keep her mind off what she had to do.

"Funny little thing," she said. "But for my mother it was kind of a principle. She'd be damned if she'd let the *boches* eat it or tell her to get rid of it. That simple!"

"What happened?" Aimée asked, dabbing alcohol around the ugly chunk of shrapnel protruding from above her hip, where her Kevlar vest had stopped.

"Stupid thing got incinerated by a panzer with a flame-thrower," Inés winked. "Maman was mad for days. I think she's never forgiven the *boches* for that."

"Where was your father?" Aimée asked, gripping the chunk with her tweezers and taking as big a breath as she could. She pulled, and gasped at the searing pain.

"Never came back from the work camp near Düsseldorf," Inés said. "We're not really sure where he ended up. That had some-thing to do with Maman's anger."

Aimée didn't get it out on the first try. Or the second. The stubborn thing had lodged deep from the force of a Magnum. The searing pain would be nothing, she knew, compared to the infection if she couldn't get the thing out in one piece.

"You're feisty, I can tell," Inés said. "And you act tough. Weren't you watching your tail?"

Thanks for rubbing it in, Aimée wanted to say.

Determined this time, she caught the piece and pulled it out slow and straight, trying to last through the knife-edge pain.

Right away Inés slid a large gauze wrap around it. "Tape it closed, and you'll be fine," she said. "I only helped because you looked like you might topple."

"Right." Aimée leaned against the cold marble wall until she'd stopped shaking.

"All kinds come here; the *mecs*, the scammers, small-time hustlers," Inés said. "For a smart-looking one, seems like you made a mistake."

Inés had a wealth of information and advice.

"I trusted the wrong person," Aimée said.

Samia had set her up, and she, a *stupide*, had walked right into it. Eagerly. She was supposed to protect Samia, but she was the one who got shot with a bullet in her hip.

Inés nodded. "See," she said, pointing in the mirror. "No trace."

The lump had gone down. And the pounding in her head had subsided to a reasonable ache. She'd taped her side tight, wrapping several strands of tape back and forth. She retired the glasses, pulled out her makeup, and did a repair job on her eyes. Kohl and lots of concealer.

Aimée noticed Inés watching her. Back in the café Aimée sat down and tried Samia on the cell phone again. No answer.

"Magnesium," Inés said, slipping her a green salad. "You need it."

"*Merci*," Aimée said. She picked at the salad and *frites* and kept trying Samia's number. She was thinking of the elephants. One of whom could have crushed her into burlap pulp.

"How about the General?" Aimée asked. "Have you heard of him?"

"How about you're out of your league?" Inés said, grinning.

Was the pastis clouding her perception or had Inés turned more smartass?

Not to mention the downright humiliation. First she got ambushed; then a woman old enough to be her mother reiterated how dumb she'd been.

"Make that out of your division," Inés said, her eyes crinkling.

Now Inés was making fun of her.

Pathetic.

She closed her eyes and laughed.

"Speaking of the General, he's way out of my universe," she grinned. "But if I don't find him, he'll do this again."

Inés brought her crossword and sat down next to her.

"Why didn't you say so?" she said. "He comes in those cars with the special license plates—"

"Diplomatic plates?" Aimée interrupted.

"No one likes him," Inés shrugged. "That's all I know."

Aimée wrote down her number on a napkin, then stood up to leave. "Call me if he comes again, please."

"Watch your tail," she replied.

AIMÉE WAS feeling better. "Feeling better" was a relative term, but the painkiller was taking effect. She crossed the narrow street and entered the back of the *cirque.*

In the circus ring she passed a fire-eater using his toes to adjust the blaze angle on a gasoline can pump. Heat emanated, and he sucked the air. She stood back in awe as the fire-eater blew billowing yellow-white flames over the sawdust. As he turned she saw a hose snaking up the back of his skinny T-shirt.

The rehearsal audience had thinned to technicians. Aimée

searched for the licorice-chewing man and his crew but was disappointed. Gone. She walked amid the red velvet seats where they'd sat. Nothing. Not even a cigarette stub.

"I need an assistant," said a deeply accented voice from the small stage.

She looked up to see the speaker's lined face, caked with flesh-colored makeup. Tall and gaunt, he wore a turban with a gleaming cabochon in the center and a black satin cape. He cocked his large head, fixing his gaze on her. "Will you assist me?"

"I'll try," she said, aglow with the sudden sparkle of circus wonder. It was the same way she'd felt sitting with her grandfather, who'd whispered "Watch, Aimée . . . look at the magician's sleeves . . . can you see how he does it?" But she never had, could never see the sleight-of-hand trick.

He brandished an iridescent scarf, waved it in the air, and balled it up. He clapped his hands and showed her. Empty.

"Smoke and mirrors, right?" she asked.

"I have no smoke," he said. "And at my age—no mirrors, please!"

His black satin cape flashed as he pulled the scarf from behind her ears.

Her mouth fell open. How did he do that?

He grinned at her reaction.

"Stanislav the Stupendous?" she said.

He bowed. "The third wonder of Budapest is available for parties, business luncheons, or that special affair needing just the right touch."

"You're not part of the *cirque?*"

"My act requires a more intimate surrounding," he said, gesturing toward the tiered red velvet seats. "We close off part of the *cirque*, making a half circle, and I perform on that platform."

A workman hammered ringside.

"Those men who sat over there," she said, gesturing toward the spot where the military types had sat. "Know where they are?

I'm supposed to meet them . . ." she trailed off, hoping Stanislav would finish it for her.

"The General?" he said.

Aimée nodded.

"Funny bird, that one," Stanislav said. "My following is loyal."

"The General's a fan of yours?"

"I'm big with the Algerians."

Algerian military? Aimée held her surprise in check.

The workman appeared and tapped his wrist, vying for the magician's attention. "You've been a delightful assistant, Mademoiselle, but I must rehearse, if you'll excuse me," Stanislav said in a practiced breathless tone, indicating that he was too busy and rushed to have even a smidgen more time.

Aimée stepped from the sawdust over the raised ring, puzzling how to elicit information about the General.

"You'll think me helpless, but the purse with my address book was stolen, and I'm at sea how to find him," she said stepping back into the ring.

"I wish I could be more helpful," Stanislav said, following the carpenter.

She sniffed around backstage, but no one knew of the General—or if they had, they wouldn't tell her. Even the grinning horse trainer who said, "I keep my eyes on beautiful females." He winked. "Like you."

AIMÉE DROVE to Samia's apartment. No answer. The *hammam* was closed, and it began to rain. Her head ached, and her spirits matched the grey drizzle. She sat in René's car near Place Jean Timbaud, the rain spattering on the windshield. People emerged from the Métro, turning up their collars, and running down the street. She must have nodded off, because the next thing she knew, there was a loud tap on the passenger window.

"*Allez-y!*" A green-suited *égoutier* shouted, his dark face beaded with rain. "Move along. Quit blocking the truck."

"*Pardon,*" she said, turning on the ignition. The Citroën roared to life, and she hit the wipers.

That's when she saw Samia, scurrying out of the dingy hotel on Impasse Ouestre. She shifted into first and cut Samia off before she could enter Jean Timbaud.

"Get in!" Aimée said, leaning over and pushing the door handle open.

Samia blinked, like a deer caught in the headlights. She tried to back up, but her heels slipped and she grabbed the door.

"I can't—"

The garbage truck's horn blared.

"Hurry up, we need to talk," Aimée said.

Samia looked for an escape. The rain beat harder. Her only option was the passage she'd emerged from.

"*Now!*" Aimée yelled.

Either the rain or Aimée's voice convinced her to get in and slam the door. They took off down Jean Timbaud. Aimée reached Passage de la Fonderie, a narrow ivy-walled lane, and pulled in. She parked and turned off the ignition.

"You don't look too good," Samia said.

"Smart girl," Aimée said, reaching for Samia's bag. She turned the beaded pink bag upside down. "Considering I got shot, I don't think I look half bad."

Samia's eyes widened.

"Smart girls don't betray their friends."

"You're not my friend," Samia said, but she winced when she spoke. She brushed her shoulders, sending a wet spray over the upholstery.

"Even for an acquaintance, that's not very nice."

Samia looked down, "I'm sorry. They just said . . . well, you weren't supposed to get hurt."

"Why do I have a hard time believing you?"

"Just warn you off, they said," she said, her voice sullen.

"Who?"

"Let me out."

The passage was quiet except for occasional footsteps. The fogged Citroën's windows shielded them from prying eyes.

Aimée had to get Samia to talk.

"What does *bent al haram* mean?"

"Bent al haram?" Samia said, closing her eyes as if in deep thought. " 'Interfering slut' comes pretty close."

Great.

"Doesn't the General like me?"

Samia reached for the door handle, but Aimée pulled out her Beretta.

"It's been a rough afternoon, Samia," she said. "Time for you to brighten my day." With her other hand she poked around the strewn items from Samia's bag. A package of pink condoms, hotel keys, an illustrated ten-franc pocket romance, and a pearl hair clip. Aimée shook the bag again, and a hand of Fat'ma tumbled out. Just like Eugénie/Sylvie's.

"Where did you get this?"

"The Fat'ma?" Samia asked.

Aimée nodded.

"Belonged to my mother," she said. "Lots of people have them."

"Like who?" Aimée asked.

"You probably can't even use that," Samia said, looking in the visor mirror at the Beretta, and ignoring the question.

"Even if my aim was bad, it'd be hard to miss with you so close," Aimée cocked the trigger. "Want to find out?"

Samia flinched.

"Some *flic* taped us talking," Aimée lied. Anything to get Samia to talk. "He's watching you on video surveillance. He wants my hide, but I think he's nailed yours already. He's just waiting, Samia."

Samia's bravado shriveled.

"Sergeant Martaud?"

Aimée nodded. The stale air inside the car and Samia's perfume were getting to her.

"Is the General's number in here?" Aimée asked, holding up a pink fur address book. "I'll deal directly with him."

Samia blinked in fear. "They're big—"

"Who?"

"Leave it alone," she said.

"Samia, don't you see my finger's still on the trigger?" she said.

"You don't know about—" she stopped.

"About what?"

Samia's lips tightened.

"Fine, I'll let Martaud know Zdanine supplies the *plastique*," Aimée sighed, pocketing the address book. "That will get me off his hook." She turned the ignition key. "Since Zdanine's claiming sanctuary in the church, you're the perfect connection."

It was a guess, but by the look on Samia's face it hit home.

"*Attends*," Samia said. "I called a number. That's all." Her chest heaved. She faced Aimée, her eye makeup smeared. "You leave my kid out of it, *compris*?"

Aimée wondered why Samia would say that—was her young son used to keep her in line? A pang of remorse hit her for using Samia, a mother who couldn't have been more than eighteen.

"Zdanine used you, didn't he?"

"Only two times," she said. "That's why I didn't believe you."

"You want to believe Zdanine instead of me . . ." Aimée let that trail in the air.

Silence except for the steady thrum of rain on the windshield.

"Something's about to happen, isn't it?"

Samia shrugged.

"What's Eugénie's connection?"

Samia rubbed the foggy window and turned away. "What time is it?"

"For a moment you were so helpful," Aimée said. She leaned over, the Beretta still in one hand. "Who murdered Sylvie?"

"Sylvie . . . who's that?"

Anger flared in Aimée, then died. Why would Samia know about her double life?

Aimée turned Samia's chin toward her.

"Was it the General?" she asked.

"Who's Sylvie?" Samia blinked several times.

Exasperated, Aimée pounded the steering wheel.

"What does Eugénie have to do with it?"

"She stayed at the apartment." Tears streamed down her cheeks.

"Who met her there?" Aimée said, knowing she had to pull information from Samia. Bit by painful bit.

"People dropped things off," Samia said, wiping her face. "I've told you nothing. Nothing."

"Of course you haven't," Aimée said soothingly. "Is someone making you afraid to tell me what you know?"

"The *Maghrébins* used that place. They scare me," she said. "I told Zdanine, I don't want to mix with them. He does."

"What for?"

"They have places like that," Samia said. "You know, all over. Like an octopus."

Aimée remembered the flyer with "Youssef" written on it. She felt as if she were grasping for straws.

"Did Eugénie mention Youssef?" she asked.

"Youssef? I think so: Someone called Zdanine while I was there. But I only met Eugénie once," Samia said. "That's all."

"Did Eugénie give you this?" Aimée asked, holding up the pearl hair clip.

"I owe her a hundred francs," Samia said, her voice contrite. "Look, it's Marcus's birthday. He'll be hurt if I don't make the school party. Didn't even have time to buy him a present."

Samia looked as if the world had fallen on her shoulders.

Aimée slipped the Beretta into her bag. She looked at her watch.

"Here," she said, unstrapping the happy-face watch. "This suits you more than me. Give it to your son."

Samia blinked and looked unsure.

"Take it," she said. "Just don't set me up again."

"*Chouette!*" Samia's face burst into a big smile. A big-kid smile, happy with a new toy, putting it on eagerly. "*Merci!*"

Aimée was amazed how childlike Samia seemed when her defenses were down. For a moment Aimée saw the young girl whose mother probably worked *horizontale*, who'd grown up in a housing project and then hooked up with a maggot like Zdanine. It reminded her of what Molière had said about writing: First you do it because you like it, then you do it for some friends, then you do it for money.

Samia had pulled the visor down and begun wiping off her makeup in the mirror.

"I need to get to Gare du Nord," she said. "Catch the 1:30 train for Marcus's party."

Of all the things Samia had told her, she believed this 100 percent.

"Tell me more en route to the station," she said, turning on the ignition. "What's your connection to Morbier?"

"Who?"

Surprised, Aimée kept driving. She decided to describe him, so if Samia had seen him she wouldn't necessarily know he was a *flic*.

"Morbier's an old *mec*, salt-and-pepper hair, moustache, and he wears suspenders over his big gut."

"Sounds like one of my mother's friends," Samia said. "She knew lots of old farts."

Aimée picked up on the past tense.

"Knew?"

"Passed away," Samia said.

"I'm sorry," she said.

Curious, she wanted to explore more. At least find out why

Morbier wanted her to protect Samia. She circled Place de la République, then gunned up boulevard de Magenta.

"What was your mother's name?" she asked.

"Fouaz, like mine," Samia said, her mouth crinkling in a sad smile.

Aimée was about to ask more when Samia turned to her.

"Keep this between us, but fifty thousand francs buys a hostage situation."

Aimée's heart skipped. Her fingers clenched the steering wheel. "Go on."

Samia's face, now scrubbed clean of makeup, made her look younger than she probably was. A demure peach skirt and twinset emerged from under the black coat. Aimée wondered how Samia placated her conscience, if she had one.

"Who orders this *plastique*?"

"Zdanine says it's Balkan crazies who like to blow each other up," Samia said. "They do that shit all the time anyway."

Aimée nodded. Too bad it wasn't true in her case.

"Was it Duplo last time?" Aimée asked, hoping against hope that Samia knew.

"Semtex duds out sometimes, unreliable. The fundamentalists don't seem to mind," Samia said matter-of-factly. "Zdanine uses Duplo—only quality, he says."

"What about the General?"

She shrugged. "I don't know."

"But why pick Eugénie?"

"That was a one-off." Samia's eyes slit in suspicion. "He sells to outsiders. No locals." She shook her head. "Don't look at me. Zdanine was in the church—he couldn't have blown her up."

Rain coursed down the windshield in silvered rivulets, like mercury. Aimée flipped the wipers faster. Samia's casual tone made her angry. But she had to play it cool or Samia would bolt.

"It's scary," Aimée said, staring meaningfully at her. "I mean, look what can happen."

"Just don't rub anyone the wrong way," Samia said, but her lip quivered. She looked uneasy. "I called a pager number—that's all I did."

"When?"

"They said, 'Call in four hours—if no answer, try in another two hours.' Someone called back with a delivery location."

Aimée pulled in to the taxi line. She had an idea.

"Contact Zdanine before you go."

Samia took Aimée's phone and called Zdanine.

Samia's voice changed; not just the cloying, soothing line to a pimp but an earnest overtone as if convincing him. For a full two minutes she argued, her words a mix of gutter French, *verlan*, and Arabic.

Abruptly she snapped Aimée's phone shut.

"What happened?" Aimée asked.

"He'll come around," she said.

Aimée didn't care about Zdanine's list of potential clients; she wanted the suppliers who'd been at the Cirque d'Hiver.

"Zdanine says it's too dangerous, doesn't he?"

Samia shook her head.

"What then?"

"He thinks your cut's too big," she said. "It should be split so he gets a nice slice. After all, he says, he's Khalil's cousin, and the contacts are his."

Spoken like a true pimp, Aimée thought. If Samia translated correctly. Outside in Place Napoleon III, people emerged from Gare du Nord, opened their umbrellas, and ran to the taxi line.

"Nothing happens until I wire Khalil to front the money," Aimée said. "How do I know your people can deliver the *plastique*?"

"They're not my people," Samia said, "I told you, I don't like them. Zdanine does the connection."

"Until you give me the supplier's name, I don't cough up the front money."

Samia shrugged. She buttoned her coat and gripped the door handle before she turned back.

"What's the number?"

Samia opened the car door. A sheet of rain sprayed in. "Marc's school is outside Paris, not far. I'll be back soon." Samia slammed the door shut and disappeared toward the train platforms in the cavernous station.

Aimée lowered her forehead onto the steering wheel. This stank. Samia had made a deal. Aimée felt it in her bones.

Here she sat at a taxi line outside Gare du Nord, the windows fogged, and no closer to Eugénie or the explosive suppliers than before.

Her gloom matched the gray sheeting rain whipping across the square. Extraordinary—she couldn't remember when April had been this wet. It had rained incessantly all week. She took several deep breaths and thought. If those men were the explosive suppliers, why wait for Samia to get back?

She switched on the ignition and took off back down boulevard de Magenta. In record time, she parked in Cité de Crussol, on one of the passages branching from behind Cirque d'Hiver.

She punched in Morbier's number. He answered after several rings.

"Morbier, call it intuition, but Samia's playing me," she said. "Your little friend got me shot!"

"Shot?"

"I pulled the shrapnel out but—"

"She's young, Leduc," he said. "And the young don't know left from right."

"No conscience, more like it," she said.

"*Bien sûr,*" he said. "Tell me about it."

She explained about Cirque d'Hiver and her abrupt departure at Gare du Nord. "I didn't like the big guys in the circus."

"Nice groundwork and setup," he said.

She paused, surprised at his comment. He rarely said anything complimentary. "But I'm still in the dark. Samia became helpful too quickly."

"She'll come through," he said.

She wondered why he kept excusing her.

"Why do you let her off the hook so easily?"

"No questions, remember?" he said. "Marcus must be six or seven, eh?"

His comment didn't surprise her. Morbier had an immense memory, like her father and those of his generation possessed. No computer files or central storage systems; they kept it all in their head: a *mec*'s street record, an unsolved murder in their arrondissement years back, whose palm oiled the important palms, a pimp's harem, and their children's names.

"Where are you going now?" Morbier asked.

"To church," she said. "Zdanine might be more helpful."

"Will he talk to you?"

"I won't know until I try."

A LIGHT DRIZZLE BEADED Aimée's glasses. The smell of wet wool rose from the damp pavement in front of Notre-Dame de la Croix.

In the midst of the rain, the noise, and pushing bodies, she felt someone staring at her.

Aimée's throat tightened. Had someone followed her from the circus or was she some street *mec's* target?

She looked up.

Yves stared across the barricade, his navy anorak glistening with rain droplets.

His gaze pulled her in as if it were a homing signal. Caught in his magnetic field, she was powerless to resist.

And then she was next to him.

"New perfume?" he muttered, as the police pointed them toward the barricade's end.

"Does this have to do with the way I change the air?"

"The other night you wore lemon verbena," he said, nodding at the other reporters.

"Quite a memory you've got," she said.

"You'd be amazed," he said, "at what I remember."

She turned away.

"Slumming or trying to meet me?"

"Working," she said.

"You ought to charge your cell phone," he said, flashing his press pass at the barricade. "Makes it easier for people to reach you. I've been trying since this morning."

"Other people can reach me, why not you?"

Dumb. Why let him know it bothered her?

She felt his hot breath on her earlobe, and his bristly chin brushed her neck as he turned back to a policeman. He smelled the same. The dusky Yves scent.

She had no time for someone who popped in and out of her life when it suited him. Most of all she didn't want these feelings; couldn't deal with them at the best of times.

But he could help her.

"Look, I need to get into the church," she said. "Say I'm with you, just for now."

"You want to use me," he said. He didn't wait for her to answer. "Make sure you abuse me later."

"If you're lucky," she said, trying not to smile.

"Let me do the talking. Nice touch."

"What do you mean?" she asked, pushing her feelings aside.

"The glasses," he said.

She frowned and briefly felt disappointed.

He leaned over and whispered, "The police think you're Martine's assistant. Keep it that way for now."

She followed him, threading past an old woman with ill-fitting dentures who yelled at a reporter waving a microphone. Shouts of "Let the *sans-papiers* stay!" arose from the swaying crowd contrasting with the CRS riot squad: silent impassive faces behind clear, shatterproof visors, hands clutching billy clubs. Legitimized by the press credentials and with Yves escorting her, Aimée crossed the wooden police barricades.

Once inside the church, Yves motioned for her to wait. He approached a bearded man guarding the confessional. Apprehensive, Aimée crouched by the marble holy water font. What if she couldn't find Zdanine?

Incense mingled with sweat. Obsidian-faced men in bright pastel polyester shirts sprawled in the wooden pews. The whites of their eyes caught the gleam from dripping wax candles. Murmured conversations echoed off vaulting pillars. A plump, honey-colored woman in a maroon *djellaba* wrote on a chalk-board. Teenagers in tracksuits sat before her on the stone floor. She admonished them in Arabic, and several raised their hands.

Aimée felt a tug at her elbow and turned. A longhaired man in a priest's collar, corduroy pants, and worn loafers smiled at her.

"I'm *Abbé* Geoffroy," he said. "My hope is that you report on the plight of these people." He gestured around the gothic church.

"*Bonjour, Abbé* Geoffroy," Aimée said, shaking his hand. "I understand a minister is negotiating, granting permission for these immigrants to stay in France."

"I hope it's not too late," he said. The priest's brow furrowed and he brushed a stray hair behind his ear. "The ten hunger strikers are in the twentieth day."

She'd noticed how thin and listless the men were who lay on the pews. She and the priest walked toward high-backed dark wood stalls.

"Pacifists," he said. "Many are political refugees from Algeria, Mali, and Senegal. To send them back would mean certain execution."

"That's what I don't understand, *Abbé*," she said. Ahead of them, the carved altarpiece lay bathed in a mauve glow from the stained-glass windows surrounding the nave. "Seems to me this goes against their philosophy."

"I offer my prayers hourly for them."

"Please don't be offended, but isn't there something more concrete that can be done?"

"Dissident factions took over," he shrugged.

"Can you point out Zdanine for me?"

Abbé Geoffroy's expression grew pained.

"Gone," he said.

"Can I reach him somehow?"

"I can't keep track," the priest said, shaking his head. "I'm sorry."

Aimée wanted to ask more, but Yves beckoned her. She excused herself and joined him.

"They've just finished their prayers," Yves said, handing her a black veil. "Put this *hijab* over your head. Hamid's like an *imam*, and this shows respect."

She knew about *imams*, Muslim religious leaders or persons officiating in a mosque. Every *bidonville*, or shantytown, had one.

"Will this level the playing ground or score points?" she asked draping it over her and raising her eyebrows.

"Forget it," Yves said. "In Islam, as a woman, you won't even be allowed a catch-up role. But Hamid's unique, a man who works to bridge the gap between strict Islamists and the *beurs*, tiptoeing over the French colonial legacy."

Again that word *beur*, Sylvie's bank password. She wanted to know more, but Yves strode ahead.

Back in a recessed side altar, several robed men sat on prayer carpets. Yves nodded toward Hamid, who wore a skullcap. Fatigue laced Hamid's deep black eyes. His long black beard, flecked with gray, rose and fell with his labored breath.

"I partake of no food along with my African brethren," he said before either of them could speak. "I wet my tongue for sustenance. Dead, I will serve no purpose."

Hamid's breath, a sharp acid odor, emanated unpleasantly. A characteristic of severe hunger, she knew, which indicated the body's slip into a negative balance. She shuddered. This came from the body literally consuming itself.

"We appreciate you granting this interview," Yves said, and sat down.

Aimée did the same, keeping the veil tight as she lowered her head. Hamid didn't look old, but it was hard to tell.

"Your motto—" Yves began.

"The AFL's motto," Hamid interrupted, "remains the same, forged by oppressed people who demand their rights."

"Can you speak to the situation?" Yves asked. "Comment on the fundamentalist factions rumored to be attempting to gain control of the AFL?"

"At times one must bend like the willow branch to Allah's will or stand firm like a rod of iron."

Aimée studied Hamid as he spoke. Whether it was his manner, the brief facial tick scoring his lips, or her sixth sense, she doubted he wanted this infighting or this publicity. Hamid didn't make a very good liar.

"Does the fact that your followers refer to you as a *maghour,* an 'outsider,' disturb you?" Aimée asked.

"We are all Allah's children, some his disciples," Hamid said simply.

"Forgive me," Aimée said, catching Hamid's gaze but keeping her head lowered. "How can you assure these *sans-papiers* that they will stay?"

"We await the minister's action, secure in our belief." Hamid's dark eyes filled with pain, his breathing faltered. "The AFL's aim remains the same. Mutual cooperation will solve this conflict."

"Did you know Eugénie Grandet?"

"Forgive me, fatigue claims my efforts," Hamid said.

Frustrated, she studied him. Hamid's hollowed cheekbones creased his face. His lids were half closed, and the stark white below his pupils glowed eerily. Aimée watched Hamid's eyelids flutter. Had he gone into a trance, or was he about to pass out from hunger?

She wanted to know more about his dealings with Eugénie.

"Hamid must reserve his strength for prayer. Please end your audience," an aide said to them.

"I respect Hamid's duties, but he agreed to this interview," Yves said.

"Later. Now he must rest," the aide shouldered his way toward them.

Reluctantly Yves stood, and Aimée followed suit.

"The Koran teaches the spirit how to live among men," Hamid said to Yves, his voice fading. "A code of life, harming no brethren. You must tell people this."

The aide waved Aimée and Yves back toward the vestibule. He stood guard, watching them leave.

"Not even five minutes for an interview," Yves said, distressed. "He looked ill."

"He's weak," Aimée said, pulling Yves aside. "But he's covering something up."

"You mean lying?" Yves said. "*Imams* have immunity, like priests do. They can be creative with the truth, and followers buy it. Reporters, like me, have problems with that."

On their way out she saw a Berber woman with hennaed hands and callused bare feet, asleep against the water font. The woman's mouth hung open, her tongue flicking, as if tasting the air as a snake does to find its way. Maybe I should do the same, Aimée thought, and discover who attacked me in the *cirque* and planted Sylvie's bomb.

Suddenly the woman's eyes batted open and she sat bolt upright, her frayed black caftan trailing on the floor. She glared at Aimée, then wagged her finger, a silver bangle outlined against her dark-skinned tattooed wrist.

"*Hittistes,*" she said, drawing out the first *s* into a hiss.

"*Comment*, Madame?" Aimée asked.

The woman muttered to herself. Yves tugged at her sleeve.

"Let's go," he said.

As Aimée walked past her, the woman emitted a piercing series of wails, bloodcurdling "*you-you-you*" ululations. From what she knew, Arab women in anguish or mourning did that.

Aimée knelt down on the cold stone and put her hand on

the woman's knee. Scars lined the woman's weather-beaten arms.

"Tell me what you mean, please," she said.

The woman spoke rapid and guttural Arabic. All Aimée caught were the words *hittiste* and *nahgar*, which the woman repeated over and over. She covered Aimée's hand with her tattooed one, beat her heart with the other, then let go.

Outside, past the crowds, she turned to Yves. They stood across from the parked buses in Place Chevalier. Yves leaned his backpack on a stone stanchion, tucking his tape recorder and notebooks inside.

"Got a clue to what the woman meant?" Aimée asked.

"*Hittistes* are the young, unemployed men hanging out on the streets," he said. "Holding up the walls in every *bidonville* as well as in Oran, Constantine, and Algiers."

Aimée wondered if the *hittistes* composed the dissident faction who'd joined the church. Like Zdanine.

"And *nahgar*?"

His mouth pursed in thought.

Aimée remembered his slim hips, the way he'd made her feel. Stop it, she told herself, pushing those thoughts from her mind.

"My grasp of Arabic is rudimentary," Yves said. "But it's something to do with humiliating people, abusing power."

Had the Berber woman tried to tell her the *hittistes* were undermining the immigrants' cause? "I thought the Algerian government promoted an official Islam compatible with socialist ideals. Or tried to."

Yves shrugged.

"There's a lot more going on here than a protest, isn't there?" she asked.

"In Algeria," Yves said, "the fundamentalist opponents charge Hamid's group with running guns-for-drugs operations in Europe. They accuse him of being supported by the most repressive Islamic regimes in the Arab world."

"But he's not like that at all," Aimée said. "The AFL sponsors adult education and food programs."

Aimée felt in her jacket pocket for cigarettes. None. She paused by Yves at the corner of rue du Liban and found Nicorette gum in her pocket. Yves's words made some kind of sense, but she wasn't sure how. She popped a piece in her mouth and chewed furiously.

Yves continued. "Many think the fundamentalists' broader goal is building *umma islamiyya*, an Islamic empire, countering the depraved West, which they see as doomed to hell even though they use it for asylum and access to media."

"Should I take my pick, or do you have a preference for one theory?" she asked, pulling her jacket tighter against the cooling air. He certainly knew his subject, she thought, but he was a top journalist.

"Algeria's in civil war," Yves said. He pulled out a small pad and jotted some notes. "A quiet underreported war rarely highlighted on CNN. It's a fight for power between the hard-line military and the strict Islamic forces to govern the country."

Aimée nodded. That made sense.

"*Les barbes*, among others, fuel this war. But *les barbes*, the religious scholars, and preachers in storefront mosques adopt the white robe, skullcap and beard of the traditional *mullah*. The difference is in their fanaticism. The West brands it Islamic fundamentalism."

"Does the Algerian government disavow *les barbes*?" she asked.

"Sometimes," he said. "Of course, they accuse us journalists of oversimplifying political and religious connections. Like the secular structured state pitted against religious opponents."

"I'm not sure I understand, Yves," she said. "But hear me out."

Swift-moving clouds obscured the sun again, throwing them into shadow. Chimneys dotted the rooftops. She had an idea.

"What if Hamid lost internal AFL control?" she said. "Say a

rebel fundamentalist faction splinters off for recognition and publicity. But Hamid bows to the faction so the cause isn't lost—after all, he's on a hunger strike and has principles—so the fundamentalists get media coverage, and Hamid gets the immigrant deportations halted." Aimée shook her head, "I don't think it's that simple, events stack up wrong."

"Too simple," he agreed.

"Could the crisis here mimic what's happening in Algeria?" she said.

"Nice observation," Yves said and shrugged. "Or it could all be smoke and mirrors."

Again smoke and mirrors.

Something ran unspoken between them. His wife must be taking up his time, she figured. She had the terrible feeling things with Yves led to a brick wall. A dead end. She wished she didn't want so much for him to come and spend the night again.

Act smart. Much better to cut her losses and walk away. Don't wait for him to say he's returned to his wife.

She turned and said, "Yves, I've got to go."

"Are you playing hard to get, Aimée?" he said, grinning. "That will get you everywhere." He pulled her close. She wished he hadn't done that.

"That's not what I meant," she said, struggling for words to express her feelings. Why couldn't she say it? He kept rubbing her neck and being no help. Whatsoever.

A taxi screeched in front of them. Several correspondents and photographers yelled at Yves to hurry and get in if he wanted a ride to the airport. He kissed her hard.

Then he was gone.

He'd popped in and out of her life again. And she'd let him.

She went to the nearest café, set her bag down, and ordered a glass of *vin rouge*. Maybe it would help drown her indecision.

"Mademoiselle Leduc?" a voice with a light accent asked from behind her.

She turned to face Kaseem Nwar, smiling beside her at the counter. Several men and women stood there, and for a moment she couldn't place where she'd met him. Then she remembered. He was more handsome than she recalled, in a long wool coat over a *djellaba*. As if it had been designed for him. The way he dressed revealed a pride in his heritage. She liked that.

"You probably don't remember me," he said, his smile turning sheepish. "I'm sorry to bother you."

"*Mais bien sûr*, we met at Philippe de Froissart's," she said, saddened by the memory of her conversation with Philippe.

"You looked upset," he said.

She gave him a small smile. "Anaïs was ill, things were difficult."

"I know what you mean," he said, his brow furrowed. "Philippe and Anaïs have been my good friends since the Sorbonne."

Aimée made space for Kaseem at the bar, taking a sip of wine.

"Wine?"

He shook his head and got the bartender's attention. "I'll nurse a Perrier."

She'd forgotten that Muslims took no alcohol.

"Do you live in the area?" she said, wondering why she'd run into him here.

His look turned serious at her casual question.

"Please understand, I have no political affiliation with the AFL," he said, a shadow crossing his face. "But some of my ex-wife's family claimed sanctuary, so I brought clothes and food. It's important to help them, person to person."

Aimée wondered if he could do more than that.

"Can't you help them stay?" she said, noting the muted café light playing on his features.

"Not with the present law," Kaseem shrugged, a very Gallic response. "My wife was French, but I'm naturalized. I can't help them anymore. That's the trouble."

Kaseem's mineral water arrived, and he paid for both their

drinks with an assurance that commanded attention. Kaseem appeared at ease in many worlds yet was not pompous.

"*Merci*," she said. She enjoyed standing in a café with an interesting man and talking. Face it, she admitted to herself, Kaseem wasn't hard on the eyes. And he wasn't rushing off to the airport.

"Tell me about your project involved with the humanitarian mission," she said.

"Mostly I export and import," he said, waving his long-fingered hand. "Life in the countryside is stark," he said. "We're doing all we can."

As Kaseem spoke his eyes lit up, and he gave her his complete attention. As if her every thought mattered.

"With feet in both worlds, I'm just a conduit," Kaseem said. "But I feel a sense of responsibility. Especially since I know Philippe, maybe I can help in ways others can't."

She remembered the military types among the trade delegation at Philippe's house. Broaching the subject indirectly seemed the only way.

Aimée said, "My nephew's going through an army stage," she grinned. "You know boys. You wouldn't know anyone in the military?"

Kaseem returned her smile. "Sorry, I'm just a merchant."

He laid his arm on hers.

"Right now I'm worried about Anaïs," he said, interrupting. "Philippe acts stoic, but you're her friend. Please, I want to help. But I don't even know where she is."

"Makes two of us, Kaseem," she said, glancing up at the café clock. "I've got to get back to work."

He offered her a lift to her office. Why not? He exuded an ease with himself, an elusive quality she didn't see in many men. Except Yves. But Yves was gone, and she liked Kaseem's attention. En route Kaseem said he knew where to get the best falafel in Belleville, so they stopped and ate on the street.

"Call me paranoid, but either Anaïs doesn't like me anymore or something's happened," Kaseem said as they stood munching their overflowing falafels and tossing crumbs to the pigeons. "She's never home, doesn't return calls."

Aimée knew the feeling.

"Did something happen?" Kaseem asked. "Tell me; I don't want to pester."

"Philippe's the one to ask, Kaseem," she said.

At the curb on rue du Louvre, she turned to thank him. Kaseem responded with a lingering *bisou* on both cheeks. Nice. In fact, quite nice. Her cheeks burned all the way up the stairs.

AS SHE opened her office door, the phone was ringing.

"*Allô*," she said, hitting the light switch with her elbow.

"Anaïs's all shaken up," Martine said, her voice low.

"Where is she?" Aimée tossed her bag on the desk, switched her computer on, and threw herself in the chair.

"Philippe's put her in a clinic," Martine said. "And for once he's done the right thing."

Aimée doubted that.

"Look, Martine, Philippe threatened me," she said. "Sicked a gorilla on my tail to make sure I don't investigate further."

"He did *what?*" Martine said, sounding more indignant than surprised.

"And threatened my business," Aimée said, turning toward her oval window. Rain had started to prickle the glass fronting rue du Louvre.

"Philippe's protecting his family," she said.

"Martine, he's hiding something," she said. "He's afraid."

Over the phone Aimée heard Martine sigh.

"Anaïs wants you to find out what he's hiding," Martine said. "Don't stop. I'll talk to him."

"After being beaten and shot at the Cirque d'Hiver and finding no leads, maybe he's right."

"Philippe did that?"

"My top suspect is an Algerian who has links to *plastique*," she said.

"How's that?"

"It's a long story," Aimée said, not wanting to go into a lengthy explanation.

"Condense it and tell me," Martine said.

"Now you sound like an editor," Aimée said.

But she did.

She told Martine about how she'd tried to find the *plastique* source via Samia.

"What about this General?"

"He likes magic, and he's not nice."

"Don't think I'm not concerned," Martine said, "but at least Anaïs is safe."

Aimée felt there was more to what Martine said. "What do you mean, Martine?"

"Now that I'm spending time with Simone," she said. "Maybe I want my own."

Caught off guard, Aimée heard wistfulness in Martine's voice. She'd never heard Martine talk like this. Disturbing.

"*Attends*, Martine, it's worse than having a dog," she said. "You have to make them eat, and the vet bills are much higher."

Martine laughed.

"Martine, Philippe acted strange when he heard about Hamid and the hunger strikers," she said, "Sylvie had one of his flyers."

"So you think there's some connection?" Martine asked.

"We'll find out," Aimée said. "Do you still have your friend in *Sécurité sociale*?"

"He retired," Martine said.

Too bad. She could have found information about the AFL.

"Anaïs mentioned she'd given Philippe an envelope."

"I'll ask him. Look, Aimée, I'm helping take care of Simone. That's all I can do for Anaïs," Martine said, her voice pleading.

"Find out what's got Philippe by the balls, please. You can do this."

"Get the goon off my tail," Aimée said.

"*D'accord,*" Martine agreed. "You're the only one I trust, Aimée. No matter what, I know you'll come through. Please."

By the time Aimée reached the crowded mouth of the Métro, she had a plan. She still hadn't heard from Samia, but there was one person nearby whom she could ask about Eugénie.

THE DEAD HAD IT easy, Bernard thought, shuffling his files together on his office desk.

Dead easy.

But that wasn't true. He wished it were. Outside his window, along the gravel paths, the trees' shadows wavered and lengthened. He tossed the empty pill bottle in the trash—he needed more or he wouldn't sleep.

Visions of his *nounou*, the caramel-faced Berber nursemaid who'd diapered and fed him, flashed in front of him. He saw her gold-toothed smile, warm and welcoming. Her eyes crinkling in laughter when he'd tickle behind her elbow on her soft, dark skin. How she'd save him the first of the season's figs, swollen with seeds, and a fistful of golden white grapes from Lemta. He heard the hoarse notes of her song, one he'd never understood. The song, she'd said, told of the Atlas Mountains near her village, jagged, purple, and massive. And how the *chergui*, the dry and burning east wind, whipped the land and inflamed spirits.

His *nounou* had taught him games the nomad children played in the desert. For hours they'd sit in the cool turquoise-tiled courtyard under the whitewashed arches by the fountain, playing pebble toss and hide the waterskin.

And then the last vision that he'd tried to forget—his *nounou's* head impaled on the fencepost of the Michelin factory, in a row by others accused of sabotage by the *gendarmes*. A cloud of black flies on her slack jaw revealing the gold tooth glinting in the sun, his mother's screams. How his mother made them all run to the harbor. But there were no ships.

How could an illiterate woman who spoke a Berber dialect be

a spy? he'd overheard his mother ask his stepfather over the dinner table years later. Every dinar *nounou* earned, his mother continued, she'd sent to her family in the village.

Roman had said both sides paid and made bad mistakes. "France will reap the dividends in the future," he'd said. For a former soldier that seemed charitable. In fact it was the only charitable thing about Algerians Bernard ever heard him say.

And he'd been right, Bernard thought. He dealt with that dividend in Notre-Dame de la Croix.

TWILIGHT DIMMED THE BELLEVILLE sky, canceling the magenta and orange slashes left from the fading sunset. Aimée sniffed the algae accompanying the biting wind blowing from Canal Saint Martin. The breath of spring she'd felt the other day had disappeared. Passengers erupted from the Métro like particles from a jet stream, erratic and windblown.

The security guard by the Crédit Lyonnais ATM near the Métro steps looked familiar. Very familiar, even with a leashed German shepherd beside him. Most of the guards in Paris were African, but he was of Algerian descent. It had to be Hassan Elymani, the custodian she spoke with on Sylvie/Eugénie's street.

And she had to get him to talk.

She entered the nearest café, rubbing her arms and wishing she'd worn her leather coat. She planned to watch him from a warm and caffeine-laden environment. However, the fogged-up windows blocked her view of the corner. Too bad. Over the conversational hum and tinkling of demitasse spoons, she ordered two *café-crèmes* to go. Back out on the corner of avenue Parmentier, she approached him.

"So this is your second job, Monsieur Elymani," she said, offering him a café. "Do you have a moment to talk?"

"I'm on duty, Mademoiselle," he said, his voice stiff, refusing to return her gaze.

He rubbed his hands together.

She could play this game, too. But it was a shame they were outside and it was so cold.

"And I'm a customer with questions," she said, still holding the cup. "Take it, please."

He ignored her gloved hand with the coffee.

"Don't you have something better to do than hound me?"

"Not right now," she said. "I want to know about Eugénie."

"You talk like an *amateur*!" Elymani snorted.

She certainly felt like one. And wasn't he a rent-a-*flic*?

"The men who blew Sylvie up threatened my friend," Aimée said. "They're after her."

Elymani shook his head. "You've even got the victim's name wrong."

"How's that?" she asked.

He kept silent but rolled his eyes as if she were too stupid to comprehend. His breath frosted in the air.

She pulled out the fax from the *Fichier* in Nantes. "According to this the body from the explosion has been identified as Sylvie Coudray."

"Eh," he said, then shrugged. "Call her what you want."

His remark disturbed her. Elymani had made a kind of sense, since it seemed to her the dead woman had a dual persona. Aimée popped the lid and sipped her café. The hot, sweet jolt burned the roof of her mouth.

"What time's your shift over?"

"None of your business," Elymani snapped.

A tall man tapped Elymani on the shoulder. The man's chiseled dark face shone in the sodium streetlight.

"Go make up with your lady friend, Hassan, and be nice," he said, with a West African accent. He winked at Aimée. "I don't mind starting a few minutes early, eh, *camarade*."

Elymani shifted in his work boots. "Beni, that wouldn't be fair."

The German shepherd growled, but the new man, BENI ANOUR labeled on his shirt, took the dog's leash.

"You crazy, *camarade*?" Beni said to Elymani, grinning. He eyed Aimée up and down. "A real woman and your shift's over, no one in your dormitory waitin' for ya! Has life been this sweet to ya in a while?"

Poor Elymani, faced with his manhood in question or her interrogation, stood mute and uncomfortable. Aimée heard the click of worry beads in his pocket.

"Look, Hassan, let's have coffee and walk to the boulevard, please," Aimée said, her voice low, crooking her arm under his.

"*Allez-y.*" Beni grinned. "Only Allah knows what she sees in you. Make some time before she wakes up, eh?"

ELYMANI ACCEPTED the café, his mouth tight. Halfway down avenue Parmentier they turned into narrow rue Tesson.

He shook her arm off and glared at her. But there was fear in his eyes.

"I work hard, mind my own business," Elymani said, his voice cracking. "Yet you step in and make my life . . ." he stopped searching for the word.

"*Compliqué?*" she said. "My intention isn't to get you in trouble."

"I have to take care of my father. Last month he got injured on the job site," he said, his voice different. "Look," he said, almost pleading, "My family in Oran relies on me."

Elymani's eyes were large with fear.

"We're having a private conversation. No one will know," she said. "I promise."

"The *Maghrébins*," he said, scanning the deserted street, "they know."

Aimée's stomach fluttered with apprehension, but she shook her head. "You can't be sure, now can you, Hassan?" She went on before he could answer. "Someone was blown up, you saw something, and you're nervous. Anyone would be."

He looked down, scraping the sides of his muddy boots on the cobbles.

"They'll know soon enough," he said.

"How?"

Elymani took a sip of café, sighed, then gestured toward the building opposite. Cracked plaster facades, scrolled grills fronting tall windows, and black grime in almost a trompe l'oeil design covered the ground floor of a once exquisite Haussmann-style apartment. Now the windows were cinderblocked and a *permis à démolir* sign hung above the massive doors covered with graffiti.

"In the back courtyard of that building," he said, "they run a makeover business."

She rubbed her arms again in the biting chill. What did Elymani mean?

"Makeover?" she asked.

"Say your *permis de conduire* was revoked. You visit with a roll of francs, *et voilà*, the *Maghrébins* furnish you with a new driver's license," he said. "At least they used to. They moved on."

So Elymani fed her information, not current but true.

The warrens of old Belleville, honeycombed by courtyards, passages, and stone cellars in deserted buildings held the *Maghrébin* network. At least that's what she figured from Elymani's conversational pirouette. And that could be how Sylvie had gotten ID as Eugénie. To open a bank account, she needed ID.

"So would you say they live in the housing projects?" she asked, lifting her eyes toward the tall concrete buildings a block away. "But run their business where they won't be disturbed?"

He nodded. "They find a place, maybe a building ready to be torn down or renovated. The rent's cheap. Full of Yugoslavs, Hindus, or retired people who don't ask questions. The tenants ignore who goes in and out, until problems erupt over turf or money. Things get noisy. Then the *Maghrébins* move on."

"So you're saying Eugénie was involved in this?"

A tidy hypothesis, even plausible, but how would it fit Sylvie's murder—even if they'd furnished her with a new identity?

"For good reasons, I keep my nose out of it," he said. "Those *hittistes* want easy money, a nice life. But in the end life reckons with them."

Elymani had his own survival code.

"You better be careful," he said. "You're being watched."

"By whom?"

"Look, my jobs are on the street. All I do is listen and keep my eyes down. I don't want to know what goes on." His eyes darted down the street. "What I really want to do is sleep for a week. *Alors*, the foyer is noisy, my mattress is lumpy, and I miss my wife." He shrugged. "When my papers come through I'll bring her over."

"What did you hear about Eugénie?" Aimée said, stamping her feet in the cold, wishing she had a cigarette.

"My next job starts in a few hours," Elymani said, turning to walk away. "*Merci* for the café."

"Are you a lookout or do they pay you to keep your mouth shut?"

He stiffened.

"My family would be here if I did that," he said his voice low with anger. "But dirty money brings no honor or peace."

"My friend's in danger, and now they're after me," she said. "Don't you understand? Tell me what you saw, Elymani, then I'll leave you alone."

"All I know is that Eugénie used the place. She lived somewhere else. Sometimes Dédé dropped by."

"Who's Dédé?" Aimée asked, forgetting how ice-like the air had become.

"An old-fashioned *mec* who's got a finger in every pot," he said. "Like a *giclée*, a fine ink spray coating the surface—know what I mean?"

She wasn't sure but figured Dédé bent with the wind.

"Where can I find him?"

"Café la Vielleuse." He turned toward the streetlight. "Now, leave me alone."

YOUSSEFA BOUGHT HAIR DYE at the Casino market around the corner from the apartment. Behind her chador it was as if she were invisible. But she had to be careful; few women in chadors frequented this kind of shop.

In the twenty-franc bargain bin on boulevard Belleville she found a black denim coat. Back at the apartment, she mended the broken crutches she'd found discarded in the trash.

At the bathroom sink, she read the instructions. But when her scalp started burning, she realized the chemicals had been on too long: Her hair had turned orange. Bleach was bleach, she'd thought. She did it again. In the end, when she looked in the mirror, she'd done a good job by accident. She'd fit in with the trendy crowd at Café Charbon, who sported the same white-hair, black-roots look.

Youssefa felt a measure of relief. No one paid attention to a woman in a chador or a fashionable type with a broken leg. Then the sobering thought hit her that if Eugénie'd had another identity, it hadn't helped her.

In the church Zdanine had agreed to help her. But first, he'd said, he wanted to see the photos. He'd seemed eager when she told him why she had to speak with Hamid. After Zdanine saw them, he'd acted uninterested but promised to try and get her five minutes with Hamid.

Youssefa finished her prayers, rolled up her prayer mat, and felt ready. She headed toward the church, hoping Zdanine had paved the way.

Saturday Night

AIMÉE STARED AT THE mirror to the left of the bar, cracked in four or five places, in crowded Café la Vielleuse. Painted on the mirror was a faded image of a woman holding a *vielleuse*, an old-fashioned hurdy-gurdy. The woman's blue puff-sleeved blouse and white tie bespoke turn-of-the-century fashion. The timeworn burnished wood, mosaic floor, and stumpy bar competed with seventies modernizations in the front. Café la Vielleuse straddled the broad boulevard de Belleville and the uphill, two-lane rue de Belleville, choked with buses, cars, and hurrying pedestrians.

"There must be a story behind that," she said in a conversational tone, smiling to the busy waiter behind the counter.

He nodded and stuck his pencil behind his ear, then flicked the milk steamer into high gear, filling the café with a muffled whining. Then a slow hiss as the milk frothed.

"The manager, Dédé, would know," he said.

"Have I missed Dédé?"

"He's in back. *Dédé!*" the waiter yelled over the noise.

A stocky man sat behind a large adding machine at the rear, picking his nose. The machine droned continuously, spitting out a roll of adding tape. "*Merde!*" he barked, giving the machine a shove and switching it off.

"The mademoiselle has questions about *La Vielleuse*," the waiter said, jerking his thumb at Aimée.

Dédé, a squat fireplug of a man who was a head shorter than Aimée, fluffed his thinning hair as he walked toward her. His cropped suit jacket didn't meet his checked trousers. He wore pointed-toed heeled boots.

"*Tiens*, there's quite a story to that," he said, then extended his hand to shake hers.

Aimée dropped her purse on the floor, "*Je m'excuse*," she said, quickly stooping to pick it up. The linoleum was littered with sugar-cube wrappers, cigarette butts, and lottery stubs. But anything was better than shaking Dédé's hand!

When she stood up, Dédé lit a cigarette, set down his gold lighter, and leaned on the zinc counter. She smelled wine on his breath. "In 1914 *les Allemands* encamped at Fontainebleu. Their cannon flattened the shop next door and shattered *la vielleuse, comme ça*," Dédé said. "We left her like that so people would remember."

Outside on rue de Belleville, Chinese children, a heavy-set Arab woman, and Jews in yarmulkes thronged the sidewalk. Gawking at something. Aimée wondered what drew their attention. Then she saw a figure on stilts juggling what looked like bowling pins.

"Rumor has it that the Germans' big gun got pulled back for duty on the front," Dédé said, fingering a soccer ball on the end of a keychain, "and that saved Paris from bombing."

"Lots of history here." Aimée kept a smile on her face, her tone neutral. She figured she'd better buy him a drink.

"Would you like a drink?"

"I wouldn't mind a *bière lambic*, Belgian style."

"Make that two," she said.

Dédé smiled and snapped his fingers. Every so often he jangled the keychain, as though he needed to know it was still there. Aimée wondered if he'd tell her about Edith Piaf.

She didn't have long to wait. As the froth-topped glasses of beer appeared, Dédé recounted the "Sparrow's" birth on the steps of 72 rue de Belleville. He said a plaque now proclaimed: EDITH PIAF SANG FIRST ON THE STREETS OF BELLEVILLE. MUCH LATER HER SONGS TRAVERSED THE BOULEVARDS OF THE WORLD.

A nice way to put it, she thought.

"To tell the truth, Piaf's mother made it to Hospital Tenon, behind Gambetta," Dédé said. "But the other makes a better story."

Dédé had a point. Aimée sipped the *bière lambic* letting the toasty hops mingle with the sweetness of raspberry.

Not bad.

She noticed, as they stood at the counter and Dédé recounted the story, how he'd nod to patrons, send a wink across the café, or raise a hand in greeting. He never broke his conversational thread or lost her attention. Or missed noticing a spilled glass or conveying a sharp glance to a waiter who hadn't noticed a patron ready to pay the bill. Elymani's description, the slick *giclée* type, came to her mind.

"My old boss told me that Piaf sang out front, but then so many did in those days," Dédé shrugged. "Truth to tell, she wasn't anything special until her cabaret-owner boyfriend was killed and the *police judiciare* hauled her in for questioning. Brought her major publicity."

He grinned.

"Things haven't changed, eh?" Aimée said. "People get famous any way they can."

"Belleville was different then, all *populaire*, working class. The *populaire* worked hard, played hard," he winked, draining his glass. "My papa inspected rail lines, and my mama shoved a vegetable barrow in the market. So I say I grew up in between the market and the tracks." He let out a bark of laughter and palmed his empty glass. "Raised on this like mother's milk."

Several of the staff behind the counter joined his laughter. To Aimée the guffaws sounded brittle and forced.

"*Encore, s'il vous plaît,*" she said, realizing she'd need to keep buying to hold Dédé's mouth open. Dédé seemed to relish portraying himself as a *populaire* descendant. And he probably drank all day, nourishing his memories. But he stayed razor sharp and seemed to make it his business to nurse acquaintances, know people. She wondered how he knew Eugénie.

"They say Piaf never stopped, had the energy of a humming-bird," Dédé continued as he raised his *bière*. "*Salut.*"

Aimée saw her opening.

"My friend Eugénie, who lives right near here, is just like that," Aimée said, nodding. "Sometimes it's tiring to be around her."

Dédé sipped his *bière*. His eyes had narrowed. He didn't respond.

Maybe he was used to doing all the talking, or maybe he didn't like how she'd turned the conversation. A chirping noise sounded in his pocket, and he plucked out his cell phone. Red and compact, a new Nokia. He answered, mumbled something Aimée couldn't hear, clicked it off, and slipped it back in his pocket.

"Eugénie's got a place on rue Jean Moinon," Aimée said, smiling. "*Bien sûr* you probably know her, Eugénie Grandet."

"We're the busiest café on the boulevard. There are so many people," Dédé said. His small dark eyes crinkled as he threw up his arms, revealing a gold watch and a thick rose-gold chain circling his wrist.

"*Tiens*, Dédé, be honest! You know everyone who comes in here," the young waiter piped, while he rinsed glasses and dried them.

If he'd meant to curry points with Dédé, Aimée figured the effect had been the opposite.

"Unfortunately I can't put a face to every name," Dédé said, his tone now self-deprecating. "But I make sure things run smoothly and all our clients feel at home, eh—that's my job! Thank you for the drinks, next time it's my round." He winked, giving her an oily smile. "Now if you'll—"

She had to stop him before he bolted.

"You're too humble," Aimée said. She laid her hand firmly on his wrist, covered with wiry black hairs, to hold him. "Eugénie's got short hair, like mine, only bright red."

"The one in the tight overalls," the waiter said. "She comes here—"

Dédé shot him a look that shut him up.

"Mes enfants," Dédé gave a loud chuckle, squeezed Aimée's hand with his, then removed it. "I can't keep up with you kids. Meanwhile I've got to check on the unloading. Pascal, I need your help." He gestured to the young waiter, and with the ease of a lizard removed himself.

She wanted to disinfect her hands.

But as she glanced down her eye caught a slim lighter, a luminescent pearl set on it. No ordinary pearl.

A Biwa pearl.

And Dédé had forgotten it, but then she figured it hadn't been his to forget.

She palmed the lighter, small and expensive, certain it belonged to Eugénie/Sylvie.

She must have rattled Dédé's cage for him to forget this. But he'd remember soon. She threw fifty francs on the counter and was gone.

IN THE office, René passed her the latest fax from the EDF. "We're in the hurry-up-and-wait mode," he said.

Aimée read the fax stating that the EDF had brought Leduc Detective's security system proposal under review.

"But they haven't said no."

"I'm buying lottery tickets," René said. "Could be quicker."

She told René about the conversation at Café la Vielleuse.

"So Dédé knows more than he's telling," René said.

"A lot more," she said. "Look at this, Dédé forgot it on the counter."

She put the lighter into René's stubby hand. He turned it over in his palm, feeling the bumpy pearl. "This doesn't look like a man's lighter."

"I'd be surprised if it was," she said.

"Dédé's got a nice little Nokia phone," Aimée said. "They're not the encrypted cell phones, are they?"

"Not yet. Those work wonderfully for monitoring transmissions!" René's eyes widened. "And they have such clear reception. Nice bandwidth too!"

His face gleamed with excitement.

"If you're going to follow him," René said, sliding a laptop in his case, "count me in."

"Glad for the company," she said.

Sunday Midafternoon

AIMÉE STOOD IN THE Vietnamese jewelry shop window fingering twenty-two-karat rose-gold chains and watching Dédé. He'd paused outside Café la Vielleuse, watching the traffic as he buttoned a long mohair overcoat, then turned up his collar.

At a nearby *tabac*, its torn awning hiding her view, he chatted with the shopkeeper. After a minute, Dédé went inside but the shopkeeper, his sleeves rolled up, remained outside, watching the pedestrians. She left the jewelry store and stepped onto the crowded sidewalk.

A few minutes later Dédé exited, patted the man's shoulder, then walked at a fast clip up steep rue de Belleville. He passed Cour Lesage, then turned right into rue Julian Lacroix.

Aimée's dark glasses and Gucci scarf covered the headset she wore. In her gray raincoat pocket was the power pack for the walkie-talkie she spoke to René with. Following Dédé proved a challenge. He'd stop frequently, shaking hands or nodding to men on the street. She'd pause and look down into her bag or peer at the nameplates on grimy apartment doors.

Most of the men were *beurs*. By the look of it young and unemployed. From open windows came aromatic smells—spices and oil, laced by orange blossom and the refuse in the street. She kept in touch with René as he monitored the bandwidths in the area.

"Dédé's on the phone, I can see," she said.

"I've got his bandwidth," René said.

She heard clicks, a buzzing, then Dédé's voice in short spurts saying, "Nervous, no amateur . . . emptied the flat . . . asking questions . . . Eugénie . . . move everything. General . . . get Muktar."

"René, he's turned off rue du Sénégal," she said.

Dédé's boots clicked in the distance.

"I see him," René said. "I'm below the synagogue on rue Pali Kao. He's moving fast now."

By the time Aimée made it to the corner, René appeared.

"Did you lose him?" she asked.

Dédé reminded her of a rat. A fat one.

"He evaporated," René said. "But the block isn't long. Let's go."

New angular buildings were nestled between old decrepit ones on the hilly cobbled street. Timber supports braced their buckled walls. She saw evidence of habitation in the lines of wash and rusted pots of geraniums, despite the walls appearing in a state of semicollapse.

"Don't be offended," René's eyes twinkled. "It's better if he thinks you're an amateur. Shall we try this one?" He gestured toward the oldest building, rotten beams propping up damp walls. Parts of the courtyard had been torn up, bald stones, plaster, and wood laths strewn.

"Do you know something I don't?"

"He went in there," René said.

She heard footsteps. Apprehensive, she motioned him back. Quickly they ducked into an arched doorway.

Dédé whipped past them. Aimée held her breath, counting the beads of dew on a rusty door knocker. His heels echoed off the peeling walls. They waited a few minutes before emerging into the courtyard.

"Guess I should see what he doesn't want me to," she said.

René stood watch as Aimée padded to the rear. She passed an upturned metal chair, its legs pointing skyward. Turning right, she followed a wet tunnel-like passage to a slant of gray light. A paint-chipped stairwell led to the next floor. The only sound was the drip of rain from a rotted metal gutter onto the cracked concrete.

On the right was a faded green door partially visible under the stairs. Then she saw the sign.

A dark blue handprint was stamped above the doorframe. Like in Samia's building.

Excited, she looked around and listened. Only the plop of raindrops and in the distance, a muffled radio talk show.

She pulled the Beretta from her black jeans and slipped it into her coat pocket. Thinking fast, she came up with a pretext to get inside.

"Dédé," she said, even though she knew he'd gone. "Sorry I'm late."

No answer. She leaned forward on her toes, put her ear to the door. Nothing. She touched the wood, and it creaked open. Hadn't Elymani said the *Maghrébins* used places like this?

A musty smell greeted her. The small, low-ceilinged apartment looked as if homeless people camped in it. Soggy sleeping bags emitted a reek of mildew; rags and papers littered the floor. Torn dark green plastic bags, covering the open window, fluttered.

She paused, wondering about Dédé's purpose in coming here. He hadn't stayed long. The floor was tracked by many dirty footsteps. Had it been a *Maghrébin* haven of operation? Had Dédé left because they'd moved on?

She tiptoed over a phone book and tripped, catching herself on an armoire that groaned dangerously. The slender wooden handle came off in her hand. Sooty and full of splinters, it stung her scarred palm.

She almost didn't notice the fat *Bottin Administratif* government directory on the warped linoleum floor. What a strange thing, she thought. Someone would need a handcart to carry that heavy volume.

She found her penlight and shined it along the floor. Nothing but dried-up yogurt cartons. But there wasn't the film of dust or layer of dirt she'd expect if the place had been deserted. By the old tiled fireplace sat an ancient coal bin. She shoved it aside with her boot; underneath lay a wooden trap door to the coal cellar. She pulled the worm-holed top up, shone her penlight around.

Cold, dead, empty space.

She checked the mattress in the back room, finding dried rat turds. Flakes of stucco powdered the scuffed floor. On the wall an old calendar with saints' pictures had been turned upside down.

Her walkie-talkie vibrated on her hip. Startled, she switched it on.

"You've got company," René said.

She looked around nervously.

"Whereabouts?"

"Approaching the rear courtyard," René said.

No time to go out the way she came in.

"Dédé?"

"Some *Maghrébins*," René said in a throaty whisper. "Get out of there!"

She pulled a chair to the window, leaned on the sill, kicked the chair. Digging her toes into the wall, she hoisted herself up. She prayed the building held up and she would have somewhere to land.

Outside the window she faced a wall.

A wet dripping wall to nowhere.

Sewer smells clung in the dank crack between buildings. Probably from a leaking toilet somewhere above, sweating rivulets furred by moss. Below that lay packed earth and cracked glass.

No exit.

Blindly she reached out and felt for a ledge.

Nothing.

She let herself back down into the room, her hands trembling.

Where to go?

Voices and footsteps came from the passageway. She spied the trap door, ran and opened it.

She folded herself inside and pulled the door closed. Soot filled her lungs, her legs cramped in that sliver of a space. She could hardly breathe in the frigid cellar. Footsteps pounded heavily over the floor.

She wished she understood Arabic because, from above her, the conversation was clear. They stood right over the wooden door, which creaked and groaned with their weight. To her the clunk and scraping from above sounded as if they were pulling tiles or bricks from the fireplace. Then she realized they might look down in the coal cellar. She scooted as far back in the blackness as she could. As far back as her knotted legs would push her. She wished her hands wouldn't tremble so much; she was afraid to drop her penlight. More footsteps entered the room.

She recognized the words *"Dédé"* "rue Piat," and realized they spoke *verlan*, too. The only word she recognized was *erutiov*, the inverse for *voiture*, car. At least she thought it was.

Every breath she took filled her lungs with a chalky powder. Her throat ached with holding back her cough. She inched her foot out, then leaned her back against the wall. Laboriously she stretched her other leg out into the cramped space. She managed to push her body in the opposite direction along the cold, uneven stones.

The space opened up to a larger cellar. She saw dim outlines of a chute. Above that a rotted metal grille came into view. She hoped it fronted the backstreet.

The conversational pitch carried, but she couldn't make out any meanings. The tone seemed angry, almost confrontational. One voice kept saying *"Insh'allah–bent al haram, insh'allah!"*

And then she remembered that voice. The voice hissing "bent al haram" in her ear before her head got whacked into orbit at the *cirque*.

"René," she whispered into her headset. "Take the stairs to-ward Maison de l'Air in Parc de Belleville. These *mecs* plan to meet Dédé on rue Piat."

"See you there," he said.

A welcome channel of fresh air came from the grille.

If she could just keep going! Sweat beaded her forehead and her knees weakened. She heard the footsteps again.

Above her pinpricks of light fanned from the street. She clutched for something along the slippery wall. The smooth metal chute led up. She climbed, searching for footholds with one foot while bracing the other against the wall.

And then her toe slipped, and she fell onto something hard and wooden, banging her knee. Above her the footsteps stopped. Had they heard?

She had to get out of there.

Trying again, perspiring and pulling herself up, she reached the grille. She straddled the chute's entrance, but the grille was rusted shut. At least more air came through.

Frustrated, she didn't know what to do; shuffling noises came from the apartment.

She kicked the metal latch with her heel. Nothing budged. She heard a scraping, as if the wooden door was being opened.

She kicked harder until the latch moved.

After two more kicks, she tried the grille. It grated noisily, then fell forward. Welcome fresh air filled her lungs. She grabbed the edge and shimmied through.

Outside she blinked in the light and got to her knees. She realized she'd emerged through an oval window into a crumbling courtyard.

A dark, rotund woman in a multicolored African robe, one shoulder bare, was hanging wash on a line. She stared at Aimée.

"*Je m'excuse,*" Aimée smiled, dusting herself off.

The woman returned the smile and resumed hanging clothes.

"You haven't seen me," Aimée said, placing a hundred francs in her hand. *"D'accord?"*

The woman winked, then waved, as Aimée slipped into rue Julian Lacroix. She headed to open-spaced Parc de Belleville.

Aimée paused inside the entrance by the Resistance *Mémorial aux morts*. Blue, white, and red flowers lay on the engraved slab. Memories didn't die with the victims, she thought, heartened by the fresh bouquet. She scanned the park. A few gardeners tended the beds of tulips on her left.

No *mecs*. No Dédé.

"Where are you, René?" she spoke into her headset, turning up the volume.

René's panting came from the other end.

"Near Terrasse Belvédère," René said. "My binoculars find them heading toward the vineyard, midway between us."

"How many?"

"Two *mecs*, heavy-set," René said.

She inhaled the rain-freshened air scented by damp grassy smells. Except for the gardeners and two women with strollers headed down the hill, no one else came into view. Before the highest point, Terrasse Belvédère, were benches under catalpa trees, near spreading beds of pink and yellow tulips. Vestiges of old Belleville, once dotted by vineyards and waterfalls sourced from subterranean tunnels, were evidenced by fountains and struggling rows of vines.

"Did you get dipped in charcoal?"

"Close enough," she said, brushing her shoulders and rubbing her face. Her fingers came back black. "Still up on your martial arts?"

"At the top of my dojo," he said, pride in his voice. "Got a plan?"

"Something quick and dirty should work."

"You can do the dirty," René said. "I'll do the quick."

"What are they carrying?"

"Gym bags, dark blue," René said.

Of course, she thought. Simple and inconspicuous. Everyone carried them. It gave her pause, thinking of all the foot traffic carrying gym bags along rue de Belleville.

"What are they wearing?"

"Gray tracksuits, not very color coordinated. Let's meet half-way," René said. "I've got an idea, remember those *mecs* in Canal de l'Ourcq?"

"*Alors*, René be careful!" She remembered how creative he'd gotten with his feet.

"Follow my lead," he said.

By the time she reached the second segment of trellised stairs, arched with trailing jasmine, the *mecs* had stopped just ahead of her.

René stood at the top of the stairs blocking the way, his short legs apart. Budding pink-and-white jasmine released a sweet fragrance.

"Fashion police," René said. "I've had a trend alert. Hand over those bags."

The two Algerian *mecs* paused and laughed.

"*Mon petit,*" the bigger *mec* said, looking up at René at the top of the stairs. "Are you lost? Dwarf land is that way."

"Your colors clash," René said, his tone serious.

The *mec* stepped up to swat René. His diamond ring sparkled in the weak sunlight.

Aimée went cold. She recognized that ring, in the shape of a star and half moon, and the hairy paw that went with it, from Cirque d'Hiver.

"Hey, Muktar!" she shouted.

He spun around as René shot a fancy kick to his chin. She heard a loud crack. Then another, as René's boot landed on his shoulder. Muktar twirled, struck the railing, and landed, bumping down the steps. His face etched in permanent surprise.

Aimée settled for some hard rib chops to his partner from behind. Startled, the partner crumpled, then began flailing wildly at Aimée and the jasmine trellis. Aimée ducked. René crosscut a series of punches to his kidneys, causing the *mec* to wail in pain. René stepped forward, then pushed him over.

It was easy after that to roll him down the stairs to midway in the path. At that point neither one of the them felt a thing and wouldn't for a while. Aimée and René tugged them both behind the dark green bench, covering them over with vines.

"Sorry," René grinned, moving the gravel aside with his shoe. "I had to improvise the first part."

She looked up. "We've got new company." Her heart raced. "Dédé's brought more gorillas."

MUSTAFA HAMID WIPED AT the spittle on his chin. But there was none. He must have closed his eyes. They burned, and his nose felt dry, his mouth parched. Thoughts blurred, and he felt so weak. So tired.

He slit the envelope. It took a long time, the white paper ripping and fighting him. And there it was, simple and irrevocable. The long thread back. The summons to his roots.

He'd be damned if he'd give in. The old fight blazed in him again. Human rights had to be fought for, otherwise we're all animals!

Everything he'd spent his life working for—thirty years of it— would go down the *pissoir*.

He stared at the messenger, whom he didn't know.

"No deal," he said, shaking his head.

DÉDÉ'S GAZE REACHED OVER their heads as they shouldered the gym bags. Aimée spun around. Several men who could be Muktar's relatives approached from both directions.

"Dédé," she said. "Who set the car bomb?"

"Let's talk at my place," Dédé said.

The *mecs* moved closer, their eyes locked on her and René as if they were rabbits. Rabbits caught between their crosshairs.

"Crowds make me nervous," René said.

"Me too," Aimée took his arm, edging out from the trellis toward the open grass. Three uniformed CRS, armed with machine guns slung over their chests, were visible through the grilled fence on rue des Couronnes.

Almost a shout away.

"Keep going, René." She and René kept edging over the grass. Large signs proclaimed PELOUSE INTERDITÉ, but she didn't care if she stepped on the grass.

The way the *mecs'* jacket pockets bulged bothered her.

She and René were out in the open; to their left was a wooden playground structure. If only they they could get the attention of the CRS.

"Put those bags down," Dédé said, his chest heaving. Several of his shirt buttons were undone, revealing gold chains.

"Dédé, I asked you a question," she said, ready to pull out her Beretta.

"Try to behave, eh?" Dédé said, his teeth white and smiling. "Let's work out the misunderstanding. Just hand those over. Let's keep this civilized, eh."

"Civilized?" she screamed. "Muktar called me nasty things in Arabic."

The men Dédé summoned had disappeared up the trellised steps. An unreadable look crossed his perspiring face.

"You little *salope!*" Dédé said.

"Little?" she said. "I'm taller than you."

"You're dead," Dédé said, his eyes vacant. "And you've dug a lot of graves next to yours," he added before disappearing.

The CRS headed through the open gates toward the grass.

"Some trouble here?" asked one of the stout-legged CRS.

"Yes, officer," she said. "Thank God you're here."

And she meant it. She wasn't often happy to see the CRS.

BERNARD SPRAWLED AT HIS desk, opening a new pill bottle, the phone on hold to the *interministériel* hot line cradled in his neck. That evening heightened media attention had erupted into a free-for-all when film stars, a rock mogul, and a political observer from *L'évènement* joined the hunger strikers. Channel France 2 demanded access for news coverage inside the church.

Meanwhile Guittard kept the ministry in limbo, back-pedaling on the arrest and roundup order but still not rescinding the eight-hour deadline.

His other phone hadn't stopped ringing. Finally he picked it up.

"*Directeur* Berge, can you speak to speculation as to whether Mustafa Hamid's AFL links to the fundamentalists in Algiers will influence the power struggle with the Algerian military?" The reporter's grating voice continued, not waiting for a response. "Being a pacifist, does Hamid eschew the military's stance in Algiers?"

"Why are you asking me about Algeria?" Bernard asked in surprise. "We're dealing with *sans-papiers*, an internal French immigration issue under *le code civil.* Defining who is a citizen and allowed to stay in France presents no forum for civil unrest in Algeria."

He slammed the phone down. Who had started that rumor?

Bernard put his head down on his desk. How far could this go? Hamid's reputation in all communities over the years was stellar. It could be said that he practiced what he preached more than anyone. He thought back to Hamid, remembering his remark about violence. Was Hamid a pawn? Could this affect Algerian politics?

Even if Bernard cared, what could he do about Algeria anymore? Deep inside, Bernard realized he'd given up long ago.

He'd said good-bye from the crowded ship's deck. He remembered the smoke from the burning medina, the stench from the hanging bodies rotting in the sun on the Esplanade, and the port shaking from the oil-storage-tank explosions. He'd clutched his slain father's watch and held his mother's hand as the sun died over the port of Algiers.

ON THE FLOOR OF René's studio, Aimée and René emptied the gym bag. A Prada purse, sleek and black tumbled out. The perfect match to the Prada shoes she'd found in Eugénie's trash. Not many could afford to throw away Prada shoes with a broken heel.

"ST196" said the cover of a folder. She opened it. Black-and-white photos were stapled together. Shots of dark-skinned Algerian men, in front of a concrete background. Numbers attached by safety pins to their shirts.

But why?

Something bothered her.

"Doesn't this all seem strange to you?"

"In what way?" René asked, as he sliced a large, crusty slab of baguette stuffed with tapenade, slivers of smoked salmon, goat cheese, and ruby tomatoes. He handed one half to Aimée.

"Why keep it in that dump I escaped from?" she said, taking a bite. "Why didn't the boss have it? Why threaten me at the circus?"

"They deal in explosives," René said. "Suppose they're in at the deep end—not used to blackmailing ministers or their mistresses. Let's say it's not Dédé's specialty."

That made sense. She ate looking out his window onto dimly lit rue de la Reynie, which narrowed into a passage to Place Michelet. A man's shaved head, like a thumb, caught the light.

"But I know what you mean," René said, wiping mustard from his goatee.

She kept watching the figure. When the headlamp from a passing motor scooter illuminated his face she recognized Claude, Philippe's goon.

She rolled the fat sandwich in nearby computer paper, stuck it in her pocket, and gathered the photos.

"Hate to eat and run but . . ." she said, buttoning up her black three-quarter-length leather coat. "I'm going to give this to Philippe. See if this will loosen someone's grip on his nuts."

"Succinctly put," René said. "Meanwhile?"

"I'd like to leave gracefully," she grinned, "without any fanfare from that bald *mec* Claude, who's watching the apartment."

"Philippe's thug?"

She nodded, ruffling Miles Davis's furry neck.

"He knows your car, René."

René tossed her a set of keys to his old motor scooter. "Take the underground passage from the basement to my garage."

"Can Miles Davis stay?"

"*Bien sûr,*" René said.

"Mind your manners, furball," she said, slipping the keys into her pocket.

SHE DROVE René's Vespa, an apple green remnant of his Sorbonne days. Passing the curled metal lanterns in Place des Vosges, she saw Claude following her in a small van, his lights visible in her wobbling side view mirror.

Why hadn't Martine spoken to Philippe and gotten Claude off her tail? She gunned up boulevard Richard Lenoir wondering how to get rid of Claude. Where had he been when they'd been cornered by Dédé in Parc de Belleville?

She stayed close behind the green bus traveling up the boulevard. Claude kept a discreet distance, but she realized he was pacing his truck. He probably thought she didn't notice him, the *stupide*! Well she'd make that work to her advantage.

Continuing up boulevard Richard Lenoir, she maintained an unhurried pace until rue Oberkampf, where she jumped the curb. There she zoomed down the wide pedestrian way, which had been paved over Canal Saint Martin. Claude couldn't follow her there, but he could see her until she turned left into rue Crussol, zipping into the warren of narrow streets she remembered behind the Cirque d'Hiver. Streets fronting the *cirque* headed to République or Bastille. She chewed the sandwich, crumbs sprinkling her legs, as she waited in a darkened doorway. Café des Artistes lay dark—Inés had closed. She saw the truck's taillights heading toward République. Feeling it was safe, she shot back over the boulevard to Belleville.

"*MAIS*, I didn't call the SAMU," Jules Denet said, ten minutes later. "I called the *flics*."

Aimée wanted to be sure her and René's theory of two SAMU vans fit. It did.

And make sure Denet recognized Sylvie in the morphed photo. She didn't want to show up at Philippe's and have made a huge blunder.

Jules Denet poured herbal *tisane* into Aimée's cup, a steaming gingery concoction. Blanca perched on the back of his chair, pecking her feathers, bits of plumage wafting onto the floor.

"When did you last see Eugénie?"

He rubbed his unshaved jaw, making a scratchy sound. "Must have been that afternoon—she was hauling trash into the courtyard. Said she was leaving."

"Leaving?"

"The *permis de démolir* was to be posted." Denet offered Blanca an apple slice. Blanca nibbled the white bit, ignoring the green skin. "The building's about to be torn down. Poor Eugénie, she seemed excited."

"How's that, Monsieur Denet?" Aimée said, sipping her tea.

"Things had changed, that's all she said."

"Had you noticed any visitors?"

"You asked me already," he said, stroking Blanca's head. "But there was a truck parked out front a day or so before."

Aimée's antenna went up.

"What kind of truck?"

"Blue, maybe gray. No," Denet shook his head. "Brown."

Frustrated, she gripped the underside of his chrome table, then breathed deeply.

"Any specific reason, Monsieur Denet, that you remembered this truck, a delivery service, a company name, or some kind of logo, perhaps?" Her smile was thin.

"Wings by the letters," he returned her smile. "That's it."

"Do you remember the name?" she asked.

"Like Euro-Photo," he said. "But I'm not sure. Eugénie knew the young man."

"How do you know, Monsieur Denet?" she asked.

"He carried things back and forth," he said. "Seemed funny to be a moving man, I thought."

"In what way?"

"Bad limp," Denet said.

Aimée's mind went back to helpful Gaston. A cold fear coursed through her. Had Gaston led her off track the whole time, sent her to a car bombing, then fed her useless information?

"An older man with a limp, Monsieur Denet?"

Blanca pecked at corn kernels on the coffee table. Denet seemed lost in thought.

She wished he'd answer her.

"Young like you," Denet said. "Dark skin. Funny hair, like yours."

Aimée smiled, relieved, partly because she hated to think herself such a bad judge of character, but also because she liked Gaston.

She filed his information and got on with her purpose in visiting Denet. She pulled out the digital composite René had made, setting it by his teapot.

"Please look at the this, Monsieur Denet."

He looked at the photo, then shook his head.

"Monsieur Denet? Isn't that Eugénie?"

"Leave me alone!" He shook his head violently.

Aimée stood up.

Jules Denet sat unmoving, his head down.

"I'll see myself out, Monsieur," Aimée said.

She slung her leather coat over her arm. The only sound was the dance of Blanca's talons on the glass-topped table.

"Yellow roses. I'd like to send roses," Denet said, his eyes welling with tears.

"That's Eugénie, isn't it?" she said, sitting down.

He nodded. "Could I make a copy of the photo? I'll be sure to give it back," he said, his voice low.

"You keep it, Monsieur," she said.

Blanca had gone to his shoulder and he stroked her absent-mindedly. "Eugénie loved yellow roses. They were her favorite."

"I'll make sure there's a dozen," she said. "You have my word, Monsieur Denet."

Even if I have to pick them myself from the garden at 78 rue du Guignier, she thought as she let herself out and walked to rue Jean Moinon. She remembered those yellow roses. Those had to be Sylvie's roses in Sylvie's house.

"PHILIPPE," SHE said, leaning down and speaking into her cell phone outside Denet's door. "We need to talk."

"What the hell have you done?" he said, his speech slurred.

Taken aback, Aimée paused outside Denet's apartment. She stood in his doorway, keeping alert to movement on rue de Ménilmontant. Her eyes scanned for Claude.

"Where's Anaïs?"

Aimée heard splashes, then a thud. Silence.

"Ça va, Philippe?"

"Leave Anaïs out of this," he said.

"Wasn't Sylvie protecting you?" Aimée said.

"Let me h-h-handle this," Philippe interrupted. "You're trouble—complicating things!"

"*Alors*, you might be in trouble," Aimée said, raising her voice. " 'ST196'—do you understand?"

"Quit meddling." Philippe slammed down the phone.

She had to make him understand. And find out why Sylvie had another persona. Grabbing a wool *foulard* in her bag, she wrapped it around her neck and drove to his house.

By the time she reached Villa Georgina, the de Froissart home lay in darkness. She went up to the side door and knocked.

Silence.

Old metal-framed windows looked onto the garden. A dim light shone from over the blue Aga stove in the kitchen. Peering through the bubbled-glass window, she saw Philippe half-sprawled across the pine kitchen table. Distorted, motionless.

Panic rippled through her. Was he hurt?

She pounded on the door.

No sound. No movement.

She tried all the windows. Finally the farthest metal-framed one jiggled. Grabbing a long twig in the garden, she inserted it and shoved it up again and again until she felt the hasp flip. The window scratched open.

She hitched her coat up, climbed in, and sniffed. Whiskey lay in an amber puddle on the floor. Philippe snored loudly, dead drunk. Relieved, she shook him several times, he sputtered and drooled. His graying hair was matted and plastered on one side of his head.

Philippe had passed out. Frustrated, she wanted to pound him in the head—he'd triggered this whole mess because he couldn't keep his pants zipped.

Or had he?

With Philippe passed out, only Anaïs could tell her—and Anaïs had disappeared.

Aimée searched the kitchen, the phone table in the hallway, Philippe's mahogany-walled study, and every drawer in his desk.

Nothing to indicate where Anaïs could be. She looked under the piled folders on his desk, through ministry directives and business prospectuses.

And then she saw "ST196" labeled on the outside of a brown envelope. Inside were hundreds of small black-and-white photos. Algerian men with number cards safety-pinned to their shirts. Just like the ones in the gym bag.

What did this mean?

She looked closer. Some cards were pinned directly to the skin on their chest. But what got her were the mostly expressionless faces, interspersed by the ones with fear shining from their eyes. Unnerving.

No text. Just the faces.

On the back flap, she saw something written in pencil. Smudged. "Youssef," and a number. Again the same name and phone number.

She went back to the kitchen table where Philippe still snored, dead to the world. Aimée opened the stainless-steel fridge and helped herself to a fresh Badoit. She sucked the bubbly mineral water, then rifled through Philippe's pockets. Stuck in his pants pocket was a receipt from Centre Hôpitalisation d'urgence en psychiatrie Esquiro for Madame Sitbon. Of course, that had to be Anaïs. Sitbon was Anaïs's maiden name!

Aimée recognized the hospital, noted for its *centre de crise*, not far from Père Lachaise on rue Roquette. She chugged more Badoit. Then she propped her card with a scribbled "Call me" near Philippe's curled hand and left.

On the fourth floor of the clinic, Aimée brushed Anaïs's cheek with the back of her hand.

Anaïs's eyes fluttered open.

"It's so good to see a familiar face," Anaïs said, smiling weakly at Aimée.

"Sorry to disturb you."

The private room overlooked the manicured trees on Square de la Roquette. Beside the hospital bed, a monitor beeped, slow and steady.

"How's my Simone?"

Aimée started guiltily—she hadn't checked.

"*Bien*, but missing you," she lied. "Look at these."

She held another photo René had morphed together—of Sylvie with the red wig.

"Sylvie wore wigs," Anaïs said. "Some men like that. Philippe did."

Poor Anaïs.

"There's more to it than that. I'm sorry," Aimée said, controlling her excitement. "But I found some odd photos."

Tears ran down Anaïs's cheeks.

"What's the matter?" Aimée said. She couldn't understand why Anaïs wasn't interested.

"Philippe's changed. He's dead inside."

"He's trying to forget," Aimée shook her head. "*Tiens*, if he were dead inside he wouldn't be drinking himself into a stupor."

"Nothing will be over until the killer . . . ," Anaïs's chest heaved, then the tears spilled down her pale cheeks, "until you catch them. If Sylvie pretended to be someone else, you've got to find out why—what's the reason. Nothing will be over until then. I hired you to find out who murdered Sylvie."

Aimée sighed. "Look, Anaïs, I'm doing my best, but you and Philippe haven't helped me. I've been working in the dark. If you knew about the photos, why didn't you tell me? It's like you gave me half a deck and want me to play cards!"

"The General," Anaïs said, rubbing her wet cheeks.

Aimée's hand tightened on the bed's railing and she leaned forward. "What's that?"

"I remembered . . . someone saying "general," maybe it was Sylvie . . . but then the explosion."

What did that mean? "Did Sylvie say this upstairs in the apartment?"

Anaïs nodded. "Sylvie said terrible things happened in Algeria. Philippe knew about them."

Did it have to do with those photos? she wondered.

"What did Sylvie give you?"

"Some envelope," Anaïs rubbed her eyes.

"The envelope with 'ST196' written on it?"

"Philippe has it."

"Did you see the General?"

Anaïs shook her head.

"Did you hear a voice, a sound?"

"The smell," Anaïs squinted, as if trying to remember could force it to come back.

"What smell?"

"I feel so stupid," Anaïs said. "My brain's so mixed up."

"Which smell, Anaïs?"

"I can't remember," she said. "Philippe says I should recover without worrying about Simone," Anaïs shoulders slumped under her hospital jacket. "Martine's taking Simone to the *école maternelle*, but I want to take her to school and be with her. It's safer for me here, he says, but I want to go home. He's afraid, Aimée. But I don't know why."

"If someone is blackmailing him I've got part of the evidence," she said, trying to get that through Anaïs's skull. "You're safe. He'll come and get you tomorrow."

"Licorice," Anaïs said.

Aimée froze. Her mind went back to the military man chewing licorice at the circus.

"You smelled licorice in Sylvie's apartment?"

But Anaïs's eyes had closed. Little whistles of sleep escaped her lips.

As Aimée walked into the cold Paris night she wished she felt it was true that Anaïs was safe.

Sunday Night

HAMID STARED AT THE torn green-and-white Algerian flag. "Where did this come from?"

"Discord within the AFL mounts. If you don't comply . . ." Walid left the rest unfinished. He pointed at the broken red crescent moon enfolding a star. Walid, another *mullah* in his cause, looked defeated. He shook his head.

Hamid's years of work, the ties he'd established, the movement he'd created—all would be sabotaged if he didn't comply with his enemy. Such a close enemy. The French had no idea.

Hamid gently fitted the sickle-shaped red moon on the green-and-white cloth, then folded the pieces together. If only he could weave his people together so easily.

He nodded at Walid; he couldn't ignore the warning. "I must rinse my mouth; please pass me water."

After he partook from the beaten bronze bowl and washed his face, he prayed, for the first time, that the *sans-papiers* would forgive him.

Late Sunday Night

A<small>IMÉE COULDN'T SLEEP.</small>

From outside her bedroom window came the low hum of a barge, its blue running lights blinking on the Seine. Reflected in her bedroom's mirrored french doors, she saw the dark rooftops of the Marais across the river.

Her laptop screen, perched on her legs as she sat propped up in bed, held a jumble of numbers. Sylvie/Eugenie's Crédit Lyonnais balance.

She'd been trying to make sense of the withdrawals and deposits, but her eyes blurred.

The courtyard, overlooked by her other window, held the pear tree's budding leaves and bird's nests. Miles Davis curled in the bed beside her, growling in his sleep. His white fur chest rose and fell in the midst of an intense dream.

With her other laptop on top of the large medical texts she used as a night table, she'd been online for hours searching for links to the Crédit Lyonnais account. She'd entered the account number, then checked it for links corresponding to other bank accounts, a tedious job. So far she'd tried fifteen banks and found no connections.

The money had to come from somewhere, and she knew Sylvie banked on-line. The Minitel had paved the way for that. She had narrowed her list of banks to those who had client online capabilities. But since all French banks were regulated by the Banque de France, she didn't see how Sylvie could launder or obtain money without its knowledge.

Dejected, she had only two more numbers to check when a

routine thousand-franc deposit responded to her link query. Immediately a series of numbers appeared on her screen.

Of course, this had to be interest paid into the account!

She sat up excitedly, pushing the goose-down duvet to the side. Following the number source to a transit account, she found a thread to the Bank of Commerce Ltd., headquartered in the Channel Islands. A convenient offshore account destination, Aimée thought. Nice and anonymous. Why hadn't she thought of that?

She dug deeper and accessed the Channel Island account. Three large cash infusions had swelled the Bank of Commerce balance since last September. But like the ebb and flow of the tide, as a significant amount was withdrawn another would replace the void. However, the current balance of nearly five million U.S. dollars—or roughly three million pounds sterling—stood out. Aimée gasped. No wonder Sylvie could afford Biwa pearls and to throw away Prada shoes.

Surprise mingled with a feeling of being in over her head. Something smelled very dirty. She scrolled back, checking the deposit amounts over the past twelve months. Several large deposits had brought the amount, at one time, to twenty million dollars.

The phone rang, startling her. Miles Davis snorted awake.

"Aimée," René said, his voice tight with excitement. "Hold on to your laptop."

"Did you find out what I just did?" she asked.

"Sylvie was born in Oran," he said. "That's why the identification from the *Fichier* in Nantes took time."

Surprised, Aimée hit Save on both her laptops, then stroked Miles Davis.

"Bravo, René," she said. "Go on."

"Get this," he said. "Her real name is Eugénie Sylvie Cardet, her family left Algeria at the exodus. She ended up at the Sorbonne, in one of Philippe's classes."

"I'm impressed, René," she said. "Did you crack the *Fichier* code?"

"A few hours ago," he said. "They're a storehouse of information. Seems she joined the Socialist Party then the Arab Student League, which according to my Arab friends on the net later became the AFL."

Aimée grabbed her notebook. She filled the gridblock sheet diagramming Sylvie's connections to Hamid and Philippe.

"So there's her connection to Hamid," she said. "She's known him since the late sixties. Her address is 78 Place du Guignier, right?"

"Fast work, Aimée," René said. "But the most interesting item was her father," René said. "Léon Cardet, a *caporal* with the OAS."

Miles Davis nestled in the crook of her arm, his ears perking up at René's voice. She sat up straighter.

"*Attends*, René, wasn't there a Cardet in the coup to oust de Gaulle?"

"One of many attempted coups." René chuckled. "But you're right, Cardet got caught. Very nasty *mec*."

"So if Sylvie had a father like that and joined Hamid, then became Philippe's mistress, she could have been rebelling against her father and what he stood for," she grew excited. "Sylvie could have been helping the underdog!"

"Exactly," René said. "Seems Cardet and his OAS cronies liked the Canal Saint Martin for body dump-offs in the sixties."

Aimée shivered. She pictured the narrow tree-lined canal, the metal locks, and eddying scum on the surface.

"There're some problems with that theory, René," she said. "Gaston told me that warring Algerian factions dumped bodies there. Those helping the French or not contributing to the FLN got a watery grave."

A pause on the other end.

"Cardet could have played both sides," René said slowly. "Or he used the cover to dispose of OAS targets, attributing them to the FLN."

"Good point," she said. "You could be right." She remembered the grainy photos of Cardet at his trial, a sneering arrogance even on sentencing. "But if Sylvie was helping Hamid, why does she have millions in an offshore account?"

René whistled when she told him what she'd found in the Channel Island account. Miles Davis yelped at the sound.

"Wait a minute," René said. "What if Sylvie received funds in an offshore account in the Channel Islands and passed it to the AFL?"

"Hold on," Aimée paused. "The AFL connection isn't clear," she said, racking her brains to think of what was eluding her. "The AFL seems more of a grassroots, shoestring operation. They address issues of all immigrants, not just those from Algeria."

She stepped into her black leather pants, "René, let me try something. I'll call you back."

"*Bien,*" René said. "I'll dig for more links from the *Fichier.*"

After pulling on her oversize wool sweater, she carried the laptops, individually, to her home office. Her desktop computer held more memory and within thirty minutes, she had all three computers working on projects. Both laptops steadily ran software encryption programs to access the link bank that paid into Sylvie's offshore account.

Aimée sat at the large computer, delving into the AFL's financial source. The only account she located was an AFL business account in the Credit Agricole for less than a quarter of a million.

"AFL'S ACCOUNT IS CHUMP change compared to Sylvie's!" René said thirty minutes later on the phone. His voice rose. "Why don't you talk with Philippe?"

"Believe me, I'm trying," she said.

"Can you hyperlink it over to me?" he asked. "I'd like to try something."

"Be my guest," she said.

Miles Davis growled and pawed at her window frame.

The sun had risen in golden glory over the Seine. Dawn painted the rooftops. Below her window she saw several men in blue jumpsuits with German shepherds along the quai. Her heart raced. They watched her window.

"René, I don't like what's happening outside my window," she said.

"What do you mean?"

"Can you meet me in the office?" she said. "I'm leaving now."

She E-mailed Sylvie's and the AFL's account information to her office, called a taxi, and put her laptop in her bag. She left the lights on and a bowl of food for Miles Davis, put on a black curly wig, and a long raincoat over her leather one. As the taxi pulled up on the curb of quai d'Anjou, she ducked into the taxi's backseat.

SHE WANTED a cigarette desperately. Instead she entered the Pont Marie Métro, slid her ticket into the turnstile, and marched toward the nearest platform. Before the stairs, she pulled off the wig, slipped out of the raincoat, and dumped them in the trash bin.

She joined the early Monday morning commuters filing past her. The voices of panhandlers singing for a handout echoed off the tiled walls.

She sat down on the plastic molded seat, watching and thinking. Were those Elymani's cohorts outside her window or men sent by Philippe?

She leaned against the Métro wall map, the station names erased by the rubbing of countless fingers. A shiny red Selecta vending machine on the platform blocked her view of the other end. But after five minutes she figured she'd lost the men tailing her.

She punched in her office number.

René answered on the first ring.

"You might want to get over here, Aimée," he said.

"I'm doing my best," she said. "What's happened?"

"Things have gotten dicey," he said, his voice low. "Thanks to Philippe."

"What do you mean?"

"There's a big *mec* sitting here who says we're out of compliance."

"Compliance?"

"Some ordinance infraction," René said. "Has to do with the space we rent and the tax we pay."

"Tell me, René," she said. "Does the *mec* have a shaved head and fish eyes?"

"Exactly," René said.

"Tell him our last adjustment should suffice," she said. "Matter of fact, let *me* tell him."

She heard the muffled sound.

"*Allô?*"

"Claude, what's the problem?"

"I represent the tribunal verifying rent according to space and convenience," he said. "Your last *surface corigée* assessment is invalid."

"Not according to their report," Aimée said. "Take it up in the appeals section."

"I already have," he said.

Her reply caught in her throat.

Dédé marched along the opposite Métro platform, his boots echoing off the tiled walls with their giant arching posters. Muktar's clones eased among the commuters. Coming right toward her.

"Claude, this is between Philippe and me," she said, scanning the crowds. "Tell René I might be held up, but I'm on the way."

She clicked off. She sat in the middle of the platform, a few seats taken up by an older woman and high school students. Commuters in business suits clustered around her but would board the next train. Granted, they'd be looking for a black-haired woman first, but Dédé and the other *mecs* knew her face. If she stood up she'd be seen.

Should she rush into a car when it pulled into the station? The ominous bulge in the coat pockets of the two *mecs* weaving toward her made her think they had silencers on their guns. And what did she have? A Beretta in her faux-leopard coat—at the office.

BERNARD PAUSED AT THE massive doors of Notre-Dame de la Croix. Charcoal stubble shadowed his chin, he'd worn the same suit for two days.

This time his entry to the church had been barred. Cameras whirred and flashed, reporters stuck microphones in his face, and news cameras captured the event. Captured every tic and twitch in his face. Uniformed CRS flanked the steps in formation behind him. For once the April sun glared mercilessly, illuminating the square, the protesters, the police, and the reporters. The protesters loudly chanted, "Don't break up families—let them stay!" to drown out the reporters.

Guittard had ordered Bernard to empty the church, put the *sans-papiers* en route to the airport, and escort the rest to the Vincennes detention center if they resisted.

Bernard couldn't really hold Hamid; the man had papers, and so far he'd broken no law. Bernard didn't want any of them bound for prison; they'd become martyrs for the cause and defeat the purpose. Of course Guittard didn't agree.

In the hubbub and turmoil surrounding him Bernard felt curiously detached, as if he hovered cloudlike above, watching the scene unfold.

The bull horn was thrust into his hand. Nedelec, poised and immaculate in a Burberry raincoat, nodded at him. Bernard stared, immobile. He was aware of Nedelec's thin moustache, and the set jaw of the CRS captain.

Bernard opened his mouth. Nothing came out.

Nedelec elbowed him discreetly.

"Monsieur Mustafa Hamid," Bernard began, his mouth dry and

his voice a whisper. "Monsieur Hamid, the authorities have reexamined all the immigration cases." Bernard cleared his throat, spoke louder. "So far they've determined permission to stay will be granted to thirty or forty percent of the *sans-papiers* due to extenuating circumstances. Specifically those married to French citizens or who have children born in France before 1993."

No response.

"I'm very sorry to inform you that under orders from the minister of the interior and in compliance with the laws of France, I must ask you to evacuate the premises."

A heavy silence broken only by the sound of a flag with HUMAN RIGHTS NOT WRONGS crudely written on it, flapping in the wind.

Moments later Bernard cringed as a police ax came down on the church door, splinters flying. The chanting protesters roared. And then the square erupted.

The CRS, attacked by the mob, rushed headlong, billy clubs raised, into the church. Peaceful *sans-papiers* screamed, thinking they were being attacked and prepared to defend themselves. Bernard was flattened against the church wall between a cameraman and his videocam.

"Look what you've done!" the cameraman yelled at him, referring to his smashed equipment.

But the feed was live, and the accusation against Bernard was broadcast across France into millions of homes.

The women and children were handcuffed together and escorted out. As they filed past him, he saw little Akim asleep in his mother's arms. Though her chador-hidden face revealed nothing, the hiss of angry words issuing from her veil needed no translation.

If he wasn't hated before, he certainly was now.

TENSE AND WARY, AIMÉE stood on the Métro platform as the train blared its arrival. She heard the wheels clacking, smelled the burning rubber. She held her leftover newspaper over her face. Neither Dédé nor the *mecs* had spotted her yet. But when the platform emptied, she was afraid.

She realized what she had to do.

As she broke the red glass door on the emergency box with her miniscrewdriver, she screamed, "My baby fell on the tracks," and yanked the switch. Every face turned toward the electric line—the train's brakes screeched and whined, shuddering to a painful, jolting stop. Passengers were thrown against the windows.

The platform passengers looked around, asking, "Where's the baby?" Over the loudspeaker came a recorded message, "Standard procedure allows no train to proceed without Métro personnel clearing the track."

The anxious buzz turned into a disgruntled murmur. She wanted to melt into the crowd. Dédé and the *mecs* trolled the platform, bumping into people taking a good look before excusing themselves. She turned to the men standing near her, in suits, with briefcases and newspapers under their arms. She picked the one with the nicest eyes, wearing a large trenchcoat.

"Pretending you don't remember me?" she said, sliding into the folds of the man's coat and wrapping her arms around him. He wasn't bad looking on closer inspection. And he smelled nice, as if he'd just showered with lavender-olive soap. She put her finger to his lips. "*Shh*, it's our secret."

"Do I know you?" the man asked, a look of happy surprise struggling with suspicion on his face.

"Don't be coy," she said. "I've never forgotten." She pulled his head down, shielding herself from view and started kissing him. She kept her eyes open, scanning the platform. Another of Dédé's *mecs* had stopped by her elbow.

"You're even better than I remember," she breathed into the man's ear, pulling his arms around her, and guiding him back into the tiled Métro wall. She saw the wedding band on his finger. "Let me enjoy it once more: Your wife will never know."

"You know, you've got the wrong person . . . ," he murmured. But he didn't pull away.

She pulled him tighter, edging toward the exit stairs, "I've heard that before. Play along with me, okay?"

His eyes crinkled in amusement. "Who said anything about stopping?"

"I'm going to slip away," she said, walking backwards up the stairs. "*Merci* for your help."

"Anytime," he grinned, digging in his pocket for a business card.

But she'd gone.

TWENTY MINUTES later Aimée slammed her office door.

Startled, René dropped the book he was reading.

"You just missed Claude," he said, shaking his head. "That man has unsettling eyes."

She picked René's book up off the floor. "Reading again?" she asked, looking at the title, *Life with Picasso*, by Françoise Gilot.

"Picasso appeared and disappeared in her life," René said. "A stormy relationship."

Aimée gave a wry smile.

"Like Yves," she nodded. "Too bad he's not around long enough for the stormy."

She threw off her wet clothes and kicked the radiator to life. In the armoire she found wool tights, black skirt, ankle boots, and a striped silver ski parka to wear over a black sweater.

Back in the office she opened her bag, thrust some disks into René's hand, and pulled out her laptop. Logging on, she glanced at the clock.

"Let's get to work," she said. "We may not have much time."

"Are we catching a plane?"

"Dédé's getting a little too close for comfort," she said. She told him about the men watching her apartment and the Métro.

René climbed into his orthopedic chair, then logged onto his terminal. Aimée's phone started beeping.

"Let me give you a proper battery, Aimée," he said, handing her a new one. "Try that."

"My phone has been messed up," she said. "My watch, too. Ever since the EDF."

He set the battery on her desk.

"Right now," she said, "I want to know why Sylvie dealt with Dédé."

"Figure this. If Dédé knows everybody in Belleville," René said, "he might be the one people use to reach the *Maghrébin* network."

"Good point," she said. "But first we've got some bank tunneling to do."

By the time she'd checked the links from Sylvie's Channel Island bank, she'd found the money transfers.

"Look René, the deposits come from the Bank of Algiers," she said, excited. "Several million each time."

René pulled up the Bank of Algiers account on his screen then clicked away. "I found them," he pointed. "Here, wire transfers come from AlNwar Enterprises."

Aimée peered at his screen, seeing a long list of wire transfers. She sat back down; something familiar tugged at her.

"Why would AlNwar Enterprises pass amounts via the Bank

of Algiers to a Channel Island account in Eugénie Grandet's name," Aimée said. She swiveled her chair to the office terminal and logged on.

"Smells bad to me," René said.

"Guess it's time to find out about AlNwar."

After she dug into an Arab net server, she'd discovered the company's charter and by-laws of incorporation, required by the French government for any contract.

Nothing illegal in that.

Then it hit her. The night of the explosion. Philippe introduced her to Kaseem Nwar. Kaseem had been with Olivier Guittard, both intent on Philippe's passing some project and humanitarian mission. She remembered Philippe's strained reaction and how he got her out of there quickly. Then she'd seen him again in the café in Belleville. Was Kaseem Nwar part of AlNwar?

She accessed the company records. Downloading took time.

Aimée thought back to those photos of people with numbers pinned to them. All Algerian.

Curious, on her office computer she started accessing information about AlNwar while René concentrated on Philippe de Froissart's account. She kept digging for the company structure, list of shareholders and employees. When she found them, she stood up and whistled.

"Kaseem Nwar's the director," she said. "Appears he's into nepotism."

"Why?"

"Most of the employees and shareholders are Nwars, too."

"What kind of firm?" René asked. "Heavy machinery or something to do with oil?"

She shook her head.

"Jewelry importer," she said. Odd. "How does that fit with a project in connection with humanitarian aid?"

"Pearls for the masses?"

"That's it, René," she said, grabbing his arm excitedly. "Pearls! The Lake Biwa pearl. I keep saying you're a genius. And you are."

He grinned. "I'm never one to refuse a compliment, but where does that fit?"

"I don't know yet, but I'm getting there," she said, unable to sit down. She paced back and forth.

It was all there. Somehow. She had to piece it together. Figure out where the odd bits went. One big piece was Mustafa Hamid and the AFL; she felt they were part of it. In some way they belonged.

"AlNwar sent huge sums to Sylvie," she said. "Why? Were they bribes for Philippe so contracts went AlNwar's way?"

"But a jewelry business?" René asked. "Unless AlNwar fronts another kind of company?"

She sat back down and searched AlNwar's records. Two firms were listed as subsidiaries; NadraCo and AtraAl Inc.

But she could find nothing more.

René couldn't break into the Banque de France. They were blocked at every turn.

He stood up and stretched.

"Aimée, if the bribes came in, they're hidden," René said, sucking air through his lips. "Takes time to unearth them. All my tools sit in my database at home."

René left, promising to call her when he found anything.

Frustrated, she knew more information existed. How to find it was the problem.

Start simple. Go with what she knew.

She logged on to the Ministry of Defense. Using a secure government password, one of many René kept current, courtesy of his ever-changing connections, she found a list of ministry-funded projects. Then she refined her search to projects under funding consideration.

Hundreds.

She took a breath and narrowed her topic to those involving Algeria. The list slimmed down considerably. While the list printed out, she sat down at René's desk.

On his terminal she accessed the *National Fichier* via René's connection, because if the government didn't catch you when you were born, they always caught up when you checked out.

She knew that Algeria, at the time of Mustafa Hamid and his brother Sidi's birth, was regarded by France as more than a colony. Even more than an extension of France across the Mediterranean—a department. However, this wasn't reckoned with in actual voting terms. Unable to vote, Algerians belonged to the République like a member of the wedding but never the bride.

If Hamid or Sidi emigrated to France, she figured, they would probably have paid some application fee, surcharge, or tax.

In Hamid's case she found his *carte bancaire* via his date of birth and *Sécurité sociale*. No names were listed as next of kin, only a Sidi, H., as father, and Sidi, S., for mother, both entered as deceased. She entered Djeloul Sidi's name. His wife's maiden name, El Hechiri, appeared.

Aimée's eyes widened as she saw a cross reference to Kaseem Nwar. That seemed odd.

Further on, records indicated that El Hechiri had been married to Kaseem Nwar from 1968 to 1979. Aimée peered closer, then scrolled back. Sidi's records showed he'd been married to El Hechiri during 1968–1979, the same years.

Aimée sat back and whistled. He'd changed his name, and the computer hadn't caught it—just cross-referenced it.

She remembered him appearing in the café, telling her how he'd brought food to the *sans-papiers*—why hadn't he just said, "I saw my brother."

Come to think of it, why hadn't he admitted he sent Sylvie millions of francs and Lake Biwa pearls? But then she hadn't asked him, either.

She scanned the Algerian project list, running her fingers over the names, ticking them off until she found a name that struck her.

Taking the list to her wall map of Algeria, she followed the course of the Atlas Mountains and pinpointed the area south of Oran. Once a rebel *fellagha* stronghold against the French, the area had then become a munitions-dump wasteland, now declared off limits by the military.

Staggered, she sat down. It was hard for her to believe what she'd discovered.

She knew what she had to do.

Her charged phone signaled several voice mail messages. She tried not to hope, wondering if Yves had left her a message. But when she listened, all three were from the same person.

"Aimée," Samia's voice, high, shallow-breathing. "Pick up!"

Again the same message. Samia's voice rising, sounding frantic.

The last message just a phone number, mumbled quickly. Samia. Very frightened.

Aimée listened to the number several times to make sure she'd written it correctly. Had Samia come through with the explosives connection? And should she believe her? The last time she had, Aimée had been shot.

Aimée hit the call-back function. A woman answered, saying this was a pay phone in rue des Amandiers, but if Aimée would like to buy Ecstasy she'd give her a good price.

She hung up and dialed the number Samia had left.

"*Oui,*" a voice answered after six rings.

"Samia gave me this number," she said, keeping it vague.

A pause. "Who is this?"

"Aimée. Is Samia there?"

Another long pause. "I expected her by now."

"I'd like to come over."

"Call back."

The phone went dead.

No one answered on her next three tries.

Had Samia given her the number to the explosives? She recognized the phone number. In her bag she checked the folder—"Youssef" was written above the matching phone number. Her heart raced. And she remembered Denet's words. On her minitel she searched under EuroPhoto. She found the same number with an address for a lab on rue de Ménilmontant. So now she knew that they connected.

She redialed the number. The same voice answered.

"Please don't hang up, listen to me," she said. "I think you have something I want to see."

"Who are you?" the voice said.

"I found your name in the 'ST196' folder," she said. "Did you take the photos?"

The phone slammed down.

She stuck the Beretta in her waistband, pulled on her gloves and long wool scarf.

In the hallway she climbed down the back fire escape and made her way to the Métro.

EUROPHOTO'S GRIMY lab entrance stood in the rear of a courtyard filled with trucks and vans.

Inside Aimée leaned on the Formica counter. She smelled the acidic photographic chemicals and heard the chomp of print machines. On the office walls hung huge photos of white marble mosques and shots of sugar-sand beaches with sapphire slivers of the Mediterranean.

Through an open grime-stained window, Aimée noticed a company van pulling into the courtyard.

"Dropping an order off?" asked a smiling dark-eyed young woman, her head covered by a scarf. From behind the counter she passed an order form toward Aimée.

Aimée returned her smile.

"Actually I need to talk with Youssef about some processing," she said. "Does he have a moment?"

She backed up, shaking her head. "There's no Youssef here."

"But I talked with someone—"

"Orders come in all the time," the woman said, turning away. "You must have misunderstood."

This woman was scared, Aimée thought, hiding something.

"Yes, of course, you're right," she said, thinking fast, "I'm terrible with names. A man helped me, he seemed about my age. He limped."

Loud buzzing erupted from the back of the lab. Lights blinked green. "You're in the wrong lab, I think," the woman said, gesturing toward the rear. "Try the one on rue de Belleville."

The woman headed quickly toward the back.

"But please, can't you—"

"Excuse me," the woman said, her mouth tight and compressed. "I've got a production schedule to meet."

By the time Aimée made her way toward the back near the van, she'd come up with a plan. She jiggled the van door open, grabbed some large boxes of photographic papers, then entered the back.

Loud arguing in Arabic reached her ears. The scarf-clad woman stood by another stocky woman, pointing toward the front counter. In front of Aimée a massive printing machine spat out large-format posters, shooting them onto a spinning wheel. Aimée knew she had to move quickly. The women would throw her out before she found Youssef.

Men filled cartons as the posters came off the wheel. None of them sported spiky hair like Denet had described, so she kept going. Mounting the spiral staircase in back, leading to more of the lab, she discovered a warren of cluttered offices.

"Youssef's supposed to check this order," she mumbled to an older man busy working an ancient adding machine.

"Let me see," he said, pushing his glasses up his forehead.

Aimée leaned the carton on the edge of his desk, making a show of how heavy it was.

The man's phone rang; he picked it up and immediately began punching the adding machine.

"Sorry, but I've got more deliveries," she said, tapping her nails on the box.

He looked up, then motioned Aimée toward a long hallway.

"Down there. I don't recognize the order," he said. "Check with me on your way out."

Aimée shot ahead before he changed his mind. She figured that this nineteenth-century building joined apartments in the back. Below her the floor vibrated from the machines.

After checking four dusty offices in the next wing, she saw a figure hunched over a photo layout, marking shots with red pen.

"Youssef?" she asked, setting down the cartons.

A young short-haired woman in her mid-twenties looked up, her eyes unsure.

"I'm Youssefa," she said. "What do you need?"

Now it made sense. No wonder the women downstairs had told her there was no Youssef here.

Denet had mistakenly taken Youssefa for a man in Eugénie's courtyard. Youssefa looked young, Aimée thought. Her dark skin stood out against her chalk white hair. Half-moon scars crossed from her temple to her left eye.

"Where's Samia?"

"She left," Youssefa said, her look guarded. "Who are you?"

"Her friend."

Youssefa's eyes flicked over her outfit. "You don't seem her type," she said.

"Samia left a message. She sounded frightened," Aimée said. Youseffa shrugged.

"Can you tell me about the 'ST196' photos?"

Youssefa's brown face passed from curiosity to terror in seconds. She dropped the pen, backed into a chair.

"I know you went to Eugénie's apartment—did you develop those photos for her?"

Youssefa moved fast, around the corner of the table. She started running, her limp noticeable, out into the hall.

"Please, Youssefa, wait!" She shoved the carton on the floor and took off after her.

Aimée barreled into a stack of old film cans, sending them shooting across the wooden floor. She slipped and fell over the metal canisters, wincing as she landed on her aching hip.

Youssefa was gone.

Aimée got up slowly. She figured Youssefa could only have gone into the warren ahead of her, since the hall dead-ended behind her. The windows overlooking the courtyard parking area were open. She heard an unmistakable voice from below. She stopped and listened. A voice described her hair, her jacket, and how she owed his boss.

Dédé.

How could he have found her, unless he'd seen her leave from the back of her office. Or—her heart quickened. She didn't like to think of it. Unless he'd gotten to René and threatened him. But René didn't know where she was going—she hadn't told him.

She heard scuffling down the dark hallway. That was the only direction Youssefa could have gone. She followed the noise.

Youssefa was pounding on a fire exit door, but it was jammed. When she saw Aimée, she reared back like a cornered animal about to attack.

"Let me help you, Youssefa," she said. "Someone's after me too."

"I destroyed the negatives," she said, her voice cracking. "Leave me alone."

Why destroy the proof?

"I'm on your side, but as soon as we get out of here, I will," she said. "A *mec* called Dédé's after me."

Youssefa blinked her good eye.

"Look out the window, check for yourself," she said. "Dédé's determined to find me, but he's not my type either."

She figured if they got out of here, she'd corner Youssefa and sit on her chest until she told her what the photos meant and why she'd destroyed the negatives.

She aimed several heel kicks until the exit door sagged open.

"Lead the way," she said.

"Dédé's a piece of shit," Youssefa said, hesitating, then limping ahead.

"No argument there," Aimée said, following her.

She wondered why the sign said EXIT when this web of narrow halls, roofed by skylights, clearly led to another building instead of outside.

Youssefa opened the last door at the end. They entered a hallway, yellowed and scuffed, passing a dim stairwell. She took out a key and unlocked a door.

Uneasiness washed over Aimée but she figured this had to be better than what lay behind her. They entered the back rooms of a small apartment.

Red-flocked wallpaper, old gas sconces, and small upholstered chairs gave the rooms a busy appearance. But the huge black-and-white photos of Edith Piaf on stage and candid shots, filling the walls, lent the rooms a 1940s feel. A scratchy recording of Piaf played from another room. In the corner, tacked onto a dressmaker's dummy about shoulder height, hung an old-fashioned black dress. Bizarre.

Everything was on a smaller scale, as if made for a little person. René would feel right at home, she thought.

"Where are we?"

"At my friend's," Youssefa said.

"What is this place . . . a shrine to Piaf?"

"Close," Youssefa said. "It's the Edith Piaf Museum." She motioned her toward the back, putting her finger on her lips.

She followed Youssefa into a small modern kitchen, all white and stainless steel.

"Go on." Youssefa gestured toward the back window. "That leads to rue Crespin du Gast."

She started toward the window, then turned back and pinned Youssefa's arms behind her back, sliding her onto a wobbly kitchen stool.

"Tell me what 'ST196' means," she said, leaning over her. "Or I go nowhere."

A momentary hint of regret hit her as Youssefa's chest heaved and she burst into frightened sobs. But Aimée couldn't stop now.

"Youssefa, Eugénie passed something to my friend before her car exploded." She loosened her grip on her arms. "My God, Youssefa, it happened in front of me! I have to know why," she said. "Not only Dédé, but someone else is after me and my friend."

"They'll k-k-kill me," she said, choking on her sobs.

"Why?"

"I took those photos—they made me!"

Aimée's mouth felt dry. "Who did?"

"He's not a general, but they call him one," Youssefa said. "He likes people to call him that. He likes to hang around with the military."

Had he sat in the *cirque*, wearing a uniform?

"What's his name?"

"He's known as the general, that's all."

"Youssefa, why did they make you take the photos?" she said. Part of her didn't want to know why. It was too horrendous to contemplate.

"D-d-documentation." She closed her eyes.

Aimée remembered the looks on the faces in the photos. The way the numbers were pinned to the shirts or the skin of the bare chested. Pinned to their skin. Like temporary branding.

She sank down on the stool next to Youssefa.

As a child, she'd seen cattle in the pasture next to her grand-mother's Auvergne farm. Numbers were clipped on the cows' ears to distinguish them from herds en route to the *abbatoir*. She gasped.

"ST . . . that stands for 'slaughter,' doesn't it?" she said, not waiting for her answer. "And 196 would be the military division of the area, according to Algerian military maps."

Youssefa covered her face, her body quivering with spasms.

That was answer enough for her.

"They wanted you to record it, didn't they . . . or he did, the man they refer to as 'general?' " she said. "Villagers, dissent-ers, and anyone they could lump together as fundamentalists, right?"

Finally Youssefa nodded. "My family owned a photo shop. We sold cameras, developed film. Then one day the military rounded everyone up in the square, called us Islamic zealots," she mut-tered. "Herded us into grain trucks and took us out in the *bled*. Dropped us near big hangars storing wheat. Someone had told them I knew photography." Youssefa rubbed her good eye. "They shoved a Minolta in my hand, put a box of film at my feet, and said, 'Shoot.' "

Horrified, Aimée thought of all those faces.

"It took days," Youssefa said, her voice growing curiously de-tached. "At the end my fingers didn't work, and I couldn't stand up. They did this." She pointed to her scars and her eye. "But I lived. I owed the victims. That's why I hid the negatives. The military didn't care, all they wanted were prints recorded in black and white."

Like Cambodia, Aimée thought, sickened. Wholesale mass killings of innocents by the military. Slaughtered by their own forces, which spoke to the madness of the military mind.

"How did you get out?"

"She helped me," Youssefa said simply.

"Eugénie?"

"She's my AFL contact's cousin."

Of course! Aimée remembered the AFL's hunger-strike flyer with Youssefa's name on it, and Sylvie's membership, starting in the Sorbonne. Now things added up.

"Sylvie Cardet was known as Eugénie Grandet," Aimée said.

Youssefa shrugged, "I don't know."

"But what was she doing with those photos?"

Youssefa looked down.

"I showed them to her, told her about the massacres," she said. "Then Eugénie found out that everything was a sham."

"A sham?" she asked worriedly.

"The humanitarian mission," she said. "The fund goes to the military—they turn around and buy surplus military ware."

Aimée shook her head. She had a hard time believing the second part.

"What do you mean?" she said. "How can that work?"

"French military surplus; I saw trucks filled with night-vision goggles," Youssefa said. "Some idiot boasted there were thirty thousand pairs, at only two francs a pair! So cheap, he said, the General had bought the lot."

The humanitarian mission—Philippe was involved in that. No wonder he'd wanted to keep her quiet.

"What's it got to do with the AFL hunger strikers in the church?"

"Eugénie trusted Mustafa Hamid," Youssefa said. "Several times she told me if I got in trouble to go to Hamid. That's all."

"What happened to them?"

"I gave the rest of the photos to Zdanine," Youssefa said. "He said he'd give them to Hamid, get me time to speak with him."

Zdanine! For a price he must have hid the photos, left them for Dédé in that abandoned house. Dédé's *mecs* recovered them, but she and René had surprised them in the park.

"You didn't destroy the negatives, did you?"

She averted her gaze. "In good hands."

"Give me a contact sheet."

Youssefa turned away.

"I need to have proof if you want me to stop them."

She shook her head. "That's what Eugénie said."

Gently she turned Youssefa's disfigured face toward her.

"Trust me," she said, mustering as much bravado as she could. "Believe it or not, I do this for a living. And they're after me as well."

She saw agreement in Youssefa's sad eyes.

Youssefa led her toward the room they'd first entered. The room with the Piaf photos and the black dress. Youssefa opened a wooden armoire. Musty smells laced with lavender wafted out. On the shelves Aimée saw a row of little black shoes, some T-strapped, others open-toed, all from the thirties and forties. She stared. The pairs of shoes couldn't be bigger than her hand.

"Piaf's?"

Youssefa nodded.

For such a tiny woman, Aimée thought, Piaf had touched the world.

Youssefa reached to the upper shelf, where rows of yellowed kid gloves lay.

In good hands, she'd said.

Youssefa pulled out an envelope, checked it, then handed it to her. "These show the piles of bodies." She looked down. "Other than this, the proof lies in the desert, fifty kilometers outside Oran. Bones bleached by the sun."

She thought about Gaston's words. His experience in the same part of Algeria. History repeated itself in sad, twisted ways.

AIMÉE SLID out of the back kitchen window, climbing down the rusty fire escape to an asphalted yard. Following the yard, she exited onto rue Crespin du Gast and walked the two blocks to Samia's apartment.

She knocked on the door. No answer.

"Samia, it's Aimée."

All she heard was pounding Raï music with a techno-beat.

She tried the handle. Locked.

If Samia was scared, why play the music so loud?

Aimée tramped back down to the courtyard. The rain was coming down hard. She rolled up her collar, passing the boarded-up butcher shop. Peeling posters lined the facade. She headed toward the spot overlooked by Samia's kitchen window.

And then she saw the orange-pink phosphorescent watch on the stones. She bent down, picked it up, her heart quickening.

"Are you here?"

Water rushing from a rain gutter answered her.

She edged toward the passage, reeking of urine, that bordered the *hammam*. And then she saw Samia sprawled against the stone wall.

"Samia, *ça va?*"

But when Aimée got closer she froze.

A dark red wound blossomed on Samia's chest, staining her peach twinset, her eyes open to the falling raindrops. Aimée gasped and knelt beside her. "You're too young," Aimée whispered, reaching for Samia's hands. Cold.

Dead cold.

Guilt stabbed at her. And was supposed to protect the streetwise, childlike Samia.

She closed Samia's eyes, saying a prayer, promising her justice.

She punched in 17 for SAMU on her cell phone, gave the location, then waited until she heard the siren scream before she slipped into the street.

Where had Samia been going? Why here? But that was for the *flics* to chase, she thought grimly. Dédé had been two blocks away looking for her; he'd meant business when he'd warned her others would die.

She dreaded calling Morbier, debating when to tell him. But in the end she stood on the rainswept corner a block away on rue Moret and tried him on her cell phone. She didn't want him hearing it on the news or over the *flic's* radio.

"I messed up, Morbier," she said.

"Any good news, Leduc?"

She heard the flick of a match, and heard him inhaling.

"Bad. Samia's gone."

Morbier's silence seemed to last forever. She knew this news had pierced him.

"Nom de Dieu," he sighed. "I'm so stupid."

"Désolée, Morbier." The tears welled in her eyes. "My fault."

Why hadn't she made Samia stay in the car, baby-sat her until she'd made the *plastique* connection.

"You took a bullet too, didn't you, Leduc," Morbier said finally, his voice sad and tired. "Where are you?"

She told him.

"Get out of there, Leduc. Start walking. Now!"

She stumbled against the street sign, then ran all the way to rue de Belleville and flagged a taxi. They'd be after her now, double strength. An icy determination took over; she could play hardball too. She handed the taxi driver a hundred francs and told him he'd make another if he got to the Ministry of Defense in under thirty minutes.

TWENTY MINUTES later in the ministry reception area Aimée told Philippe's secretary, in a hushed polite tone, that she needed to see *le Ministre immédiatement!*

The secretary reluctantly acknowledged that the minister was busy. He had high-level meetings but would get back to her within the day.

Aimée continued, her tone just above a whisper, that if she couldn't be accommodated the secretary would have the blood of innocent people staining her silk blouse. No amount of dry cleaning could take care of that.

The secretary blinked but still refused.

However, when Aimée threatened to burst into the meeting she rose up in alarm and showed her into an adjoining office.

"*Oui?*" Philippe said, coming in a moment later.

His haggard eyes and stooped shoulders projected an air of defeat. A new experience for Philippe. Pathetic, she thought, and pitied him. But only briefly.

"Philippe, I've got proof that the humanitarian mission's bogus," she said. "And someone's blackmailing you."

Alarm shone in Philippe's eyes. He stepped back. Voices buzzed in the background, papers rustled under a glowing chandelier. He turned and shut the door.

"There's a conference going on, officials from my department," he said, his voice tight. "I can't talk."

He hadn't denied it. And he looked pale.

"Don't talk, Philippe," she said. "I can help. Just listen."

He'd changed after his threats on Canal Saint Martin. He looked almost tame and so beaten. Maybe she had a chance. She pulled a gilt upholstered Louis XV chair close to him.

"Sit down. Give me three minutes," she said easing him toward the seat.

For a moment, she thought he'd refuse, but he sat down. That was a start.

"You didn't know the funds went to the Algerian military, did you?" She didn't wait for an answer. "Of course not, you trusted Hamid, Kaseem, and Sylvie. Why not? They'd been your friends since the Sorbonne. When the late sixties revelations about French repression came to light, the legacy left in war-torn Algeria—you joined what became the AFL."

She watched Philippe. He blinked and rubbed his thumbs together.

"What proof do you have?"

"Hear me out, Philippe," she said. "Hamid followed Islam his own way. I'm sure you admired his peaceful means and how he embraced a broader humanity. You contributed discreetly to the AFL as you rose in the ministry."

She paused: now the ugly part.

"Kaseem had returned to Algeria. Made money supplying the military, somehow. But you didn't know that. Six years ago Sylvie came back into your life."

Philippe shook his head. "She wasn't my mistress."

"I know. She talked you into funding this humanitarian mission while sweetening your bank account. The project revitalized the 196 sector, a land ravaged and barren since the Algerian war in the sixties. Provided irrigation, remapping the area, building roads, a power station, and housing. After all, it helped those most affected, you thought. You believed in the mission, wanted it to succeed. This was for the disenfranchised tribes in the *bled*, not the politicians or the military. You believed Kaseem. So did Sylvie and Hamid. He was your friend. Your old friend."

She had Philippe's attention, she was reaching him.

"But the reality hit when the photos of 'ST196' appeared. No new settlements, roads, or irrigated fields. Just death-squad executions and weapons for the military. Sylvie grew a conscience quickly. You did, too, Philippe. But Dédé, one of the generals' hired *mecs*, blew her up when she threatened to expose the truth."

His shook his head.

"You stopped funding the project. That's why you're hiding Anaïs," she said. "They planned to kidnap her, use her as bait to force you to fund the project. But I got in the way."

Anger blazed in Philippe's eyes. "You're always in the way!"

The door opened, and the light from the hallway streamed in.

"Philippe, we're waiting," said Guittard, the blond man she recognized from Philippe's kitchen. He ignored Aimée, tapping his designer loafers, and faced Philippe. "They've tabled the resolution. Get up, man! Unless you propose a new initiative, the mission goes down the *pissoir*."

"Why shouldn't it, Monsieur?" she said.

But she spoke to their backs.

Two women had been murdered but that didn't seem to grease the wheels of the government. Money did. At least the mission wouldn't be funded. But someone had to pay, Aimée told herself.

BERNARD STOOD INSIDE THE gate of the Vincennes detention center, where a busload of men awaited forced repatriation. Other buses had taken those without any papers to chartered planes at Creil, a military air base. Bernard stamped his feet on the frigid packed earth. Cold—he always felt cold. His body never warmed up until July. Then there were one or two fitful months of what they called "heat" until the cold resumed again.

The barred media waited outside like hungry carrion to fill their newsfeeds. Inside Bernard was numb. These men had come to France years ago, seeking asylum from repression, and stayed on illegally after their applications were rejected. What could he do?

"*Directeur* Berge, please sign the transport receipt," said the hawk-faced detention official.

Bernard hesitated. He wished he could disappear.

"Just a formality, *Directeur* Berge," the official put the pen in his hand. "But we've got regulations."

Bernard could have sworn the man guided his hand, forcing his signature.

Then it was over. Officials marched him through the receiving yard, past the buses disgorging the eighty or so *sans-papiers*. They formed into lines waiting to be processed. Bernard felt like a war criminal, like a Nazi who'd been released because he'd agreed to talk. Hadn't he acted, as his mother had pointed out, like the Gestapo?

And then above him he heard the sound of helicopter blades. Grit and sand shot over the yard, spraying everyone as it landed. A RAID officer jumped out and ran toward them.

"*Directeur* Berge," he shouted, making himself heard over the rotor blades. "*Ministre* Guittard needs you."

Bernard stumbled.

The officer caught him.

"But why?" Could things get worse?

"Hostage situation, *Directeur* Berge. Orders are to proceed immediately."

Bernard began to shake his head but the officer held his arm, propelling him to the waiting helicopter.

AIMÉE WALKED FROM PHILIPPE'S office all the way to her own. She kept alert down the narrow streets. No one followed her. The biting wind had risen from the Seine. She pulled her coat closer.

The scent of flowering lily of the valley reached her from a walled garden nearby. For a moment her mother's blurred face floated before her. All her mother's clothes had been scented with lily of the valley, the room full of it long after she'd left. And then the image was gone. The gusty wind snatched the scent and her memories away.

Aimée's cell phone rang in her pocket.

"*Allô*," she said, her frozen fingers fumbling with the keypad.

"Everything's my fault, Aimée," Anaïs sobbed.

"What do you mean?" Aimée was surprised. "I thought you were in the hospital?"

"Hostage situation . . . Simone," Anaïs's voice faded, then came back. "*École maternelle* . . . in the Twentieth Arrondissement. I need you."

Aimée's blood ran cold.

"Rue l'Ermitage, up from Place du Guignier." Anaïs's voice broke. Aimée heard the unmistakable *rat-a-tat-tat* of a semiautomatic, people screaming, and then the shattering of glass.

"Anaïs!" she shouted.

Her phone went dead.

AIMÉE RUSHED to the tree-lined nineteenth-century street, buzzing with *La Police* and the elite paramilitary group RAID. To her left the *école maternelle*, a building with iron-railed balconies bordered the north side. The adjoining *école élémentaire* held the entrance for both schools on rue Olivier Métra.

Nervous and scared, she wondered where Anaïs and Simone were. What could she do?

An old man, his winter coat thrown over a bathrobe, clutched a parrot cage and complained loudly at being evacuated from his apartment across the street. Paris in April still hadn't shaken off winter's cold cloak, she thought. Frost dusted the cobblestones and wedged in the cracks of the pavement.

"I must speak with the commissaire in charge," she began.

The businesslike plainclothes *flic* listened to Aimée's story, checking her PI credentials. He spoke into a microphone clipped to his collar, then finally directed her past a police barricade. Somewhat relieved, she ran ahead. She knew she had to persuade the officer in charge that she could help.

Inside a Belle-Epoque building housing the temporary commissariat command post, she waited for the inspector in charge. Glad of her wool sweater and parka, she rubbed her hands together in the mirrored building's foyer, the hallway echoing with the tramp of boots and radio static.

She felt another presence and looked up. From the spiraling marble staircase expanding like a nautilus shell, Yves stared down at her.

For a moment the world stopped; scurrying police and walkie-talkie static around her ceased. "What's going on here?" she said.

He edged down the stairs toward her.

"Who wants to know?" said a stocky blue-uniformed policeman beside her.

She turned and showed the *flic* her PI license, glancing at the badge with his rank. "Sergeant, my friend Anaïs de Froissart called me from inside the *école maternelle*. Is she in danger?"

"You could say that," he said. "*Attends*, I'll get the inspector." He walked over to a knot of uniformed men in deep discussion.

Yves's deep brown eyes met hers.

"Some things never change," he said, coming down the stairs and standing beside her.

"I thought you were in Marseilles," she said returning his look, taking in the flak jacket over his bullet-proof vest. "You're still undercover, aren't you?"

"And you're still smack in the middle of things," he said.

She felt her face grow warm. "Why didn't you tell me?"

"Certain things are better left unsaid."

"Like your wife?" she said. Right away, she wished she'd bitten her tongue.

"My ex-wife?" he said, his eyes narrowed. "Did you think—?"

"Policy must have changed," she interrupted, "if they let you come front-line on hostage situations."

"I pulled up before the area got cordoned off," Yves said. "To meet Martine when she dropped Simone at school. We planned to interview Hamid."

She didn't believe him for a minute. A brown curl escaped from his jacket collar. She'd almost forgotten the curving nape of his neck.

"Why was Anaïs taken hostage?" Aimée asked.

"Everything's unclear," he said, rubbing his eyes. He shook his head. "The *sans-papiers* were removed from the church, and Hamid's been taken to the hospital. I'm going to meet Martine there."

The smell of burnt grease hovered near the marble staircase. Someone had forgotten to shut off their stove. Aimée struggled to look away from Yves's face. A man motioned to Yves from the barricades. "There's my colleague. I've got to go," he said. "But I know where to find you."

"Don't count on it, Yves," she said turning away, now determined. "If you can't speak the truth, forget me."

"The less you know the better," Yves said. "The other part doesn't work."

"What doesn't work?"

"Trying to forget you."

Why did everyone have secrets and keep her in the dark?

"I forgot you until you popped up in my flat," she said, unable to meet his gaze.

"Liar."

But she'd turned and strode toward a knot of men in the foyer. By the time she looked back, he was gone.

Technicians and RAID teams speaking into headsets hurried past her. The hell with Yves. She had to get back on track, talk to the head honcho to find out how to help Anaïs.

"Who's the commissaire in charge here?" she asked.

"Mademoiselle Leduc, I understand a hostage has been in contact with you," the clipped voice of Hubert Sardou, a former commissaire in the Twentieth Arrondissement, came from behind her. His long, sallow face hovered near hers.

"Please elaborate as to whom and when," he said.

She recalled Sardou, once a colleague of her father's, from his three-inch platform shoe, which fooled few as to his clubfoot. But now he wore the distinctive badge identifying him as part of DST, the French Internal Security Service. "Hubert feels he must prove he's the equal to the rest of us," her father had said. "Every day."

"*Oui*, Monsieur Sardou," she said. "Anaïs called me on my cell phone twenty minutes ago. She wants my help. Why has she been taken hostage?"

"Seems the AFL wants a bigger audience," he said.

In stunned disbelief she stepped back. "But the AFL policy is peaceful." Aimée wondered if Hamid's power had been usurped by factions. Or if the "ST196" photos played into this.

"We believe an AFL member's holding everyone in the school hostage, but so far," Sardou shrugged, "there's been no contact." Sardou crinkled his face, whether in distaste or indigestion, she found it hard to tell. "We'll take it from here. Your cell phone, please," he said, snapping his fingers at her.

"Won't help much," she said, keeping her expression neutral with effort and handing it to him. "Dead battery."

Sardou studied her phone, raised it in the air, and barked, "*Alors*, anyone have a battery for this phone?"

Aimée could have sworn everyone in the foyer reached in their pocket to check. The French obsession with phone communication produced a matching battery. Sardou inserted it, beckoning to a man with NEGOTIATOR in large black letters on a flak jacket. An officer copied down the number while another hooked a wire from the cell phone into a tape recorder. Several pairs of headphones were connected, and the commissaire donned one quickly.

"Call Anaïs, tell her—and this is very important—to identify which room they're being held hostage in. An experienced negotiator wants to speak with him." He hit Call Return and nodded to Aimée as he handed her the phone.

She heard the phone ring several times before it was answered. "Anaïs?"

No answer, only heavy breathing.

"This is Aimée, Anaïs's friend. Who is this?"

Sardou nodded, then put his finger to his lips.

A sob erupted, sniffles, then a child's voice lisped. "I made pee-pee . . . on my new dress. Maman will be mad at me!"

Surprised looks painted the commissaire and police officers' faces. The negotiator put his hand forward but Aimée shook her head.

"Simone?" Aimée asked. "I'm Aimée, remember me? I'm your maman's friend."

Loud crying answered her. Obviously Simone knew her mother was in the building. Had Anaïs come to see Simone after being released from the clinic?

Aimée kept her voice even. "Simone, that's happened to me before too. I'll clean your dress. Where are you?"

"Can you?" The sobbing ceased.

"Of course. I'll do a good job," Aimée said. "No one will know the difference. Where's your maman?"

"The clown took her."

"A clown?"

"He took her away."

"Took her where?"

Aimée looked to Sardou, who signaled to keep talking. Outside the window, apart from the sun-dappled trees, no sign of life showed behind the school windows. Near Aimée in the foyer, a line of marksmen stood, checking their rifles and telescopic sights.

"Maman gave me her phone. The clown got angry with her and pushed her. She whispered it was part of the game, we were playing hide-and-seek with him, so we should all run away."

Aimée wondered what had happened to Anaïs.

The commissaire's face tightened. A worried expression appeared in the negotiator's eyes.

"Where are you and the other children now?" Aimée asked.

"I'm in the closet under the stairs. Everyone else ran away with my teachers," she said. "The clown looked funny. Not like a real clown."

"What do you mean, Simone?"

"He didn't have balloons," she said. "Only fat sticks that you can light like candles. He said they'll go *boum*!"

Dynamite.

Aimée froze. How would they defuse a terrorist carrying dynamite in a preschool full of hiding children?

Sardou barked an order to the waiting marksmen, who straightened to attention. Blue lights flashed outside in the narrow street as a truck screeched to a halt. That meant only one thing in Paris these days: the bomb squad. Aimée forced herself to keep her voice steady.

"Simone, you're being such a big girl! Can you remember if

your maman said something? Maybe something the clown wanted?"

"He wants Bernard, the bad man. If Bernard comes we get a big *glacé*."

She heard sniffling. "You're so brave, Simone. I'll get you an ice cream too. Did you see where they went?"

She heard rustling. Aimée figured Simone was shaking or nodding her head. "Can you tell me yes or no, Simone?"

"Up the stairs. I thought he was going to hurt her, but she said it was part of the game. I must remember one thing."

"One thing?"

"It's secret."

Aimée's knuckles were white from gripping the phone so hard. Her hands trembled. "Of course! But I can keep a secret, I'm your *tante* Martine's best friend—you can tell secrets to best friends."

"How do I know you can keep a secret, Aimée?" lisped Simone.

Aimée felt the air stir as the row of marksmen single-filed past her in their stiff military boots toward the roof. Another RAID team assembled near her. For a moment Aimée wanted to shout, "Do what your maman told you—get out, run like hell!" But she needed little Simone to guide them.

"Martine and I used to make pinkie promises. Can we pretend to do that over the phone?"

The phone tinkled, then scraped. "*D'accord,* Aimée. Pinkie promise."

Aimée paused. Sardou nodded to her and motioned to keep talking. "Good, Simone. What was the secret?"

"That's between you and her."

"What do you mean, Simone?" Exasperated, Aimée managed to keep her voice level.

"Maman said, 'Aimée knows how to do this, she'll get us out.' "

"Do what, Simone?"

No answer.

"*Allô?* Simone?"

Simone must have set the phone down, because Aimée heard quick little footsteps, as if running, fainter and fainter. With difficulty she unclenched her fingers and handed her phone to Sardou.

Aimée watched Sardou, his head down deep in conversation with a blond-haired man.

"Pardon, Monsieur, may I talk with you?" she said.

Sardou looked up briefly, his eyes small and squinty in annoyance or anger.

"Simone is *Ministre* de Froissart's daughter," she said, "and Anaïs is his wife. Does he know?"

"That's just been brought to my attention," he snapped. "The minister's en route."

"Please, I have to go inside the *école maternelle!*"

He seemed to ponder briefly, then shook his head. "Trained personnel will be more effective."

"Anaïs wants me. Simone's message . . ."

"Impossible," he interrupted. "Only the bomb squad and the special mine sweeping unit can enter the target area."

"I don't like going over your head, Monsieur Sardou, but who's your superior?"

"That would be me, Mademoiselle," the blond man said, straightening up.

Startled, Aimée stared into the face of Guittard, the man who'd ushered Philippe back into the meeting. He wore a navy blue pinstriped suit and was holding a pair of padded overalls stenciled with *BOMBE BRIGADE* in large letters.

"Minister Guittard of the Ministry of the Interior," he said. His hard green eyes crinkled in amusement. "I neglected to catch your name, Mademoiselle."

"Leduc, Aimée Leduc. But we've met twice, *Monsieur le Min-*

istre," she said. "A week ago in Philippe de Froissart's kitchen."
Already she liked him less than before, and that wasn't much.
It had nothing to do with his perfectly brushed hair or once-
over look of appraisal.

"But of course," he said, perplexed for an instant. "Aren't you
an actress?"

"Does this hostage situation involve the project you were
meeting about in de Froissart's office?"

"Aaah," he nodded, recognizing her. "That was you. I don't
know what you mean."

"That's Philippe's daughter in there. Does it have something
to do with—"

"It's the AFL, Mademoiselle."

Guittard turned, stepping into overalls.

"Minister, there's something only I can do."

"Now what would that be?" He bent to snap on the overalls
and cocked his head toward her. As if, she thought, encouraging
whispered confidences. She imagined he spent most of his week-
ends in a country house.

"You heard what Simone said—"

"That you 'know how to do this'?" he interrupted. "Enlighten
me, please, as to what 'this' is."

"Believe me, if I could, I would," she said. "For the life of me,
I don't know." Her eyes lit up. "If the school has a computer, I
can get in the system."

Sardou shook his head. "The school's philosophy dictates only
wooden materials. No plastic, nothing machine made. An elite
preschool, where the pampered ones are allowed to get dirty and
elemental. They go home to the Barbies and computers."

Minister Guittard rolled his French cuffs under the flak jacket.
"Beside computers, what else can you do?" His amused expression
had returned. An aide approached with a cell phone and handed
it to him.

She thought back to the taxi ride with Anaïs, and Sylvie's

Fat'ma. The Fat'ma had turned into a dead end. But Aimée had discovered the "ST196" photos and Youssefa's statement about the humanitarian mission being a sham. And she remembered Anaïs's words in the clinic. "You've got to find out why . . . nothing will be over until then," and her mention of the General.

"You've thought of something, haven't you?" Guittard's eyes bored into hers.

Aimée started guiltily. "Are you sure the school office has no computer?"

He turned to Sardou. "Find out."

But maybe Anaïs had meant something totally different.

"Stay here. If you get any more ideas, tell the commissaire." He trundled a headset over his head.

"Where are you going, Minister Guittard?" she said.

"To tempt the fox," he said.

"How can you do that?"

The whirring of helicopter blades came from outside the foyer. Fine sprays of dust rose; heavy aviation fuel exhaust blew in from the street.

"With the golden goose," he said.

The flash of photographer's bulbs caught Guittard near the helicopter, and she figured he'd suited up specifically for the photo op. The man bundled out of the helicopter looked no more goose-like than golden. Wiry, tall, and with dark pouches under his eyes, he appeared more like an advertisement for the perfect Club Med candidate in need of serious *vacances*. His crumpled suit hung off his body, and the wind from the helicopter blades whipped his gray hair across his face. He looked as if he hadn't slept in days.

"Who's that?" someone asked.

"Bernard, the bad man, would be my guess," she said.

Behind her an earnest Sardou spoke into his headset. He motioned her down the hall as the Guittard entourage mounted the stairway. Aimée figured they were going to freeze her out of the action. She had to remedy that.

A RAID worker in a Kevlar suit escorted her to a deserted part of the landing, around the corner, and away from the crowd. She stumbled on purpose and grabbed his vest for balance, pocketing his ID badge.

"*Ça va?*" he asked, not unkindly.

"*Merci*, I'm so clumsy," she said.

He left her there. For the first time she realized that she had no bomb protection, not to mention being the only woman.

Shunted out of the way, Aimée started planning her own route into the school building. Nobody would help her; she'd have to figure one out herself.

BERNARD BERGE STOOD IN the scurrying sea of police activity. Around him buzzed two-way radio static, the clomp of boots, and the low, meaningful hum of whispered asides. If only he could get his fingers to work and put this headset on, his lifeline, they'd called it, whereby he'd be assured of constant communication with the negotiating team.

"What do I say—I mean to the hostage taker's demands?" His hands trembled attempting to mount the headset.

"Discuss the ramifications," Minister Guittard said, snapping his flak jacket closed and turning to his entourage.

"But, Minister, will he understand?"

"Berge has a point," Sardou said, consulting a printout. "This man, Rachid, twenty-six years old, is a recent immigrant from Oran, Algeria. He's a dishwasher in the mosque tearoom."

"Find out what he wants, what the AFL wants," Guittard turned back to Bernard. "Agree to anything he says."

Bernard swallowed hard. "You mean, I have the power—"

Guittard cut him off, "Promise him a Swiss bank account, a private jet back to Oran, whatever it takes to get him in front of that window." He pointed to the window directly in the crosshairs of the crack shot team on the opposite roof. "Do you understand, *Directeur* Berge?"

Berge nodded uneasily. He noticed Sardou's hawklike gaze.

"Then I've made myself clear, *n'est-ce pas?*" He grinned and slapped Berge on the back. "The ministry counts itself fortunate to have men such as you!"

A loud clamor of shouting reached their ears. The CRS captain joined them, breathless. He wore plastic gloves and held an envelope.

"Thrown out of the third-floor window, sir," he said.

Sardou yelled orders to a white-coated technician, who spread plastic over a wood-planked table. A lab crew assembled powders, brushes, and chemicals in assorted colored vials.

"*Merci*, captain. Put the envelope on the table."

While one technician treated the envelope to a quick array of powder tests, the others extracted the contents with tweezers.

Guittard, unable to disguise his impatience, appeared ready to grab the contents.

"We must see if this is from Rachid, Minister," he said. "It could be from one of the hostages, giving us clues to their location."

Bernard Berge winced.

A crayoned picture of what was clearly a spired church, brown-skinned people inside, and a man with dark bags under his eyes, holding a little navy blue book. A small stick drawing of a man, tubes drawn about his chest was signed in a crude hand, "*le Bombe Humain.*" The negotiator studied the drawing.

"He's calling himself the Human Bomb," he said.

After a few more minutes he turned to Bernard. "That's you. He knows your face well. I'd guess the navy blue book would be residence permits. He'll give himself to you if the immigrants are released from prison." The negotiator turned toward the group. "He's illiterate also. That's my interpretation."

Minister Guittard's piercing eyes held Bernard's. "Good," he said, rubbing his hands. "You know what to do."

Bernard Berge nodded. "Minister, there's one issue I want to clarify."

"*Vite,*" Guittard said, tapping his fingers on Bernard Berge's shoulder. "You must go inside now."

"If he's wired with dynamite," Bernard paused, "won't the building explode if he's shot?"

Sardou watched Guittard. So did Bernard.

"Not if you disconnect him, talk him out of his plan," Guittard smiled grimly.

"Excuse me, minister, it's not quite that simple," said the bomb squad commander stepping from behind Sardou. "Berge must look for a dead-man switch. It's something the man would hold all the time. So if he lets go, the circuit completes."

Bernard's eyes widened in fear. Sweat beaded his upper lip.

"However, a command detonation is different," the commander continued. "Usually it's a pair of wires with a handle, maybe a red button. Like a bike handle, with wires and dangling switch. Something he'd have to signal manually."

Bernard knew he would die.

He hoped that his underwear was clean and that he'd updated his will. Most of all he hoped his mother would bury him in a Christian cemetery.

"Look on it as a typical ministry meeting," Guittard said, slapping Bernard's shoulder in bonhomie. "Like when you have to handle an upstart. It's the same principle, *Directeur* Berge. *Bonne chance!*"

Minister Guittard whisked past the group and down to the waiting crowd of reporters eager for an update.

Monday Early Afternoon

AIMÉE LOOKED DOWN FROM the broad first-floor window, trying to figure out how to get into the school. Scurrying figures entered a mobile truck on the street. They emerged wearing jackets, carrying weapons.

She edged backward; none of Sardou's men paid the slightest attention to her. But if anyone noticed, she'd say she was trying to find the bathroom. Behind her lay several wood-paneled doors, housing utility closets and garbage chutes. She gripped the brass handle in the door closest to her, pulled it open, and felt cool air. She prayed she'd gotten lucky. Once inside she saw a curving narrow staircase and sighed in relief. She had.

Going down the stairs, she figured Anaïs must have been trying to tell her something—but what?

She didn't know how to get Simone and the children out—the area teemed with antiterrorist squads, trucks, and equipment.

Worried, all she knew was that Anaïs counted on her.

Again.

The paramilitary RAID was notorious for blazing its way in, fudging the body count later in hostage situations, only intent on neutralizing its target. Judging by Bernard's appearance, the goose brought in by helicopter, that could make sense. Maybe Anaïs felt that Aimée was the only one who had a real chance. Or, knowing Aimée, would be crazy enough to try.

"Keep moving," said a helmeted figure, motioning her toward the barricades blocking narrow rue Friedel.

The first step would be to access the building adjoining the *école maternelle*, get inside, and find a way from there into the school. She flashed the CRS badge, then sidestepped through the colonnade to a group of about ten hastily assembled CRS and *flics*. With any luck the plan she'd started hatching in her brain would trap the terrorist.

"Inform me on the latest—have demands been made in the hostage situation?" she said to a guard.

The guard hesitated, then jerked his head toward several figures bent over a police car's hood. "Talk to LeMoine, chief of operations."

Next to them stood the open van lined with black jumpsuits and flak jackets. Inside the van a stocky woman chewing gum ticked off items from her clipboard. She nodded when Aimée flashed her badge, then gestured toward the rack, "One size fits all, Captain. I suggest rolling up the cuffs and sleeves."

Aimée lifted the light swat suit, which crinkled in her hands. "Fabric seems flimsy, Lieutenant . . . ?"

"Lieutenant Vedrine." The policewoman winked. "Use the resistant liner." She handed Aimée an aqua Goretex-type gunnysack. "You might want to slip off that skirt and shimmy this on."

"How long has the situation existed?" Aimée asked as she stepped into the outfit, snapped the Kevlar vest, and zipped the black jumpsuit.

"No one briefed you?" Lieutenant Vedrine's gum popped constantly while she helped Aimée.

Aimée thought quickly.

"They paged me during my anniversary dinner with my husband."

"*C'est dommage!* How many years?"

"Five, and it was the first time we'd had a babysitter in ages—give me the quick and dirty." Aimée inspected the contents of various flaps and panels on the jumpsuit.

Lieutenant Veldrine helped Aimée into the flak jacket. "A disgruntled tearoom employee from the Mosque Paris went *bal-*

listique when his *sans-papiers* sister got bused to prison. He joined the AFL." She shrugged, intelligence and humor behind her gaze. "Pretty routine operation. If you're lucky, shouldn't be long."

Aimée covered her surprise. What about the children? But maybe everyone figured the units were biding their time until RAID marksmen got their shot. Aimée pointed toward the rack of locked low-light sensor rifles.

"Weapons authorization number?" Lieutenant Vedrine asked opening her weapons log.

Aimée racked her brains for Morbier's number—what was it? Creature of habit that Morbier was, he usually picked his birth-date for such things, at least he had for his apartment digicode entrance and his office locker. She forgot if he was a year or two years older than her father.

"It's 21433. Listen, I know one of the hostages." Aimée took a deep breath. "We were in the *lycée* together. Her sister's my closest friend."

Lieutenant Vedrine paused, her mouth still.

"Who's that?"

"Anaïs de Froissart, wife of the minister."

"I'll check that." Lieutenant Vedrine bent and talked into her collar radio. "Confirm identity of hostage."

The static from the radio competed with the sirens from another arriving bomb-squad truck. Blue flashing lights swept the streets.

Lieutenant Vedrine touched the headphone to her ear, straining to hear. Then she nodded to Aimée, chewing again in a deliberate fashion, looking impressed.

"From what command gathers, about twenty children and two teachers could be in either of three classrooms facing south," she said. "Marksmen are positioned on rooftops lining the street."

Aimée broke into a sweat. She had to find those children!

Lieutenant Vedrine activated the mobile radio linking Aimée's unit to the others. She handed Aimée earphones and
clipped a tiny microphone to her jumpsuit collar.

Aimée's gut told her that this was her one shot in hell and
she'd better take it.

If she didn't find them, the body count would be higher and
the bodies smaller. She joined the others quickly assembled on
rue de l'Ermitage.

"We make a sweep of next door," the sergeant said. "Make
sure of total evacuation before sharpshooters lock these windows
in their crosshairs, eh?"

Most nodded or murmured assent. As the group moved forward, Aimée sidled near a pillar and melted into the ranks. They
entered the older building, an elder-care facility. Private and
posh, by the looks of it, much more upscale than a *maison de
retrait* retirement home.

Inside, members fanned out, and Aimée headed across an
empty dining room; the tables were set with half-empty glasses
of wine and plates of food were still warm. She entered the
kitchen, which had stainless-steel counters, a *jalousied* grille scal-
loping the window.

Smoke and burning onions filled the stovetop area, making
her cough. Copper pots simmered with soup stock on the blackened industrial stove, but the culprit was a large frying pan sizzling with rapidly deteriorating clumps of onion. Careful to avoid
the searing-hot handle, she killed the fire, then lifted the frying
pan with a towel into the sink of water. The hiss and smoke
billowed, but she was already past the sous-chef's butcher block
littered with chopped vegetables and crushed garlic.

She exited into a dark back hall. With the building behind
her, she faced what looked like an old theater. Behind her she
heard doors shutting, and she realized that the CRS would enter
soon.

This theater shared the back half of the elder-care building.

Aimée hesitated; the sergeant hadn't instructed them to climb to the next level. However, she figured the only way to reach the school would be to gain entrance to the theater attic and find the roof.

Her heels clicked on the marble as she wended her way to the mezzanine. The only other sound came from the old sconces, buzzing like insects, lining the *grande* mezzanine. She mounted the wide marble staircase. Dim, deserted hallways branched off the mezzanine level, barely lit by the central chandelier.

She heard rumbling and then a tinkling of glass. She tiptoed across the marble but stopped when the sound ceased.

Aimée saw the glint in the tall smoky mirror. She turned to feel a machine gun's cold metal in her temple, and froze.

"Mademoiselle, seems you're lost," said a black-jumpsuited RAID figure wearing night-vision goggles and resembling a giant fly. "The CRS forces monitor the the lower quadrant. Not up here." He stepped back and gestured with the gun toward the staircase.

"*Bien sûr,*" she said, recovering her composure and stepping ahead. "But since I took a stage class in this theater years ago, and I'm familiar with the layout—"

"We'll just make sure of that now, won't we?" he interrupted. "*Vite!*" He gestured again toward the staircase.

BERNARD BERGE'S heart pounded so loudly that he thought the RAID team flanking him would notice—even with their thick helmets and headgear. A little voice in his head cried, "Why me??!" while Sardou, via a headphone in Bernard's ear, repeated instructions. Rue Olivier Métra, deserted except for the CRS stationed behind pillars, shone in the weak April sunlight.

"Do you understand, Berge?" Sardou repeated. "Get him by a window."

Bernard assented, wondering again if his mother would relent

and bury him even if his body was unidentifiable after the explosion.

The team melted away as Bernard approached the deserted
concierge's loge by the school entrance. Ahead of him lay the
école maternelle courtyard, lined with potted red geraniums and
filled with tricycles. Shuttered windows and skylights in sloping
mansard roofs looked down on him from three sides. The fanatic
could be behind any of them! An eerie silence hung over the
courtyard. He took a deep breath and a faltering step before
clutching the limestone wall. His hands shook.

Bernard Berge prayed for a miracle, as he had as a little boy
on the ship leaving Algiers. He prayed that the burning city
would be whole and that everything was a dream. Now he prayed
he'd wake up and find this was a dream too. But he knew it
wasn't.

"Get moving," someone hissed from behind. He heard the
clicking metal sounds of triggers being cocked. "We're covering
you."

He made his legs move to the center of the courtyard. He shut
his eyes and raised his arms high.

"I'm Bernard Berge," he said. "From the ministry."

Silence.

He opened one eye. Something red fluttered behind a ground-
floor classroom window. Then a small head popped up briefly.

"Monsieur Rachid, I have authority to reverse the immigration
orders."

A parrot's squawking erupted from the concierge's loge, and
Bernard jumped. He looked up. The windows stared vacantly
back at him.

"In my pocket. I want to show you—may I enter?"

The only answer was the parrot's shrill cry.

A little hand waved from the window, then disappeared.

"Monsieur Rachid, I'm coming in, and I'm keeping my arms
high so you can see them."

He concentrated on moving his feet toward the window. Before he could reach the door, it opened, and a small red-sweatered boy in short pants barreled into Bernard's legs.

"Run!" Bernard said, keeping his arms raised.

"Loulou," the little boy sobbed. "I can't go without Loulou."

"Don't worry, I'll get her," Bernard said.

"Loulou's a boy!" he said.

"Hurry up," Bernard said, irritated. He pried the little boy from his legs. "Do as I say!"

The boy ran and tripped over the cobbles. He landed, crying, by the wall. "I can't leave Loulou!"

"Go on!" Bernard snarled, raising his eyes and scanning the windows.

The little boy stood up and stumbled but made it to the concierge's loge. From the corner of his eye Bernard saw the RAID man scoop the boy up.

Bernard entered the long classroom, edging past white walls plastered with children's watercolors, a sand table littered with wooden shovels and an empty rabbit cage with *"Loulou"* scribbled on a sign in crayon. *Merde!* Bernard thought. The little boy would put everyone in danger for a rabbit!

He passed through a yellow-tiled bathroom, stools set in front of washbasins and tiny toilets, into a darkened room filled with nap cots. Where should he go now?

He knelt down, feeling his way past the cots toward a double door. Something wet and sticky clung to his fingers, and fear shot up Bernard's spine. He didn't want to look.

In the crack of light from the door he saw the blood on his hands. Bernard gasped. A vision of his little brother, André, came to him, his small face floating in the village well. Bernard didn't try to wipe his hands. Now he knew he'd never get the blood off them.

* * *

"NICE LITTLE stunt, Leduc!" Sardou said. "You're banned from the area."

The RAID man had escorted her back to the command center. Her grim feeling was highlighted by sobbing parents waiting on the periphery.

"The bomb unit has set procedures," Sardou said. "We will not put anyone in jeopardy."

"But look at Berge," Aimée protested. "Standard procedure wouldn't put—"

"Him inside?" Sardou interrupted. "Of course not! But the hostage taker set the rules, since Berge was responsible for the deportations."

She struggled to make Sardou understand. "The AFL wouldn't do this," she said. "A radical faction took over. The real reason is the funding loss for the humanitarian mission."

"You're banned from this area," Sardou said again, nodding to a nearby CRS, who escorted her to the barricade.

Her heart sank. How could she get them out? She didn't trust RAID, Guittard, or the sharpshooters. 'Trigger-happy' took on a new meaning with highly trained marksmen who ached to take out suspects quickly. Bombs and hostage situations had become too common in Paris.

Defeated, she walked down rue de l'Ermitage. She slumped on the curb, oblivious to the stares of passersby. If something happened and she did nothing, she'd never forgive herself. Anaïs had said she knew how to do it . . . but how to do what?

She had to get them out.

Aimée noticed the pearly pink oil rivulets snaking through the cobble cracks, pooling in slick puddles. She glanced at her watch from force of habit. Her dead Tintin watch.

She stood up, called René from the nearest phone, asking him to gather equipment and meet her at Gaston's café, four blocks away. Then she started running.

*   *   *

"MAY WE use your café as headquarters, so to speak, Gaston?" she said. "I've got a plan to disarm the bomb."

"If you let me watch you use one of those," Gaston said, pointing to the laptops René began unpacking on the glass-ring-stained tables.

"I'll even teach you," René said, his smile widening. He looked around. "First we need an outlet so you can see how surge protectors work. I'll show you in a moment."

Aimée stuck the new cell phone René had given her on her waistband.

Something didn't add up.

"I have a terrible feeling," she said, explaining about her conversation with Philippe. "He denied nothing, just looked beaten."

"So you think this is another blackmail route?" René asked.

"His daughter's in there, René," she said. "And his wife."

"But how?" asked Gaston. "Haven't the AFL claimed credit?"

"Mafoud and the AFL are grassroots, cranking out leaflets, organizing soup kitchens and child care for strikers," she said. "Hostage seizure isn't their style. Even though this Rachid claims it is."

René clicked Save on his laptop and looked up. "Rachid could be a loose cannon. What if his baguette's sliced a little thin and he decided to carry the cause further?"

"Sliced a little thin . . . ?" Gaston winced.

She could see Gaston didn't like the implication. She didn't either.

"Quite possible, René," she said. "But I'd say he's smart and with some kind of explosives training." She paused. "He's got about two hundred police, including sharpshooters and the RAID squad, in a holding pattern, so his baguette can't be sliced too thin."

"You've got a point, Aimée," Gaston said. He leaned against the zinc counter, wiping it with a wet rag. "Perhaps he trained in the army."

Outside the café windows rain glistened on a grime-encrusted banner with BIÈRE FORMENT in block letters rustling in the wind. The Arab trio moved into another doorway to conduct business as a postman cycled by.

She nodded. "Do you remember last year when some young Moroccans with French passports, trained in Afghanistan, were sent first to fight in Bosnia, and then told by their bosses to 'go to Morocco to kill a few tourists' because this would destabilize Morocco?"

René and Gaston both nodded.

Aimée stared at the frayed photo wedged in the mirror frame and thought about all the things that didn't add up. Or did they? Hadn't Berge been dispatched to the site with authority to offer guarantees of residence status to the immigrants?

"Go on," René said as they both watched her.

"Seems similar. Kind of the same off-the-wall rationale," she said. "I think they're hired hands." She shrugged. "Just a feeling."

René's brows furrowed. "I trust your intuition, Aimée."

"The Battle of Tlemcen attests to that," Gaston said, reaching for tissue. Tears slid down his cheeks.

"What's the matter, Gaston?" Aimée asked.

"A medical problem," he said. "My tear ducts dilate and I spurt at the slightest occasion." He winked. "Gets me an extra half kilo of melon at the market."

"There's another thing," she said. "What if he's not alone?"

"Of course he's not alone," René said. "Teachers, children—"

"He has to eat and defecate, right?" she said.

"He'll make someone test his food," Gaston said. "Pull one of them to the bathroom with him."

"True, Gaston," she said. "More important, he'll get tired. Of course it depends on how long he holds them hostage—but he'll have to sleep."

"So what are you saying, Aimée?" René asked.

"He's got an accomplice," she said. "And unless he's on a suicide mission, he's got an escape route."

René nodded. "Let's get to work."

Bernard Berge stared at his bloody hands—the blood of little children on them. Why? he wondered. Bluebottle flies buzzed over dark red clumps on the marble stairs. Viscous and smeared, emitting the sweet stench of meat gone bad. Bernard gasped and turned away.

He saw the velvety gray ear stuck between the thick banister. Poor Loulou. But at least the blood belonged to a rabbit, not a child. He wiped his hands on the marble and climbed.

"Monsieur Rachid, the immigration releases are in my pocket," he said, his voice cracking. "As soon as the children are released, the CRS will escort everyone to a processing site for residence papers, I promise you!"

Bernard's steps echoed off the marble. No other sound reached him but the distant buzzing of the flies.

"Please, we're meeting your requests, Rachid." He kept speaking as he mounted the once grand staircase, now with traces of crayon and signs pointing "Silkworms to Butterflies group every Friday," "Mademoiselle Mireille's Gazelles in Motion on Tuesday mornings."

Bernard paused on the landing. Where were the children? His arms ached from being raised; blood had trickled down his white sleeves, but he was afraid to let them down. The foyer led down a high-ceilinged hall, narrowing to another wing. He paused. Muffled noises came from behind a door labeled ART ROOM. Should he enter?

He hesitated before turning the cracked porcelain doorknob. All of a sudden he felt hands grab him from behind.

"Rachid," he sputtered. "Talk to me."

His shoulders were harnessed in strong arms, his eyes covered, and a loud tearing reached his ears. A sticky band was taped over his mouth. He heard guttural words in Arabic, glottal and harsh.

His last conscious thought was of an ethery smell as the damp cloth covered his face, reminding him of when he'd had his tonsils out.

Sometime later, he didn't know how long, Bernard's mind unwrinkled, as if each tissue papered layer of consciousness relinquished its grasp with an effort. His eyes opened, and he became aware of silvery bubbles rising to the surface by his nose. He realized he was eye-to-eye with a gurgling fish tank, his back supported against a wall. He was breathing, but he couldn't get enough air into his lungs.

Opposite him on the floor a masked figure in black, with sticks of dynamite ringing his girth, built Legos with a little girl wearing pink tights. The masked face looked up.

"Welcome to school, Monsieur Berge," the man said, his black ski mask unmoving. "*Merci* for these releases. However, new issues have cropped up, and we'd like your help in fixing them."

Bernard realized that his short breaths and gasps meant he was hyperventilating. "I can't breathe!"

"*Calmez-vous*; we'd like to request a few concessions when you're more *tranquil*," Rachid said. He barked something in Arabic to another masked man clad in a black jumpsuit emerging from an alcove, a machine gun slung over his chest.

"We'll release the three youngest children to show good faith, Monsieur Berge. But you must stay and help work on our demands."

Bernard nodded. "I'm authorized—"

"Right now you're authorized to listen," Rachid interrupted.

*   *   *

OUTSIDE CAFÉ Tlemcen the drizzle had grown into a down-pour, wind whipping the leaves and twigs into a frenzy. They stuck in Aimée's hair. She set down the radio antenna on the table and spread her wet coat over a clump of chairs. René and Gaston huddled over the architectural drawings of the *école maternelle* on the round café table.

"Aimée, good news. The *école maternelle* has a computer," René said. "Ready for the bad news?"

She groaned.

"The computer's down," René said.

Computers going down weren't the end of the world; they both knew that.

"But that's never stopped us before, René," she said. "Just a little work and some time."

"Time is something we don't have," he said, his voice lower.

She heard the shift in his voice and worried.

"*Tiens*, has something else happened?"

"You could say that," he said. "The building's security system has been wired to the human bomb! Check out this map, Aimée."

While sheets of rain fogged up the café windows, she stared at the map revealing the building's structure. The only entrances or exits in the building plans were connected to the main system. How could she get in there?

Aimée paused and pointed her finger to several XXX's by the old sewer lines.

"Can you decipher those, René?" she said.

He nodded. "Old sinkhole shafts," he said, peering closely at the plans. "Bricked up."

"Sinkhole shafts to where?" she asked.

"A tributary to the nearby canal," he said. "Boulevard Richard Lenoir is the paved continuation of Canal Saint Martin."

Aimée quelled her rising excitement. "Any idea when these were bricked up?"

René scanned the plans, "My guess would be when the canal was paved over. Let me check." He clicked several keys on his nearby laptop. Aimée watched as a nineteenth-century structure grid was superimposed over a modern-day Belleville map on his screen. She stared transfixed. "What kind of magician are you, René?" she said.

"Just a new program I found." He chuckled. "The best is yet to come."

The crystal-clear resolution highlighted narrow lanes and streets cleared by Baron Haussmann in the nineteenth century to become the broad, clear boulevards and avenues of today's Belleville.

"Incredible!"

His eyes lit up as he hit more keys. "There's more."

A below-ground system of streams and tributaries to the Seine, like branches from a tree, spread in varying colors. "That thick blue line indicates the old tributary to Canal Saint Martin, those green ones are the old springs in Belleville."

Aimée's heart jumped. "If we could get in somehow, how navigable is a sinkhole?"

René shrugged. "Since it's porous ground composed of old river silt, who knows? The ground settled, then sank. Old sinkholes exist all over Paris especially in the Tenth, Eleventh, Nineteenth, and Twentieth Arrondissements. Everybody forgets."

Aimée paused. "Belleville is where they all meet, isn't it?"

"Looks like there's a bricked sinkhole in the cellar," he said. "Leading from the *école maternelle* into the street. The Belleville reservoir and water towers are only a few blocks away."

His eyes widened. "Are you thinking what I'm thinking?"

"We enter via that sinkhole," she said, punching the spot on the laptop screen map. "Power up the computer, hook the bomb wiring from the security design to the computer, transfer the connection, and enter the blocking code," she paused and took a breath. "All that's left is to shepherd the kids from the sink-hole."

"Whoa, Aimée!" he said. "Great logic if the computer functioned. How this theory would play in practice is another story." He hit Print. "No one knows what it's really like down there."

She pulled out her cell phone from her waistband. She tried to hide her shaking hands from René.

"Sewer rat isn't my style. I didn't like it last time in the Marais, either," René said. "Children and unstable underground holes weren't involved either."

She studied the map and kept her shaking hands in her pockets.

"Think of the concept, René," she said. "Simulate the computer connection, fool the system, and enter the security-blocking code."

René's brows knit together. "Aimée, I'm worried—there's no guarantee that way."

"No guarantee exists, René. But if we disable the explosive device, Anaïs and those kids have a chance. With RAID's sharpshooters, I'm afraid they could be machine-gun fodder."

René shook his head. "We can't do it alone."

Her heart hammering, she watched the underground plan emerge from René's printer.

"The question is do we enlist help or do it ourselves?" she said.

René rolled his eyes. "I'm too short for those commando outfits. Besides, my plumbing source moved to Valence. We'd need dynamite."

"Gaston's a military man, aren't you?" she said, turning to Gaston. "And you're handy with a plunger."

"Apprenticed with the Army Corps of Engineers," he said. "Before I chose intelligence."

"Perfect," she said.

"Bombs make you nervous, Aimée," René said, concern in his voice. "Let the big guys get us in. Then we'll have a better chance."

Before she could reply, they heard a gunshot in the distance.

"You might have a point, René." She grabbed the wet raincoat and opened the café door.

Two blocks later she ran into a solemn crowd of women by the barricaded square. One of the anxious mothers, her face mirroring the fear of a silent group around her, had collared a riot-geared policeman.

"What's happening?" she asked. "Tell us what's going on."

"*Tiens*," he said. "We'll have them out soon." He led her and the others further back. "Three more just came out!"

Loud shouts of "Take the right perimeter!" came from the school courtyard direction.

"My boy's asthmatic," the woman begged. "He needs his inhaler."

"Give me his name, Madame," the uniformed CRS man said, not unkindly. He copied it down, then repeated the name into his collar-clipped microphone.

Aimée overheard an official pleading to offer himself as a hostage in exchange for the children. Middle-aged and well dressed, he kept insisting to be taken.

A small group of people, who she figured were child pyschiatrists, stood at alert next to him. She looked up, examining the mansarded roof bordering the theater, when shots ricocheted off the square's metal guard rail. Everyone hit the cobblestones. Except Aimée. She'd seen a face in the fourth-floor attic window. A flash of blond hair, and then it disappeared. Was it Anaïs?

"*ENCORE!*" Bernard's mouth widened in surprise as the young teacher, wearing a paint-spattered smock, her face flushed, wound the music box, which tinkled a nursery rhyme. Children giggled as they paraded around a line of small chairs. When the music halted abruptly, all made a mad scramble. The lone child without a seat gave up, laughing, and joined the clapping throng circling the remaining chairs as the teacher again cranked up the music.

A small wooden sword was thrust in Bernard's lap.

"*En garde*, Monsieur!" said a serious-faced boy, his button eyes shining, with a black-and-scarlet cape tied under his chin.

"Michel, perhaps the monsieur is tired. Slaying dragons and wolves all day can be exhausting," said a calm voice behind him.

Bernard turned to see a brunette woman in a denim smock, entering the class room with a tray of biscuits and pitchers of juice, escorted by a man in a black ski mask.

"A *table*, *mes enfants*," she said. "After that we take our nap, as usual."

The first masked man, wired to a pile of dynamite sticks on a basket of wooden blocks, motioned for Bernard to rejoin him. Bernard saw the man's hands move and realized the explosive device must be a command-detonation type.

"Are you helping the hunter?" asked the caped young boy.

"*Alors*, Michel, it's a big job to catch the wolf," the teacher nodded to Bernard. "Our hunter needs some help!"

Bernard nodded as if he slew wolves and dragons daily. So the teachers made everything a game, he thought. Smart. And a good way to avoid panic and ensure cooperation.

A redhaired girl, freckles splashed over her face, wore a feather boa twined around her shoulders. She emerged from the dress-up corner and stumbled pigeon-toed in oversize ruby-red high heels.

"Gigi's hungry," she said, a large tortoise in her arms. The tortoise's mouth snapped.

Bernard saw wires trailing from the dynamite. Afraid she'd trip over them, he yelled, "*Stop!*"

The teacher looked up. "Lise, don't forget you get three points for your team every time you jump over those wires!"

Lise nodded, set Gigi down, and calmly jumped over them. Bernard's heart hammered, and he knew he was hyperventilating again.

He'd conveyed Rachid's demands to Guittard, who reiterated that he must remember his "goal": Get them by a window. However, neither of these men went far from the dynamite. Guittard had agreed to Rachid's demands for the immigrants' release and implied that Bernard should play for time.

"Monsieur Rachid, Minister Guittard agrees to your demands," Bernard said, parroting Guittard's commands. "We're recalling the planes, which stand by on the runway."

"Three hours," he said. "Every hour after that I shoot a teacher."

Bernard flinched but kept his countenance firm. "Monsieur Rachid, we're complying with your demands—"

"And you lose a limb," he interrupted.

"Monsieur Rachid . . ." Bernard stumbled; he tried to go on.

"Do you like the sun?" Rachid interrupted. "Because when we leave we might bring you with us."

Bernard's hope sank. He'd been doomed from the start.

"RENÉ, COULD we disengage the security by a remote source?" Aimée asked, standing at the Café Tlemcen window.

He shrugged.

"But you're right, René," Aimée said. "It's time to work with the big boys on this."

They had no other choice.

"Commissaire Sardou, I can help you," Aimée said into her cell phone.

"You again?" Sardou snapped.

"Let me talk with Minister Guittard," she said. "We can disable the *école maternelle* security system."

"Don't mess things up. We're meeting the hostage takers' demands," Sardou snorted. "You're not needed."

"I suggest we simulate the computer connection," Aimée said, "fool the system, and enter the security-blocking code."

Guittard got on the line.

"Talk to me, Mademoiselle Leduc," he said.

"No fuss, if my partner and I work with your engineers. The children will walk out alive."

"I'm listening," he said.

She outlined her plan, sketching in the details after he'd paused and told her to go on. "But the computer must be up to do this."

Guittard sounded worried, she thought.

"*Un moment,*" Guittard said, putting her on hold.

"Rachid gave them three hours," René said. He looked at his watch, shaking his head. "Two hours left."

"Forget it. The tactics team run this operation," Guittard said, coming back on the line. "Their men coordinate this. The terrorists booby-trapped the computer against a simulation like that. There's no way to defuse the bomb via the security system."

Frustrated, she kicked the floor tiles. If their information was true, there was no way around it.

She'd never been on friendly terms with the *gendarmerie*'s specialized computer services. This unit, a quietly kept secret of the Defense Ministry, had a large budget. Paradoxically, the government's red tape never allowed the branch to keep pace with private sector developments; René was always several computer years ahead of them. Every dealing she'd ever had with them had been fraught with resentment and roadblocks.

"So we wait," Guittard said. "For every ten *sans-papiers* they release one child."

Frustrated, she wanted to scream at him that terrorists didn't play by the rules. Instead she said good-bye and paced Gaston's café.

"Bernard Berge was a top graduate of ENA," Gaston said, sipping mineral water. "Have some confidence in him."

Crème de la crème, Aimée knew. No other country had an equivalent. The only close comparison had been from a friend of her father's who'd likened it to Princeton, Harvard, and Yale all rolled into one, only more exclusive.

Graduates, referred to as *enarques*, stepped right into ministry posts. Aimée remembered a newspaper comment referring to the government not as *socialiste* but as *enarquiste*.

"Bernard followed the *enarque* path true to form," Gaston continued. He took another sip, then set down the glass, careful to place it on the coaster. "Appointed first to the Ministry of Finance, he worked on the budget, then moved to law. He was a judge for a long time."

"So *enarques* move around the government?" she asked, surprised.

"Bien sûr," he said. "They're all friends, like to keep the jobs inside the family, so to say. Keep them exclusive. They all live near one another, fancy flats in the Seventh Arrondissement so they can walk together to the ministry."

But to her mind Bernard hadn't seemed to fit that crowd. Remembering his haunted look, she became lost in thought. If he'd had some balls, he would have had everything.

The fading afternoon light hit and sparkled in Gaston's glass. He looked up again; this time his lined eyes were serious. "His father served under Soustelle in Algérie. For a *pied-noir*, Bernard Berge has attained the top."

Maybe what she'd mistaken for Bernard's cowardice was a conscience. How had he felt to be part of this rarefied echelon? What had it cost him to perform this mission?

"Rumors had it he'd taken a leave earlier this year to avoid a nervous breakdown," Gaston said. "He holed up in his flat and wouldn't come out. Until they snagged him for this job."

*   *   *

BERNARD WATCHED the hands edge toward the 4 on the large wall clock. Around him little snores in the nap room kept time to the Mozart tape that had lulled many to sleep. The teacher, whom he'd heard called Dominique, sat in the middle, writing down Rachid's whispered dictation, as she rubbed a child's back.

"In order to escape," Rachid said, "we demand that the police announce our deaths. Once sure of our safety, we will release the last of the children."

Dominique held up the paper, written in red crayon, for him to see. Dark circles ringed her eyes.

"Sign it 'the Human Bomb,'" Rachid said. "Then stay with the children."

She complied and lay down on a cot.

Rachid stuffed the note in a biscuit tin and crawled over to Bernard. "Go with him," he said jerking his head towards the other terrorist. "Throw it out of the attic window facing the square."

"Why not call Guittard?" Bernard asked. "You can explain your demands to the minister."

Rachid slammed his fist on the counter. The fish tank shuddered. "When I want suggestions, bureaucrat, I'll ask for them."

Bernard flinched. He took the note and crept past the sleeping children. Rachid's accomplice nudged him with the machine gun up the staircase, poking him in the ribs every time he paused.

Bernard was sweating as they reached the fourth floor. All the way up, his mind fixed on how to get the terrorist near a window. A creaking sound on the wooden stairs alerted him . . . a rat, another escaped school pet, or a hiding child? The terrorist paused, he'd heard it, too.

"Wait here," the man barked.

Bernard stood on the worn steps, breathing hard. This pampered childhood world felt foreign to him.

The hungry postwar years he remembered were in rented

rooms with a toilet shared by two floors. And that, his mother had considered a luxury. His real father had died in a desert skirmish with rebel *fellagha* when he was little.

His stepfather, Roman, also a *pied-noir*, said little. But when he spoke everyone listened. Bernard had always likened Roman's speech to the tools of his butcher's trade—sharp and cutting.

He'd once asked his mother, before he'd learned better, why his Papi's words cut like a knife. She'd sighed, then pulled him close, something she'd rarely had time for. She told him his Papi bottled everything inside and that some people showed their love in different ways. His Papi, she continued, showed it by working hard. They had a home now, she'd said. She'd gestured toward the room around them. Peeling plaster in two narrow, high-ceilinged rooms, the only water source a pump in the courtyard.

But when Roman spoke, he used language as a weapon. Whereas Bernard learned to use language as a shield, living in the ether of ideas.

His mother said she was sure one day he'd make his Papi proud and show him how smart he was. She'd run her hand down his cheek, smooth down his hair and the stubborn cowlick that never took orders. Her tone had been wistful when she'd asked him if he'd take care of his Papi when he got older.

But he never had. Roman died broken and tubercular seven years later. Before Bernard earned entrance to École Nationale Administratif, and his brother passed the entrance exam for medical school. However, Roman's fierce silences and cutting words were imprinted on his pysche.

These children would never know his deprivations. And for once, bypassing the envy that lived in his heart, he experienced gratitude. Gratitude that no child would know those days . . . but then he thought of the Balkans, the blank-eyed orphans. War never stopped, it just took different forms. And these children, weren't they victims forged from battles of the long-lost Algerian war?

There was a loud shattering of glass ahead of him.

"In here, bureaucrat!" the man yelled. "Now!"

Bernard fought the impulse to flee, ducked his head, and entered the doorway. The terrorist had broken the window. Glass shards blanketed the attic floor, giving off a bluish tinge. Used, musty air and waist-high wooden storefront letters filled the narrow attic. Weak sunlight flashed off the glass, creating a diamond carpet. What if the sharpshooters thought he was signaling? Bernard felt panic, his breathing coming in short gasps.

No, they'd wait—they wouldn't shoot at anything that sparkled—he felt sure. The bands of tension in Bernard's head relaxed a fraction. Until he saw the disheveled woman in the corner, tied to a chair, struggling to kick at the terrorist's shins. She sent him a look that Bernard couldn't read.

"Take me to the bathroom," she yelled. "Or I'll do it on the floor."

The terrorist whacked her across the face with the back of his gloved hand. "Suit yourself, *infidéle*, just shut up!"

Bernard saw her hands clutch the splindly chair back behind her and realized her wrists were untied. She was signaling him. There were two of them and just one big semiautomatic-toting terrorist.

"Look," Bernard said, edging toward the terrorist, "I'd suggest—"

"Cut the small talk."

Bernard gestured toward her. "Can't you at least let her go to the bathroom?"

Bernard wondered who she was.

The terrorist pointed to a window, jagged splinters of glass peeking from the corners.

"Hurry up," he said. "Throw it from here! Bureaucrat, I'm losing patience," the terrorist growled. He hawked and spit, coming over and nudging the machine gun into Bernard's ribs. "Didn't you hear me? Throw the box out the window."

Bernard winced as the cold metal barrel poked through his thin suit jacket. He took a step. Shattered glass crackled under his shoes. He froze.

He looked over at the woman for help, but her heavy-lidded eyes stared vacantly. Her nose bled bright red down her chin, spattering on her once white silk blouse.

Bernard knew he was a coward. Schoolyard fights and tauntings had proved that. The idea of standing as a window target for RAID sharpshooters was not appealing. Right now he wanted to get on his knees under the skylight, in the chill air among the skewed letters, and beg the man for mercy.

"The police will shoot me," he said, his veined hands shaking. "I can't—"

"Makes no difference," the terrorist yawned. "I'll use her."

Bernard's legs wobbled; they didn't support him any more. Lightheaded and dizzy, he reached to steady himself against the woman's chair. He missed. Around him the angle of light spun and shifted. He hit the ground heavy and hard. What must have been moments later, he grew aware of myriad sharp splinters in his arms.

The woman erupted from her chair screaming, kicking at the terrorist's legs. He tripped over the dazed Bernard and let out a roar. He landed headfirst against the wall and crumpled onto his machine gun. Deafening shots erupted into his chest. His black torso twitched as the round drilled into him. His body fell sideways.

Bernard realized the woman had gone. He was alone. Alone with a dead terrorist oozing guts onto the pebble-like plaster. What should he do? Wouldn't Rachid have heard the bullets?

He rolled the stocky corpse over and slid out the machine gun, sticky with blood.

Bernard pulled off the man's black mask. He saw the stubbled slackjaw and vacancy of death. For the first time in Bernard's life, he felt no fear at death. A curious relief flooded him.

And then Bernard decided. He would no doubt join little André, who had beckoned him at night for so long. But first he would save the children, since he hadn't been able to save his brother.

He would make up for the past.

Bernard unzipped and removed the terrorist's jumpsuit, a laborious process, rolling down the sleeves, then shimmying the cloth over shoulders and thick, lifeless hips. Then the heavy boots, which he wiped off, then put on. He put on the ski mask. In the zippered side pocket he found a fresh bullet cartridge.

By the time he trailed down two flights of stairs wearing the black mask, his fingers had clamped rock steady on the trigger. He liked the way the solid curve molded to his finger. A creaking on the narrow landing caused him to stop.

Light from a wall sconce illuminated a trail of greasy fingerprints. Wedged under the metal-railed staircase, almost unoticeable, was the outline of a small door. He tiptoed across the floor, cocked his ear to the door, and listened. From time to time, he heard childlike whispers and strident beeping.

"Stay calm, I'm a friend," he said, opening the door slowly. A figure crouched behind cleansers and dust mops. "Let me help you, little boy."

"My name's Simone," said a glaring little face. She emerged slowly, holding a cell phone and cradling a worn brown-furred teddy bear in her arms. "This game is boring," she coughed and choked back sniffles. "I want to go home!"

Bernard knelt down, stiff and awkward in the jumpsuit, his arms full with the gun. "So do I," he said.

"You're not allowed to!" she said wiping her runny nose with her sleeve.

"My name's Bernard."

"You're the bad man."

"Let me explain—" he began.

"Where's my maman?" she lisped.

Was this the woman upstairs? "Tell me what she looks like."

"You pushed her," Simone said, her voice climbing higher. "I saw you. Not fair. Everyone knows you're not supposed to push people."

"But it wasn't me."

"Liar!"

As Bernard reached to brace himself, Simone shut the door on his fingers. He lurched in pain, pulled his hand out, and stumbled backward. With a sharp crack his head hit the railing and he crumpled. The machine gun slid from his grasp, and the cartridge round clattered from his pocket onto the parquetry.

Crouched on her knees, Simone peered out of the door. The bad man looked asleep. She'd hurt him. Good—that would teach him not to push people! Rules were rules, but sometimes you had to learn the hard way, like Papa said, give people doses of medicine. . . . What had he said? Anyway, something like that.

Her stomach growled, and it was too hot in that closet. Time to find her maman and a buttered *tartine*. She'd won over the bad man. They could go home now.

Just in case no one believed her she lifted the gun. So heavy and ugly. Too bad; it would never fit in her Tintin bookbag. She slung the strap over her shoulder but the gun scraped the floor. Looping it three times around her neck did the trick. She picked up the smooth black cartridge filled with bullets and shoved it in the empty gun slot, like they did on the *télé*. She sighed. So heavy, and what a lot to carry!

And teddy bear, he didn't like all this bumping. She stuck him between the gun straps and hoped he wouldn't mind such tight quarters. After taking the stairs one at a time and holding the rail with her free hand, she remembered the phone and trudged back. Teddy would get cross with all this to-ing and fro-ing. She grabbed the phone from the metal mop pail in the closet and a green light flashed. Maybe it worked now. She hit the button Maman had showed her, the one with the big letter she couldn't remember.

AIMÉE'S NEW cell phone, connected to her previous number, rang. Even though she'd told Yves to get lost, she hoped it might be him. Get ahold of yourself. No time to be waylaid by visions of Yves's sideburns.

"Aimée Leduc speaking," she said, making her tone business-like.

"A *flic's* picking you up!" Sardou barked. "Get over here now!"

She started to speak, but a siren announced a motorcycle policeman outside the café.

When she arrived at the temporary headquarters, Sardou looked ready to spit bullets.

"Simone will only talk with you," he said thrusting the cell phone at her.

Aimée took a deep breath.

"Simone?" Aimée said, her knuckles white as she clutched the phone.

"Tell everybody I won, Aimée," the tired child's voice said.

Something clacked in the background, heavy and metallic sounding. A brief series of clicks, and Aimée realized that Sardou was monitoring the call. What a primitive tracing system these *flics* had—René would laugh, but this wasn't funny.

"You can talk to me, Simone, I'm a policeman and want to help you," Sardou said.

"That's what the bad man told me," Simone said, sounding more tired. "But I took care of him. So stop talking."

"Simone, tell me what's happened, okay?" Aimée coaxed, keeping her voice light. "Just a little. You'll tell me more over hot chocolate in the café, eh?"

Simone yawned. Sardou kept silent.

"Aha, you must be the Orangina type, eh?" Aimée giggled, hoping her giggle sounded real.

"Do I get a *grande* Orangina even though Maman says I get a stomachache from cold drinks?"

"How about a double?" Aimée asked.

"I put a bad man to sleep and took his gun," Simone said.

"Where are you?" Sardou interrupted.

"But Aimée," Simone sobbed, tears caught in her throat. "Where's Maman?"

"Look Simone, my name is Sardou. I can help—"

"You're with the bad man, I know," Simone said. She hung up with a loud click.

Here was four-year-old Simone wandering around with a gun, and Sardou had pissed her off! And no contact from Anaïs. Aimée shuddered, she pushed possible scenarios from her mind.

Sardou muttered over the buzzing line. Her hands tensed around the phone. She must remain calm and collected. She took a deep breath.

"Sardou, when I hit the Return Call button, let me do the talking. Don't you agree it's called for in this situation?"

That sounded diplomatic, she thought. For what seemed a minute all she heard was the buzz and click of the other line. Sardou must be conferring with others.

"Make sure she gets Rachid by the window," he finally said.

Flustered, Aimée measured her words. "How do you propose a little girl would do that? Rachid isn't stupid."

"Sounds like she got rid of one terrorist."

Sardou could have a point.

"Would a courtyard window suffice?"

"Facing south," Minister Guittard said, cutting in on the line.

She punched the Return Call button on her cell phone. A recording came on: "The party is unable to answer your call momentarily or has stepped out of range. France Telecom thanks you for your patience and requests you try again momentarily."

Great.

"She trusted me, Sardou; you blew it," Aimée said. Sardou

and Guittard's conversation had wasted time and proved useless. Until Simone answered they hovered in a holding pattern.

"Call again. Keep trying, Mademoiselle Leduc," Guittard said and hung up.

She'd pretty much figured that out.

And then she looked at her new cell phone with the battery . . . her dead Tintin watch . . . her mind raced. When she'd dropped the proposal off at the EDF site, the manager had warned her to turn off her cell phone since the electromagnetic rays from the HERF generator interfered with systems. Flattened them, he'd said. The electromagnetic fields were quite high due to all the unshielded equipment and the heavy iron reinforcement in the station walls. No reason it couldn't do so now.

"Sardou," she said, her voice certain and calm. "I know how to dismantle the bomb without touching the computer."

BERNARD AIMED for the staircase, which tilted dizzily as he crawled toward it. His hand throbbed. Where had the little girl gone? Where was the gun?

The terrorist's overalls clung to him. He shivered. If he could just get downstairs he'd pretend to be the other terrorist, wounded and unable to talk. He'd get Rachid by the window. With that thought, Bernard almost tumbled down the stairs headfirst.

And then the sun blazed for a brief moment as the clouds parted. Bernard smiled. The sun at last. He heard a zinging crack as a fine tinkle of windowglass powdered him. And then Bernard felt warmth on his face. The wonderful warmth, the heat from his childhood. Everything danced before him; his *nounou*, the slim grinning mother he knew as a child, his papa driving a jeep. Little teething André beckoned, and Bernard joined him.

RENÉ WALKED into the command center with a small shopping bag. He set the bag down and started pulling items out.

"Everything's here," he said, strapping on the Walkman-size

HERF generator in his waist bag. With the power emanating from this he could knock out communications systems in the surrounding buildings.

Aimée helped adjust the antenna up his left sleeve so he could easily slide it out.

"From Simone's conversation, we know one of the terrorists was knocked out," Aimée said. "René resembles a child from this distance. If the doors Berge entered are closed, René can go to the window. Aiming the HERF gun at the device controlling the bomb, he shoots high-energy radio frequencies. He interferes with the detonation device, defusing the—"

Aimée never finished.

Sardou and every man wearing headsets rushed to the window.

"Green light," someone muttered.

She saw a black-suited tactics team pause at the door, simultaneously heard the crack of rifles.

"Don't do it!" she yelled. "The building will blow up."

"They've got three to five seconds before the reaction time sets in," Sardou muttered. "They better make it count."

In stunned disbelief she watched the team enter the building. No explosion. More cracks from the rifles. She could see bullet holes pepper and shatter the glass.

Aimée gasped, "Please God keep the children and Anaïs away from the windows! What happened?" she asked, turning to Sardou.

"Three minutes ago Rachid agreed to the demands," Sardou said. "We recorded him dismantling the wires. Your plan was backup."

"Then why shoot him?"

Aimée's knuckles whitened as her fingers clutched the windowsill; she still braced herself for an explosion.

"We'd taken out the other one," Sardou said. "RAID doesn't like taking prisoners."

Sixteen children with their teacher and a shaking Anaïs holding Simone were led out through the courtyard. Relief flooded Aimée until she remembered.

"What about Bernard Berge?"

Aimée's answer came as three bodies were rolled out into the cobbled courtyard: one burly man in his underwear, and two men in black jumpsuits.

Three terrorists?

The tactics team stripped off the ski masks of the other two.

One was a bearded man, a small black hole over his cranial vault. Dead instantly, she figured. A surgical shot to the skull, which wouldn't have affected his nervous system and prevented him from tripping the wire. Bernard was the other, in a stained jumpsuit. A dark red spot, like a third eye, dripped down his forehead. His features were relaxed, and he looked at peace. Aimée felt the oddest sensation, as if Bernard's soul fluttered on wings above the cobbled courtyard and toward the weak sun.

"Nom de Dieu!" Sardou snorted, looking at Berge. "Berge will go from sinner to saint all in one day!"

"Berge was expendable, wasn't he?" she said, angry. "Guittard always planned to shovel him in the dirt, one way or the other."

Sardou's eyes glazed. He turned and walked into the courtyard. As the stretcher lifted Bernard's corpse, Aimée whispered a prayer. Poor Bernard had been terrorist fodder.

Outside, Guittard was holding a press conference, so jammed with media that she and René had to wait near the SAMU vans where tearful relieved parents were hugging their children. Martine had arrived, joining Simone, and was helping Anaïs to a temporary first-aid station at the rear of a fire truck.

Disheveled, Anaïs sat on the truck's fender, her wounds receiving attention.

"We were going to dismantle the system, Anaïs," Aimée said. "We'd figured it out."

"I knew you could, why didn't you?" Anaïs said, her blond hair matted to her scratched and swollen face. "My suit's ruined."

Aimée saw Kaseem Nwar. He stood smiling, rocking on his heels, as Philippe hugged Simone.

And then Aimée knew.

Everything fit together. Philippe had made a deal with the grinning devil. Seething inside, she stared at Kaseem Nwar, who bent down and patted Simone's head.

"Philippe gave in to Kaseem," Aimée said, turning to wide-eyed Martine and Anaïs. "He funded the mission, didn't he?"

Anaïs shrugged, then winced with pain as a paramedic swabbed her face.

Aimée shook with fury. For the second time she'd been about to save Philippe's family but he'd dealt with the devil. The smiling devil who sold out his own brother, Hamid.

"The DNS knew the terrorist defused the bomb," she said. "But they killed them anyway, even Bernard."

Anaïs bit her lip as the paramedic treated her.

"What do you mean?"

"Kaseem held you and your daughter hostage until Philippe caved in," she said.

Anger flashed in Anaïs's eyes. Then she softened as she looked at Simone and her husband. "I didn't know it was Kaseem, Aimée. I'm sorry. I just wanted you to find out who was black-mailing Philippe."

"Maybe you could have helped me more, Anaïs."

Aimée strode over to Kaseem and Philippe. Philippe ignored her, holding Simone tightly.

"I owe you an Orangina, Simone," she said, keeping her voice even.

Simone nodded, her eyes serious. "A big one."

"Let's take Maman home, Simone," Philippe said.

He didn't look Aimée in the eye.

Simone pulled her father's hand.

"It's not over, Philippe," Aimée said, through her clenched teeth. "I'm seeing to that."

But Philippe and Simone threaded their way past the emergency crew toward Anaïs. Philippe enveloped Anaïs in his arms. For a moment the de Froissarts huddled. Then Philippe led them to the debriefing area.

"Let things go, Mademoiselle Leduc," Kaseem said.

"You risked little children," she said. "Before that you tried to have me killed at the *cirque*. You sabotaged the AFL and your own brother Hamid's cause!"

Kaseem shook his head. "No one believed in him anyway."

Aimée felt pity for poor Hamid, starving himself for a cause to help immigrants. The irony being that Kaseem, his brother, supplied arms and assisted the massacres the immigrants had tried to avoid.

"The 'ST196' photos—"

"Tell nothing," Kaseem interrupted. "They're just photos."

Aimée shuddered. His cruel arrogance unnerved her.

"Piles of bodies in the desert," he said. "So what. That's been happening for years. Since the eighties. No one cares about Algerian infighting."

"There's a difference when surplus French weapons are responsible and French taxpayers foot the bill," she said. "At least, the French might think so."

Kaseem buttoned his wool coat; he snapped his fingers at a man leaning against a car. "The ministers turn a blind eye. So should you. You know, I enjoyed being with you. We could—"

"This whole thing was a hoax," Aimée interrupted. "Sylvie discovered what 'ST196' meant so you killed her, meanwhile Philippe cut the funding. Philippe hid Anaïs, so you used your brother Hamid. You engineered a hostage situation blaming the AFL. All this to pressure Philippe so he'd give in, fund the mission because his daughter was inside. Then Anaïs checked herself out of the clinic, a bonus for you. And no one would know. No one would put it together. But I did."

"I'll take that for a no to dinner." Kaseem smiled and didn't blink once. "Theorize all you want. You can't prove it."

Powerless, she wanted to nail him there on the spot. His patronizing smile got to her.

"You're a wannabe general, aren't you, playing with the big military boys," she said. "As long as you supply the weapons, you get to play. Without toys from Philippe's funding you're just a *maghour* holding up the dusty wall!"

His eyes flashed.

She knew she'd hit home.

"Say what you like," he said. "I've got what I want."

And then he was gone.

The cobbles glistened below her, slick and gummy, as the *panier á salade*, the van to carry out the dead, pulled up. Kaseem was right, and he made her sick. The bad guys had won. And she'd thought she could stop them.

As they loaded Bernard's corpse onto the stretcher, she whispered a prayer.

There had to be some way to get Kaseem. Discredit him.

By the time Martine had joined her, she'd figured out a way.

"Kaseem's not your favorite, I see," Martine said. "What are you going to do about him?"

"Make him very uncomfortable," she said. "With your help I can do some damage."

"How?"

"Let's go back to your office for a start," Aimée said. "I'll fill you in on the way."

"Not if this involves Anaïs," Martine said.

"Don't worry," Aimée said, pulling out her laptop. "The big fish will get caught, hook, line, and sinker. Not only that, you'll sell more papers with my insider report. I've got the negatives to prove it."

"Point me to the newsroom," Martine said, flipping open her cell phone. "I've got a firsthand hostage report to write."

THREE WIRE SERVICES, IN addition to Agence France-Presse and CNN, had picked up Martine's story by the time Aimée opened the door of Leduc Detective. She heard the radio say fingers pointed to an Algerian jewelry importer, rumored to be in the pay of Afghani-based terrorists and sympathetic to the militant fundamentalists. He was alleged to supply the Algerian military with inferior-grade weapons and military surplus. His Swiss bank account, the article continued, buried under an alias, hid a multitude of sins.

Aimée logged on to her terminal and René's. From hers she accessed Sylvie/Eugénie's account using the *beur* password. The five-million dollar balance was still there and she hit Save.

On René's terminal she followed the maze he'd established to the Bank of Algiers. From the Bank of Algiers she linked to the AlNwar bank account and the two other subsidiary companies. Aimée withdrew all but the minimum balance of ten dinars from each account.

In the same fashion as Kaseem and Sylvie had previously established, she transferred the sums to Sylvie's Channel Island account. However, instead of their procedure, she transferred that balance, all fifty million francs, to the AFL's account.

Now Kaseem and his businesses were broke. But the Algerian military would think he'd hid it all in Switzerland.

To foil attempts at wire tracing, she pulled out the police report of Sylvie Cardet's death, highlighted the name "Eugénie Grandet" and the bank statements and faxed this to the records department in the *Fichier* in Nantes. The *Fichier* would declare the Eugénie persona dead and freeze the account.

She logged in to the Ministry of Defense, the humanitarian mission funding. Marking the shipment as time-dated medical supplies and perishable, she red-flagged the containers. This ear-marked them for inspection prior to departure from the port of Toulon. Toulon was the largest naval center and adjoined a military complex. If the shipment contained the surplus military arms she figured it did, the inspectors would seize them.

Kaseem wouldn't get his shipment.

She brushed off her black leather pants and reached for her jacket.

Now she figured she should pay Hamid a visit and tell him some good news.

HAMID'S WARD bed in L'hôpital Tenon overlooked leafy lime trees on the street below. Color now tinted his cheeks; his eyes had lost their listless quality.

"*Salaam aleikum,*" he said, shaking her hand, then touching his heart.

"*Aleikum es-salaam,*" Aimée returned his greeting. She pulled an orange from her bag, setting it on his enamel hospital tray. "May I peel this for you?"

"*Merci,*" he said. "I've given my life to the AFL, but I couldn't save the *sans-papiers.*" Hamid said, his face still haggard. "But the new immigrants, the young ones, they think differently. I never heeded them. Now I must rebuild."

"I know the truth," she said, digging her fingers into the firm orange flesh.

"What do you mean?" Hamid's eyebrows rose like accent marks over his deep-set eyes.

"Kaseem pressured you." She peeled the skin, the segments fanned out in her hand. "Like he does everyone. But you're his brother, as *maghours* you only have each other."

She offered the orange pieces to Hamid. He slipped his worry beads into his other hand and accepted the orange. His eyes lit up with curiosity.

"Your brother killed Sylvie," she said. "Blew her up."

Hamid's hand shook, but he didn't drop the orange on the worn green linoleum. "I don't believe you."

"I'm sorry. He didn't know Sylvie gave this to Anaïs," she pulled out the photos. She spread some of them over the hospital blanket. "Isn't it south of Oran, where you were born?"

Hamid nodded slowly and stared.

"Now it's a wasteland labeled 196," she said. "Just a number. Not even a name. A cemetery of bleached bones mingled with sunken munitions. As young men you two fought there once. You lost to the French."

Hamid nodded. "Yes, a lifetime ago."

"Kaseem calls himself the General," she said. "He still likes to play war. He has to find toys so he can play with the big guys."

Fear shone in Hamid's large eyes. "There's no proof." His tone was hesitant.

"But Kaseem can't do that anymore. I took care of those toys," she said. "Sylvie's money and his are back in the AFL."

Hamid's face registered disbelief.

Rectangular shadows crossed the linoleum in the long ward. Few beds were occupied. A smiling ward matron in a starched white uniform nodded as she passed them. The matron's clogs clicked busily away.

Aimée passed him some more orange segments, then stood up.

"Now you can rebuild, Hamid," she said. "Hire lawyers to fight deportation, run a day-care program, a newspaper, a meals on wheels—do it the way you want. Even attract the young kids with a modern center, a gym, Arabic classes, video games. You name it."

"I don't really know you," Hamid said. His eyes were unsure.

"Sylvie would have wanted it like this," she said. "To make

up for her father's work in the OAS. The murdered innocents, things she hated."

"Funny." Hamid's eyes turned wistful. "That's the last thing Sylvie told me."

"What's that?" she asked.

"She wanted to make up for what her father did."

"Sylvie must have been a special person."

"A rare star," Hamid said.

Touched, Aimée remembered Roberge saying the same thing. In fact, almost everyone but Anaïs had loved her.

"Where is Kaseem?" she asked.

She remembered how Hamid's face twitched when he lied.

"On the plane," he said, his mouth slightly askew. "Why?"

"I only want to tell him what I did," she said. "Prepare him for what's in store back in Algiers."

She wanted to serve Kaseem justice on a platter, personally. See the look on his face, even if it was long distance.

She thought she'd have to battle with Hamid for hours but he seemed to come to a decision.

Hamid watched her, expressionless.

"Just don't hurt him," he said.

She nodded. She'd let the military he liked to play with handle that part.

"He's at a wedding," Hamid said.

STREET LIGHTS shone over the news kiosk as Aimée bought the special edition of *Le Figaro* with Martine's lead story. Harrowing images of prisoners tagged with numbers, their numbers recognizable on piled corpses, filled the lower half of the front page. The sidebar column related the story of the alleged surplus weapons supplier, sympathetic to fundamentalists. *Parfait*, she thought. I just want to see Kaseem's face.

Patrons milled around the busy Kabyle Star restaurant on rue de Belleville. Aimée threaded her way past diners to the back banquet room. From inside she heard traditional music accompanied by a tambour coming from the private wedding reception.

"I'm with the in-laws on the groom's side," she said to the curious bouncer.

Kaseem stood by the buffet, his arm around a uniformed man, laughing and toasting with a glass of juice. A furious gaiety spilled over the room of a hundred or so guests. Small children ran between the tables, old men in caftans scooping them up every so often.

"There, see him." She pointed, and waved at Kaseem, knowing he couldn't recognize her from the darkened distance. "Kaseem Nwar, my sister's brother-in-law . . ." but the bored bouncer was already waving her inside.

Aromas of mutton and cloves from the steaming clay *tajines* tempted Aimée from the buffet. She saw platters of *bistilla*, flaky spiced pastry frosty with sugar and shaded by cinnamon. The air was dense with perfume, sweat, and orange blossom water.

Aimée hugged the wall, melting into the draperies as she surveyed the room. She saw the bride and groom spotlighted on the dance floor. The bride wore an ornate blue-and-gold caftan, her neck shimmering with gold necklaces. As the wedding couple danced by, guests stuck money in the laughing bride's hair and around her shoulders.

"Such a gorgeous *ta'shi ka*," said a heavily kohl-eyed woman who'd appeared next to Aimée. "The gold sets off her hair and the blue highlights her eyes." She eyed Aimée knowingly. "The third day of the wedding *fête* is always the best. The best spread!"

Aimée nodded, trying to move away from the woman.

The woman elbowed Aimée in the ribs. "Just like I told Latifa the other day, don't worry. Everything will be perfect, everyone will come, the buffet will be wonderful, and your baby will pass the virginity test!"

Aimée wished the woman would shut up. Her voice kept increasing in volume.

"The groom's family is so traditional." The woman leaned forward, her tone becoming confidential. "What can they expect from girls born over here, eh? But they can hope, I say."

"May I ask you a tremendous favor?" Aimée said, feeling out of place. She didn't wait for the woman to answer. "Hand this to Kaseem, please!" she said thrusting the paper into the woman's jeweled fat fingers. "That man there."

She pointed toward Kaseem, who was seriously stuffing franc notes in the giggling bride's hair. "He's my friend's uncle, and he wanted the paper for some reason. I've got to go back out and park the car. It's on the curb and I'll be towed. Please!"

The woman shrugged. "Why not? I want to find out if he has a son my daughter's age anyway." She let out a loud laugh, nudged Aimée in the ribs again, and worked her way to the other side of the room.

Aimée thought Kaseem might want that money back when he realized his bank account status. She'd enclosed a copy of his new statement as well. She edged along the velvet curtains dividing the banquet room from the dining area.

Aimée never got to see the look on Kaseem's face.

She felt something stick in her spine. Pointed and sharp.

Her heart pounded.

She reached back for her Beretta but an iron grip imprisoned hers.

She turned slowly. The knife edge grazed her skin. Dédé's eyes locked hers. Cold and dead. Sweat prickled her spine.

"Make a move," Dédé whispered, "and I gut you like a fish."

"It's over, Dédé," she said, her voice hoarse. "Kaseem's history. Read the paper."

Out of the corner of her eye she saw Kaseem holding the newpaper while the woman pointed toward where Aimée had stood. Several uniformed men had gathered, peering over his shoulder, yet agonizingly Aimée couldn't see his face.

"*Qu'importe?*" Dédé said. "I always finish the job."

He hustled her through the swinging kitchen doors to the left. They followed a white-aproned waiter past bubbling saucepans in the hot steaming kitchen.

Aimée wriggled, but every time she did, the knife came closer to her flesh. For a little man, Dédé had a grip like iron.

"*Tiens*, you can't come in here!" a waiter said, his arms laden with a huge couscous platter.

"I know the chef," Dédé said, barreling past him with Aimée.

They stumbled past yelling waiters and sweating cooks who shook slotted spoons at them. Aimée grabbed at some knives on the chopping block but Dédé seized her hand, shaking them out one by one. One of the chefs rushed forward as the knives clattered to the floor.

"Stand back," Dédé yelled, waving the Beretta and letting go of her arm briefly.

Aimée's one thought was to grab another knife. Instead her hand came back with greasy steel kabob skewers. She worked them under her sleeve before Dédé caught her hand again.

If only she could get away, escape out the back exit. But Dédé's truck waited in the back passage, an old *deux chevaux* delivery truck, battered and rusty. He opened the back doors, slammed her inside.

"Let's go for a ride," he said.

Dédé whacked her again. This time so hard that she flew against the hard plastic cartons racked on the truck's wall. White-hot pain shot through her body. Then he kneed her in the back, knocking the wind out of her. She gasped, trying to get air. The last thing she remembered was her head hitting the floor and seeing the blurry pavement through a rusted-out hole in the floorboard.

SHE BECAME aware of her heels dragging over stones, gravel popping, and dirt. Everything was dark except for curiously shaped white slabs shining in the moonlight. Her head ached.

Every breath was like the stab of a needle in her rib. Dédé's voice came from somewhere.

"Thought I'd save everyone the extra trip," he said, huffing and setting her down. "Kill you here."

She realized she was in a cemetery. And Dédé held her Beretta.

"Cimetière de Belleville," he said. "Not many famous people buried here, and a little out of the way, but you'll have a nice view."

She wouldn't give him the satisfaction of whimpering, but her head felt ready to explode with pain.

"Dédé, your contract's over," she said, her voice not much above a whisper. "Forget this."

"Maybe it's my *proletariat* upbringing—some work ethic, but when I start a job, eh, I finish it," he said sitting down on a low marble crypt. He smoothed down his short jacket, dusted off his pants. "That's what they pay me for."

In the slants of moonlight she saw Dédé's hands find the bald soccer-ball key chain in his pocket. He fingered it, worrying it nonstop through his fingers.

"Please listen, Dédé. Kaseem's finished," she said.

"*Alors*, my work is my life. There's a pride and satisfaction in it. Eh, I like doing an even better job than my employer asked for. I make it personal. Kids today . . . just don't have it."

Her hands shook, but she could hardly move them. He'd tied them up. How could she get away? She felt the kabobs jabbing her somewhere above her elbow. But couldn't reach them.

"After you screwed up the car bomb," Dédé clucked his mouth, shaking his head, "I had to do a lot of work. But when you stole the pearl lighter and embarrassed me in front of my *mecs*—that did it."

Her mind grew clearer. The pain had receded so she could think. She felt a metal cross behind her. She started sawing the rope that tied her wrists.

"What about the other Lake Biwa pearls?" she said, remembering there'd been four of *les Maudites*. She wanted to keep him talking until her hands came free.

"My collection has grown," he said. "I have them all." Dédé slipped the key chain back in his pocket and pointed the Beretta at her.

Behind the dark cemetery wall two tall water towers loomed, standing outlined against the yellow glow of Belleville. In the moonlight she saw piles of dirt and pipe holes in the lot under the towers. Muffled voices came from a nearby gravestone.

She started screaming but her voice came out only a low croak.

Dédé stuck his sleeve in her mouth to shut her up. She bit as hard as she could. He yelped. And she bit harder.

He tried to shake her off, swatting her head against the marble. She wouldn't let go. Blood filmed one of her eyes, but she hung on like a pit bull until her hands came free. Then she shoved him over the wire cross, struggling to her feet.

"*Salope!*" he swore, still gripping the Beretta.

What sounded like a whistle came from the wall.

Aimée started running, dodging the gravestones.

Her head throbbed, but she could run. She skidded through an abandoned gate in the wall. Her labored breaths stung sharply, but she made herself gulp air, her mind clearer the more she did so. She made it halfway across the gravel lot between the water towers before Dédé caught her ankles. Her body slapped the ground. She came face-to-face with a hole, her neck stinging.

"Look what you've done!" Dédé hissed, pointing at his ripped jacket.

She'd almost gotten away!

"Kaseem used you," she said. "Like he uses everyone."

Dédé marched her to the nearest water tower, six or seven stories high. The tower loomed robotlike, with spindly legs webbed by ladders and pipe.

"Climb!"

The Beretta felt cold against her temple.

Aimée looked up, her hands shaking on the side of the ladder. "But I'm afraid of heights."

"Too bad," Dédé said. His gold chains glinted in the moonlight, his perspiring face glistening with sweat. "I need target practice."

He was going to pick her off like a fly.

"Look, Dédé—"

"This is taking too long, I've got other jobs." He cocked the trigger, shoved her toward the ladder. "Move."

She took several steps, faltered. Her greasy hand slipped and she grabbed the railing. Her leather-soled boots slid down the steps.

The heavy skewers rained from her sleeve, tinkling down the metal steps.

Gone.

Her heart sank as her last hope rained over the gravel.

"What's that?" Dédé grunted, leaning forward and grabbing them. He laughed, short and barklike. "Kabobs? You belong on these."

"No, you do!" She turned quickly, not caring anymore what he'd do.

But she spoke to the air. She'd knocked into Dédé. His finger pulled the Beretta. Shots drilled into the concrete water tower supports. She ducked as he spun and staggered. In his other hand he held the skewers. He tripped into a hole. She saw him land with a loud *ouff*! then a piercing cry.

A skewer rammed through his temple.

He clutched his face in surprise, a skewer handle poking out above his ear. He convulsed in a burrowing motion. Trickles of blood pooled into the dirt, and then Dédé lay still.

Aimée collapsed and grabbed her gun from the dirt. She tried not to look at his face.

"I told you I'm afraid of heights."

"YOU STILL LOOK LIKE you've been hit by a truck," René said.

"Just got slammed into the back of one, like I told you," Aimée said as she limped into her office.

Miles Davis scampered beside her and jumped onto René's chair.

"Why don't you recover at home?" René asked.

"Work heals me," she said, hanging her leather jacket on the hook. "What's the EDF status?"

"Last night they talked about us doing a vulnerability scan of their software system," he said, with a little smile. "Today they mentioned hardware. *Tiens*, no signatures on any dotted line yet." René buttoned his Burberry raincoat. "Guess where Philippe's money went."

Aimée looked up.

"Into his vineyard," René shook his head. "Château de Froissart turned into a veritable money pit. His vines have root disease."

No wonder he needed a lot of money.

"Time for my practice at the dojo," René said. As he opened the door, he paused, concern on his face. "*Ça va?*"

"Fine, partner," she said.

"Someone's here to see you," René said.

Morbier walked into her office, hand in hand with the boy from the photograph in Samia's apartment.

"Leduc, meet my grandson, Marc," Morbier said.

"*Enchanté*, Marc," she said, rising to greet him. She wasn't too surprised.

Marc's round black eyes shone in his honey-colored face when Miles Davis appeared.

"Would you like something to drink, Marc?"

Marc's shy smile got hidden in the folds of Morbier's coat. He leaned down to pet Miles Davis, who'd pranced up to sniff him.

"We'll take a raincheck, Leduc," he said. "We can't be late for the special event at the Vincennes Zoo. Just wanted to drop this off." He thrust a grimy folder on her desk. "Now you know what I know," Morbier said, giving her a meaningful look. "That's if you want. Drop it off later."

After the door shut she sat down. She stared at the folder, dog-eared with a coffee stain on the cover.

Her cell phone rang several times. Miles Davis barked and jumped on her lap. She ignored the phone. She reached for the folder, but her hands shook and she couldn't grasp it. The shadows lengthened. She didn't know how long she'd sat staring at it before she grew aware of the streetlights shining in from rue du Louvre. Miles Davis growled. Pounding sounded on her office door. Loud and insistent.

Aimée opened the door.

Yves stood on the landing, his suitcase behind him. Charcoal stubble shaded his chin. He wore black jeans, a black leather jacket, and looked good enough to eat. And he was going away.

"You stole my thunder, Aimée, grabbing the front page and bumping my Defense Ministry exposé," he said, coming in. He grinned. "But if anyone did, I'm glad it was you. Reuters seems interested. They're making the appropriate noises."

"Is that why you disappeared?" she asked.

"I couldn't tell you what I was doing, you were working for the minister's wife. Martine wasn't too happy with me either. She won't run the story. But I understand, it's family. She knows I'll go elsewhere with it."

Before she could speak he handed her a thick envelope.

"You could come with me," he said, his dark eyes locking on hers.

"It's just not that easy."

"True. It's very simple," he said, brushing her spiky hair down. He ran his fingers along her chin. "There's an open-dated ticket in there, departure and return good for a year."

She stiffened. "I've got a business . . . Miles Davis . . ."

"There's computer crime in Cairo. Matter of fact, all kinds of crime, too," he said. He held out another ticket. "Miles Davis has a seat but he'll have to spend some of the flight in a doggie carrier."

He enveloped her in his arms and kissed her hard. Hot and searching. She didn't want him to stop, but he did. "My taxi's waiting."

From her window she watched the red brake lights as Yves's taxi pulled away on rue du Louvre. To the right the western palace of the Louvre lay dark and tomblike. But on the lighted quai the trees had flowered, fragrant and leafy.

She set the tickets next to the folder on the desk and opened the window. As she sat down to ponder the course of her life, the late-night traffic hum reached her ears, Miles Davis nestled in her arms, and she inhaled the first breath of spring.

OTHER TITLES IN THE SOHO CRIME SERIES